P9-DXC-359

GOODBYE TO THE DEAD

GOODBYE TO THE DEAD

A JONATHAN STRIDE NOVEL

BRIAN FREEMAN

Quercus

New York • London

Quercus

New York • London

Copyright © 2015 by Brian Freeman
First published in the United States by Quercus in 2016

ISBN 978-1-62365-911-0

Library of Congress Control Number: 2015956914

Distributed in the United States and Canada by
Hachette Book Group
1290 Avenue of the Americas
New York, NY 10104

Manufactured in the United States

10 9 8 7 6 5 4 3 2 1

www.quercus.com

For Marcia

We are healed of a suffering only by experiencing it to the full.

—MARCEL PROUST

PROLOGUE

THE PRESENT

Serena spotted the Grand Am parked half a block from the Duluth bar. Someone was waiting inside the car.

Mosquitoes clouded in front of the headlights. The trumpets of a Russian symphony—something loud and mournful by Shostakovich—blared through the vehicle's open windows. Serena smelled acrid, roll-your-own cigarette smoke drifting toward her with the spitting rain. Beyond the car, through the haze, she saw the milky lights of the bridge arching across the harbor.

Only the two of them haunted the late-night darkness of the summer street. Herself and the stranger behind the wheel of the Grand Am. She couldn't see the driver, but it didn't matter who was inside. Not yet.

She was here for someone else.

This was an industrial area, on the east end of Raleigh Street, not far from the coal docks and the paper mill. Power lines sizzled overhead. The ground under her feet shook with the passage of a southbound train. She made sure her Mustang was locked, with her Glock securely inside the glove compartment, and then she crossed the wet street to the Grizzly Bear Bar. It was a dive with no windows and an apartment overhead for the owner.

Cat was inside.

Serena felt guilty about putting tracking software on the teenager's phone, but she'd learned quickly that Cat's sweet face didn't mean she could be trusted.

When she pulled open the door of the bar, a sweaty, beery smell tumbled outside. She heard drunken voices shouting in languages she didn't understand and the twang of a George Strait song on the jukebox. Big men lined up two-deep at the bar and played poker at wooden tables.

Inside, she scanned the faces, looking for Cat. She spied her near a table at the far wall, standing shoulder to shoulder with an older girl, both of them head-down over smartphones. The two made an unlikely pair. Cat was a classic beauty with tumbling chestnut hair and a sculpted Hispanic face. Her skinny companion had dyed orange spikes peeking out from under a wool cap, and her ivory face was studded with piercings.

Serena keyed a text into her own phone and sent it. *Look up.*

Cat's face shot upward as she got the message. Her eyes widened, and Serena read the girl's lips. "*Oh, shit.*"

Cat whispered urgently into her friend's ear. Serena saw the other girl study her like a scientist peering into the business end of a microscope. The skinny girl wore a low-cut mesh shirt over a black bra and a jean skirt that ended mid-thigh. She picked up a drinks tray—she was a waitress—and gave Serena a smirk as she strolled to the bar, leaving Cat by herself.

Serena joined Cat at the cocktail table where she was standing. The girl's smile had vanished, and so had all of her adultness. Teenagers drifted so easily between maturity and innocence. Cat was a child again, but she was also a child who was five months pregnant.

"I'm really sorry—" Cat began, but Serena cut her off.

"Save it. I'm not interested in apologies."

She stopped herself before saying anything more that she'd regret. She was too angry even to look at Cat. Instead, by habit, she surveyed the people in the bar. It was a rough crowd, not a hangout for college kids and middle-class tourists like the bars in Canal Park. Hardened sailors came to the Grizzly Bear off the cargo boats, making up for dry days on the lake with plenty of booze. She heard raspy laughter and arguments that would spill over into fights. The bare, muscled fore-arms of the drinkers were covered in cuts and scars, and the men left greasy fingerprints on dozens of empty beer bottles.

In the opposite corner of the bar, Serena noticed a woman who didn't fit in with the others. The woman sat by herself, a nervous smile on her round face. Her long blond hair, parted in the middle, hung down like limp spaghetti. She had an all-American look, with blue eyes and young skin, like a cheerleader plucked from a college yearbook. Maybe twenty-two. She kept checking a phone on the table in front of her, and her stare shot to the bar door every time it opened.

Something about the woman set off alarm bells in Serena's head. This was a bad place for her. She wanted to go over and ask: *Why are you here?*

She didn't, because that was the question she needed to ask Cat.

"Why are you here, Cat?"

"I wanted to go somewhere. I'm bored."

"That's not an answer."

"Anna works here," Cat said. "She and I know the owner."

Cat nodded at the waitress who'd been with her at the table. Anna was playing with her phone as she waited for the bartender at the taps. One of the sailors made a grab for her ass, and Anna intercepted his hand without so much as a glance at the man's face.

"She used to live on the streets, like me," Cat told Serena. "We'd hang out together. If she found a place to sleep, she let me crash there, too."

"I get it, but that's not your world anymore."

"I'm entitled to have friends," Cat insisted, her lower lip bulging with defiance.

"You are, but no one from your old life is a friend."

Serena knew the struggle the girl faced. Not even three months ago, Cat Mateo had been a runaway. A teenage prostitute. When someone began stalking Cat in the city's graffiti graveyard, she'd gone to Duluth police lieutenant Jonathan Stride for help. Serena and Stride had been lovers for four years, and she knew he had a weakness for a woman in trouble. They'd helped capture the man who'd been targeting Cat, and when the girl was safe, Stride made a decision that surprised Serena. He suggested that the teenager live with them, have her baby there, and grow up in a house with adults who cared about her.

Serena said yes, but she'd never believed that it would be easy for any of them. And it wasn't.

"You're a sight for sore eyes in this place," a male voice announced.

A man in a rumpled blue dress shirt and loosely knotted tie stopped at their table. His eyes darted between Serena's face and her rain-damp T-shirt. He wiped his hands on a Budweiser bar towel.

"This is Fred," Cat interjected. "He owns the bar."

The man shot out a hand, which Serena shook. His fingers were sticky from sugar and limes. "Fred Sissel," he said cheerfully.

Sissel was around fifty years old, with slicked-back graying hair and a trimmed mustache. He wore the overeager grin of a man who'd tried to smile his way out of everything bad in life. Fights. Debts. Drunk driving. His cuffs were frayed, and his shirt and tie were dotted with old food stains. His face had the mottled brown of too many visits to a tanning salon.

"So, what's your name, and where have you been all my life?" Sissel asked. The teeth behind his smile were unnaturally white.

Serena slid her badge out of her jeans pocket. "My name's Serena Dial. I'm with the Itasca County Sheriff's Office."

Sissel's mustache drooped like a worm on a fishing hook. The sailors at the other tables had radar for the gold glint of a badge, and the tenor in the bar changed immediately.

"Sorry, officer, is there a problem?" Sissel asked, losing the fake grin.

"Do you know this girl?"

"Sure, she's a friend of Anna's."

"Do you know she's seventeen years old?"

Sissel swore under his breath. "Hey, I don't want any trouble," he said.

"You've already got trouble, and if I find her in this place again, you'll have even more."

"Yeah. Understood. Whatever you say."

The bar owner raised his arms in surrender and backed away. Serena saw emotions skipping like beach stones across Cat's face. Shame. Guilt. Embarrassment. Anger.

"Fred's a nice guy," the girl said finally. "You didn't have to be mean to him."

"Does he serve you alcohol?"

"No," Cat said, but Serena didn't trust her answer. She leaned closer to the girl, and although there was no booze on her breath, cigarette smoke laced her beautiful hair like stale perfume.

"You've been smoking."

"Just one."

Serena wanted to scream at the girl, but she held her voice in check. "You're pregnant. You can't smoke. You can't drink."

"I told you, it was just one."

Serena didn't answer. She couldn't fight teenage logic. As a cop, she'd seen good girls make bad choices her entire life. She knew how easy it was to cross the line. At Cat's age, she'd been a runaway herself, living with a girlfriend in Las Vegas after escaping the grip of a Phoenix drug dealer. Not a month had gone by in Vegas when she hadn't fended off the temptation to gamble, buy drugs, steal, or sell herself for the money she needed. She felt lucky that the only serious vice she carried from those days was being a recovering alcoholic. But luck was all it was. A bad choice on a bad day, and her life would have taken a different turn.

Across the bar, Serena saw the young blonde—the school cheerleader type—grab her phone suddenly and get to her feet. She was nervous and excited and couldn't control her smile. She smoothed her long, straight hair and moistened her lips. If there was a mirror, she would have checked her reflection in it. She took a breath, and her chest swelled. She headed for the bar door but backtracked to retrieve a baby-blue suitcase from behind her table.

To Serena, it felt wrong. Visitors didn't come to Duluth and wind up in this bar on their first night. Her instincts told her to stop the woman and ask questions. To intervene. To protect her.

"Are you going to tell Stride?" Cat asked.

Serena focused on the teenager again. She knew that Cat was afraid of Stride's disapproval more than anything else in her life. He was like a father to her, and she was terrified of disappointing him.

"Yes," Serena said. "You know I have to tell him."

Cat's eyes filled with tears. She was a typical teenage girl, using tears to get her way, and Serena worked hard to keep her own face as stern as stone. Meanwhile, the bar door opened and closed, letting in the patter of rain from outside.

The blond woman was gone.

"It doesn't matter what you tell him," Cat said, rubbing her nose on her sleeve. "He's going to kick me out sooner or later."

Her voice was choked with self-pity. She was smart and beautiful and eager to believe the worst about herself. She looked for any reason to assume that her life wasn't worth saving. To sabotage the second chance she'd been given. That was part of her guilt over who she'd been.

"That's not the point," Serena told her calmly, "and you know it."

"When he was married to Cindy, Stride didn't want kids," Cat protested. "So why would he want me now?"

"You're wrong about that, but even if it were true, it doesn't matter. He took you in, Cat. He wants you there. We both do. What happened in the past, what happened with Cindy, has nothing to do with who he is today."

"You wish," the girl snapped.

The words shot out of Cat like a poisoned arrow. Funny, how teenagers could always find your weak spot and apply pressure. If there was anything in Serena's life that made her feel like an insecure child, it was the thought of Cindy Stride. The suspicion that Jonny was still in love with his wife.

Still in love with the wife who died of cancer eight years ago.

Cat knew what she'd done. She looked upset now. "I'm sorry. I didn't mean that."

But she did. And she was right.

"Come on," Serena said, shoving down her own emotions. "Let's get out of here."

She took Cat's arm in a tight grip, but then something made her freeze. A woman screamed. It came from the street, muffled by the clamor of the bar. She almost missed it. The cry stopped as quickly as it started, cutting off like the slamming of a window, but Serena knew exactly who it was. She cursed herself for not listening to her instincts when she had the chance.

Serena told Cat to stay where she was. She shoved through the crowd and broke out into the street. Outside, the drizzle had become a downpour, blown sideways by the wind. The Grand Am she'd spotted earlier was still parked half a block away, its headlights white and bright, steaming in the rain. Immediately in front of the sedan was the woman from the bar, her body flailing as she fought to free herself from a man who held her in a headlock.

Serena shouted, and the woman saw her. Soundlessly, in panic, she pleaded for rescue. Serena marched toward them to break up the assault, but she'd barely taken a step when a gun blew up the night. One shot. Loud and lethal. The blond woman's pretty face, twisted in panic, became a spray of bone, brain, blood, and skin. Her knees buckled; her body slumped to the wet pavement. In shock, Serena threw herself sideways toward the outer wall of the bar.

The bar door opened, and Cat called out, curious, "What was that? What's going on?"

Serena yelled with the protective fury of a mother, "*Cat, get back inside right now!*"

Then she was running. She saw a tall man in a hooded sweatshirt, his back to her as he escaped. The killer. She didn't stop for the woman lying in the street. There was nothing she could do to help her. She charged after the man, struggling to match his steps, but the effort weighed on her chest, where she'd taken a bullet a few months earlier. Rain soaked her black hair and blurred her vision. The asphalt was slick. The man sped into the darkness of a side street that ended in dense trees, with Serena ten feet behind in pursuit. Matchbox houses on both sides bloomed with light as people crept to their windows.

Serena closed on the man when he slipped and lost a step. The woods loomed directly ahead of them. She knew where she was; the street ended in sharp stairs that led down over a creek into the grassy fields of Irving Park. She took a chance, and she jumped. Her body hit the man square in the back, kicking him forward, bringing both of them down. He slid onto the moss-slick concrete steps. She scrambled to her feet and dove for him, but he was ready for her. He spun around in the blackness and hammered a fist into her stomach. He grabbed her head. His fingers drove her chin into the rusty railing bordering the stairs, where bone struck metal. Her teeth rattled as if driven upward into her skull. She collapsed to her knees.

He skidded on his heels and jumped down the rest of the stairs. She heard his footsteps splashing into the creek below them. He was gone, breaking free into the wide-open land of the park. She hadn't even seen his face.

People from the bar ran toward her, shouting. Somewhere among them, Cat called her name over and over in fear. Serena tried to stand, but she was too dizzy, and she fell forward, tasting blood on her tongue. She was on all fours now. Her hands pushed blindly around the muddy steps, hunting for the railing to use as leverage as she stood up. She felt rocks and tree branches and bug-eaten leaves beneath her fingers, and then, finally, she brushed against the iron of the railing.

Except—no.

What she felt under the wet skin of her hand wasn't the railing mounted beside the steps. It was something else. Something metal and lethal and still hot to the touch.

When her brain righted itself, she realized it was a gun.

THEN

1

NINE YEARS AGO

Cindy Stride noted the clock on the dashboard of her Subaru Outback. 9:32 p.m.

Eventually, everyone would ask her about that. Jonny would pepper her with questions, not as a husband but as a cop. *What time was it? When did you leave the party at the Radisson?* The county attorney, Dan Erickson, would interrogate her about it months later on the witness stand. *Mrs. Stride, exactly what time was it when you took the defendant back to her house that night?*

She didn't know why she noticed the time or why she remembered it, but she did. 9:32 p.m. Friday night. January 28.

Cindy glanced at the woman in the passenger seat beside her. Dr. Janine Snow. She couldn't look at Janine without a twinge of jealousy. If you were a short woman, you wanted to be tall. If you had black hair, you wanted to be blond. If you were a physical therapist, like Cindy, you wanted to be a surgeon. Janine was all of those things.

"I'm sorry to make you leave the party early," her friend said, with a little hint of her Texas roots in her voice. "I'm not feeling well, and I didn't think I should drive myself."

Cindy shrugged. "Don't worry about it. I wished the chief a happy birthday. I kissed his cheek. My duty was done."

She squinted through the windshield of her Outback. She hated driving at night, and the hillside trek to Janine's house made her nervous. Duluth was a city that made no sense in the winter, when ice turned the steep streets into luge tracks. Janine owned a Frank Lloyd Wright–style mansion high above Skyline Parkway, with a million-dollar view and drop-offs that made you hold your breath trying to climb the slick streets to get there. With each switchback over the treetops, the glazed roads felt as if they were a stairway into the clouds.

"Could you stop?" Janine asked suddenly.

"What? Why?"

"Please. I have to throw up."

Cindy punched the brakes, and the Outback shimmied. Janine flung open the door and fumbled with the seat belt. Subzero air roared into the car, making Cindy shiver. She saw Janine sway on the shoulder of the road, where the frozen ground dipped sharply at her feet.

"Are you okay? Be careful!"

Janine sank to her knees and vomited the contents of her stomach. She tried to stand, but her heels slipped, and she nearly fell. She clung to the car door as she dragged herself back inside. The smell of puke came with her. Her untucked lavender blouse and her Paige jeans were soiled with dirt, snow, and regurgitated remnants of banquet shrimp. She put her fists on her knees and laid her head back with closed eyes.

"I am so sorry," Janine murmured.

"It's okay," Cindy replied. "These days, it seems like eating anything makes me sick, too."

The wheels of the Outback churned for traction as Cindy accelerated. She had nightmares sometimes about navigating the Duluth streets; in the dream, she kept pushing the gas but could never get up an impossibly steep hill. She peered at the cliffside over the terraced road. Icicles dripped from the rocky ledges, remnants of a brief, early-month thaw. Somewhere above her was Janine's house. The mansion's frame butted over the hillside, as if floating on air. It was a crazy place to live. She preferred the drafty cottage that she and Jonny owned on the spit of land between Lake Superior and the inner harbor. She liked living at sea level.

Beside her, Janine's skin was ghostly white. The annoying thing about Janine was that she could be sick and still look good. Her natural blond hair swished about her shoulders like waves of sunshine. It didn't matter whether her hair was styled or messy; somehow it always looked right. She was the perfect weight and the perfect size, and at thirty-nine years old, she seemed to stay that way effortlessly. She had ice-blue eyes that hardly ever blinked. It was unnerving when those eyes looked at you and made you stutter like a fool because you were standing in front of someone who was so beautifully put together.

Yes, Cindy was a little jealous of Janine Snow.

"Where's your husband?" Janine asked. "I'm surprised he'd miss the chief's party."

"Jonny and Maggie got stuck on top of the Bong Bridge coming back from Superior. A semi overturned on the ice. Shut the whole thing down. It's a mess."

Janine gave a thin smile. "So, is his little Chinese partner still in love with him?"

"Maggie? Oh, yeah. She is."

"Does that worry you? They spend a lot of time together."

"No, it doesn't bother me. Maggie may be in love with *him*, but Jonny's in love with me."

Janine pursed her lips as if she wanted to say something more, but she held her tongue. She wasn't always blessed with social graces. If anyone else had insinuated a relationship between Jonny and Maggie, Cindy would have cut them off at the knees, but she made allowances for Janine's prickly side.

They'd been friends for five years, ever since St. Anne's recruited Janine from Texas to a top spot in cardiac surgery at the downtown hospital. Cindy worked as a physical therapist in an adjacent building, and they'd met in the cafeteria. Janine didn't make friends easily, particularly with other women, but Cindy took pride in the fact that she herself was impossible to dislike. The two of them soon became close. Or as close as a doctor like Janine could be to anyone else.

Janine made no secret of her Texas-size libido, but she was one of those women who always seemed to have the wrong man in her life. She'd already been divorced twice before relocating to Duluth. One marriage was teen love, naive and doomed. One was mercenary, to pay for medical school. Through both marriages, she'd kept her own name. Snow. And, like the Duluth snow, she was cold, driven, and blinding.

Two years after arriving at St. Anne's, Janine married again. This time it was a newspaper columnist named Jay Ferris, and the two of them were from Mars and Venus. Jay was black, and Janine was white. He was an Iron Range Democrat, and Janine was a Lone Star Republican. Their differences made the attraction hotter. Janine freely admitted to Cindy that her interest in Jay was rooted more in lust than love, but after the heat between them flamed out, their passion had veered to the other extreme. Cindy didn't need to ask why Jay hadn't accompanied his wife to the party at the Radisson. Janine and Jay never went anywhere together. Not anymore. Not for months.

Cindy turned toward Janine's house. The last hill was the steepest of all. Three houses perched at the summit of a dead end, built to soak up views of the city and the lake. Janine's house was the most recent, the most modern, and the most expensive. It had flat roofs, heated to melt the snow. The back of the house, built on columns mounted into the hillside, featured a wall of floor-to-ceiling windows. The rounded porte cochere extended over the semicircular driveway like a flying saucer.

Lights were on in the house. Jay was home. The garage door was open, revealing his new Hummer and an empty space where Janine usually kept her Mercedes, which she'd left behind in the parking garage at the Radisson.

Cindy stopped in the driveway. "Here you go."

"Do you mind coming in with me? I'm feeling pretty unsteady."

"Sure."

Cindy got out. The hilltop wind swirled her long black hair and pinked up her cheeks. She went to the other side of the Outback and helped Janine out of the car. The taller woman put an arm over Cindy's shoulder to support herself. Janine still walked with a limp after a painful fall on the ice the previous year. Cindy didn't understand why her friend insisted on wearing heels, but to a Texas blonde, leaving her heels at home was like suggesting she go to the party naked.

"Do you have your key?" Cindy asked.

"Yes."

But Janine didn't need her key. Through the glass front door, Cindy spotted Jay coming to meet them. She noticed a visceral reaction in her friend's body when she saw her husband. Nothing brought this strong woman low the way the man she'd married did. Cindy wondered how long people could live that way before they did something about it.

"I'll come inside with you," Cindy told Janine.

"No." Janine's voice was hushed and shaken. "No, you don't need to do that. I can handle it myself from here. Thank you for bringing me home."

"Are you all right?"

"Actually, I'd like to throw myself into the canyon," she said.

"Janine."

"I'm kidding. I'm fine."

"Come home with me. You don't have to stay here with him."

Janine shook her head. "Yes, I do."

The front door opened. A jazz clarinet sang from hidden speakers inside. Jay had a glass of red wine in his hand. He was slim and three or four inches shorter than his wife. He wore an untucked white silk shirt and gray dress slacks. His feet were bare. He cast a withering glance at Janine and paid no attention to Cindy.

"Look at you. Is that puke? Very nice."

Janine squared her shoulders and pushed past him. He slammed the door without acknowledging Cindy. Through the glass, she saw Janine kick off her heels in the marble foyer. She could hear their loud voices, already arguing. Jay reached for his wife, and she watched her friend violently shake him off. Cindy thought about ringing the bell to intervene, but Janine looked back through the glass and mouthed: "*Go.*"

Cindy returned to her Outback and steeled herself for a slow, slippery drive home. She gave a silent prayer of thanks, not for the first time, for the husband she had and the life she led.

The streets around her were empty. No one else was foolish enough to be out on a night like this. It was just one of the details they would eventually ask her to remember.

As you left the house that night, Mrs. Stride, did you see anyone else?
"No. There was no one else there. I was alone."

Cindy awoke to the smell of cigarette smoke.

Their small bedroom was dark. She didn't know what time it was. Through the half-open window, she heard the roar of Lake Superior yards from their back door. She shivered with cold in her nightgown as she sat up in bed, and the blanket slipped down her chest. She pushed tangled hair out of her face.

Where the moon made a triangle of light on the floor, she saw the silhouette of her husband. He was tall, almost six-foot-two. Strong and fit. His black hair wavy and untamed. He'd shrugged clothes onto his lean frame when he should have been getting undressed. He put a cigarette to his mouth—a habit she hated but which he'd been unable to quit.

His side of the bed was cold. He hadn't climbed in with her yet.

She asked, "What's up?"

When he realized she was awake, he sat down beside her. He flicked his cigarette lighter, and it cast a flame. She could see his eyes now. She adored his eyes. Dark, teasing, fierce, funny, and so in love whenever they looked at her.

But his eyes weren't happy.

"Bad news," Jonathan Stride said. "I have to go out."

"What's going on?"

"Did you see Janine at the chief's party tonight?"

"Of course. I took her home. She wasn't feeling well."

Stride stroked her cheek with the back of his hand. "*You* drove Janine home? What time was that? When did you leave the party at the Radisson?"

The time popped into her head. "Nine thirty-two p.m."

"Almost an hour and a half ago," Stride murmured. "Did you see Jay when you got to their house?"

"Briefly, yes. Why?"

Stride kissed her forehead. He stood up again. "Jay's dead. Janine called 911 a few minutes ago. She says someone shot him."

2

"The thing about dead husbands and dead wives is that the cases are always like a knock-knock joke," Maggie Bei said.

Jonathan Stride eyed his tiny partner, who stared up at him from behind her black bangs. He played along. "How's that?"

"Knock, knock," she said.

"Who's there?"

"We know."

"We know who?" Stride asked.

Maggie cocked her finger like a gun. "Yes, we do."

Stride smothered a laugh. Maggie was right. He was hard-pressed to remember a dead spouse at home who hadn't been shot, stabbed, or bludgeoned by a loving husband or loving wife. The investigations typically didn't take long to produce enough evidence to lay in front of a jury. However, Dr. Janine Snow wasn't an ordinary suspect.

She was rich.

She was a local hero who saved lives on the operating table.

She was one of his wife's closest friends.

Stride ran his hands back through his wavy hair and blinked to stay awake. He was tired and cold. The temperature hovered around zero, and here on the high hillside, the lake wind hit his skin like acid.

They'd already spent two hours outside this evening, up on the arch of the Bong Bridge that connected Duluth to its Wisconsin twin port town, Superior. A semi had spilled over on the icy bridge deck, closing the span and stranding cars for hours. One woman had freaked out at the height and begun threatening to throw herself into the water. A typical January evening.

He'd barely had time for a hot shower at home when Maggie called about the murder of Jay Ferris. Now he was cold again, but in Duluth, the chill of winter never really went away. You lived your life cold. Even under a wool blanket, your bones never forgot the cold. They reminded you with a little involuntary shiver.

Stride stood with Maggie next to his Ford Bronco, which was crusted with dirt and road salt. He studied the street and the house. His team had already closed off the scene, and it was remote enough and late enough—after midnight—that news of the murder hadn't leaked to the media yet. That blessed silence wouldn't last long, though, particularly given the prominence of the husband and wife involved in the crime.

The road banked sharply downward from where he was parked. The street was free of snow, but plows had piled six-foot drifts on the shoulders. There were three houses here, all on the cliffside overlooking the lake, all worth in excess of a million dollars. He knew the families who owned them. Janine and Jay. Next to them, another surgeon, along with his gay partner and their three adopted children. Next to them, behind a wrought-iron gate, the owners of a successful restaurant chain located in the tourist heart of the city in Canal Park. Duluth's upper crust was a small community, and the chief made it a point that he and his lieutenants keep good relationships with them.

"I want you to interview the neighbors yourself," he told Maggie.

"Sure."

"Be polite."

"Me? I'm always polite."

Stride smiled at her. Another joke. Maggie was, in fact, foul-mouthed and sarcastic. He was amazed at how much she'd changed in the few years they'd been working together. She was a whip-smart

Chinese immigrant and criminology grad from the University of Minnesota, but Stride had been reluctant to hire her because she came across as too straitlaced for his rowdy team. That didn't last long. She loosened up, learned how to swear, and learned how to boss around colleagues who were at least a foot taller than she was. She dressed in trendy clothes from the teen racks, wore ridiculous block heels that made her sound like a clog dancer when she walked, and constantly had to blow bangs from her mop of black hair out of her eyes.

"Come on," Stride said, "let's go inside."

Janine Snow's house was three stories high, but the entrance was on the uppermost level, and the other two floors were built below them into the side of the hill. They walked up the semicircular driveway past an open, three-car garage. Gravel and salt littered the sidewalk. At the front entry, where a uniformed officer guarded the door, they donned gloves and plastic coverings over their shoes. The marbled foyer opened into a living area with a high ceiling that was decorated with African-themed paintings and abstract onyx sculptures. A triptych portrait of Malcolm X loomed over a black-and-white sofa, and the modern chairs looked uncomfortable. The living room stretched to the back of the house, where high windows overlooked the city lights and the dark mass of Lake Superior.

The view was stunning, but right now, it was overshadowed by the body of Jay Ferris, which lay sprawled on a gray-striped area rug. A circular wound was burned through the middle of his forehead, and the carpeting under his head was matted with blood. None of the blood had stained his shirt, which was cloud-white against his black skin. Aside from the hole in his head, he was still a handsome man. Shaved scalp. Tightly cropped goatee.

"Jay Ferris," Stride murmured. He had to be honest. He'd never liked this man.

Jay was a Duluth lifer, like Stride. He'd grown up in the city's Lincoln Park area and tangled with the police as a teenager over drugs and theft. Even so, Jay was a smart, ambitious kid. He'd studied at UMD on a scholarship, gotten a journalism degree with honors, and worked his way up at the *Duluth News Tribune* from the copyediting desk to a gig as a daily columnist. He knew that controversy sold newspapers, and he supplied a lot of it. In a city that smoothed over its racist past, Jay was a crusader against the white elite. Stride didn't mind that—there were skeletons in any town's closet that needed to see the light of day—but he resented the carelessness with which Jay used his bully pulpit to destroy ordinary people.

One of his own cops had wound up in Jay's crosshairs. A young police officer named Nathan Skinner had gotten drunk in the Wisconsin Dells and been pulled over on the highway. That was bad enough, but Skinner used an ugly racial epithet in the course of the arrest. It was outrageous, drunken behavior, and Stride suspended him for a month and sent him to diversity training in Minneapolis. That didn't satisfy Jay Ferris, who beat the drum over Skinner's arrest in his newspaper column. He made Skinner the poster boy for racism inside the city's police ranks, and the chief finally ordered Stride to fire Skinner as a way to get the story out of the papers. Stride didn't excuse what Skinner had done, but he didn't think the mistake justified taking a young man's entire career.

Neither did most of his other cops. Jay Ferris wasn't popular with the Duluth Police Department.

Stride examined Jay's body. The full report would come from the St. Louis County medical examiner, but he'd seen enough gunshot victims to recognize the obvious details. Powder tattooing on the forehead indicated an intermediate-range wound; the shooter had been within a couple of feet of Jay when firing the shot. Based on the location and position of the body, the shooter had stood between Jay and the front door.

A glass of wine lay tipped on the rug beside him, leaving its own stain of red. Another glass, smeared with lipstick, sat on a mahogany coffee table.

"No gun," Maggie said. "We're still searching."

"Search harder," Stride said. "We need that gun. Where's Janine?"

"Downstairs in her office. Archie Gale is already with her. She wouldn't say a word until he got here. Smart." Maggie rolled her eyes.

"I'll talk to her." He added again, "Find the gun."

Stride took spiral stairs down to the next level of the house. The staircase was modern, made of chrome and stone. Janine and Jay had built the house less than a year earlier, but according to Cindy, it was Janine's baby. Her dream. She'd worked with an architect for months on the design. The mansion on the hill was one of the perks of being a surgeon.

Janine's home office was about the square footage of Stride's whole house. She had a huge and impeccably clean desk near the windows. He could see the lift bridge in Canal Park shimmering far below. An entire wall of the office was dedicated to built-in bookshelves stocked with medical volumes, and she had another wall filled with photographs of people. These were her heart patients. People whose lives she'd saved. He didn't think it was an accident that she was waiting for the police here. She wanted to remind him who she was and how important she was to the city of Duluth.

It also wasn't an accident that she wasn't alone. Archibald Gale was with her, and Gale was the northland's leading criminal defense attorney. As Stride entered the office, Gale sprang up from the leather sofa. For a large man—six feet tall, at least 275 pounds—he was nimble on his feet. He had receding gray hair, curly and short, and blue eyes that twinkled behind tiny circular glasses. Despite the hour, he wore a pressed suit, with a tie neatly knotted to pinch his thick neck where his beard ended.

"Lieutenant!" Gale exclaimed cheerfully, as if they were old friends. Which, to some extent, they were. They were on opposite sides of the game, but Gale was also a difficult man to dislike.

"Archie," Stride replied. "Nice suit."

Stride's own tie was loose at his neck, and he'd pulled an oxford shirt out of the dirty-clothes basket. He still wore his old leather jacket, which had seen more than a decade of use and had a bullet hole in one sleeve.

"I was still at the office," Gale explained. "Lieutenant, I believe you know Dr. Janine Snow."

Stride nodded at the surgeon. "Dr. Snow."

"Lieutenant Stride."

It was strange, being so formal with her. They were otherwise on a first-name basis. She'd been in his house. She had lunch or played golf with his wife a couple of times a month. They'd done community fund-raisers together. Even so, she was a suspect in a crime now. They both knew it.

The first thing he noticed about Janine was that her blond hair was wet. She'd showered. That was what you did when you arrived home from a party, sick and disheveled. Or it was what you did when you had just shot your husband and you wanted to make sure your skin and hair kept no residue chemicals from firing a gun.

He sat down on the sofa next to her, in the spot where Gale had been. The attorney leaned his wide backside on the corner of Janine's desk and watched them with the fussy concern of a mother superior. Janine waited for Stride's questions, and she was exactly the woman he remembered. Smart, beautiful, emotionally distant. She shed no tears. Made no pretense of sadness. For her, this was a practical exercise. Her husband had been murdered. Innocent or guilty, she needed to make sure that this incident didn't rob her of the rest of her life.

"I'm surprised you felt the need to bring in an attorney so quickly," he said to her.

"Oh, let's not travel down that tired old road," Gale interjected before Janine could answer. "If you were hiking in the Alaskan wilderness for the first time, I imagine you'd want a guide, wouldn't you, Lieutenant? There are always bears feeding in the shallows."

Stride shrugged. Janine knew that hiring a lawyer made her look guilty. She was savvy enough not to care.

"Tell me exactly what happened tonight," he said.

Janine glanced at Gale, who nodded his approval.

"Cindy brought me home early from the party," she explained. "I wasn't feeling well. In fact, we had to stop along the way for me to throw up. After she dropped me off, I talked to Jay for a while. Argued, is more like it. I'm being candid with you about that."

"What did you argue about?"

"Nothing of consequence. Jay and I could argue about anything, and we usually did. Mr. Gale probably wants me to pretend that everything was fine between us, but you wouldn't believe me if I said that. I'm sure Cindy has told you that the relationship between me and Jay was strained. You knew my husband, Lieutenant. If you think he was difficult as a journalist, trust me, he was even more difficult to live with."

"How long did you argue?" Stride asked.

"I have no idea. Ten minutes? Fifteen? I had some wine."

"Even though you were feeling sick?"

"Vomiting has a way of improving your outlook," Janine replied.

"Then what?"

"I took a shower."

"Where is the shower located in the house?" Stride asked.

"The lowest level, off the master bedroom. Jay and I have separate bathrooms. I built mine as something of a spa and retreat. Husbands have man caves. I have my bathroom."

"And when you got out?"

"I noticed something strange."

"What was that?" Stride asked.

"The drawers of the jewelry case in the bedroom were open. I hadn't left them that way. When I looked, several expensive pieces of jewelry were gone. I called for Jay but got no answer. I went back upstairs, and that was when I found him."

It wasn't a convincing story, but she told it as if it were gospel.

"So you're saying that in the time you were in the shower, someone came into the house, shot and killed your husband, walked down two levels, found your bedroom, stole jewelry, and then escaped."

"That's correct," Janine said.

"You must take long showers," Stride said without humor.

"In fact, I do."

"How long?"

"I didn't time myself, Lieutenant. I sat in the spray for a long time."

"Did you hear anything? Did you hear the gunshot?"

"No."

"What did you do when you found Jay's body?" Stride asked.

"I was in shock," Janine replied. "The front door was open. I ran to the doorway, and I heard the noise of a car on the streets below us, but that's all. I didn't see anyone or anything."

"What next? Take me through it."

"I confirmed that Jay was dead, although the wound made that obvious."

"And then you dialed 911?"

Janine hesitated. "I believe some time passed."

"Some time? How much time?"

"Again, I don't know. There are no clocks in my house. I'm not interested in what time it is when I'm home. I sat on the sofa and stared at Jay. As I say, I was in shock. When I was myself again, I called the police."

"And Mr. Gale," Stride said.

"Yes, that's correct."

"Anybody else? Neighbors? Friends?"

"No."

"Did you go anywhere? Did you leave the house?"

"No."

Some time. Time enough to hide a gun. Time enough to hide jewelry. Time enough to craft a story.

"Do you own a gun, Dr. Snow?"

"No, I don't," she replied.

"What about your husband?"

"He used to, but I asked him to get rid of it when we got married. I didn't like the idea of a gun in the house."

"What about enemies? Threats? Either directed at you or your husband?"

Janine shrugged. "You know who Jay was. The way he was. He collected enemies like stamps."

"Where are your clothes?" Stride asked.

"Excuse me?"

"The clothes you wore home from the party. Where are they?"

"In the washing machine."

"You already washed your clothes?"

"Having thrown up on them? Yes."

"I would have pegged you for more of a dry-cleaning-only kind of woman, Dr. Snow."

"In Dallas? Maybe. In Duluth in January? No."

She spoke down to him with all the superiority and impatience of a surgeon doing rounds with her residents.

"Was Jay abusive?" Stride asked. "Did he ever hit you?"

Gale broke in sharply. "Enough of that, Lieutenant. We're not discussing their relationship."

"It's all right, Archie," Janine added calmly. "No, he wasn't physically abusive. Jay was many things, but he never touched me."

Stride watched her face, expecting a crack in her facade. Instead, she was calm and deliberate.

"Is there anything else you want to tell me?" he asked.

"I think that's everything."

He leaned closer and lowered his voice. "Janine, if something happened between the two of you—if there was a fight, if things got out of hand—the best thing is to tell me now. We can work things out if we know the truth. Lying only makes it worse."

Gale opened his mouth again, but Janine held up a hand and silenced him with the tiniest smile. Her robe nudged forward, offering a small V of bare skin. Damp blond hair caressed her face. He smelled her soap and shampoo.

"I've already told you the truth, Jonathan," she said. "I didn't shoot my husband. It wasn't me."

3

"She did it," Carol Marlowe announced to her husband.

Howard Marlowe didn't hear his wife at first. His eyes were glued to the Gateway monitor on his desk, where he'd zoomed in on a photo of Janine Snow on the screen. Finally, he glanced at Carol, who'd wandered into his basement office from the laundry room in her slippers.

"What?" he said, distracted.

"That rich doctor. She killed her husband. That's what you're looking at, aren't you? More stories about her? You haven't talked about anything else for days."

Howard shrugged defensively. Carol was right, but he wasn't going to say so. His mouse was poised to close the window on his screen if she came any closer. "You don't know that she killed him. Nobody knows what happened. She says she's innocent."

Carol flopped down on the threadbare sofa on the other side of the room, underneath posters of the Great Wall of China and the statues of Easter Island. Places he'd never been but had always wanted to visit. His wife pulled out an emery board and worked on her fingernails. "Do you think she'd admit it if she were guilty?"

"No," he acknowledged.

"Well, there you go. Everyone at Super One is talking about her. They all think she killed him."

Super One was a local grocery store. Carol had worked there as a cashier since she was in high school. They'd met at the store when Howard tried to take fifteen items down the ten-items-or-less aisle, and Carol refused to let him through.

He found himself getting annoyed. "Oh, so the detectives at the store have it figured out. I'll call the police and tell them you cracked the case."

Carol rolled her eyes. "Come on, Howard. A mysterious stranger sneaks in while Dr. Perfect is in the shower? He blows away her husband, steals some jewelry, and escapes? She must think we're idiots." She leaned forward and lowered her voice. "It just goes to show you, a rich white doctor marrying a black man like that? Nothing good is going to come of it."

"Don't talk like that," Howard snapped. "It's offensive."

"I'm just saying what everyone is thinking."

"Well, don't say it."

"Whatever." Carol shrugged and kept filing her nails. The dryer tumbled in another part of the basement, and he heard a zipper banging on the metal drum.

His wife wore a long-sleeved Minnesota Vikings T-shirt and gray sweatpants. She always wore loose clothes to cover the extra ten pounds she complained about. Her mousy brown hair was pushed back behind her ears. She grabbed a tissue to blow her nose, which was a little too large for the rest of her face. Her eyes were brown, and her winter-pale skin sported a few freckles.

"I booked the Dells for our vacation in July," she told him.

Howard picked up his high school bowling trophy from the desk and rubbed a little dust from the base with a shirtsleeve. "Do we have to go there again? We've been there three years in a row."

"I love it there. So does Annie."

"Well, we've done it already," Howard complained. "We should go someplace else."

"Well, what about Branson?"

Howard frowned and didn't answer. They'd been to Branson three times, too. Everything about their lives was as predictable as an assembly line. Same vacations. Same television shows. Same meals. It was Wednesday, and Wednesday was meat-loaf day. Every week, all year. For Carol, routine was like a suit of armor against change. Change was bad. Change was scary. She wanted her world to stay exactly the same.

He understood why she felt that way. At twelve years old, Carol had walked into the garage and found her father hanging by his belt from an overhead beam. Her perfect suburban childhood had been stolen from her. She was never going to let that happen again.

Howard put down his trophy with a frustrated little bang. Janine Snow stared at him from his computer monitor. Dr. Perfect.

"Fine, we can go to the Dells if that's what you want," he said with a sigh. Surrender was the easiest way to keep the peace.

"Good. It'll be fun. We can go to that supper club you like. The one by the lake."

"Uh-huh."

Carol got up from the sofa. She looked pleased with herself. "You coming to bed?"

"I want to work on tomorrow's lesson plan," he said.

"Howard, you teach ninth-grade history. It hasn't changed since last year. Here's a hint: the North won the war."

He knew that she didn't mean to be nasty when she teased him about his job. To her, there was no shame in being an ordinary teacher in an ordinary school. Even so, her jokes bothered him. They reminded him of everything he hadn't done with his life.

"I'll be up later," he muttered.

"Okay, 'night." She wiggled her fingers at him.

Carol would be asleep when he climbed into bed. That was how it usually was. They had sex a couple of times a month. She was cheerful about it, but he knew she looked at sex as more of a wifely obligation than as something she did because she enjoyed it.

His eyes went back to the photograph of Janine Snow. Blond hair, long and luscious. Icy blue eyes that made you shiver. Rich. Hands that brought people back to life. What would it be like to be someone like that?

What would it be like to be *with* someone like that?

Howard turned off his monitor, because her face made it impossible to think about anything else. He opened the high school textbook and tried to write questions for the test, but he couldn't focus. Carol was right. History didn't change. In the end, he would use the same test he'd used the year before and the year before that.

He took a pencil from his desk and threw it across his office in annoyance. It landed on the pea-green shag. He got up and paced in front of the Easter Island poster. The empty eyes of one of the giant statues stared back at him. That was the place to take a vacation, on the storm-swept shore of some desolate island, examining clues to one of history's great mysteries. Growing up, he'd imagined himself as a famous archaeologist, leading digs around the world.

Instead, he taught bored kids about things he'd only read about in books. He'd never done anything himself. Not really. At age thirty-two, he'd complained to the Super One manager about the annoying cashier in the Express Lane who refused to ring up his groceries, and the manager had made her apologize to him. Carol had cried so hard that Howard asked her out for coffee as a way to make it up to her. One year later, they got married. Another year after that, they had their daughter, Annie, who was now six. And that was that.

Nothing about his life was going to change.

He retrieved a juice box from the mini refrigerator under the bar. He stared at himself in the mirror as he sucked through the tiny straw, making dimples in his cheeks. Not a bad-looking guy, he told himself. Five-foot-ten, not tall but not short. Curly brown hair parted in the middle, no gray yet. Long face, long chin. Clark Kent glasses, but those were fashionable again. He wore a striped Kohl's polo shirt, and you couldn't really see the paunch.

He went to the file cabinet and grabbed a copy of last year's Civil War test.

This battle, fought in Maryland on September 17, 1862, is also known as the Battle of Sharpsburg.

A. Gettysburg

B. Antietam

C. Bull Run

D. Saratoga

It depressed him, after weeks of study, how many students usually chose D. Bad enough to get the wrong battle, but the wrong war? He didn't blame them. Teaching the kids was his job, and he was decidedly mediocre at it.

Howard knew why he was depressed. Six days earlier, he'd turned forty years old. Forty—the burying place for all of your younger dreams. He was celebrating with a pity party. *Welcome to the Middle Ages*, Carol had written on his birthday card, which was another joke that he didn't find funny. He was halfway through life, and it was February, and the gray Duluth winter felt as if it would go on forever. He defied anyone not to be depressed in the face of that.

He sat down at his desk and turned on the monitor again. Janine Snow stared back at him. If you had a face like hers, if you had that kind of money, if you lived in a big house on the hill, it would never feel like winter. According to the papers, she was almost forty years old, too. She didn't look it.

He asked the question that everyone in Duluth was asking.

Did you do it?

4

One week after the murder of Jay Ferris, Stride's team still hadn't found the gun.

"We tore that house apart from top to bottom," Maggie told him. "I had guys tramping through the snow and climbing the cliffs on both sides. We searched every Dumpster within a mile around the place. Nothing. The gun's gone."

Stride leaned back in the old vinyl chair. They were in the basement of City Hall in downtown Duluth, where the Detective Bureau's investigations were headquartered. It was late, and the rest of the office was dark, but they had fluorescent lights blazing over their heads. One of the lights flickered like a strobe. The table was strewn with half-empty cans of Coke, Lays potato chip bags, and sauce-stained wrappers that smelled of Subway meatballs. File folders on every chair bulged with papers and photographs, and evidence boxes were stacked against the conference room's walls. This was the war room for everything they knew—and didn't know—about Jay Ferris and Janine Snow.

He stared at the ceiling and thought about the missing gun.

"So you kill your husband," Stride said. "You have an argument, you go find a gun, you shoot him. Now there you are with his body on the floor, and you have to figure out what to do next. You don't have much time. Fifteen minutes? Half an hour? You can't be sure a neighbor didn't hear the shot, and if too much time goes by before you call 911, people will wonder why."

"Nobody heard the shot," Maggie pointed out.

"Right, but Janine doesn't know that. She needs to get rid of the gun, and she grabs a bunch of jewelry to make it look like a robbery. Then what? Throw it all down the canyon? Someone's bound to find it when the snow melts. Does she get into Jay's car and drive somewhere? Maybe, but what if someone sees her on the road?"

"So what do you think she did?" Maggie asked.

He shook his head. "I don't know. Chances are, Janine already had a plan. She's not the kind of woman who does anything on the spur of the moment. She probably thought about this for weeks."

"Or she's innocent," Maggie pointed out.

"Yeah. Or she's innocent."

It was possible—but Stride didn't believe it. He'd looked into Janine's eyes that night and seen the truth. She was guilty. She'd killed her husband.

He got up and wandered through the darkened office to the pop machine, where he bought another can of Coke. He popped it and drank most of it quickly. A noisy furnace vent rattled over his head, but it did little to warm the drafty basement. He leaned against the wall, waiting for the rush of caffeine and sugar.

Stride was almost forty, and on most days, he still felt young. His face had been weathered by the Duluth winters, but he could be boyish when he cracked his quick, easy grin. His hair was jet black, short on the sides, messy and cowlicked on top. He didn't have perfect features. He would never be a smooth-skinned, blow-dried model. Cindy said she liked his flaws because he didn't try to hide them. She said you could look at her husband and know exactly who he was: honorable, headstrong, brooding, and bold—a man who would give his life trying to do the right thing and who would feel every failure deep in his bones.

He knew half the people in the city, thanks to his job, but he didn't invite many people into his life. He had no siblings. His parents were dead. When he was a boy, he'd lost his father to the lake, and his mother had passed away ten years ago. Since then, his world had mostly been him and Cindy, but he didn't need anyone else. He only kept a few close friends other than his wife. His doctor and college buddy Steve Garske. And Maggie.

Stride smiled at the idea of Maggie. As cops, as friends, they were good together. They were as close as two people could be who had never slept together. Which was something that he would never let happen.

He returned to the conference room and sat down.

"So what do you think, Mags?"

"She did it," Maggie said, "but I wish we could find that gun."

"We will. In the meantime, we need to track down anyone else with a motive. I don't want to give Archie Gale room to run when this gets to court."

Maggie nodded. "I'm meeting Nathan Skinner tomorrow. I don't like thinking that an ex-cop could have done this, but—"

"No, you're right. Talk to Nathan. Make sure he's got an alibi. I'm meeting Jay's brother, Clyde. He wants to know why we haven't already arrested Janine. What else do we have?"

Maggie grabbed her notebook from the table, although she didn't really need to consult it. She had one of the best memories of any cop he'd ever met. "We're still waiting on bank and phone records, and we're reviewing video dumps of ATMs and store cameras in the area, in case Janine took a drive to get rid of the gun. Guppo's going through everything we pulled from the house. Jay got a lot of hate mail because of his newspaper columns. It's going to take a while to clear those people."

"What about the neighbors up on Skyline?" Stride asked. "And their coworkers at the newspaper and the hospital?"

"According to them, Jay and Janine's marriage wasn't good. Lots of fights. Lots of arguments. Most people didn't understand why they were still married."

"Do we know if there was a prenup?" Stride asked.

"Unfortunately, yes," Maggie told him, "and a good one. If Janine and Jay got a divorce, he'd walk away with squat. And their friends said that Jay was very fond of having money. If anybody had a motive to pick murder over divorce, it was Jay, not Janine."

Stride frowned. "What else?"

"We got a Good Samaritan call," Maggie said. "A teenage boy and his girlfriend were heading along West Eighth Street to Skyline on Friday evening. He says they passed a white SUV parked on the shoulder. He couldn't tell me exactly where this was, but if it was close to the intersection at Skyline, it wouldn't have been too far from the spur leading up to the doctor's house."

"What time was this?"

Maggie shook her head. "He wasn't sure. After ten, he thought, but he didn't check the clock."

"Did he see anyone?"

"No, he's pretty sure the van was empty."

"Pretty sure?"

"Yeah. Except it was dark, so he doesn't really know. That's helpful, huh? He's also pretty sure the SUV didn't have a Minnesota plate, but not one hundred percent sure."

"I don't suppose he knew what kind of SUV it was."

"Actually, he was *very* sure of that. This kid is sort of a car geek. He said it was a Toyota RAV4. He recognized the silly spare tire on the back."

"Well, there couldn't be more than a few thousand of those in the northland," Stride sighed.

"Yeah. It's a needle in a haystack, but it's worth a look, just in case Janine *is* telling the truth and this was a home-invasion robbery. I asked our buddy Lynn Ristau on the Wisconsin side of the bridge to cross-reference white-RAV owners with criminal records. She didn't sound too happy about it. You're going to owe her a burger at the Anchor Bar when we get the results."

Stride smiled. "Well, I already owe her. She was a big help with the bridge closure on Friday."

He and Maggie both turned toward the conference room door when they heard the bell of the elevator arriving in the basement. The doors slid open, and Sergeant Max Guppo waddled toward them with a laptop computer in his arms and a monster bag of Fritos tightly clamped between his teeth.

"Yoogzgonnwnsds," he said as he shouldered into the office.

Stride grinned at him. "Excuse me?"

Guppo opened his mouth, and the Fritos dropped onto the conference table. He plugged in the laptop.

"You guys are going to want to see this," he told them.

Guppo was only about as tall as Maggie and shaped like a snowman. His perfectly round head had a black comb-over that routinely flew like a pirate flag at the slightest breeze. He sported a pencil mustache underneath a nose that was mashed flat against his face. He'd been a Duluth police officer even longer than Stride, and despite his girth, Guppo was one of the most versatile investigators on the team.

"We found a bunch of SD memory cards in Jay's desk at the *News Tribune*," Guppo told them. "I've been going through the photos he took."

Breathing hard, Guppo sat down, squeezing himself into one of the wheely chairs. He turned the monitor so that Stride and Maggie could see it, and then he grabbed a handful of corn chips and pushed them into his mouth until his cheeks swelled like a squirrel's. He crunched loudly.

Stride watched as Guppo's thick forefinger scrolled through a series of photos that had been taken in parkland during the Minnesota fall, when the colors of the trees were at their peak. He recognized the wilderness not far from the ski slopes of Spirit Mountain. Leaning forward, Stride saw a man in the photographs, but the man was too distant to identify. Whoever it was wore camouflage pants and a black T-shirt. As the pictures scrolled, Stride saw that Jay had crept closer to the man in camouflage. The guy looked young—probably in his twenties—and in the best of the pictures, Stride picked out details in the man's profile. He had a shaved head, a trimmed beard, and a mass of tattoos on his neck and his bare forearms. It was difficult to estimate his height, but he looked bony and underfed. A small man.

He also held an assault rifle in his arms.

"So Jay took these photos?" Stride asked.

"Yeah."

"Do we know who this guy is?"

Guppo shook his head. "No. It looks like he spotted Jay and took off."

"Do you know when the pictures were taken?" Stride asked.

"Last October."

"That looks like Ely's Peak," Maggie said.

"Yeah, that's what I thought, too," Guppo replied. "The whole thing rang a bell with me, so I went back to police reports from the fall. We had a call from Jay on file from October 5. He said he'd been hiking in the woods near Ely's Peak, and he heard gunfire. He chased the guy and took pictures, and he sent us a couple of photos. We handed it off to Abel Teitscher, but he wasn't able to identify the man in camouflage. He staked out the location for a few days, but whoever it was didn't come back. That was the end of it. However, according to Abel's report, Jay was right about the gunfire. There was a lot of it. He followed the trail and found hundreds of shell casings in a clearing. Somebody went on a shooting spree."

Stride arrived home late, which wasn't unusual.

He lived with Cindy on a finger of land beyond the Duluth lift bridge known as the Point. They'd owned the house since they got married. It was a squat, two-bedroom cottage that could have been plucked from a Monopoly board. Detached garage, sand driveway, peeling paint. The backyard butted up to the dunes of Lake Superior. Everyone told them they should move to a larger place on Miller Hill, but they loved the location on the water, and Cindy loved the timelessness of an old house. She always said you shared a place like that with everyone who'd lived and died there before you.

He parked his Bronco in the snow and ice of their driveway. Inside, he hung his leather jacket on the hook near the front door and wandered into their tiny bedroom, which was behind the first door in the stubby hallway. He found Cindy in a lotus position on a throw rug on the wooden floor. Her eyes were closed, and she wore nothing but panties. She knew he was there, but she didn't react, and he simply watched her, smiling. Cindy was a pixie, not more than 110 pounds. Her black hair, parted in the middle, draped long and perfectly straight on either side of her face, all the way past her shallow breasts with their pretty pink tips. Her face was narrow, her nose as sharp as a shark's fin.

He could hear the shower running in their bathroom. They didn't have much water pressure, and it took forever to get hot water dripping into the tub.

"Hey," he said.

"Hey, babe," she replied cheerfully.

He no longer apologized for being late or missing dinner. That was just part of their lives.

She unfolded her legs and hopped nimbly to her feet. She came up to him, her forehead only reaching his chin, and got up on tiptoe to kiss him. Her arms slid around his waist. She had big brown eyes, with irises so large, there was almost no room for the whites around them.

"I'm going to hit the shower," she said.

"Want company?" he asked.

"I'd love it, but not this week."

"Oh."

"Yeah, back on the red river. Big surprise."

He heard the frustration in her voice. They'd been trying to get pregnant for two years with no success. Cindy was rarely moody, but the first day of her period always left her feeling sorry for herself. It was taking so long that he'd begun to wonder whether God was sending them a message, but he would never say so aloud. The need to have children was so much a part of who Cindy was that he didn't like to rain on her chalk-painting dreams. She came from a small family. Her only sister had been murdered as a teenager. If she'd had her way, she already would have had three or four kids of her own.

He followed her into the bathroom, where she brushed her teeth and tied her hair in a ponytail behind her back. She slid down her panties, and he watched as she climbed into the shower and pulled back the old plastic curtain.

"Any progress on Jay's murder?" she called.

"I can't really talk to you about that."

"Why? You talk to me about all your cases."

"You took Janine home. You'll be a witness when this goes to trial."

Cindy was silent in the shower for a long time. He wondered if it was the first time she realized that she was a part of this case, whether she liked it or not. Finally, her damp face poked around the side of the shower curtain. Her brow crinkled into an angry knot. "Assuming there is a trial," she told him. "Assuming she did it. Which she didn't."

"Cin," he said, but she swept the curtain closed again with a dismissive shake.

He left the bathroom, rather than argue with her. He was still hungry, so he went to the kitchen and cut himself a blond brownie from the pan Cindy had made over the weekend. He ate it in two bites.

Their house had a drafty screened patio facing the lake. Technically, it was a three-season porch, unheated, but he sat out there throughout the winter season anyway. He didn't bother turning on the lights. He sat in one of the chaise lounges and watched the windows. Snow flurries dotted the glass, making icy streaks. He must have dozed off, because when he opened his eyes, Cindy lay in the other chaise beside him.

Her eyes were open. She wore a pajama top and boxer shorts, and her tiny feet were poked into moccasins. Like him, she was unaffected by cold.

"I really don't get it," she murmured.

"You were there with Janine—" he began, but she shook her head.

"Not that."

"Oh."

He understood. Kids. Babies. He slid off the lounger and knelt beside her and took her hand, which was warm from the shower. "It'll happen."

"No," she said. "I don't think it will."

There was no point in trying to convince her. He didn't know, and she didn't know. Instead, he wrapped her small body up in his arms, the way he had for most of his life, since they were teenagers. At first, she was motionless, simply numb. Then her body began to shake, and she cried into his chest.

5

The next morning, Cindy Stride was annoyed with Cindy Stride.

She had no time for self-pity, and she was irritated with herself for giving in to negative emotions. She got out of bed while it was still dark, leaving Jonny to sleep. Despite the cold and the slick glaze of snow on the street, she went jogging, and she returned home red-faced and refreshed. She made a pot of coffee and drank a cup, leaving the rest for her husband.

Jonny was still asleep when she left. He usually was, because he kept late hours. Sometimes she woke him up to have sex, but not this week. On her way to work, she stopped at the basement bakery called Amazing Grace in Canal Park, and she talked with the college kids behind the counter while she ate a cranberry-walnut muffin. They all knew her. She stuck her nose into their lives and gave them advice. The kids probably rolled their eyes when she was gone, but she didn't care. Unlike her husband, Cindy was an extrovert who felt energized by other people.

She arrived at the clinic before everyone else, which was part of her routine. Turned on the lights. Made more coffee. She caught up on insurance paperwork at her desk. This was her peaceful time of the day, when she was alone to think. She read the newspaper for a while, and then she stared at the photographs pinned to the fabric wall of her cubicle. Jonny, of course. Their neighbor and doctor, Steve Garske. Jonny's boss and Cindy's friend, the deputy police chief Kyle Kinnick, looking ridiculous in his golfing outfit.

Cindy's sister, Laura.

She only had a teenage picture of Laura, because her sister had been killed when she was just eighteen. They hadn't been particularly close, but sometimes she found herself looking at Laura's face and wondering what she would have been like as an adult. It wasn't that Cindy felt alone. Not really. She had Jonny, and she had tons of friends. Even so, she wished that her relationship with Laura had been stronger when they were kids.

Her morning was busy with physio appointments. She worked with a seventy-two-year-old woman recovering from a hip replacement. She taught exercises to a thirty-something man dealing with a pinched nerve in his neck. A sixteen-year-old girl who'd broken her ankle playing soccer came in for work on the weight machines and got an extended lecture from Cindy about safe sex.

At lunchtime, she wandered around the corner of 3rd Street to St. Anne's to eat in the cafeteria, but when she spotted the cardiac wing on the hospital sign, she took an impulsive detour and headed for Janine Snow's office. She hadn't seen her friend since the night of the murder.

Cindy asked the receptionist to get a message to Janine, and she sat down to wait. It was a typical doctor's office. Old magazines. Soothing paintings on the wall. A few children's books and toys. The only other people in the waiting room were a black woman and her son. The boy was around ten, and he had his face pushed against an aquarium, making nose prints as he watched the brightly colored tropical fish.

"Sherman," the woman called to her son. She was probably in her late twenties but had the tired posture and foghorn cough of an older woman. When he didn't answer, she spoke more sharply. "Sherman, you look at me right now."

The boy turned away from the aquarium and folded his arms across his chest. "What?"

"See if this nice woman here would like a cup of coffee."

Cindy smiled. "Oh, I'm fine, thank you."

"No, it's the polite thing to do," the woman said. "He has to be polite. Sherman Aloysious, what did I say?"

With an exaggerated sigh, the boy wandered to a coffee urn on a corner table and filled a foam cup. The woman winked at Cindy. "We named him after his grandfathers, but truth to tell, he's not so fond of either name."

Sherman Aloysious brought Cindy a cup of coffee, and she thanked him profusely. He was at that little-boy stage where his ears had grown faster than the rest of his head, and his skinny arms and long legs looked out of proportion. Even so, he was cute. She won him over enough to get a shy smile, and he returned to his previous job of studying the fish.

"You here to see Dr. Janine?" the woman asked with a hint of concern. People who came to see Janine typically had big problems.

"I am, but I'm not a patient. Janine's a friend."

"Oh, I'm glad she has friends. Awful thing she's going through. She's a good woman."

"Yes, she is," Cindy said.

"The police should just leave her alone," the woman announced defiantly, "instead of hassling her the way they are. Damn cops."

Cindy didn't identify herself or her husband. "The police have a job to do. I'm sure everyone just wants the truth to come out."

The woman shook her head. She had a narrow face with too much eye makeup, a big pile of dark hair, and a curvy, overpadded figure. "Wish I could believe that's true," she said, "but you know how it goes. Woman gets too uppity, men want to tear her down. That husband of hers is no big loss."

"Did you know Jay?" Cindy asked.

She shook her head. "I know his type, that's all. Think a white wife makes them God's gift."

"Well, the whole thing is a tragedy," Cindy said.

"You're right about that."

Cindy got up and crossed the small office and sat down next to the woman. "Is he your only child?" she asked, nodding at the boy.

"Lord, no, three more back home. All girls. He's the oldest. My husband's watching the others. Didn't think Dr. Janine needed the whole clan running around. My boy was born with a heart problem. Started getting worse last year. We thought we were going to lose him, but Dr. Janine saved his life. Believe me, I love that woman to pieces. It makes me mad to see the police and the newspapers talking about her the way they do. Anybody says something bad about Dr. Janine around me, I'll kick their ass."

Near the aquarium, the boy giggled at his mother's language. Looking at him, Cindy could see the top of a zipper scar on his skin, where his loose T-shirt hung on his chest.

"Want the truth?" the woman went on. "I don't much care whether Dr. Janine killed her husband or not. Everything that woman does for people? All the lives she saves? I say, put that man in the ground and move on. Give her a medal or something for who she is. The world needs her doing what she's doing."

Cindy gave the woman a weak smile but didn't reply. The trouble was that even people who defended Janine still thought she'd pulled the trigger. This woman didn't believe that Janine was innocent. She simply didn't care if Janine was guilty.

"Cindy," said a Texas voice. "This is a surprise."

Janine stood in the doorway in a white coat over her blouse and skirt. She looked better than she had on the night of the party. She was calm, strong, a professional—not a woman suspected of murder.

"I'm sorry to barge in on you," Cindy said. "Do you have five minutes?"

"I suppose." Janine nodded at the woman next to Cindy. "Toiana, do you mind?"

The woman waved a hand. "You two friends take all the time you want. We're just fine here."

Janine led her into her office. Cindy had been here many times, but it felt different now, and she felt out of place. Janine sat down behind her desk and said what Cindy was thinking. "You probably shouldn't be here, you know. We shouldn't be talking. Your husband and my lawyer wouldn't be happy with us."

"I don't care," Cindy said. "Do you?"

Janine laughed, showing a little bit of her old self. "Not really."

"So, how are you?"

"Trying to go on with my life as if nothing was happening," Janine replied. "Which is impossible, of course."

"Sure." Cindy bit her lip and then said, "I just wanted to tell you that I believe you about Jay. I told Jonny you didn't do it."

"I appreciate that. Most people seem to have their minds made up about me."

"You have lots of defenders."

"I'm not so sure. Everywhere I go now, people suddenly stop talking. I realize it's because they were gossiping about me and Jay. And not because they think I'm innocent."

"That woman outside thinks you're a saint."

Janine didn't look comforted. "Oh, patients, yes. You save a life, they love you forever. Mind you, if you fail, they hate you just as much. I'm not comfortable with it either way."

She got up and went to the window. She put a hand on the glass, and when she took her fingers away, the warmth left behind a ghost of steam. "I'm not looking forward to facing a jury of my peers," she added. "I don't have peers. I know how arrogant that sounds, but I don't. I'm not sure an ordinary person could understand my life."

"It won't come to that," Cindy said.

"Yes, it will. Let's not kid ourselves. There's a courtroom in my future."

"Jonny won't ignore evidence that exonerates you."

"Maybe not, but it's hard to dislodge an idea in someone's head, once it puts down roots."

Cindy wanted to say something more, but Janine held up a hand to stop her. Her friend came closer. For a moment, Cindy thought Janine might hug her, but she stopped short. Janine wasn't a physical woman in that way. She shied away from sentiment.

"Listen, you should probably go," Janine told her. "I appreciate your coming to see me, though. Really. No one does now, if they don't have to. I'm a pariah."

"I'm always here if you need me. If there's any way I can help you, I will."

"Thank you." Janine looked at her in a strange way, as if seeing her for the first time. Cindy wondered what she saw. For a woman who was typically self-confident and happy with her life, Cindy felt a nagging sense of inferiority around Janine Snow.

"You know, I envy you," Janine went on.

Cindy was so surprised that she laughed. "Me?"

"Absolutely."

"Why is that?"

Janine reached out and touched Cindy's long hair. It was a meaningful gesture for a woman who was particular about personal boundaries and distances. "You're a woman first. A wife. You're more than your job."

"So are you."

"Oh, no," Janine said, shaking her head emphatically. "That's not me at all. I don't think of myself as a woman. And definitely not a wife. I've never been good at that. No, I made my choice a long time ago. I'm a doctor. A surgeon. That's me. That's what I do, and it's who I am. There's nothing else."

She gestured around the office as if it were her home. Her sanctuary.

"All this," she said, "this is what I live for."

6

"So why isn't that doctor in prison yet?" Clyde Ferris asked Stride. "C'mon, man, if she was black, you'd have closed the book, and she'd be rotting behind bars already. We both know it."

"The investigation is still in the early stages," Stride replied.

Clyde grabbed a lit cigarette from a crinkled piece of aluminum foil on the concrete floor of the garage. Both men were smoking, and the bitter smell clouded over their heads. The wooden garage door was open, letting in cold air and the noise of a truck engine on Grand Avenue. Jay Ferris's brother sat among the disassembled parts of a rusted snowblower. He ran a small engine shop out of his house in West Duluth, repairing snowblowers during the winter and lawn mowers during the summer. The garage walls were covered with spare motor parts hung on hooks.

"You saying she didn't do it?" Clyde asked. "Or is it just that she's a rich white doctor, so you have to treat her like the queen?"

"I'm saying we're still gathering evidence, and that takes time. We have to work our way through a lot of potential suspects."

"Including a few cops," Clyde said.

Stride didn't respond to the taunt, even though it was true. "Jay made a lot of enemies with the things he wrote."

Clyde labored on an overtight screw with a wrench that had seen a lot of seasons. He wore coveralls that were greasy with oil stains and a pair of old Converse sneakers. He was shorter and skinnier than his handsome older brother. He wore his hair in a bushy Afro that looked like a throwback to the 1970s. His beard was scraggly and untrimmed. He had a reddish birthmark on his cheek shaped like a turtle with its head and legs poked out.

"Yeah, Jay was honest, and that scares people," Clyde said. "People around here don't like a black man messing with their privileged little lives."

"I'm not sure many people in Duluth see themselves as privileged," Stride said.

"Well, that's the point, right? Jay was just telling it like it is. Like about that cop of yours. Skinner. Jay knew what that boy was all about."

"Nathan Skinner made a mistake," Stride said. "I never said he didn't."

"His mistake was getting caught. You know Skinner came after Jay after you gave him the boot, right? Took a swing at him over by the Saratoga bar?"

"I do. Nathan was drunk. He spent a night in jail."

Clyde spit on the floor. "One night."

"We're talking to Nathan," Stride said. "We're talking to everyone who might have had a grudge against Jay. Is there anyone *you* think wanted Jay dead?"

"Other than that bitch of a wife? Yeah, okay, it was a long list with Jay. He pushed people's buttons. Got everybody riled up. That was his *job*. Remember that column he did on suburban drug addicts last July?"

Clyde got to his feet and wiped his hands. He strolled to a bulletin board in the back of the garage. Stride could see that Clyde kept many of his brother's newspaper columns pinned there with thumbtacks. The man pawed through yellowed clippings and grabbed one, tearing it and leaving a scrap behind on the board. He brought it to Stride.

"Folks were talking about this one for weeks," Clyde said.

Stride read it, and he remembered the column.

Think you're safe? You're not.

Think you know who you should be afraid of? You don't.

Case in point: I was in line behind a woman at a pharmacy this week. Me, I like my New York steaks, and if that means 40mg of Lipitor a day, so be it. This woman ahead of me, let's call her Holly. That's not her real name, but it doesn't matter. You know who she is. She could be your next-door neighbor. Your wife. Your sister. Your boss. Ms. Everywoman.

Holly had a prescription for Vicodin. The pain med that makes you feel no pain. Weird, she didn't look like she was in pain, but I guess you can't always tell. Holly paid cash. Sometimes you just know something's not right, and my radar told me that Holly wasn't right. Ping, ping, ping—that's how it works. I picked up my all-the-meat-you-can-eat drug, and then I followed Holly. To the parking lot. To her car. Followed her all the way across town to another pharmacy.

That's right. You guessed it. Another prescription. Vicodin. Cash.

Yep, sweet-faced, all-American housewife Holly is an addict. Don't be so shocked. There are Hollys everywhere. But who cares, you say, right? If she's a pill popper, nobody gets hurt except herself. We've all got our vices.

Oh, but I left out the best part. Guess what Holly does for a living? She drives a school bus. You hand your kids over to her every day, and she's an addict. She could fall asleep at the wheel. She could forget to stop at a railroad crossing. Maybe she already has.

How are you feeling now?

All right, cards on the table. I lied. I don't know who Holly is. Or what she does. Maybe she's a secretary. Or a waitress. Or a pilot. Or a cop. That's the point: she's the only one who knows.

But I've got your number, Holly. I can rat you out any time I want to. Get help, okay?

Clyde laughed. "I bet half the pill poppers in town started looking over their shoulders at Walgreens after this column came out."

"Did Jay ever tell you who Holly was?"

Clyde shook his head. "No, he'd never spill something like that."

"Did you and your brother have a close relationship?" Stride asked.

The man wiped sweat from his brow and grabbed an open can of beer from a metal shelf.

"Me and Jay? Not so much, really. I saw him every couple of months. He had better things to do than hang out with me."

"When was the last time you saw him?"

"Right after New Year's. Dude almost killed me."

Stride cocked his head. "How so?"

"Jay took me ice-fishing in the harbor. Didn't look safe to me, but Jay wanted to go. Winter started out pretty warm, remember? Next thing you know, ice started cracking, shanty started going down. We barely got out with our necks. He lost his truck and his fish house, but that was Jay. He liked risks, liked going all in. It was the same way when he was growing up. Smart as hell, way smarter than me, but all you cops knew his name because of the stupid shit he pulled. He near got thrown out of UMD half a dozen times, but they were scared he'd write about them in the college paper."

"Jay made something of himself," Stride said.

"Oh, sure, Jay was going places. He had the looks, the brains, the mojo."

"What about Dr. Snow?" Stride asked.

"What about her?"

"I gather you don't like her."

"Oh, hell, no. Rich Southern bitch, that's who she is. I warned him off her when they started dating, but he didn't care. I met her exactly once. Treated me like a turd she was stepping around on the sidewalk."

"So what did Jay see in her?"

"You can't figure it out? That face, that body? Jay said she was wild in the sack. And let's face it, the money was a big thing. Jay liked money. Everybody knew his name because of the newspaper, but he didn't have a dime to call his own until he met her."

"I heard their relationship was rocky," Stride said.

"Oh, yeah, the two of them could fight."

"Jay signed a prenup, though, right? If he walked out, he got nothing."

"Jay wasn't walking out," Clyde said. "No way. Fact is, for all the shit, he loved her. Or maybe he just loved shoving it in everyone's face, white doc with her black stud. He didn't want a divorce. No, sir. He was never going to give her up. If anything, he wanted to break her."

"What about Dr. Snow? Did she want out of the marriage?"

"Yeah, she offered to buy him out with a fat settlement. He didn't want it. I told him, take the money and run, but he was stubborn. Both of them were. Neither one wanted to lose to the other, you know? Guess she finally figured out there was only one way to get rid of him."

Stride frowned. "You know we haven't found the murder weapon."

"So? She's smart. She dumped it somewhere good."

"Dr. Snow says there was no gun in the house."

"She's lying."

"You know that for a fact?" Stride asked.

"Damn right. Jay had a gun. Big fat old revolver. Had it for years."

"She says she made him get rid of his gun when they got married."

"I don't know what Jay told her," Clyde said, "but he didn't get rid of it. No way. He always had his gun with him. He didn't like going to certain places in the city without a little protection."

"Do you know what kind of gun it was?"

"Like I said, a revolver. Beyond that, who knows? You may not believe this, but not all black folks know about guns."

Stride smiled. "Okay."

Clyde retreated to his bulletin board again. He grabbed a photograph and brought it back and put it in Stride's hands. "I want this picture back at some point, but for now, you take it. I don't want anyone taking Janine's word over mine about that gun. See what I mean?"

Stride studied the photograph. It was a picture of Clyde and Jay in a Duluth bar, along with half a dozen other men. Jay had his arm slung around the shoulder of his younger brother, and where his sport coat fell open, Stride could see the black grip of a revolver poking out of a shoulder holster. Clyde wasn't lying.

"When was this taken?" he asked.

Clyde shrugged. "Last October, maybe? Not long ago. It was a bachelor party for one of the boys there. I'm telling you, I never saw Jay without his gun."

7

Maggie sat in her Avalanche in the shadow of Ely's Peak.

The craggy hilltop looming over the highway was dotted with trees clinging to the earth against the bitter wind. It was raw and wild, like most winter days. Duluth in the cold season was a black-and-white movie, as if all the colors of the world had been leached away. Black trees met the milky gray sky, and the white ice of the lakes blended into the snow-covered hills. Hoarfrost deadened the clustered needles of the pines, turning green to silver. Most of the time, the sun didn't dare show its face.

She'd been up since before dawn, and she typically didn't sleep until one or two in the morning. So far, the pace hadn't caught up with her. All she did was work, but she didn't really miss having a social life. Twice since she'd moved to Duluth, she'd had one-night stands, and two years earlier, she'd had a relationship that lasted three months before it crashed and burned. That was it. Most men couldn't deal with her insane work hours. They also couldn't deal with her attachment to Stride. Anyone who spent ten minutes listening to her talk about him knew that her feelings ran deep.

Stride had taken a chance on Maggie right out of college, when she was a stiff kid who knew a lot about books and not much about people. She was grateful for the opportunity, but she wasn't sure when gratitude had morphed into something else. Most days, she pushed those thoughts out of her head. Stride was the boss. Cindy was his wife. End of story. It was one of those fantasies that was best left in the back of a closet somewhere.

Maggie saw a dented pickup drawing closer on Becks Road, and she switched off her radio, which was blasting Aerosmith. The truck slowed and turned into the parking lot near the train tunnel overpass where Maggie waited. The door of the pickup opened, and Nathan Skinner climbed out.

The two of them had never been friends. Maggie scared the hell out of most cops, despite her size. She was smarter than they were, and she had a wicked tongue. One of the newbies, Ken McCarty, said a meeting with her was like sticking a finger into boiling water. Nathan was different. He was a UMD hockey hero, with a chip on his shoulder from the day she'd met him. Politicians and businesspeople in the city fawned over him because of his victories on the ice. He was part of the boys' club, and he resented Maggie because she was small, young, a woman, and Chinese. To him, if you weren't a white male with Scandinavian roots, you didn't really belong in Duluth.

When Jay Ferris leaked a videotape of Nathan's highway arrest near the Wisconsin Dells, Maggie wasn't surprised by the man's drunken rant. Nathan wasn't really a hard-core racist, but he oozed privilege, which was the worst kind of arrogance for a cop. He thought he could do anything and say anything and never pay a price. When Stride finally fired him, she was glad to see him go.

Nathan knew it.

He wore the drab uniform of a security guard as he climbed into her truck, but his demotion hadn't wiped the self-satisfied grin from his face. Nothing dented Nathan's ego. She would never have admitted it to anyone, but she felt the attraction of his physical magnetism. He was an asshole, but he was a good-looking asshole. He was still built like a college athlete, with muscles testing the seams of his uniform. He had short blond hair, and his face bore the dents of hockey sticks to his nose and chin, but the effect was to make him look tough. Which he was. He had a casual smile that didn't hide what he wanted, and

though Maggie would never have gone to bed with him, she knew lots
of women who would have jumped at the chance.

"Let's get this over with, Nathan," she told him. "You know why
you're here."

"Sure, I figured you'd be calling. What a shame about Jay, huh?"
The edge in his voice made it clear that Nathan didn't consider Jay's
death a shame at all. "Why meet out here in the middle of nowhere?
Are you afraid people would talk if they saw us together?"

"Don't flatter yourself. Jay filed a report about a shooting incident
near here. I'm checking it out. Besides, I figured you wouldn't want
anyone to know the police were questioning you. You don't want your
name in the papers again, do you?"

"Oh, I don't really care. If people think I shot Jay, they might give
me a medal for it."

"Did you?" she asked.

"What, shoot him? No. Unfortunately, I don't have much of an
alibi for last Friday. Sorry."

"What were you doing?"

"I was sick. Flu. I spent the evening alone in my apartment."

"Did you go to a doctor?"

"No."

"Can anyone confirm that you were home that night?"

"I had a Sammy's pizza delivered," he said. "The driver will remember me. She was cute."

"What time was that?"

"Too early to make a difference," he said. "I still could have gone
out later and blown Jay's head off. But I didn't."

"When did you last see Jay?" Maggie asked.

"See him? When his face was at the other end of my fist at the Saratoga last April. After that, he took out a restraining order, so I stayed
away from him. Look, my gun is in my truck. If you want to test it,
feel free. I didn't shoot him."

"Okay," Maggie said. "Go get it."

Nathan looked surprised and annoyed. He climbed down from the
Avalanche, kicked through snow back to his pickup, and retrieved a
Smith & Wesson .357 Magnum revolver with a wooden grip from his

glove compartment. He emptied the cartridges and shoved them into his pocket. When he returned to the Avalanche, Maggie held an open evidence bag, and he put the gun inside.

"How long do you plan to keep that?" Nathan asked.

"Until the test is done. Few days. Couple years. Somewhere in there."

She shoved the evidence bag with the gun into her glove compartment, and Nathan swore under his breath. She grabbed a printout from her dashboard of one of the photographs taken from Jay's camera. She showed the picture of the man in camouflage to Nathan.

"Ever seen this guy around town?" she asked.

His blue eyes squinted at the paper. "Nope."

"Either on the force or after?"

"Like I said, no." Nathan checked his watch. "Are we done here, Maggie? I've got a shift starting soon. Nothing like minimum wage and no benefits. I live the glamorous life."

"Where do you work?"

"Wherever they send me."

"Yeah, we're done here," Maggie said.

Nathan stalked back to his pickup and drove off with his tires spinning. Maggie watched the truck disappear northward toward Interstate 35. She knew the test would come back negative on Nathan's gun. He wouldn't have offered it up if it was the murder weapon. Even so, the streets of Duluth were a little safer with him disarmed.

She got out of her truck and swapped her clog heels for a pair of winter boots. She zipped up her burgundy jacket, which wasn't much protection against the cold. She didn't bother with a hat. When she shut the door, she saw the dents and scrapes tattooing the yellow paint of the Avalanche. She was a terrible driver.

Maggie climbed from the parking lot into the deep snow lining the shallow slope. Dead weeds poked out of the drifts. She crossed under power lines where a strip of land had been cleared in the woods and headed for the next line of birch trees, whose black-and-white trunks were speckled like snake skins. The dark mountain loomed above the trees like a slumbering bear. She heard a lonely train whistle below her, near the river. Her face felt blistered by the wind.

Four months earlier, Jay Ferris had been here. He'd tracked a man wearing camouflage and carrying an assault rifle. Maggie had checked other police calls since then. Two other reports had come in of gunfire in this area. One was only three weeks ago. Whoever the man was, he was still around. He was more careful now, but he kept coming back.

She pushed through the trees. The snow got inside her boots and made her socks wet. She dug in her pocket for some of the photographs from Jay's camera, and when she compared them to the landscape around her, she thought she was in the right place. She studied the ground and the trees but saw nothing unusual.

Ten more minutes passed as she climbed higher. She couldn't feel her feet or her fingers. She was about to turn back when she glimpsed a fleck of red winking in and out of the black-and-white forest. She waded into the thicker trees, and as she got closer, she heard the flapping of plastic. What she'd spotted was a red bull's-eye target laminated and nailed to the trunk of a birch. The center of the target had a jagged hole where it had been shot away with numerous bullets, and the wood of the tree underneath was splintered and broken.

She looked deeper into the forest, and she saw other red targets. Six, eight, ten of them. One by one, she tracked them, and each one bore the marks of a hunter who had used them for practice. In the snow, as she walked, she found spent shell casings, too. Dozens of them, like dirty gold cigars at her feet. Dozens became hundreds.

She didn't like it. Not one little bit.

After a quarter-mile following the targets, she came upon the carcass of a deer in a small clearing. It was a doe, frozen and stiff in the snow, its tongue drooping from its mouth. The deer had been dead for days. Its fur was a mass of darkened blood, and the animal was surrounded by more spent casings. The hunter had shot it and then come upon the body and kept firing. And firing.

Maggie started counting the bullet wounds in the dead deer, but she stopped after two dozen.

Someone was very angry.

8

"A deer?" Stride asked.

He leaned on the metal handle of his shovel. He'd cleared eight inches of snow from his driveway on the Point, and he was sweating. A quarter mile away, the tower of the Duluth lift bridge shimmered over the ship canal like a monster of gray metal. Lingering snow flurries spat through the lights. In February, the bridge mostly stayed anchored to the ground, so the residents of the Point enjoyed a respite for several icy weeks from getting trapped by the coming and going of cargo boats.

"Yeah. A deer. Shot to pieces."

Stride didn't answer immediately. He wiped his brow with one sleeve. On the street, he spotted the sedan of his friend Steve Garske passing behind Maggie's Avalanche. The two men waved at each other. Steve's Chrysler kicked up slush, and as his wheels hit the metal bridge deck, the whine sounded like a pack of stinging wasps. It was nine o'clock at night. He figured that Steve, who was a musician as well as a doctor, was off to a gig with his band at Amazing Grace.

"I'm not sure what we can do other than notify the Department of Natural Resources," Stride told her.

"I did that," Maggie said, "but that's not what bothers me."

"Then what is it?"

"This wasn't hunting. This was rage."

Stride frowned. Hunting out of season wasn't uncommon, and neither was the occasional hunter who used his weapon to live out a Rambo fantasy in the forest. Even so, he'd worked with Maggie long enough to trust her instincts.

"What else did you find?" he asked.

"He had plastic targets scattered in an unusual pattern. The heights varied. It was what you'd expect from someone walking through a crowd, picking off targets." She added after a pause, "Human targets."

"That's a big leap, Mags."

"I'm just telling you what it looked like to me. I mean, I know we're all sensitive after Columbine—"

"No, I hear you. Do we have any idea who this guy could be?"

Maggie shook her head. "I passed Jay's photos around. No one recognized him. Whoever he is, he's flying under the radar. I'm having a couple of the uniforms collect shell casings so we can see if he left any prints."

"Well, let's make sure our guys keep their eyes open around town, too."

"Do you want more bad news?" Maggie asked. "Jay wrote about this guy in his column."

"The guy in camouflage?"

"Yeah, Jay did a column in November on gun control and the expiration of the assault-weapons ban. Camo Guy was Exhibit Number One. Jay talked about gun nuts carrying military-style hardware in our parks. Talked about chasing this guy, reporting him to the cops. And, naturally, how the cops did squat."

Stride leaned against the yellow Avalanche next to Maggie and lit a cigarette. He stared at the pack in his hand with disgust, then shoved it into the rear pocket of his jeans. "Do you think this guy is a legitimate suspect in Jay's murder?"

"Probably not, but if we don't rule him out, it's raw meat for Archie Gale. Plus, I want to find him and see what makes him tick. He worries me."

"Okay. We'll let the dogs out. Speaking of Jay's columns, what about this prescription-drug addict he wrote about last summer? The woman he called Holly. Do we have any way of tracking her down? He threatened to blow up this woman's life in his column. That's certainly a motive if she thought he was serious."

"Unless he made up the whole thing," Maggie said.

"Is that possible?"

"Jay wrote that he was picking up Lipitor at a pharmacy when he saw this woman Holly. The thing is, I checked, and there weren't any pharmacy charges on his credit card last year. His medical records don't show that he was taking any prescription meds. He wasn't on Lipitor. So if you ask me, Holly is a fake. He made her up to make a point about prescription-drug abuse."

"Okay. Well, that's one we can cross off our list." Stride blew smoke into the night air. "How's Nathan?"

"You know what I think about him," Maggie said.

"Yes, I do. Does he have an alibi?"

"Sort of. I found the Sammy's driver who confirmed that she delivered a pizza to Nathan at his apartment that night. It was too early for an alibi, but she said he looked half-dead and was hacking up phlegm. He put the moves on her anyway, which she said was pretty gross."

"Some things don't change," Stride said. "How about the tip on the white Toyota RAV? The one that the kid spotted on Skyline Parkway?"

"We've got a list of RAV owners in the northland who have some kind of criminal record. We're working our way through them. So far, no one looks promising. I re-interviewed the kid, too. He admits smoking a few joints at Enger Tower that night. I'm not sure we can rely on his memory for details."

"Great."

"I've been backtracking through home break-in reports around the state, too, and I can't find any MOs that look similar. The idea that this was a murder-robbery seems far-fetched. We've been watching pawnshops, but none of the missing jewelry has shown up."

"I think if we find the gun, we'll find the jewelry, too," Stride said. "Wherever Janine hid it."

"I agree," Maggie replied. "But as much as I like Janine Snow for this, we keep digging up new suspects faster than we cross them off."

"Like who?"

Maggie fished in the pocket of her red jacket. She pulled out an evidence bag with a handwritten piece of paper inside. "Guppo was going through papers from Jay's desk. He found this. It's a letter to Janine from last May. Jay had it in his top drawer."

Stride glanced at the paper. The script handwriting was impeccable, but it was too dark outside to read the text. "What does it say?"

"It's from a woman named Esther Rose. Basically, she accuses Janine of murdering her husband."

Stride's eyebrows rose. "Excuse me?"

"Esther's husband, Ira, had a heart problem. He went under the knife at St. Anne's. He didn't make it. Janine was the surgeon. Esther blames Janine for his death, and despite some very ladylike handwriting, she makes threats like a crime boss. In fact, she says specifically that she'd like to see Janine's husband die so that she knows how it feels."

"What do we know about Esther Rose?" Stride asked.

"She has a place on the North Shore. Expensive. Ira was an IP attorney in the Twin Cities, so he made a bundle. Driver's license record shows a very proper-looking sixty-year-old lady."

"Not exactly your typical gun-toting killer, but I'll talk to her," Stride said.

"You might want to bring backup. Those grandmotherly types can surprise you."

Stride smiled and crushed his cigarette under his foot. "Dan Erickson called today."

"Lucky you," Maggie said.

Dan Erickson was the St. Louis County Attorney. He hadn't been in the job long, but he'd already contracted the disease most common to county prosecutors. Ambition. Dan was politically hungry, and he saw the county attorney's job as a stepping-stone to higher office in Minnesota. He had the suave looks of a politician—blond hair sprayed into place, dark suits and shined shoes, a Florida tan even in February.

He was smooth and effective in front of juries, but Stride didn't trust him. Dan saw every trial through the lens of how a win or loss would affect his career.

A trial for Janine Snow would be a media circus. Putting a woman like her in prison would be a publicity boon for Dan all over the state.

"He wanted to know if we were any closer to making a case against Janine," Stride said.

"What did you tell him?"

Stride shrugged. "Thanks to Clyde, we can put a gun in Jay's hands. And the fact that we haven't found Jay's gun is bound to leave a jury wondering where it is. After all, if his gun wasn't the murder weapon, it should have been in his house or in his truck, right?"

"That must have made Dan happy."

"It did. It's also obvious that Janine's relationship with Jay was on the rocks. According to Clyde, Janine wanted a divorce, but Jay didn't. So a jury might believe that she didn't see a way out other than murder."

"Guppo dug up a couple more tidbits about them," Maggie added. "He's been interviewing Jay's friends. One of them told him that last summer, Janine got fed up with Jay's extravagant spending. She cut him off. Shut down his credit cards without telling him. Jay was eating dinner at a downtown restaurant on July 3, and his card came back declined. There were local heavy hitters around who saw the whole thing. Jay was humiliated. And furious."

"Interesting."

"Yeah, it's weird, though. Janine turned the credit cards back on a couple of weeks later. After that, Guppo says Jay spent even more than he did before. And here's another thing. We went through their phone records. Last December, right after Thanksgiving, Jay put in a call to an attorney at the Stanhope law firm downtown. A woman named Tamara Fellowes."

"What's her practice area?" Stride asked.

"Family law. Including divorce."

"Did you talk to her?"

"Yeah, but she's a lawyer. She wouldn't tell me anything."

Stride shoved his hands into his pockets. "Clyde insisted that Jay didn't want a divorce. He says Janine offered to pay him off, but Jay said no."

"Maybe he changed his mind."

"Maybe, but if he did, then there's no reason for Janine to kill him," Stride said. He shook his head, pulled out the pack of cigarettes, but then returned it to his pocket without taking another one. "I'm convinced she killed him, Mags, but none of this makes any sense. What the hell was really going on between those two?"

Janine made sure she wasn't being followed as she left the hospital.

She turned left out of the parking ramp in her Mercedes. She eyed her mirror, looking for headlights behind her, but she didn't see anyone. It was dark, after ten o'clock. She headed for downtown, past the city's old buildings. The Union Gospel Mission. Antiques and pawnshops. Liquor stores. A Cantonese restaurant. The brick-lined streets were slick with fresh snow. On the side streets, cars nudged their way up and down the steep hills.

At Sammy's Pizza, in the middle of downtown, she turned right. That wasn't the direction she wanted to go, but she checked to see if anyone turned behind her. No one did. She coasted around the next corner, still watching the mirror, and then she parked and waited with her engine running. Paranoia.

No one showed up. She was alone.

Janine retraced her route to 1st Street. She continued several more blocks, then turned downhill to Michigan Street, which was more industrial than the rest of downtown. She pulled into a deserted bank parking garage and took the ramp to the open-air roof, where she parked in a corner.

She got out. Despite the darkness, big sunglasses covered much of her face. A scarf was wrapped around her chin, and she pulled the fur-lined hood of her winter coat low on her forehead. She didn't look any different from other Minnesotans bundled against the cold, so no one would recognize her. These days, people stared at her wherever she went. She was that woman from the TV news.

The woman who shot her husband.

On the street, Janine limped in the snow. She wore calf-length black boots. Her head was down, and her hands were in her pockets. The spasms in her leg reminded her of the fall she'd taken the previous winter, in which her ankle had broken and the tendons torn. She would never lose the slight limp that dogged her steps.

She crossed under the skywalk that led to the convention center and checked the street again. When she was convinced that she wasn't being watched, she crossed to an unmarked black steel door in a four-story brick building. Using a loose key, she opened the heavy door and let herself inside. The interior smelled of paint and dust. There was no elevator, just stairs. She climbed to the uppermost floor and pushed through another door into a carpeted hallway. She took two steps to an unmarked apartment and used another key to open it. She slipped inside and closed the door firmly behind her. The pain in her ankle was excruciating.

Janine began to breathe again. She went to the kitchen and poured herself a large glass of wine. She took it back to the living room, where the windows faced the lake. Light and snow swept the glass. In three long swallows, she finished the wine. She went to the bathroom and then returned for more. She settled into a white armchair and closed her eyes.

It had been days since she'd been here. Her getaway. She hadn't wanted to take the chance when someone might be following her. Part of her knew that the smart thing was to stay away forever, but she couldn't. The need to be here drew her back irresistibly. Especially now. The apartment was small, clean, elegant. It wasn't big, but she didn't need size. She simply needed a place that no one knew about. Not Jay. Not anyone. The deed to the condo was in the name of a shell company. The correspondence went to a drop box. Only one other person knew about it, and he had no incentive to admit it to anyone.

Janine smiled as she relaxed. She hadn't smiled in days. And then she laughed. And then she cried. Life was a crazy, crazy business. She had no illusions that she could hide from the truth forever.

She thought about Texas. Hot, backward, wonderful, awful Texas. Twenty years ago, she'd been a teenager living outside Austin, serving drinks at a country bar to save money for college. Her first husband,

Donny, who was no older than she was, had looked down her blouse and fallen in love. He wasn't particularly handsome, but he was as hardworking and loyal as a puppy. Donny adored her. She felt bad that, for herself, he was mostly a stepping-stone on her way to somewhere else. The things he wanted—a horse ranch, three kids, vacations in Orlando—simply weren't part of her DNA. Five years later, Donny was gone with a broken heart, and Lionel took his place.

Lionel was an entrepreneur with a pot of venture capital to pay for Janine's medical school. They were clear from day one about what they needed from each other. Lionel got a sexy, intelligent wife who could wow his board. She became an MD without a dime of debt. Who else could say that?

There was little emotion between them, but Lionel understood her dreams better than most. He was the same way about his med-tech start-up. Most people didn't have passion like that—something that consumed them and ate up every waking hour and left nothing in its place. From the time she was a little girl, Janine Snow had been focused on only one thing. Being a doctor. Being the best surgeon that any human being had ever been. Saving lives.

And she did it.

But the price was giving up a normal life.

She spent two hours alone in the condominium above Michigan Street. Two blissful hours in absolute silence. That was what she needed. When she finally left, she was singing quietly to herself, and the shake had disappeared from her hands. The pain in her ankle was gone. Her confidence was back. She could do anything, defeat anyone, win any battle. After the dark days following Jay's death, when she had felt nothing but despair, she was floating on air again, and she believed for a moment that she might not lose everything. She could almost see a future for herself through the storm.

Her Mercedes was where she had left it, on the top floor of the ramp garage. Flurries blew around it. A streetlight cast shadows. It was a pretty night. She walked with a lightness in her heart, breathing in the cold air, until she realized that someone was waiting for her.

A man appeared near her car and walked toward her. Janine froze.

"Don't worry, Dr. Snow," he called.

She didn't move. She had no weapon and no rape alarm, and even if she did, she couldn't afford to use them. Not when it meant answering questions. Such as what she was doing downtown at that time of night.

The man seemed to know her dilemma.

"I just want to talk to you," he said. He stopped ten feet away with his gloved hands in the air.

"Who are you?"

"My name's Melvin Wiley."

"What do you want?"

"It's pretty cold out here," Wiley said in a reedy voice that was hard to hear above the wind. "Would you prefer to talk in your car?"

"We'll talk right here. If we talk at all."

Wiley shrugged, but he wasn't put off. He was the kind of man who didn't get noticed in a crowd. You could pass him at the grocery store and not remember he'd been there. He wasn't short; he wasn't tall. He wasn't fat or thin. He had windblown brown hair with a high forehead and a bushy mustache. He had metal glasses that could have been worn by any man on the street. He wore chocolate-brown corduroys, old sneakers, and a blue down coat that he kept half-zipped. Underneath was a flannel shirt. She decided he was in his forties.

"What do you want?" Janine repeated.

"I knew your husband," Wiley said. "I did some work for Jay."

"What kind of work?"

"You sure you wouldn't be happier in your car?" he asked.

Janine said nothing. She waited.

"People like Jay come to me when they have questions," Wiley said.

"Questions?"

"Yeah. Typically, the question is, who's been banging my wife?"

Janine felt the shiver in her body from her feet to her neck. "You're a private detective."

"I call it matrimonial research. That's funny, don't you think? You have to have a sense of humor for this job. I used to work for the Department of Revenue, but I wanted a career where I could feel good about myself."

He laughed at his own joke. Janine's face was dead.

"Most people are easy targets," Wiley went on. "You follow them for a day or two, and there they are, kissing outside the motel room or in the car. Stupid. You're much better. Really, that's a compliment. For a doc, you were pretty good at shaking a tail. I bet it was a month before I found the place across the street. Even when I did, it looked like you were always alone. Smart, you going in the back while he went in from the front. Very smart. So I had to get creative. I put a camera in the air vent in your bedroom. That new HD technology is expensive but amazing. Once I had that in place, things got interesting."

Janine took two steps and slapped him hard across the face. He took it without flinching and rubbed the red welt she left behind. She didn't think it was the first time he'd been slapped.

"Got that out of your system?" Wiley asked. He dug in the pocket of his coat and pulled out a manila envelope. "Here, take a look: These are your greatest hits. I printed stills, but I've got video, too."

Janine opened the envelope and slid out one page. She recognized her own bare skin. And her lover's. Her closed eyes. His naked back and her legs wrapped around him.

"You're disgusting," she snapped. "What do you want? Money?"

"Well, I'm feeling a little torn here, Dr. Snow. I showed Jay what I got with my camera inside your little love nest. Since the police didn't find it, I'm guessing he destroyed what I gave him. Or maybe you did—who knows? Anyway, I figure it's my civic duty to do something with this. Jay's dead. I should really hand everything I found over to the police, you know? Or, heck, if I was a mercenary kind of guy, I might sell it. The tabloids would pay big bucks for this kind of thing."

"How much do you want?" Janine asked. Her voice was drained of life.

"Oh, I don't know. I'm sure we can come to some kind of arrangement. You might want to put me on retainer. A monthly stipend to do research for you. You'd be surprised how handy it can be to have a detective on the payroll."

"I'm leaving," Janine said.

"Sure. No problem. Take the envelope with you. I've got more where those came from." Wiley reached into his pants and slid out a business card. "You think about it, Dr. Snow, and then you give me a call, okay? We'll work something out."

She said nothing.

Wiley strolled away, disappearing in a cloud of snow. She heard his footsteps descending the ramp. She was alone again. The lightness in her soul had turned to lead, dragging her back into a black hole. Twenty years had passed since she was a Texas blonde, dreaming that she would make something of herself. Twenty years, and nothing in between seemed to matter at all.

9

Cindy slipped out of bed after midnight. Her skin was moist with sweat, and she shivered, because the house was as cold as a drafty barn. Jonny slept heavily, with one bare leg outside the blankets. He always slept like the dead after they made love. Normally, she did, too, but not tonight. She felt restless, but she wasn't sure why.

She went to her closet and grabbed a robe, which she pulled around her naked body. Her long black hair was a mess. She padded in her bare feet to the kitchen and switched on the light over the sink. Quietly, she unloaded the dishwasher, pushing up on tiptoe to reach some of the cabinets. There was something about an empty dishwasher that gave her a feeling of accomplishment.

She sat down at their small kitchen table. Reaching over to the counter, she turned on the radio to the Duluth MPR station and listened to classical music at a volume barely louder than a whisper. It was something dreamy and soft. She listened to it along with the persistent ticking of the clock over the refrigerator.

Jonny's old leather jacket was draped over one of the chairs. She shook her head with a smile. She'd teased him for years about getting rid of it, but Jonny never gave up anything from the past. She saw the bullet hole in the sleeve. She still remembered the night when Jonny's mentor, a cop named Ray Wallace, had shot himself in a northwoods cabin rather than face corruption charges. Ray had shot Jonny before putting the gun in his own mouth. She remembered the call from the hospital. Remembered her husband's ashen face. Those were the calls you feared when you were married to a cop. You woke up every morning, and you wondered if this would be the night you went to bed alone and in tears.

It was hard to imagine her life without him. And yet she lived with that perpetual shadow.

He'd brought papers home with him from the Detective Bureau. Documents. Files. Evidence. He usually did. He'd intended to work through the evening, but she'd interrupted his good intentions by straddling his lap. From there, they went to bed, and he never left. The evidence in Jay's murder investigation was spread all over the table, and although she didn't usually pry—well, who was she kidding? She pried all the time.

Cindy grabbed the topmost paper and turned it over. It was a photograph, taken somewhere in the Duluth woods. The picture showed the figure of a man, blurry because of the distance. He was young, scrawny, tatted, in camouflage, holding what appeared to be an assault rifle. In the first picture, he was in profile, but when she grabbed another page, she saw his eyes. She couldn't really see the details of his face, but his eyes reminded her of a shark's. Utterly empty. Not ferocious, like a wolf on the hunt. Eyes devoid of life. Eyes that saw nothing but the gray darkness of the water.

Jonny had written on a Post-it note on one of the pictures: *Who is this guy?*

And on another: *Find him.*

Cindy turned the photos facedown again. She didn't want to stare at them anymore. Something about the man's face left her with a hollow pit of anxiety in her stomach.

She got up from the table. She went to the hall closet and retrieved her heavy winter coat and her furry boots. She retreated to the porch at the back of the house and let herself out through the rear door. Their backyard was really nothing but a sand dune. She pushed through snow and rye grass, climbing to the top of the slope and then down to the beach by the Great Lake.

The city glowed on her left. White lights marked the buildings, and red lights blinked on the antenna farm high on the hillside. At her feet were boot prints, the tracks of dogs, and the parallel trails where cross-country skis had slid up and down the snow-covered shore. The lake was loud, but it was invisible behind a wall of ice taller than she was. Each winter the waves built a mountain range. It made the lake scary, because she couldn't see it. Somehow, with every bellow of thunder, she expected a tsunami to crest the wall and wash her away.

Cindy stood there with her hands in her pockets. The few inches of skin where her legs were bare felt raw. She had the beach, the city, and the night to herself. There was something hypnotic about the noise of the wind and the waves. She thought about everything. Her mind was a grasshopper, jumping this way and that.

She thought about Jonny. She could still feel him inside her, could still feel his hands on her body afterward. They had such a familiarity with each other. He was still a little repressed about sex after all these years, but to her, it was as natural as breathing or crying. She could remember all the way back to their first time, on a summer night by a small lake in a city park. The two of them, teenagers, naked in the water. And then making love with sand on their bodies and mosquitoes biting at their skin. Magic.

That was so long ago. Funny, how you took each day and put it on top of the one before, and before you even knew it, you had a lifetime.

She thought about her family. Hardly a family. Her mother, who'd died young, leaving them alone. Laura, taken from her that same summer night she fell in love with Jonny. Her father, a sanctimonious old hypocrite who used God as an excuse for his meanness to everyone who was close to him. It was hard to say she didn't miss him, but she didn't.

She thought about Janine. They'd known each other for five years. Her friend could not take a gun and shoot her husband. She didn't believe it. And yet Jonny always said you could never really know another person. Every individual was unfathomable, living inside their own soul, sharing it with no one else. She would never have said it aloud, but she wondered if she was being naive.

Was she wrong about Janine?

She put those doubts out of her mind. She had strength of will, which was something that her faith had given her. You could choose to be happy or unhappy. It was up to you. Jonny didn't share her devotion to religion, but she didn't need him for that. Her beliefs were for her and her alone.

Cindy thought about better things. Golf. It was winter now, but soon enough, she would be on an emerald-green fairway, 3-wood in hand. She reflected on her clients and their problems and what she could do next to help them with their rehabilitation. There were always other things to try. She thought about country music and Jonny's little crush on singer Sara Evans. She thought about her Outback, which needed a wash. She thought about Sammy's sausage pizza. They were all the little things that meant nothing and made up a life.

And then, from nowhere, the pain came.

No, this was not pain. She'd experienced pain before.

This was a spike catapulted upward between her legs, lifting her off the ground, sucking a cry from her chest, driving her to the snow. If she could have died right then to obliterate the agony splitting apart her insides, she would have picked death. She had no warning as it hit. It was simply there, and then it was gone, leaving no memory, as if it had been a phantom. She found herself on her knees, sweating, trying to understand what had just happened to her.

The strange thing was, she knew.

Deep in her closet of terrors, she knew.

10

Howard Marlowe heard glass breaking.

It came from upstairs in the front of the house. It wasn't a small noise, like a wineglass breaking in the sink. Something shattered, something big. He bolted to his feet from behind his desk, and he felt scared and ridiculous, wearing nothing but his white underwear. Goose bumps rose on his arms.

The empty eyes of the Easter Island statues stared at him from the poster on the wall. *Do something*, they told him.

Howard crept on tiptoe on the green shag carpet, as if he needed to be quiet in his own house. At the doorway, the basement hallway was cold and damp. The lights were off. He told himself that maybe he'd imagined the noise, but he could hear more glass breaking now, like rain. He reached behind the office door and grabbed a softball bat made of red aluminum. With the bat cocked over his shoulder, he stutter-stepped down the carpeted hallway to the stairway leading to the main level of the house. The wooden steps were unfinished, and the wall was unpainted plasterboard. He climbed two steps and listened.

Someone was overhead, moving around in their living room.

"Hey!" he shouted as loudly as he could, in the deepest voice he could summon. "Hey, get the hell out! The police are coming! I've called 911!"

Which he hadn't. He had no phone in the basement, and his cell phone was in the bedroom. He gripped the rubber handle of the bat with sweaty hands and took two more steps toward the closed door above him.

"Did you hear me? Get out!"

Carol screamed from upstairs. His wife's voice was gutted with fear. "Oh, my God, Howard! What's going on? Where are you?"

He reached the top step and grabbed the handle of the plywood door. He found he couldn't summon the courage to twist the knob. He listened and heard footsteps, barely six feet away on the other side of the flimsy piece of wood. Voices, too. More than one. The footsteps thumped, and he heard his front door open and felt the house seize with the change in air pressure. Icy drafts blew under the door and chilled his legs.

"Howard! Howard!"

Other than the half-finished basement, their house was on one level. A hallway off the living room led to three bedrooms. Carol was trapped in one of those bedrooms, steps away from the people who had invaded his house. His six-year-old daughter was in another bedroom.

"The police are almost here!" he shouted. "You'd better get out!"

The noises had stopped. There were no more voices, nothing but the rush of air from the open front door. He pushed an ear to the door, and when a minute of silence passed, he twisted the knob and inched the basement door open. The lights were off, but the glow of the streetlight revealed a shower of glass like diamonds on the hardwood floor. He didn't see anyone, but he could smell the sweaty odor that strangers had left behind. His finger flicked the light switch, and he squinted. The intruders had fled. The front door was wide open, letting in snow and wind. He took tentative steps into the middle of the room, twisting his head to check in every direction and feeling ripples of cold and fright down his back.

Carol's laptop was missing from the dining room table. She'd been using it there before they went to bed. The three drawers of his grandmother's oval accent table had been pulled out and dumped. He kept almost one hundred dollars in cash there for pizza deliveries, and the money was gone. Next to the living room sofa, two of their tall casement windows had been kicked inward, leaving shards around the frames.

"They're gone," he called to his wife. "It's okay."

He grabbed the phone and dialed 911. When he hung up the phone, he realized that Carol hadn't come out of their bedroom. He went to check on her, but the bedroom was empty. The sheets were rumpled. A flicker of concern flashed in his heart. He rushed to the closed door of the next bedroom, which belonged to Annie, and flung it open. The nightlight was on. Carol was in a rocking chair, and Annie was asleep in her arms, utterly undisturbed.

His wife's face was a mask of tears. Her eyes were wide open and red. Mucus dripped from both nostrils. Her lower lip trembled, and she clutched their daughter so tightly that Howard was afraid she would suffocate her. He knew Carol, and he understood. The bubble had popped. The wolf had come. Carol cherished their ordinary, predictable life, and now its sanctity had been violated. Certain things, when they were taken away, never returned.

"They're gone," he repeated.

She opened her mouth and closed it. She wiped her nose on her wrist. "You weren't in bed. You weren't there."

"Sorry, I was working in my office. I couldn't sleep."

Carol leaned her cheek against Annie's hair. "They could have murdered us."

"Carol, they were probably just kids," Howard told her. "They took your laptop."

"That's what you're concerned about? A laptop? I could have been raped! Killed! They could have taken Annie!"

"I know. The police will be here soon. I'm going to check if anything else is missing."

Howard left Annie's bedroom. He returned to the icy living room and realized he would need to board up the broken windows tonight. The temperature was around zero. He went to the front door, which was still open. Looking out through the storm door, he saw footprints running across their yard in the snow. Kids, he told himself.

He closed the door.

Howard returned to his empty bedroom and slipped on sweatpants and a white T-shirt. He checked the other rooms and made sure nothing else had been taken. Just the computer and the cash. His shouts had interrupted the robbers before they made their way deeper into the house.

Just kids.

I could have been killed.

Howard heard his wife's voice in his head as he stood in front of the broken windows and waited for the police lights to appear on the street. He thought to himself: And what if she had been killed? What if he'd gone into the bedroom and found his wife's body there?

Shot. Or strangled. Or stabbed.

Howard thought about Janine Snow.

That was her story, too. She took a shower, and when she came out of the bathroom, she found her husband dead on the living room floor. An intruder had come and gone. Murdered Jay Ferris. Taken jewelry from their bedroom. So she said.

It was such a long way from Howard's little house to that mansion on the hill. He had nothing in common with a woman like Janine Snow. Except now he did. A burglary could happen to anyone. He thought about her photograph, her blond hair, her put-together look, her arrogant beauty that was so intoxicating. And then he imagined her standing over her husband's murdered body.

No one believed her.

Howard thought: Would anyone believe *him*?

What if those kids had killed his wife? You're living your life, and suddenly a random act of violence changes everything. People start tearing apart your whole world. The police. The media. Pretty soon, they find out your secrets. Things that make you look guilty, even when you're not. Everybody had things like that. You could take anybody's ordinary life and turn it into something dark and criminal.

Look at Howard Marlowe. He murdered his wife.

Look at Janine Snow. She murdered her husband.

He heard movement behind him. Carol stood there, arms folded across her chest. She looked like someone who'd opened a closet door and seen the devil hiding inside.

"I want to get a gun," she said.

Howard cocked his head. His wife hated guns. She'd told him over and over that if you brought a gun into the house, sooner or later, it got used, and someone got killed. Accidents happen. Arguments happen. Kids play games.

No guns.

"Are you sure about that?" Howard asked. "I thought that you—"

"Didn't you hear me?" Carol screamed at him. He barely recognized her. "I'm never going through something like that again! Get me a gun, Howard! *I want a gun!*"

11

The North Shore home of Esther and Ira Rose had a for sale sign in the snow. A moving van was parked in the driveway, and Stride saw two men struggling to relocate an oak china cabinet from the house to the interior of the truck. As he headed for the front door, he saw moving boxes through the picture window.

The Roses had a perfect location on the North Shore highway. Their large yard sloped toward the scenic drive, and the entire house looked out on the blue expanse of Lake Superior. Every day offered a sunrise on the water. However, Esther Rose had obviously decided to move on with her life somewhere else, after her husband died under Janine Snow's hands on the operating table.

Esther met Stride at the door. She didn't look like a murderer, but she also didn't look like a woman who would send a threatening letter in exquisite penmanship—which is what she'd done. *You stood there and watched Ira die. You killed him. I hope you can feel something in that cold, cold heart of yours. I hope you suffer the same fate someday—standing helpless over the dead body of someone you love.*

She was in her sixties. It was mid-morning, but she could have been dressed for a country-club dinner, in silk blouse, skirt, and heels. She was small in stature, almost birdlike. She had no gray hair; it was well-colored to an attractive auburn and stylishly bobbed. She wore makeup and knew how to use it. The diamond ring on her finger was large and gaudy, and her earrings sparkled.

"I appreciate your taking the time to talk to me in the midst of your move," Stride said.

Esther's expression wasn't warm, but it wasn't unfriendly. "Yes, well, I know why you're here."

"Do you?"

She waved him into the house. With a small gesture of her hand, she directed the moving men outside to have a cigarette in the sun. Stride followed her into the living room that overlooked the lake, and despite the scattered boxes, there were chairs in which to sit. Esther took the end of a yellow sofa that was positioned to take full advantage of the view. A rose-colored china cup sat on an end table next to her. Her knees were pressed together, and she sat with a rigid posture.

"I assume you found my note," she said, looking embarrassed.

"Yes, we did."

Esther stared at the water. White ice hugged the shore, and the sun-dappled water beyond it was so blue that it was almost black. "Obviously, I regret what I said to Dr. Snow after the surgery. It was foolish to give in to my emotions that way. However, I understand your concerns, Lieutenant. I talked about wishing that she would experience the pain that I did in losing my husband. And now she has. It raises questions."

"Why don't you tell me what happened," Stride said.

She glanced around the house with a look of sad nostalgia. Every surface had memories. "This was supposed to be our summer retirement home. Ira and I love—loved—Duluth. My children wish I would keep it. They still see it as a place for the family to gather. And my grand-children love coming up here. But, no. I'll be living permanently in our condo in downtown Minneapolis now. There's an energy and excitement to the city that helps me. I don't need a reclusive lake getaway anymore. Being alone, with time to think—well, that's the last thing I want now."

"I understand." Stride glanced at the mantel over the stone fireplace and saw that one photograph hadn't been packed yet. He saw a man in a tuxedo, with curly graying hair, a leathery, lined face, and jutting nose and chin. The man's smile was white and broad. He looked happy. "Is that Ira?" he asked.

"Yes." Esther got up and retrieved the photo, and she had a hard time looking away. "Ira needed heart valve replacement surgery. As you might guess, resources were not an issue for us. We could have gone to the Mayo or any of the finest hospitals in the country. But we had friends up here who expressed the highest vote of confidence in Dr. Snow. We put our trust in her. Tragically, that trust was misplaced."

Stride was silent. He'd seen people place blame many times. For crimes. For accidents. He said softly, "There are risks in any surgery, aren't there? Especially something as complex as cardiac surgery."

"Of course. We both knew that. But this was negligence. The surgery itself seemed to go well, but there was evidence of postoperative bleeding. The nurses saw it. Dr. Snow didn't take it seriously. She delayed taking action. When it was clear there was a serious problem, she finally opened him up again, but by then, it was too late. Ira didn't survive the second surgery."

"I'm very sorry."

Esther placed the photograph facedown in her lap. "I was angry. Bitter. That woman stole our future. The surgery should have been a new beginning for Ira, and, instead, it was the end. I admit, I didn't deal with it well. I said things—I wrote things—that were inappropriate. By July, I'd calmed down. Now I let my lawyer do my talking for me."

"You're suing Dr. Snow?" Stride asked.

"Of course. It's not a question of money. I don't need money. It's about justice. It's about making sure that no one else suffers the way Ira and I did." Esther stared at the lake, and then she turned back to Stride. "Believe me, I feel bad for Dr. Snow and what happened to her husband. No one should lose a spouse like that. Are you married, Lieutenant?"

"I am."

"And is she the light of your life?"

Stride smiled. "She is."

"That's as it should be. Ira and I were very much in love and had been for decades. Long before we had a dime to call our own. Of course, if you believe what you read in the newspaper, Dr. Snow and her husband had a much more troubled relationship. That's a shame."

"Did Dr. Snow talk to you about her marriage?" Stride asked.

Esther shook her head firmly. "Oh, no. Our relationship wasn't personal. It was strictly professional. To be very candid with you, both Ira and I felt that Dr. Snow was an unusually cold woman. She had no bedside manner. If our goal had been to find someone who had a caring way about them, we certainly would have gone elsewhere. However, we choose surgeons for their hands, not their warm, fuzzy side, don't we? We believed that she was the best."

"When did the surgery take place?" Stride asked.

"Last May. I've been coming to terms with it ever since. I only recently made the decision to sell this place."

"And how did you hear about the death of Dr. Snow's husband?"

"The morning news, like everyone else."

"Were you in Duluth?" Stride asked.

Esther allowed herself a small smile. "You know, Lieutenant, you don't need to be coy. You could come right out and ask me if I shot him. But, really, do I look like a woman who would be traipsing through the streets of Duluth at night with a gun?"

"No."

"No, and I wasn't. I wasn't in Duluth at all. I was in Minneapolis at the Guthrie seeing *Lear* with three friends. They'll be happy to confirm it. We even have pictures of us together. I learned of the murder on WCCO the next day."

"I'll need the names of your friends," Stride said.

"Yes, of course. Does that resolve your concerns?"

"Well, you're obviously a wealthy woman, Mrs. Rose."

"True," she acknowledged. "Is that relevant?"

"It means you have the resources to hire people to do things for you. Things you might not do yourself."

"Are you suggesting I hired a hit man?" Esther asked. She giggled, genuinely amused. "Well, I don't deny that I could afford it. Or at least

I assume I could, since I don't know the going rate for such things. However, women in my circumstances don't often come into contact with hired killers. People like that don't exactly advertise on the bulletin board at temple, do they? And Ira was a trademark attorney, not a mob lawyer. We didn't hobnob with criminals."

"I understand," Stride said.

"You're welcome to review my finances, if it puts your mind at ease."

Stride smiled as he stood up. "Actually, that would be helpful. Just to cross things off my list."

"Consider it done. You can talk to my attorney, and he'll arrange it for you. He's here in Duluth. Peter Stanhope."

"As in the Stanhope law firm?"

"Yes, they handle all my affairs. Is there a problem?"

He sat down again and leaned forward with his hands on his knees. "I'm sorry. I have to ask, Mrs. Rose, did you ever have any contact with Jay Ferris yourself?"

She shrugged. "No, I never met him. I knew who he was, because of his newspaper columns. To be honest, he seemed like rather a vile man. Handsome enough but without much class. Why?"

"Jay Ferris contacted someone at the Stanhope firm not long before he was murdered. Do you know anything about that?"

"Peter never mentioned it to me."

"Jay called an attorney named Tamara Fellowes. Do you know her?"

"I don't. As I say, I work exclusively with Peter. He owns the firm, and he handles most of my matters personally. Peter is the attorney who is suing Dr. Snow for me."

Stride planned to call Archie Gale when he returned to his City Hall office, but he found that he didn't need to do so. Gale was waiting for him in a police conference room. With Janine Snow.

The attorney, looking dapper, hopped to his feet. "Ah, Lieutenant, sorry to barge in like this. Your assistant said you were on your way back to the office."

"I'm a little surprised to see you here," Stride admitted.

Gale cocked his head. "Well, Dr. Snow has something she wants to share with you."

Stride sat down. Janine, on the other side of the table, looked chastened, which wasn't typical for her. She stared at the table in front of her, not at Stride. Her hands were folded together. A few blond hairs strayed across her face.

"What did you want to tell me?" he asked.

She finally looked up, and her blue eyes were vacant. "It's not something I'm proud of. Honestly, if it weren't for a private detective threatening me with blackmail, I would have kept it to myself."

Stride frowned. "What was this detective's name?"

"Melvin Wiley."

"And why was he trying to blackmail you?"

"I was having an affair," Janine told him.

Stride said nothing. He looked at Janine and then at Gale. Finally, he said, "With whom?"

"Someone my husband hated," she said. "And someone you know very well. A former cop named Nathan Skinner."

12

Maggie parked on ice-covered ground and climbed down from her yellow Avalanche. A freight train clattered under the overpass of Highway 2 thirty yards away. Its cars were streaked with rust and graffiti. She was near a gritty industrial park in Superior, Wisconsin, in a residential neighborhood butting up to the train tracks. The land around her was piled high with plowed gray snow.

She saw the house she wanted to visit on the corner, protected by a soaring arborvitae that was twice the height of the roof. It was a small house, two stories, with vertical wooden siding painted in sea-foam green. A tall fence protected the yard, so she couldn't see inside. The storm door had bars.

A white Toyota RAV4 was parked on the side street.

She and Guppo had already talked to more than two dozen RAV owners in the Twin Ports over the past several weeks. The interviews had produced nothing useful. There had been a white RAV4 parked near the base of the hill leading to Janine Snow's house on the night of the murder, but they were no closer to discovering who owned it or whether it had any connection at all to the death of Jay Ferris.

Maggie crossed to the house. The steps on the deck were slick with ice, and she gripped the wobbly railing to keep from falling. She knew her clogs weren't made for winter, but she didn't care.

A black man in his late twenties answered the door.

"Seymour Pugh?" Maggie asked.

He considered her with coal eyes. "What about it?"

"That's your RAV on the street, right?"

"So?" he asked.

She introduced herself. "I'd like to ask you a couple of questions."

Pugh said nothing, but he stepped outside into the cold. Rule number one, Maggie thought: Never let cops inside your house. She took pride in the fact that she could size up a suspect as guilty or innocent within a few seconds, but Seymour Pugh's face gave nothing away except calm distrust. That was no surprise, because he'd dealt with the police plenty of times in his life.

He was tall and skinny, wearing baggy red cargo pants and a white tank top stained with spaghetti sauce. He had a wide, flat nose with flaring nostrils and a chin that was fuzzy with long, curling hairs. His cornrows dipped below his ears. He had big hands with long fingers. His left ear sported an earring, and he wore a simple chain with a cross around his neck.

"What's this about?" Pugh asked her.

"Do you know a man named Jay Ferris?"

"No."

She dug in the pocket of her burgundy jacket for a photograph. "This is a picture of Mr. Ferris. Do you recognize him?"

"No."

"He was murdered a few weeks ago. He lived in a big house up on the hill in Duluth. He wrote a newspaper column."

"Don't get no paper," Pugh replied.

She rattled off the date of Jay's death. "Do you remember what you were doing that night? It was a Friday."

"You're kidding, right? One day's like every other."

"Do you own a gun, Mr. Pugh?"

"I got kids. No guns in my house. What are you talking to me for anyway?"

"You own a white RAV," Maggie said. "A witness spotted a white RAV not far from the house where the murder took place."

Pugh chuckled and shook his head. "Yeah, how many of them trucks are there around here? Did you run through all the licenses and pick out the black faces?"

"We picked out the people with criminal records," Maggie replied. "Jay Ferris was shot, and jewelry was taken from his home. You've had a series of convictions in the last decade for burglary and auto theft, Mr. Pugh."

"True enough. You see me using a gun in any of them?"

"No."

"No, you didn't. Nobody got hurt. And fact is, the last time I was inside was three years ago. I'm clean now. I got a job."

"What do you do?"

"I drive a truck. I deliver machine parts all over the Midwest. Illinois, Wisconsin, Iowa, Nebraska, the Dakotas. Most days I'm hundreds of miles away from here. Hard being away from home, but it's a living. An honest living. I got a job, a wife, kids. Jesus blessed me."

"Good for you." Maggie eyed the house, which needed work. "Looks like you could use some extra money, though."

"Yeah, and if I was breaking into rich people's houses, I guess I could do better than this, huh?"

"Sometimes desperate people will do just about anything," Maggie said.

Pugh jabbed a finger at her. He'd chewed his nails and cuticles until they were bloody. Maggie spotted movement in the front window and saw a boy's face peering out with wide eyes. He'd pushed aside the curtain, which looked like a plastic tablecloth. A woman's arm dragged him away.

"Look, lady, don't go throwing my past in my face," Pugh snapped. "Yeah, I made mistakes. I was a stupid kid. Fact is, when I stole shit, it was to put food on the table, okay? You and me may not have the same values, but don't go thinking that means I don't have any values. My family needs something, I make sure they get it, but I don't steal anymore. We make do on what I earn."

Maggie nodded. "Back to that Friday night," she said.

"I told you, I have no idea where I was or what I was doing. Either I was on the road or I was home with my family. You can call my boss and find out. For me, Friday's just another day on the calendar."

"That was the night of the multi-car crash up on the Bong Bridge. It was closed for hours. Does that help?"

"I don't pay attention to traffic unless I'm in it. Now, are we done?"

"We're done. Thanks for your time."

Seymour Pugh retreated inside the house. Maggie heard the sound of his voice change and heard him greet his kids with the excited shout of a father. It made her smile.

She returned across the street to her Avalanche and got inside. As she headed back toward the bridge, she passed the white RAV4 on the street again, and she realized that this end of the investigation wasn't going anywhere. Most cases had dead ends you had to follow. The car on the street near Janine's house was one of those stray facts that got in the way of finding the truth.

Seymour Pugh was a white-RAV owner with a criminal record, and unless he was driving a truck between here and Milwaukee that night, he had no alibi. Even so, he had no history of resorting to violence or using a gun in any of his crimes. He didn't trust a cop showing up at his door, but she couldn't blame him for that.

More than anything else, Maggie realized she liked him.

"Nathan Skinner?" Stride asked.

He saw a flush in Janine's face as she nodded. She'd said she was embarrassed, but he also thought there was sexual arousal in her expression. Cindy had told him on more than one occasion that a man who could melt through the ice cap of Janine Snow would find a volcano underneath.

He didn't say anything immediately. Instead, he assessed her credibility. And Archie Gale's. Nothing came free with Gale. Nothing was given up to the police or the prosecutors without an upside for him. If Janine was freely willing to confess to an affair, there had to be a strategy behind it. Either Gale wanted credit for providing information that the police would have discovered anyway—or he wanted to cloud the facts by handing them a shiny new suspect in Jay's murder.

Nathan Skinner.

"You were sleeping with a man who lost his job because of your husband?" Stride said.

"Yes."

"Well, tell me how this affair came about."

Janine regained some of her composure and arrogance. Her blue eyes met his. She moistened her lips and brushed the loose hair from her face. "Nathan was working overnight security at St. Anne's last May. I often work late, and we got to know each other."

"You knew who he was?"

"Yes, of course I did."

"And yet you engaged with him anyway," Stride said.

"He approached me, not the other way around. This isn't hard to figure out, Lieutenant. Nathan's motives were transparent. He sought a friendship with me, because—how should I phrase this?—he was interested in screwing me as a way to get back at Jay for screwing him."

"I understand his motives. It's yours I'm struggling with."

"Is it a blindness of handsome men that they don't recognize it in others? You're very attractive yourself, Lieutenant, which you obviously know. I've said as much to Cindy. Nathan Skinner is an extremely attractive man, too. So, yes, I allowed him to seduce me."

"Getting into a relationship with Nathan Skinner sounds a lot more complicated than you're letting on," Stride said.

Janine shrugged. "Last May was a difficult time for me. Jay and I were struggling. I was in severe pain much of the time because I'd broken my ankle over the winter. So, to be honest, Nathan's attentions were flattering. That was exactly what I needed at the time."

"Is the affair still going on?"

"No, I broke it off in December."

"Why?"

Janine hesitated. "Jay confronted me about it. He knew. I didn't realize he'd hired a private detective, but the fact is, these things have a way of coming out. It was just a matter of time."

"What was Jay's reaction?"

"He was upset, of course. He wanted me to break it off with Nathan, and I agreed to do so. Frankly, the affair was becoming uncomfortable for me anyway. Nathan had developed an emotional attachment. He was falling in love. For me, it was just sex. He wanted more."

Stride listened to the monotone in her voice and didn't like it. "You make this confrontation sound pretty bloodless, Dr. Snow. I find that hard to believe. I would have expected a much more volatile argument with your husband over something like this. Particularly given what he thought about Nathan Skinner."

"I think Jay was saving his anger for Nathan," Janine replied.

Stride heard the emphasis in her voice. "You think Jay confronted Nathan about the affair?"

"I have no idea, but Jay didn't take humiliations lightly."

It was a convenient story. Impossible to prove. Easy to deny. It laid the groundwork for an explosive fight between two men who already hated each other. Jay found out about the affair. Nathan was in love with Janine and didn't want to let her go. Situations like that had a way of ending with a man dead on the floor.

"You said that you and Jay were struggling in your relationship," Stride reminded her. "Did you want a divorce?"

"I don't think that topic is part of this conversation—" Gale began, but Janine reached over and put a hand on her attorney's sleeve.

"It's all right, Archie. What's the point in denying it? Yes, Jonathan, I wanted a divorce. Jay and I were a mistake from the beginning. It hurts to say that now, but it's true. When we met, there was this electricity between us. I'll be the first to acknowledge it was extremely physical. We got swept up in each other, and we got married before we came off the high. But we fell far and fast. The things that attracted us became the things we hated about each other. Jay was a person who wore his emotions on his sleeve. I'm not. He became more and more desperate to draw me out, to get a reaction."

"Sleeping with Nathan Skinner sounds like a reaction," Stride said.

"I suppose you're right."

"You also cut off Jay's credit cards without telling him last July. That sounds like a reaction, too."

"Okay, yes, I was being a bitch."

"You turned the money back on not long after. Why?"

"I decided it was childish. We were playing tit-for-tat games. That wasn't a way to solve our problems. The way to resolve it was to end our relationship." She added quickly, "By divorce."

"Jay's brother, Clyde, says Jay didn't want a divorce."

"Originally, yes, that was true," Janine acknowledged. "Jay enjoyed playing the game. Frankly, I think he liked making me miserable. But eventually, he got tired of all the fighting. He wanted out, too."

"If the two of you divorced, Jay would have gotten nothing. Wasn't it in his interest to stay married to you?"

Janine shook her head firmly. "Prenup or not, we would have come to a financial arrangement. I wasn't trying to starve him, Lieutenant. I bought him a new Hummer when he lost his truck on the ice. We both wanted an amicable end."

"You're saying Jay was willing to grant you a divorce. Despite what Clyde told me."

"Yes, that's exactly what I'm saying," Janine insisted. "He consulted a divorce attorney. A woman named Tamara Fellowes."

"We know about his call to Ms. Fellowes. She wouldn't tell us what she and Jay discussed, which I'm sure you know."

"Well, I'm telling you myself. Jay wanted to talk about divorce."

"Ms. Fellowes practices with the Stanhope law firm. They're suing you, aren't they, over the death of one of your patients? Ira Rose."

"Yes, that's true. So?"

"It's an interesting coincidence," Stride said.

"Not really. Jay and Tamara were college classmates."

"What's the status of Mrs. Rose's lawsuit against you?" Stride asked.

Janine shrugged. "I have no idea. I have my own attorneys who handle those things. I felt awful about what happened to Ira Rose. Unfortunately, cardiac surgery is inherently risky. It's become so commonplace that patients don't always think through the seriousness of it. Much as I would like to guarantee a positive outcome every time, I'm just a human being, not a god. I don't resent Esther for suing. It comes with the territory. Lawsuits are an unfortunate reality of the medical profession these days. My insurer will settle, and all of our health premiums will go up. That's life without tort reform."

Stride stared at this woman and tried to understand her. She was smart. Calm. Beautiful. Sexual. She had an answer for everything. That was what bothered him. Murder was messy, and yet she could explain away all of the questions as if they didn't matter at all.

He didn't believe her. Not for a minute.

"Let's talk about guns," Stride said.

"Excuse me?" She hadn't expected him to say that. Archie Gale leaned forward, looking concerned.

"Guns," Stride said. "You said Jay didn't own a gun."

"That's right."

He dug in a folder and pulled out a copy of the photograph that Clyde Ferris had given him. "Except here's a photograph of Jay with a gun, Dr. Snow. The photo was taken just a few months ago."

The color evaporated from Janine's beautiful face.

"Jay must have lied," she murmured. Her expression turned severe. "He didn't get rid of the gun when I asked him to. Or he bought another without telling me. I didn't know he had it."

"The bullet we pulled out of your husband's head is consistent with the ammunition used in the revolver Jay is carrying."

"I don't know anything about that," she said.

"Where is the gun in this photograph?" Stride asked.

"I have no idea."

"That's odd, don't you think? Jay owned a gun, he was killed with a gun—but you don't have any idea where that gun is. It's not in the house. It's not in his car. It just vanishes." Stride spread his arms. "Poof."

Gale stood up. "This interview is over, Lieutenant. Dr. Snow was very forthcoming about an embarrassing personal matter. We don't have any more to say right now. Frankly, if you're so interested in guns, the person you should be talking to is Nathan Skinner. Now, there's a man who's extremely fond of guns. And there's one other thing you should know with regard to your ex-employee."

"What's that?" Stride asked calmly.

Gale nodded at Janine. She took a breath, and she looked in control again. As if she were about to gain the upper hand.

"One time, Nathan and I did it in my house," she said. She leaned forward and stared directly at Stride, emphasizing each word for his benefit. "We fucked in my house. Jay was away. I think it was a turn-on for Nathan. It was part of his revenge fantasy."

"And yours?" Stride asked.

Janine smiled and didn't answer directly. "The thing is, I undressed for him, Lieutenant. I did a striptease. I took off my jewelry for him. Do you understand? He saw exactly where I kept my valuables in my bedroom. If he wanted to steal something after shooting Jay—if he wanted to make the murder look like a robbery—he knew exactly where to go."

13

Howard Marlowe unzipped his heavy winter coat. The warm air inside Miller Hill Mall made him sweat. He dropped heavy shopping bags from Gap and Maurices on the tiled floor at his feet. It was Saturday, and the mall was jammed, but he and Carol were on their own. His wife had insisted on a no-kid weekend, so Annie was staying with his mother-in-law.

"An affair," Carol announced loudly as they sat on a bench outside the mall's Barnes & Noble. "That figures."

Howard looked at her. "What are you talking about?"

She pointed at an older man reading the *Duluth News Tribune*. The headline screamed about Janine Snow's relationship with Nathan Skinner.

"Dr. Perfect was cheating," Carol said, shaking her head.

"Having an affair doesn't mean she killed her husband," Howard replied.

Carol's mouth looked as if she were eating a sour candy. "Wow, do you have a crush on this rich bitch, or what? You can take her side all you want, but I don't have any more sympathy for her."

"You didn't have much to begin with," he pointed out.

Carol didn't answer, but she shot him a resentful stare. Things had been cold between the two of them since the break-in, as if somehow the robbery had been his fault. Bad moods generally didn't last long with Carol, but when she was in one, it was best to leave her alone. Or let her run up a big credit card bill.

She hadn't changed her mind about getting a gun for the house. He'd filed for a purchase permit at the St. Louis County Sheriff's Office. He had no idea what kind of gun to get, but he figured a store owner could help him. Then he needed to think about training for both of them. Maintenance. Practice at the range. He didn't want to admit to Carol that he was terrified about the idea of actually owning a handgun.

Too often, people with guns snapped. They shot someone else, or they shot themselves. Jay Ferris had owned a handgun. Without that gun in the house, would Ferris still be alive?

"There's a children's author signing books at Barnes & Noble," his wife informed him. "I'm going to get a copy for Annie."

"Do you want me to go with you?" he asked.

Carol shrugged without replying, which was as good as saying no. She gave him her back as she marched into the bookstore.

"I'll get a slice at Sbarro," he called after her. "Meet me in the food court when you're done."

Howard gathered up their shopping bags. There wasn't much room to maneuver, and people bumped into him as he walked. Little kids dodged in and out of the crowds. Teenage girls from his high school classes chewed gum, blew bubbles, and waved at him, giggling. A couple of the girls carried tiny bags from Victoria's Secret, and he wondered what they'd purchased. Panties. Sexy bra. Maybe a boyfriend would get to see them in it. Or out of it.

It depressed him to be forty.

Howard passed more stores. Suncoast. Gymboree. Wilson's Leather. He stopped at a Rocky Mountain Chocolate kiosk and bought himself a piece of milk chocolate almond bark. After the pizza, he'd want dessert. He fumbled with his bags again as he headed for the food court, and he walked carefully, because the floor was slippery with wet boot marks.

Ahead of him, he spotted an empty storefront. A line of parents and kids stretched out the door into the mall corridor. Getting closer, he saw that the vacant space had been converted into a free weekend clinic for families, sponsored by St. Anne's. Vaccinations. Strep tests. Flu shots. Massages. The clinic was a hive of activity. Nurses handled registration and gave out balloons to the children. A short, pretty woman with long black hair demonstrated muscle stretches to a young girl in a shoulder brace.

And in the midst of all of them—there she was.

Janine Snow.

Howard stopped. People bustled around Janine, but for him, she was the only person there, as if she were in the halo of a spotlight. She stood beside a portable curtain, talking to a patient who was invisible behind the white sheet. He'd never seen her before in the flesh. Real. Alive. She didn't see him watching her, which was a good thing, because he found he couldn't drag his eyes away. It made him feel like a voyeur, staring between the crowds. Others whispered as they walked by.

That's her.

She had a magnetism that wasn't like other people's. Yes, she was beautiful and blond, with fullness and curves under her white coat, but to Howard, the attraction went deeper than that. It was her life; it was the drama of being her. She was famous, infamous, gifted, cool, erotic. She was as far removed from Howard's own life as a distant star, and yet she was so close that he could have taken a few steps and touched her.

Somehow, after a while, she felt his stare. She looked up from her work and saw him, and their eyes met.

His physical reaction was immediate. A full erection squeezed its way into the pocket of his underwear. That wasn't a common event at his age. Hard-ons didn't just happen anymore. He couldn't recall the last time he'd experienced something so intimate with a woman. She was staring at him, and he was staring back. There may as well not have been a single other soul in the mall around them.

She went back to her patient. He was nothing to her again. A stranger. Even so, they'd shared a connection. Something had passed between them. It had only lasted a moment, but it took his breath away.

* * *

"Everyone looks at me now," Janine mused aloud.

Cindy put down her clipboard and glanced at her friend, who'd spoken softly from a few feet away. Janine tilted her head toward the mall, and Cindy looked out at the crowds and saw a middle-aged man eyeing her friend like a fan stalking a celebrity. He was a little doughy, and he labored under the weight of numerous shopping bags. He had a long face with puppy-dog eyes behind old-fashioned black glasses. His coat, plaid shirt, and jeans were the uniform of a suburban husband.

When the man realized Cindy was watching him, he looked away, embarrassed, and trudged toward the mall's food court.

"He's harmless," Cindy said.

Janine shrugged. "Oh, I know."

Her friend stripped off her latex gloves and nodded at the child with her, indicating they were all done with the dreaded shot. The little boy scampered to join his parents. Cindy's eyes followed him, and she felt the same old yearning that dogged her whenever she saw a mother and child together. As if she'd missed something in her life. Janine didn't seem similarly affected. When her time with a patient was over, that person disappeared from her consciousness. Cindy didn't understand it, but she'd seen it in doctors over and over again.

"You want some lemonade?" she asked her friend.

"Sure."

Cindy filled two Dixie cups from a large plastic pitcher near the check-in desk. She drank one and then refilled it, and she ate a stale butter cookie. They'd already been on their feet for hours, and she was exhausted.

"Here you go," she said, handing a cup to Janine.

"Thanks." Janine sipped pink lemonade and eyed the gawkers in the mall. "It's odd. I've been saving lives for years, and no one had a clue who I was. Now people think I shot my husband, and I'm recognized everywhere."

"Duluth is still a small town," Cindy said.

"Yes, that's what Archie says. He told me to come here today. He said it would humanize me if people saw me giving shots to little kids. I guess my compassion is just a legal strategy." She lowered her voice further and added, "You know what this means, don't you?"

Cindy looked at her, confused. "No."

"Archie is already thinking about the jury pool."

Cindy was shocked, but she realized that Janine was right. Archie knew that trials were shaped months in advance by the public perception of a defendant. Initial prejudices, good or bad, were hard to overcome. Janine's lawyer wanted the people of Duluth to see her as a doctor. A healer. Not a rich, cold adulterer who could point a gun at her husband and pull the trigger.

"I'll be back in a minute, okay?" Cindy said. "I need to splash some water on my face."

She retreated to a bathroom at the back of the empty store. It was handicapped-accessible and smelled of pine disinfectant. She left the door open and didn't bother turning on the light. She washed her hands, then her face, and she dried her skin with paper towels from the dispenser.

As she stared at her dark reflection in the mirror, it happened again.

Pain, like a lightning bolt between her legs.

Cindy couldn't hold back a loud cry. She grabbed the porcelain sink, riding the wave, squeezing her eyes shut. Nausea rose in her throat, and she was ready to bolt for the toilet. Her body felt as if it were being torn in two. She wanted to scream again, but as quickly as it had come, the wave crested and washed away. She breathed slowly and deeply, relaxing. Her body was clammy with sweat.

Opening her eyes, she saw Janine watching her closely from the bathroom doorway.

"Is everything okay?" Janine asked. "I heard you cry out."

"I'm fine."

"Are you feeling all right?"

Cindy brightened her smile. "Sure. It's just stomach cramps."

Patients lied to doctors all the time, and doctors knew it. Janine didn't believe her. "The pain looked sharp. Has this been happening a lot?"

"Every now and then."

"Have you seen your doctor?" Janine asked. "Because you should."

"I will. I'm due for a physical in a couple of months. Right now, I'm too busy."

Janine frowned. "Too busy" was every patient's excuse.

"I'm sure it's nothing," Cindy added, which was a stupid thing to say to a doctor when you weren't a doctor yourself. Her gut told her it was something, but she wasn't ready to face whatever it might be.

"Take a break," Janine told her. "Go sit in the food court for a while."

"Yeah, maybe I will." Cindy changed the subject and added, "I'm sure Archie's just covering his ass about the jury pool."

"That's sweet, but no." Janine looked behind her to make sure they were alone. "Your husband can put a gun in my hand now. That idiot, Jay, hiding his gun from me. It doesn't matter that the police can't *find* it. Jay had a gun, so the jury will assume I killed him with it."

Cindy stared at her friend. "Don't talk like that."

"It's reality. The fact is, they don't need much more than that to convict me. Archie already sat me down and told me the facts of life. Jay and I were alone in the house. We hated each other. My story of what happened is unlikely at best. That's enough to get most jurors to a guilty verdict right there."

"If something else happened, Jonny will find out what," Cindy insisted.

Janine smiled. "If."

Cindy flushed. "You know what I mean."

"I do." Janine opened her purse and closed it. She nodded at the toilet. "Well, I need to use the facilities, and you need to sit down and take a break."

"Okay."

Cindy left and heard Janine close and lock the bathroom door behind her. She threaded through the mall crowds to the food court, where she got in line and bought herself a grape Mr. Misty at Dairy Queen. She found a table and hummed along with an Alan Jackson song playing as background noise. The skylight over her head let in gray afternoon light. She felt better. As she sipped her frozen drink, trying to avoid brain freeze, she people-watched. Old men and women drinking coffee. Children playing tag. Teens in packs, boys eyeing girls, girls eyeing boys. She saw the man who'd been watching Janine at the clinic. His wife had joined him now, and she talked at him, and it looked as if her words sailed through her husband's head without stopping.

Cindy's drink was nearly gone, and she was feeling the sugar buzz, when she spotted someone else. She wasn't sure why her eyes were drawn to him, but once she saw him, she couldn't look away.

He was a young man, maybe in his early twenties. Not tall. Not buff. A skinny kid. He wore a camouflage jacket and blue jeans, and his hands were shoved in his jacket pockets. He had a navy-blue wool cap pulled low down his forehead, and he sported wraparound reflective sunglasses. He stood fifteen feet away, leaning against a column near Burger King. He studied everything in the mall without seeming to study anything at all. His head barely moved, but over the course of ten minutes, he shifted positions periodically so that he surveyed the entire food court. Every restaurant. Every table. Every entrance and exit.

She didn't know him, but he looked familiar. She'd seen him before. Where?

She racked her brain but couldn't place him, but then he withdrew a tatted hand from his jacket pocket and removed his sunglasses in order to rub his eyes with his sleeve. When he was done, she found herself staring dead-on into those eyes, and she realized who he was. She'd seen his face in photographs on her kitchen table. Photographs that were part of the evidence that Jonny had gathered while investigating the murder of Jay Ferris.

A young man in camouflage in the woods, carrying an assault weapon. A young man with gray, lifeless eyes that reminded her of a shark seeing only the black water.

It was him. This was the man that Jonny was looking for.

She realized she was still staring at him. So did he. The young man put his sunglasses on and stalked away, melting into the crowd of the mall. Acting on instinct, she leaped to her feet and followed him. She spotted his camouflaged back as he marched on like a soldier. Pushing past people, who parted to let him through. Bumping into others without apologizing. He kept his chin tilted down. Cameras wouldn't catch him. He was small, but he walked quickly, and she had to hurry to keep him in sight.

He looked back. He saw her.

She pretended to be window-shopping, but she didn't think he was fooled. He turned sharply right and yanked open a door labeled for employees only. The door shut, and he disappeared.

Cindy hurried to the same door and stopped with her fingers clenched around the metal handle. People came and went around her, oblivious to her anxiety. She looked for a mall security guard but saw no one to help her. In seconds, the man would be gone. She hesitated—what was she doing?—but then she opened the door herself, finding an empty, unfinished corridor ahead of her. She stepped inside and let the door close, shutting out most of the noise of the mall.

She was alone. She heard the buzz of machines. The walls on either side of the narrow space were plasterboard, and the floor was dirty. A single row of fluorescent bulbs stretched along the ceiling toward a doorway lit by a red exit sign.

She listened for his footsteps but heard nothing. She jogged to the end of the hallway, stopped, and peered carefully around the corner. He was already gone. She felt a chill, as if outside air was blowing in from somewhere. She followed the new corridor, which was built of brick and led her to a small utility room. The mechanical throb was louder. Gas and water pipes made a maze on the wall. She saw a tall steel door that ran up and down on tracks; it was closed. Another exit door had a crash bar. It led outside.

Cindy shivered, then pushed through the door into the cold air. She was outside the mall now, near the parking lot. Wind and rain slapped her face. She didn't see him. Her shoulders sagged, but then she heard a voice behind her.

"What do you think you're doing?"

She stifled a scream and spun around. He was there, behind a Dumpster. Waiting for her. She saw no eyes, just sunglasses. Cap pulled way down. There was nothing to see, nothing to recognize, only the hard, bitter line of his mouth. Despite his small size, his body carried menace. She felt fear down to her toes.

"Why are you following me?" he demanded.

"I'm not."

"Bullshit," he hissed.

"You looked like someone I knew, but I guess not." She went to push past him and head back inside, but he grabbed her arm. She struggled and shouted. "Let me go!"

"Who are you?" he asked.

"I'm the wife of a cop, that's who I am, so you'd better let go of me right now!"

He dropped her arm. She rubbed it and knew there would be a bruise where his fingers had clamped over her skin. For a small man, he was strong.

"People shouldn't go sticking their noses into other people's business," he warned her. He drew back the flap of his camouflage jacket, and she saw the butt of a gun poking out of a shoulder holster. "Bad things happen to those kinds of people. You hear what I'm saying?"

Her mouth was dry. She didn't say a word.

He marched past her into the parking lot at a quick, nervous pace. Her eyes followed him, but she didn't see him get into a vehicle. When she couldn't see him anymore, she ran back into the utility room and then to the warmth, crowds, and sweet smells of the mall.

People stared at her, and she realized that tears were streaming down her face.

14

Stride walked onto the ice of a small lake off Tree Farm Road in Midway Township. Evergreens and birches made a wreath around the shore. The rain left puddles on the frozen surface, making it slippery under his boots. Spring was coming. The locals had already pulled most of their fishing shanties off the water, but a few diehards always waited until the ice was practically slush before giving up on winter. Sometimes they waited too long.

He saw an old pickup a hundred yards away, parked beside a tin shanty that wasn't much bigger than an outhouse. Even at that distance, he recognized Nathan Skinner carrying provisions from the ice fishing house to his truck. Nathan saw him, too, and he offered Stride a mock salute.

Stride lit a cigarette and let it soothe his nerves. He kept trudging through the miserable drizzle.

He'd known Nathan for years, all the way back to his UMD hockey days. Most men in Duluth had. Nathan was a genuine star who'd brought home an NCAA championship for the Bulldogs. People in Duluth didn't forget that kind of thing. It was a shame that the kid had blown out his knee before he had a chance to prove himself as a pro. Nathan never claimed to be bothered about it, but Stride didn't believe him. You couldn't come that close to fame and money and not be bitter about missing the gold ring.

One day you're about to be a starting forward for the Blackhawks. The next day you're a street cop.

And not long after that, you're booted off the force, doing fill-in security in malls and hospitals.

Stride knew that Maggie didn't like Nathan. He couldn't really blame her. Nathan had the chauvinist arrogance of a man who'd had women fawning over him his whole life. Stride knew that Nathan was a sexist and probably a racist. He didn't condone the man's attitudes, but if you rejected every white male in the northland because they didn't understand women or blacks, then you weren't left with much of a hiring pool. His job was to purge those attitudes and help his cops see the complex reality of the world they policed. Sometimes it worked. Sometimes it didn't.

He'd been reluctant to fire Nathan, partly because he thought Nathan was smart enough to have long-term potential, and partly because he didn't like Jay Ferris whipping up public sentiment against his team. He gave in when the chief wanted Nathan gone, but he was stubborn enough to believe that with enough time and training, he still could have turned Nathan Skinner into a solid police officer.

"Hello, Nathan," Stride said as he approached the pickup.

Nathan nodded. His face was wet, his blond hair flat. "Lieutenant."

Stride blew smoke into the air. "You should be off the ice."

"I'm packing up now."

Stride nodded. "I've been looking for you."

"I figured. I wasn't really in a mood to be found. I can read the newspapers."

"Is it true?" Stride asked. "The affair with Janine?"

"Sure, it's true."

Nathan shrugged, as if the information were of no importance. He had a CD boom box in his hands, covered by plastic wrap, and he wedged it behind the driver's seat of his truck. He returned to the small shack on the ice, and Stride followed him inside. There was barely room for the two men. A wooden chair sat next to a hole drilled in the ice, revealing murky black water below.

"Maggie talked to you a while ago. You didn't mention your relationship with Janine."

"So? I don't think I'm under any obligation to discuss my sex life with Maggie Bei. She didn't ask. I didn't volunteer."

Stride flicked his cigarette into the open water. "Don't be cute."

Nathan sat in the rickety chair and stretched out his legs. He wore blue jeans and a down vest, but his arms were bare. "Fine. I didn't say anything about it because you guys already had Janine in your sights. I didn't feel the need to make her any more of a suspect than she was."

"Or to make yourself a suspect," Stride said.

"Yeah. Me too. I get it. The fact is, I didn't really think anyone would find out about us. We were pretty discreet. I sure didn't think Janine would advertise it."

Stride shoved his hands into the pockets of his jacket. Rain plinked on the metal roof, and drops leaked inside. A gust of wind rocked the corrugated metal. "She says you were in love with her."

Nathan snorted. "Are you kidding? No, I wasn't."

"Why would she say that?" Stride asked.

"Why do you think? To make it look like I had another reason to blow her husband away: I wanted her for myself. Real nice. I guess there's no honor among cheaters."

"You said *another* reason to kill Jay," Stride pointed out.

"Oh, come on, Lieutenant. You don't need to play 'gotcha' games with me. We both know I hated Jay Ferris. He cost me my job. He made it his business to ruin my life. So I made it my business to fuck his wife. Which I did. I already had my revenge against Jay."

"You don't have much of an alibi for that night."

"Maybe not, but I *was* sick. The pizza girl will tell you that. Besides, you tested my gun. It's clean."

"Is that your only handgun?" Stride asked. "Archie Gale seems to think you have more."

Nathan shrugged. "Okay, I've got others. You want to test all of them? You want to search my place? Go for it. Look, it doesn't matter. I'm not an idiot. If I killed him—which I didn't—I would have dropped the gun through this hole in the ice. You'd never find it. That's probably what Janine did, too."

"You think she killed him?"

"Of course she did."

"Did you know that Jay Ferris owned a gun?" Stride asked.

"Yeah. Jay waved it at me when I went after him at the Saratoga."

"Did you ever tell Janine about Jay's gun?"

Nathan didn't answer right away. He rubbed his bare arms against the cold. Stride thought he was deciding whether to lie, and he realized he couldn't trust anything that came out of Nathan's mouth. That was true of Janine, too. It would be a he said/she said between them all the way to the courtroom.

"Yeah, sure, I told her about it," Nathan said.

"Just to be clear," Stride reiterated, "you're saying that you *told* Janine that Jay carried a gun. She knew about it."

"I did. I joked about it once. I said we'd better be careful if Jay found out about us, in case he decided to blow us away."

"When was this?"

"I don't remember. Months ago."

"What did Janine say?"

"She didn't look surprised."

Nathan smiled. If he was a liar, he was good at it, but so was Janine. Nathan obviously realized that Stride doubted his story, so he added, "Janine knew how to shoot, too. I taught her. We went to a range together once. It was over in Superior, where I figured no one would see us." He dug in the pocket of his vest for his flip-phone. "I got a pic of it, actually. I took it while she was firing. It was pretty hot. She was really into it."

He pushed several buttons on his phone and turned it around so that Stride could see the small screen. He recognized Janine Snow, ear defenders over her head, goggles over her eyes, a Smith & Wesson revolver at the end of her outstretched arms. She aimed at a target, and her face was hard and focused. When Janine Snow did anything, she did it well.

"I'll send you a copy of the picture," Nathan added.

Stride nodded. "Tell me more about the affair."

"There's not much to tell. I met her when I was doing security at the hospital last May. I figured I'd take my chances getting her into bed. It wasn't hard."

"How often did you see her?"

"Not often. A couple times a month. She's a busy woman."

"Where did you meet?"

"Hotels at first. Then she bought her chill place, and we'd meet there."

Stride cocked his head. "Her what?"

"She keeps an apartment downtown. It's her getaway when she doesn't want to be home with Jay." Nathan read the confusion in Stride's face, and he grinned. "You didn't know about it, did you? How'd you miss that one, Lieutenant? Well, I doubt it's under her name, so don't kick yourself too hard."

Nathan rattled off a downtown address, and Stride wrote it down. He knew the location, and he was angry that they hadn't discovered the condo before now. It was only a ten-minute drive from Janine's house on the hill. If she were looking to stash a gun and jewels after the murder, it would have been an easy place to do so. And now she'd had time to dispose of them permanently.

"Janine says you had sex at her house once," Stride went on.

Nathan shook his head firmly. "No. Definitely not."

"You never went there?"

"Never."

"She was very specific about it. Said she did a striptease for you in her bedroom, and you saw where she keeps her jewelry."

"Well, give that woman extra credit—she's clever. I guess you do what it takes when you're trying to duck a murder charge. But come on, Lieutenant. You really think she'd take the risk of her friends or neighbors seeing me at her house? No way."

"When did the affair end?" Stride asked.

"December. Not long after Thanksgiving."

"Who broke it off?" Stride asked.

"She did."

"Why?"

"She didn't give me a reason, and I didn't ask. She just said we were done. She's a cold fish. I didn't really expect anything more."

"Did you want to keep the affair going?"

"I didn't care. I liked the sex, but I can get plenty of sex. I said thanks for the memories. We did it one last time, and we were over. It wasn't emotional."

"Janine thinks Jay was planning to confront you about the affair."

"Confront me? Hell, no. Do you really think Jay Ferris would admit to my face that he knew I'd been screwing his wife? Not him. He'd never give me the satisfaction."

"And yet he knew what you were doing," Stride said. "He hired a detective."

"Okay, so he knew about the affair. I'm sure he forced Janine to dump me. It would have driven him crazy to think of me and her together, and he would have done anything to make her stop. I mean, she always said it was a control game with Jay."

Stride's eyes narrowed. "How so?"

"That marriage was a war, and Jay wanted to win. He wanted to rule over her like some kind of king, you know? He was never going to give her up. I told her she should pay him off and divorce him, but she said he'd destroy her life before he walked away. She couldn't escape. Those were the words she used, Lieutenant. She said Jay would have to die before he let her get away from him."

15

Cindy sat with Jonny and Maggie in the basement conference room of the Detective Bureau. She had a cup of coffee in front of her, which she cradled between her palms. Jonny picked at the sprinkles on a chocolate donut, and Maggie—whose appetite belied her tiny size—wolfed down a Quarter Pounder from McDonald's. The furnace was loud through the air vents. Hours had passed since her confrontation with the man at Miller Hill Mall, but Cindy was still jittery. Her hands shook, making the coffee slosh. Her gaze darted back and forth between her husband and his Chinese partner, and the long silences made them all uncomfortable.

On the bulletin board, Maggie had thumbtacked photos from Jay Ferris's camera of the man in camouflage with the assault rifle. Beside the photos was the sketch they'd drawn from Cindy's description. Cindy was sure the man in the photographs was the same man she'd followed at the mall.

Almost sure. She couldn't swear to it.

"I talked to Colin in mall security," Maggie said between generous bites of her hamburger. "I gave him Jay's photos and the artist's sketch, but he didn't recognize the guy. Whoever he is, he's not a regular visitor at the mall. Colin will pass the pics around to his team, in case somebody knows him or the guy comes back."

Another long silence. Cindy smoothed her hair. She tried to catch Jonny's eye, but he refused to look at her. She knew he was furious.

"I pulled the CCTV footage, too," Maggie added. "You can't see the guy's face in most of the angles. When you catch a glimpse, he's got a cap and sunglasses, so there's nothing to help us. He's smart."

"Why is he hiding?" Cindy asked. "I mean, what's he up to?"

There was no answer. Cindy went back to her coffee, which was growing cold.

Jonny got up and stood in front of the bulletin board. He stared at the man in the photos. She knew her husband; he was mad, and he was focused. His black hair was messier than usual, because he rubbed it when he was deep in thought.

"So what is this really about?" he said, mostly to himself. "Jay spots a guy with an assault rifle near Ely's Peak. He takes a few pics and makes a police report. We get a couple more reports of gunfire in the same area, and the guy leaves targets behind like he's playing soldier. And now my wife tries to be a hero, following an armed stranger who may or may not be the same guy."

Cindy frowned. "I said I was sorry, Jonny."

He didn't look at her. Instead, he grabbed a copy of the sketch from the conference table and sat down. "So far, this adds up to nothing," he said.

"It wasn't nothing," Cindy snapped. "You weren't there. You didn't see him."

Again, her husband acted as if she were invisible. Cindy felt her face get hot as her temper flared. She was quick to blow off steam when she got angry. "Are you ever going to look at me?"

Her voice was loud. Too loud. Jonny turned and stared at her, and she could feel his own anger, too. She expected him to lash out, but, instead, he got up and left the conference room without speaking. His silence as he passed her had the chill of morning frost. Cindy continued to fume.

"He's mad because he's scared," Maggie said.

Cindy tapped her foot nervously on the floor. Her anger mixed with embarrassment. "I know."

Maggie finished a supersize cup of Coke with a loud slurp. She tried and failed to cover a belch. "Sorry. Not to piss you off, but he's right. What you did was pretty stupid."

"Don't you think I know that?" Cindy asked.

"So why'd you do it?"

"I don't know. I thought I recognized this guy, and I just—I didn't want him to walk away. I knew you were trying to find him."

Maggie blew the black bangs out of her face. "From a police standpoint, Stride's right. It does add up to nothing. Even so, I'd like to know who this man is. Something about him feels off."

Cindy was pleased that Maggie shared her concerns. She liked Maggie. They were friends, though not really close friends. Maggie was hard rock, and Cindy was country, and that summed up the two of them. Jonny's partner was almost ten years younger than she was, and ten years was a long time at their ages. Cindy worried about turning forty, and Maggie worried about turning thirty. Big difference.

There was the crush thing, too. Maggie was in love with Jonny. Love and hero worship were hard to separate when it came to cops. Jonny had mentored Maggie and coaxed her out of her shell, and she fed on it. Cindy trusted Jonny and didn't think Maggie would ever act on her feelings, but it paid to be careful.

Like most wives, she had a keen appreciation of her husband's strengths and weaknesses. When it came to women, Jonny felt the need to rescue them. He didn't always understand the rush of emotions he provoked in return, and he wasn't entirely immune to feelings of his own. A case the previous year had tested both of them. Jonny had become involved in protecting a woman named Michaela Mateo from an abusive ex-husband. Michaela was pretty and vulnerable—a dangerous combination for Jonny. Cindy could see easily enough that Michaela was attracted to her husband, and although she didn't believe anything had happened between them, she knew that Jonny's own feelings went deeper than he let on. When Michaela was killed, the loss cut him worse than anything she'd seen in his years with the police.

Thinking of Michaela Mateo also made her think of the woman's young daughter. Catalina. Cat. Six years old when her parents died.

Cindy had gone so far as to suggest to Jonny that they adopt the girl, because it had already become clear that her own dreams of having children weren't likely to come true. Jonny had said no. It was too much. Too soon. It made her wonder whether, in his heart of hearts, he really wanted kids at all.

She looked up. Her husband was in the doorway of the conference room. He hadn't said anything.

Maggie took the hint and got up and left them alone. He took a chair and put it beside her and straddled it backward. Their arms brushed against each other. His dark eyes were distant.

"What were you thinking?" he said quietly.

"I wasn't," she admitted.

She knew he wanted to yell, but he didn't. He reached for her shoulder and pulled her gently against him. She folded herself into his body and felt his strength. And his worry and relief, having her in his arms.

"Don't scare me like that," he said.

"I'm sorry, but you realize that's what I live with every day, don't you?" she murmured.

That caught him short, but he knew it was true. He didn't let go.

"This guy at the mall," she said. "He's not nothing, Jonny."

"He hasn't committed a crime," he reminded her.

"That you know of."

They were silent, and it could easily have disintegrated between them again. Him yelling. Her yelling. They both knew how to fight, but she didn't want to. Not now. It wasn't worth it.

"Hey, I've been thinking," she said. "I got a flier from Bobbie at the travel agency. Last-minute cruise specials. How about we go to Alaska in June? We can do it cheap."

Jonny separated himself from her and smiled. "A vacation? Me?"

"Every couple of years, I get to drag you out of Duluth."

"I know, but why now?"

"No reason," she said, which wasn't really true. She felt strange. She felt shadows around her, and it made her want to combat them with happier things. "You know I've always wanted to do this."

He looked as if he would protest, but this time, he gave in. "Okay."

"Really?"

"Yeah. Book it. Sure."

Cindy kissed him, and she didn't believe in peck-on-the-cheek kisses. Their kisses were always hot and hard. She liked it that way. "Thanks, babe," she said. "That means a lot to me."

He stood up and took her hand. "Come on, let's go home."

Cindy hesitated. "Janine was at the mall today, too. We were both at the clinic."

"You shouldn't be talking to her."

"I know." Cindy stopped herself, but then she added, "She thinks you're going to arrest her."

Jonny didn't comment. He shoved papers into a satchel. He didn't say yes, and he didn't say no, but she knew him well enough to realize that his silence was a yes. He was building a cage of evidence for her friend, and soon enough, he'd put her inside it.

Maybe that was the right thing to do. Cindy wasn't naive. Janine was probably guilty of murder. Nothing else made sense. Even so, Cindy wanted to find another explanation. She wanted to believe that Janine was innocent.

"That guy at the mall today really creeped me out," she told him.

Jonny stopped and looked at her. He didn't chastise her again. "I know. I'm sorry."

"He threatened me," Cindy went on, "and it didn't feel empty. He told me bad things happen to people who pry into his business. That's what Jay Ferris did for a living, Jonny. He pried into other people's lives. What if Jay found out who this guy was?"

16

Ross Klayman arrived at his mother's house after dark.

The old RCA television in the living room was on. It was *always* on, driving him crazy. The same sewer of reality programs. Empty-headed sluts squeezing their silicone tits into bikini tops. Rich trust-fund babies playing drinking games. Celebrities grinning for the cameras and pretending they had ordinary lives. They were destroying the country. Chipping away the foundation brick by brick, until soon they would all be living in anarchy. Unless good people tried to stop it.

"How can you watch this filth?" Ross asked his mother.

Jessie shrugged and didn't answer. She was draped across the sofa in a roomy T-shirt and yellow panties. Her feet were bare. She drank from a can of Miller Lite, and she already had two empties stacked on top of each other on the coffee table, next to an empty plastic tray from a Lean Cuisine dinner. Her eyes didn't leave the television set.

"Where were you today?" she asked.

"Out."

"Out where?"

"The mall."

He sat down next to her. The television was a noisy drone in his ears. She propped her feet on his thigh.

"Did you eat?" she asked.

"I had a power bar."

"Do you want a beer?"

"No."

Ross rarely drank. Alcohol was poison. It clouded his mind, and he wanted his mind sharp. If you were a soldier and hunter, your only real weapon was the clearness of your brain. Your gun was an extension of your arm, which was an extension of your mind. You had to know how to focus. To plan. To execute. The drugs that fouled other people's heads were the enemy.

"I've got a temp shift working a concert at the DECC tomorrow," his mother said.

"Uh-huh."

"Might turn into something more."

"Good," he said.

But it wouldn't. It never did. She couldn't hold a job.

He found himself staring at his mother's feet. She kept her nails painted red, and a callus bulged from her big toe. He knew what she wanted, so he massaged her arches, pressing deeply with his thumbs until she twitched on the edge of discomfort. It was their evening ritual. When she worked, she spent hours standing, leaving her flat feet sore by the time she came home.

Jessie gave him a crooked, slightly drunken smile. Her red hair, streaked with gray at the roots, was pulled back tightly behind her head, framing her oval face. She had a chirpy, too-happy voice. "You really are the best son in the world—you know that, don't you?"

Ross rubbed her feet without answering.

"The scale says I'm down a pound," she told him.

"Good for you."

He didn't think one pound would make any difference. Twenty pounds might, but that wasn't going to happen. His mother binged on diets to lose ten pounds, and then she binged on junk food to put on fifteen. She wasn't fat, but her panties and T-shirt were both a size too small for her current weight.

It was just the two of them. Ross and Jessie. That was the way it had been since he was eight years old, when his father took a page from a

Springsteen song and went out for a drive and never came home. Fifteen years had passed since then. Jessie in and out of jobs. Ross in and out of school. They'd spent most of those years in a little apartment in Fargo. His mother worked security at a local mall, and her boss was a former high school coach confined to a wheelchair. She spent most of her time straddling his lap. Wheels didn't turn bad people into angels.

When the boss's wife found out about the affair, he fired Jessie. She found a bus-stop-bench lawyer who wheedled a settlement out of the mall owner, and they used the money to get out of Fargo and buy a small house in the town of Gary, southwest of Duluth. That was a year ago. Jessie took part-time security jobs when she could get them. Some months were flush. Some weren't.

Ross had applied for jobs, but he couldn't wash the contempt off his face at interviews, and after a while, he gave up. He spent most days hiking in the woods. Sometimes he went far north, almost to Canada, taking with him only what he could carry on his back and living off the land for days at a time. That was how it was supposed to be. Man. Nature. Values.

He lifted his mother's feet off his legs and stood up. He slipped off his camouflage jacket and hung it on a hook behind the front door. Jessie noted the shoulder holster and revolver without comment. Her own philosophy was to make sure you had a gun within reach at all times.

He went to her bedroom at the end of the hall, where the twin bed was unmade. The gun safe was on the wall. He undid the combination lock and stored the handgun in a sleeve on the door, next to six others. The safe allowed room for more than a dozen rifles, too. It was full.

With the safe open and the hardware in front of him, Ross heard a knocking on the front door.

That was the moment he'd long dreaded. The knock on the door. He thought about the woman at the mall. The cop's wife. It seemed impossible that she could have recognized him or that they could have tracked him down so quickly. He was a phantom in Duluth. The only one who had ever come close was the black bastard at the newspaper who'd stumbled onto his practice field. He wasn't a problem anymore.

Even so. Be prepared.

Another knock.

"Ross," his mother called.

"Who is it?"

"I don't know. I'm not decent."

Ross had no way of knowing if this was the moment. This might be the beginning of the end.

He left the safe open and crept to the doorway of the living room, where he could see windows facing the nighttime yard. No flashing lights. No cars on the street. Then fingernails tap-tapped on the glass, and he saw a girl's face. Two girls. They called through the window to him.

"Hey, hello!"

He hadn't realized he was holding his breath. He exhaled.

Ross crossed to the front door and yanked it open. The girls jumped and giggled. They were taller than he was, both around sixteen or seventeen, probably sisters. Their hair was too long, their makeup too loud, their jeans too tight. He had no expression on his face, and he watched them catch their breath, smirk, roll their eyes, and whisper back and forth. They weren't scared of him. They were laughing at him and could barely hide it. He felt a roaring in his head, his fury as calm as an ocean wave gathering force as it rolled toward shore.

"Hi," the first girl said. She had red hair, cheap earrings. She twisted a curl around her fingers.

"Hi," her sister echoed.

He said nothing at all. They were strangers, but he knew their type. These were the girls at school. These were the girls at the mall. These were the girls on television. They were all the same. They didn't know who he was, but he wanted to shout at their painted faces: I AM GOD.

I am the Decider. I am the Bringer of Life and Death.

Kneel for your Judgment.

Unbidden, his fingers curled into fists, and his breath came faster.

"Um," the first girl said.

"We're your neighbors across the street," the second girl added.

He didn't know the neighbors, and they didn't know him. I AM GOD. The girls peeked over his shoulder and saw Jessie on the sofa, her T-shirt riding up her stomach. They giggled again, as if looking down their noses at both of them.

Kneel.

"Our dog's missing," the first girl said.

"Have you seen him?" her sister asked.

He could barely hear his voice over the blood pulsing in his brain. "No."

"He's a black Lab."

"We call him Ducks. He's a hunting dog. Dad hunts ducks."

Ross saw a tall silhouette in the house across the street. A man was at the window, peering out, keeping an eye on his girls. "I haven't seen the dog."

"Well, if you do, could you call—"

He slammed the door in their faces. Behind the frame, he heard silence, then an explosion of laughter. Heels skipped on concrete. He closed his eyes and measured each breath, in, out, slowly, carefully. Count to ten. Relaxation washed over him. Your only real weapon is the clearness of your brain.

Ross sat down on the sofa again, and his mother presented her feet for his attention. He began to massage them again, but in no time, she gave an annoyed yelp as he squeezed too hard.

On television, two girls on a reality show discussed the penis size of a man who lived in the dormitory with them.

Disgusting.

"Is that the dog who's been pooping in our backyard?" Jessie asked when the show went to a commercial.

"Yes."

"He's missing?"

"I guess."

Jessie's face got a curious little look. "Did you take that dog along on one of your trips?"

"No."

"I thought I heard barking when you went out."

"You're wrong."

"Oh. Well, whatever."

Ross got up from the sofa. "I'm going to my room."

"Okay." She hugged him around the waist. "I told you that you were the best son ever, right?"

"Yes."

She wanted him to say she was the best mother in the world, but he just separated himself from her and headed to the hallway. His bedroom door was the first on the left. It was painted black, and he pulled out a key to unlock the dead bolt he'd installed.

He went inside and shut the door behind him and locked it again.

It was the middle of the night when Jessie Klayman awoke on the sofa. Six empty beer cans were spilled across the table; the pyramid she'd built had toppled when she kicked it in her sleep. The TV was still on, and she used the remote control to switch it off. She stretched out a bare leg, fighting a cramp. Her head throbbed. When she stood up, she felt dizzy.

It was stupid to drink so much the day before a job. She hoped she could get in a few more hours of sleep before the alarm rang in the morning.

Jessie zigzagged to her bedroom, steadying herself on the wall.

As she passed Ross's room, she saw a crack of light under the door. He was still awake. From inside, she heard what she usually did. Gunfire. Explosions. Screams. He was killing zombies or aliens or mutants or whatever else was in the silly games he liked to play. Sometimes he was up all night, fighting his wars.

17

Dan Erickson smelled blood.

Stride hadn't known the new St. Louis County Attorney for long, but he recognized Dan's pattern. When they were close to making an arrest on a major case, Dan began taking a more personal role in the investigation, nudging the police aside and inserting himself into the news. Like most politicians, he had an addiction to television cameras.

Dan went to the judge personally to get the search warrant approved for Janine's condo above Michigan Street. He also fast-tracked an immunity deal for Melvin Wiley to get the private detective talking about his surveillance of Janine Snow and Nathan Skinner. Stride wouldn't have let Wiley off the hook so readily. The detective was guilty of breaking and entering, invasion of privacy, and blackmail, and Stride would have preferred to get the information they wanted somewhere else.

Dan didn't see it that way.

The three men stood in the hallway outside Janine's condo while Stride's team conducted a search inside. Wiley drank Perrier supplied by Dan and wiped his mustache after each swig from the green bottle. He wore a Twins baseball cap, a gray sweatshirt, and blue jeans. The man's face bore a smug grin. He was enjoying his turn in the spotlight. There was nothing a private detective liked more than having the police and prosecutors come to him for information.

Dan asked the questions himself. The county prosecutor wasn't a tall man, but he had an undeniable presence. Cindy, who didn't like him at all, called it charisma. He was blond and slick and knew how to connect with juries the way an actor would. He oozed success, confidence, and money, although the money wasn't his own. He was married to one of the city's most successful real estate developers, who'd bankrolled his career and his thousand-dollar suits. Dan and Lauren had an estate on the lake. A Lexus. Their eyes were on the prize. He was going places in state politics.

"We need to stick to the facts," Dan told Wiley. He paced back and forth between the narrow walls of the hallway. He had the kind of hyperactive personality that couldn't sit still. "Archie is going to paint you as a sleazy peeping Tom when you're on the stand. The jury won't like you. You'd better be prepared for that."

"It's a hazard of the profession," Wiley said. "Nobody pays me to be liked."

"Tell me about the video you took in the bedroom. What, exactly, does it show?"

"Like I told the doc, it shows her having sex with Nathan Skinner," Wiley replied. He drank more Perrier and added, "Me and Ferris watched it together. It doesn't leave anything to the imagination."

"What was his reaction?"

"Cold," Wiley said, shaking his head. "Ice cold. I see a lot of husbands when they face the ugly truth, you know? Most go to pieces. Big strong guys blubbering, how could she do this to me, blah, blah, blah. Not Ferris. He just got this frozen rage."

"When was this?"

"Thanksgiving week. Late November."

Stride thought about the timing of Wiley's revelation. Thanksgiving week. Janine and Nathan both said that the affair had ended shortly afterward. Jay also contacted a divorce lawyer named Tamara Fellowes around the same time. It wasn't hard to connect the dots. Wiley's video landed like a bomb in Jay's life. It was bad enough to learn that your wife was having an affair, but even worse to know she was sleeping with someone you loathed.

Janine said he was itching to confront Nathan Skinner, but Nathan said it never happened.

Nathan said Jay would have done anything to keep Janine under his thumb, but Janine said they were headed for an amicable separation.

Who was lying?

Stride left the two men and wandered inside the apartment. It was small and furnished sparsely. Janine hadn't spent much time decorating her secret space. His team was searching the rooms and screening surfaces for evidence of blood, in case Janine had tracked something from her house on the night of the murder. Maggie was at the apartment window, staring across Michigan Street toward Canal Park.

"So you've got a big mansion up on the hill," she said when Stride joined her. "Why do you buy a one-bedroom condo like this?"

"Sounds like the bedroom got a lot of use," Stride said.

"Well, yeah, it's a nice love nest. She's got a Tempur-Pedic mattress in there. Pretty good for rocking and rolling."

"Why didn't we find out about this place before now?" Stride asked.

"Janine set up a corporate entity for lab referrals. Medicare-reimbursement crap. The ownership is under the business name. There's nothing to tie it to her. She hasn't had the place long. Just since late July. You think she stashed the gun and jewels here that night?"

"It would have been easy and fast," Stride said, "and it would have bought her time to get rid of them."

"Well, we haven't found anything so far. No gun. No blood. Maybe this is just what Nathan said it was. Somewhere to unwind after surgery. No work, no papers, no husband. Nice bed when you want to bang an ex-cop."

Stride shook his head. "No, we're missing something. There's something else here."

"You sound pretty sure."

He looked around the apartment, but the walls gave up no secrets. "I know Janine, and I know Archie. If there wasn't anything to find here, they would have told us about it weeks ago. Janine kept it hidden. This place is more than a love nest."

He realized that the private detective, as nauseating as he was, might have more answers. He returned to the hallway and interrupted the conversation between Wiley and Dan Erickson.

"Hey, Wiley, when you met Dr. Snow in the parking lot across the street, did she say why she was here?" Stride asked the detective.

Wiley shrugged. "No."

"How did you find her? Did you follow her?"

"I didn't need to. She comes here a lot. Few times a week, for sure. All I had to do was wait."

Stride remembered what Nathan Skinner had told him. Janine was a busy woman. They only met for sex a couple of times a month. And yet she was here in her secret condominium regularly.

"When did you remove your camera from the bedroom?" Stride asked.

"Thanksgiving Day. After I reported what I found to Jay, he shut down the investigation. He had what he wanted, and I needed my equipment back. Holidays are good for that sort of thing. Nobody's around to see what you're doing."

"You must have captured video of Dr. Snow when she was here alone," Stride said. "Not just with Nathan Skinner."

"Sure. All the time."

"Was there anything unusual about the rest of the videos?"

"Nothing out of the ordinary. She wasn't in the bedroom much when Skinner wasn't around. Jay asked me the same thing, though."

Stride looked up. "What?"

"Jay wanted to see videos of his wife when she was alone," Wiley said.

"Did he say why? Or what he was looking for?"

"Nope."

"Did you show him?" Stride asked.

"Yeah, we watched videos for another hour or so. It was just her alone."

"What did you see?"

"Nothing much," the detective said. "She came into the bedroom—had a big glass of wine with her. Undressed down to her birthday suit. She left the room and probably showered, because her hair was wet when she came back. She put on music, danced a little, took a pill, read a book on the bed for a while. That's it."

"That was what Jay saw?"

"Yeah."

"What did he do next?"

"He thanked me and gave me a fat bonus. End of contract. For a guy who'd just figured out he was being cuckolded, he seemed in better spirits by the time we were done. I think I even mentioned it to him. I said, hey, aren't you mad?"

"What did Jay say?"

"He laughed. He said, 'I don't get mad, Melvin. I get even.'"

Stride returned to the apartment, which seemed to be the epicenter of all the problems between Jay and Janine. He ran his hands through his black hair and left his fingers laced on the back of his head. He wanted a cigarette.

"July," he said to Maggie. "Janine bought this place in late July, right? What was going on between her and Jay that month?"

Maggie grabbed the answer from her perfect memory. "She turned off the spigot on Jay's credit cards right before the Fourth."

"And then turned it back on a couple of weeks later," Stride said.

"Yeah, so? What does that have to do with the condo?"

He shook his head. "I don't know."

Stride dug in his pocket and snapped on gloves. He crossed the room and went into Janine's bedroom, where Guppo was leading the search. He saw that his team had removed the faceplate of the vent in the wall, exposing the area where Melvin Wiley had placed his spy camera, which had given him a perfect angle on the bed.

He thought about Janine spending time here alone several times a week. He saw the contents of Janine's nightstand spread on plastic sheeting across the bed, and he examined the items, seeing nothing unusual. Tissues. Condoms. Makeup. A few jewelry items that didn't match what had been taken from the house. Compact discs of Celtic music by Clannad. A Texas romance by Lorraine Heath. Nothing medical at all.

In this place, Stride realized, she wasn't a doctor.

He went into the adjoining bathroom. At her mansion on the hill, Janine's bathroom was her spa and temple, a place to escape. Not here. This one was clean but small, with a toilet, medicine cabinet, sink, built-in linen closet, and a combination tub and shower. He checked the closet, which contained luxury bath towels and shower supplies from L'Occitane. Inside the medicine cabinet, he found a toothbrush, toothpaste, and over-the-counter medications for stomach disorders.

Nothing special.

And then Stride noticed the paint on the wall.

The medicine cabinet was framed by four panels of oak trim. In two places beside the right-most panel, he saw faint scratches in the white paint. They were the kind of scratches fingernails would make. With his gloved hand, he pushed against the plasterboard and nudged one finger against the piece of oak trim.

It popped off the wall.

Beneath the trim was a set of hinges.

"Mags," he called.

She joined him in the small bathroom and whistled when she saw the hinges. Stride checked the oak trim on the opposite side of the medicine cabinet and removed the corresponding panel. Beneath it, the fringe of the cabinet was fitted into a steel rod that held it firmly in place against the wall. Two small fingerholds allowed someone to detach the entire cabinet from the rod and swing it on the hinges.

He removed the other two panels of oak trim. Without touching the fingerholds—they'd need to dust those for prints—he pried the medicine cabinet away from the steel rod, and it opened to reveal a small compartment built into the drywall.

"Whoa," Maggie said.

Stride shook his head. The truth never made him happy, because the truth of human nature was usually dark. "That's why she killed Jay," he said.

18

Stride found Janine in her surgical office at St. Anne's. The window behind her desk faced the expanse of Lake Superior. Her home, her condominium, and her office all looked out on the lake. He wondered whether she was even conscious of it being there day after day in all its changeable glory.

Janine waved him to a chair in front of her desk, but she clearly wasn't happy to see him. He could see an enlarged CT scan on the computer monitor in front of her, and she was reviewing a patient's file. Her pretty face was intense, her normally lush blond hair tied back behind her head. This was what she did. She was a surgeon, and he was interrupting her.

"It's not a good time, Lieutenant," Janine snapped. "I can't afford the distraction. I have a delicate operation this afternoon."

"I know."

Her eyebrows flickered with annoyance. "Excuse me? You know?"

"I checked your schedule."

In the blink of an eye, her mind ran through calculations. He watched concern mingle with curiosity. "You should run anything you need by Archie. If you have questions, talk to him, not me. You know how it works."

"Yes, I do."

"So if you'll excuse me, Lieutenant?" she asked sharply.

Stride didn't get up from the chair. He felt sadness that it had come to this. Dismantling anyone's life was a task he hated, even when he had no choice. "This is a unique situation, Janine. I don't have time to get a court order, so I'm relying on you to do the right thing."

"And what do you mean by that?" she asked.

"Cancel the surgery," Stride told her.

"Cancel it? Jonathan, I've been patient with you because of Cindy, but maybe you don't realize who I am or what I do here. I don't perform elective surgery that can be squeezed in between vacations and golf games. A man's life is at stake. Days count. Minutes count."

"Yes, I know. That's why I'd like this to happen without confrontation. I don't want to alarm a patient or a patient's family by talking to them myself, but I will if necessary."

"And say what? What's going on? Are you planning to arrest me?"

"We don't have a formal arrest warrant yet," he acknowledged, "but it's in process. We'll be working with Mr. Gale on a time for you to surrender yourself. However, this decision won't wait. You need to cancel all of the surgeries on your calendar."

"Well, unless you plan to haul me out of the hospital in cuffs, I don't see why—"

"Please, Janine," he interrupted her. "Don't make this harder on yourself or your patients. You know why."

He reached into the inner pocket of his coat and removed an evidence bag that he placed on the impeccably neat desk in front of her.

No bluff.

Her eyes saw it, and her eyes closed. The evidence bag contained a prescription bottle of the painkiller Vicodin.

"I'm sure you know where we found this," Stride told her. "This and about fifteen other bottles of Vicodin, Percocet, and OxyContin. You're hooked on pain pills, Dr. Snow. I can't let you into an operating room."

Janine said nothing.

She knew there was no point in protesting or denying. She knew whose fingerprints they would find all over the bottles. If she'd had the strength, she would have disposed of them weeks ago, but she couldn't bring herself to do it.

"You may find it surprising, but doctors aren't supermen or superwomen," Janine told him. "We're human. After I broke my ankle last winter, I needed pain medication. I figured I could manage the risks, because I knew more about them than anyone. I was naive. By the time I realized it, it was too late."

She reached to pick up the bag, and Stride pulled it away.

"I'm clean today," she added. "I always make sure I'm clean before I walk into the OR. It's my rule."

"That hardly matters, even if it's true."

She shrugged. He was right, and she knew it. "Yes, of course."

"What about Ira Rose? The patient who died?"

"I was clean then, too," she insisted. "My problem had nothing to do with his death. Not that anyone will care."

Janine was a realist about what came next. The fact of her addiction was enough to cost her everything she had. No doubt she'd lied on her malpractice-insurance application, and the policy would be voided. The judgment in litigation over Ira's death would cost her millions. Her fortune. Her house. Her license to practice medicine would soon be gone.

Everything she lived for—gone.

"Jay knew," Stride said. "He threatened to expose your addiction, right? That's what he held over your head."

She didn't answer. Her mental calculations had already shifted to the next battle of her life. Her career was over; now all that remained was guilt or innocence in a murder trial. She wouldn't make his job easier.

"You visited pharmacies all over the northland," he went on, "but the patient name on the prescriptions was the same. Holly Jorgenson. *Holly*. That was the name of the drug addict in Jay's column last July. It was a threat against you, wasn't it? A very public threat. You shut off his credit cards, and that was Jay's way of letting you know that if you didn't turn the money spigot on again, he'd expose your secret to the world."

"Jay," she said, and he could hear the depth of bitterness in her voice.

"That's when you bought the condo, too," Stride said. "Did you tell Jay you were quitting the pills? Instead, you just took your addiction underground. You found a way to keep it hidden from him."

She didn't break down. She didn't cry. There were very few tears in Janine Snow.

"What about Thanksgiving?" he asked. "Jay hired Melvin Wiley to follow you, but was he even thinking about an affair? Or did he suspect you were still using pills, and he wanted proof? I'm curious, what, exactly, did Jay say when he confronted you? Did he call his friend Tamara Fellowes at the Stanhope law firm and say that he was prepared to offer damaging information in Esther Rose's lawsuit? Did he threaten to destroy your whole life if you didn't give up the affair with Nathan Skinner? And what else? Did he want a slave, Janine? Did you finally realize there was no way out with Jay except to see him dead?"

Her voice was low but calm. "It must be so nice to be perfect, Jonathan."

"I'm certainly not that. I'm sympathetic to your situation, Janine, but you have to make some hard choices. It's time for you to talk to Archie about a plea. If you and Jay argued that night, if you lost control and shot him, then you're better off admitting it. This crazy story about someone coming into the house won't fly."

"I never lose control," she replied, "and I didn't shoot Jay."

"No one's going to believe you. Archie won't be able to sell that to a jury. Were you on the pills that night? Is that why you had to stop the car with Cindy and throw up?"

Janine picked up her office phone, as if he wasn't there. She'd already dismissed him. "Patty, what room is Mr. Fernandez in?" she asked her assistant. "I need to speak to him and his family about the surgery today. I'm afraid we have to cancel it. And get Archie Gale on the phone for me, will you? Tell him I need to see him immediately. I'm going to be arrested soon."

Howard Marlowe pulled into his driveway at the end of the school day.

They were talking about the 1960s in his ninth-grade Civil Rights class. Unrest. Riots. The assassination of JFK and then the Civil Rights Act of the following year. Kennedy was Howard's hero. He wished he'd been born earlier, so he could have been alive when Kennedy was president. That was an era when individuals could still make a difference.

As he got out of his car, his head was still reeling from the comment one of his students had made. Howard had shown them headlines from the day after Kennedy's death, and one of the fourteen-year-old girls had raised her hand and asked, "Why was it such a big deal?"

Someone took a rifle and killed the President of the United States. No big deal.

He'd never felt so impotent and purposeless in his life. He was absolutely certain that he was making no difference whatsoever with his stay on the planet. In a black mood, he grabbed the mail from the box at the end of the driveway, brought it inside, and sat down at the kitchen table. Carol was home, making dinner. Baked chicken and broccoli, because it was Monday. She whistled along to a pop song by Kelly Clarkson, as if it was a wonderful day. The anger over the break-in was behind her now.

Everything in their lives was back to normal, which was exactly what Carol wanted. Everything was the way it had always been and the way it would always be.

It made him want to scream.

"What's in the mail?" Carol asked.

"I don't know."

Howard picked at the letters and magazines in front of him. A credit card bill from Kohl's. A copy of *People* magazine. Carol liked to read it. A flier about recycling and trash collection. A brochure with coupons from the local restaurants. Five dollars off at Pizza Hut. They'd use that one.

He pulled an official-looking envelope out from the pile. It was addressed to him from the Duluth District Court of St. Louis County.

"What's that?" his wife asked from the sink.

Howard was curious, and he unfolded the official letter inside. "It's a summons," he said.

"For what?"

He read the notice at the top of the page.

You are hereby notified that you have been selected to serve as a trial juror in the County District Court.

19

Summer came.

In Duluth, people sometimes wondered if the ice would never melt and if the trees would stay bare skeletons forever. Spring was often no spring, just cold gray days of mud and rain. However, even Duluth seasons eventually had to bow to the calendar, and by midyear, the city became a paradise. The months spent as nothing but a cold nowhere were forgotten. Lake Superior shimmered, a vast sapphire sea, catching dots of sunlight on each wave. Blue skies met green hills. Waterfalls surged and played through the cataract down Seven Bridges Road. Tourists swarmed Canal Park, and swimmers ran through the surf and wet sand stretching along the Point. Sea brine and popcorn perfumed the air.

Thousands of runners crowded the city for Grandma's Marathon. A different festival filled up each weekend. Reggae and Blues. Tall Ships. The Blue Angels. Music floated out of the open doors of bars and clubs.

The length of the summer days almost made time hover in place, as perfect and fragile as a hummingbird. A Duluth summer felt as if it could be endless, not gone with the puff of a cold breeze. And yet everyone knew that perfection was a tease. The warmth was brief.

July. August. Each sunset came with a little warning label to enjoy the moment while it lasted.

Stride lounged in a deck chair on the sand dune behind their house on their first night back from Alaska. Cindy sat beside him, nearly asleep. He wore sunglasses on the bright evening, which gave the lake a midnight glow. People jogged, and dogs ran along the sand in front of them. He was exhausted from the long flight back and the drive north from the Twin Cities, but he couldn't recall a time when he'd felt so content with his life.

They'd had the perfect vacation. Luxurious food. Wine. Glaciers calving in front of them. Floatplanes over the remote wilderness. Hours spent in bed on a sea day, making love to the rough rhythm of the waves. Stride, who didn't do vacations well as a rule, had set aside Duluth and the job for seven whole days. Cindy called it nothing short of a miracle.

Even so, he was happy to be home. To be in Duluth in the summertime. To feel a lake breeze, to hold Cindy's hand, to drink cold beer from a bottle. His wife was quiet, and he knew a little part of her was sad to be back to reality, but he didn't mind the ebb and flow of the world. He knew you could never predict the moments that would linger in your memory, but he thought this was one.

"Favorite port?" Cindy murmured, revisiting the trip.

"Juneau."

"Favorite meal?"

"That Chinese restaurant we ate at before we sailed from Vancouver. With the noodles. What was it called?"

"Hon."

"Yeah, that one," he said.

"Favorite day overall?"

He nudged his sunglasses up to his forehead and let her see his eyes, and he just grinned. She laughed. "Sea day," she concluded.

"Definitely."

They were quiet for a while. The lake breathed waves in and out. As dusk spread shadows, the crowds on the beach thinned. Someone started a bonfire, and they could smell the wood and feel the smoke in their eyes. An ore boat glided through the nearby ship canal and rolled toward the open water. Stride wanted a cigarette, but he didn't take one.

"The trial starts next week," Cindy said.

"I know."

Back to reality.

The murder trial of State of Minnesota, Plaintiff, vs. Janine Snow, Defendant, was scheduled to begin on Monday. Stride knew that Dan Erickson planned to call Cindy as his first witness, and the idea of testifying weighed on his wife. She'd put it out of her mind during their trip to Alaska, but it was back as the clock ticked closer.

"You'll do fine," he told her, which was as much as he could say. His own testimony would follow hers. She would probably be off the stand in an hour; he would spend most of the day there. Then in the days to follow, Dan would build his house of cards witness by witness, and Archie would try to blow it down.

Eventually, Cindy said, "Do you think she'll be convicted?"

Stride hesitated. Saying nothing would have been better, but he couldn't remain completely silent. "You can never tell with juries."

That was true. Jurors were a strange bunch. Impossible to read or predict, always able to surprise. Dan said that trial attorneys were storytellers for a jury of children, and the lawyer with the best bedtime story won.

Stride respected the difficulty of what jurors had to do. They were asked to set aside a lifetime of bias, but they were also human beings, filled with prejudice and empathy. They were asked to evaluate nothing but the evidence in front of them, and yet they had to share a courtroom day after day with the man or woman whose fate they held in their hands. You couldn't vote guilty in a felony murder case if you didn't *believe* that the person behind the table ten feet away was capable of a terrible crime.

The state didn't have to establish a motive. The defendant didn't need a reason to cause the death of another person. Even so, every investigator and every prosecutor knew that jurors craved the why.

Why did respected surgeon Janine Snow murder her husband, Jay Ferris?

Because she was living under the threat of Jay stealing the only thing she cared about. Her career.

"You never found that man," Cindy pointed out.

"No." Stride knew who she meant. They'd been unable to identify the man who'd threatened her at Miller Hill Mall. He was a ghost. "Guppo saw a man matching his description at the marathon, but he wasn't able to get close. The guy disappeared before Guppo got there. But we haven't stopped looking for him."

"It's been months," she said. "If you haven't found him by now . . ."

He didn't answer, because he didn't want to argue with her. Arguing would only ruin the perfect day. She clearly felt the same way, because she squeezed his fingers with her small hand and then pulled his fist to her mouth and kissed it.

"Sorry," Cindy said.

"That's okay."

They sat, and the evening got darker, and the wind off the water developed a little bite. It was time to go inside, to go to bed. She got up first. By then, she was mostly a shadow. She leaned down over his deck chair, with her long hair falling across him, and she kissed his lips. A hard kiss. A Cindy kiss.

"I'm glad we went to Alaska," she said.

"Me, too."

"Nobody can ever take that away from us."

He thought that was a strange thing for her to say, but he let it go, because it was a beautiful summer night, full of love and life. You don't question such things. Even so, something in her voice made him shiver and think of winter.

20

Juror #5.

That was Howard Marlowe's identifying number. He stood along with thirteen other men and women—twelve jurors, two alternates—to swear their oaths to the court. With that, the trial began.

The judge, the Honorable Jeffrey R. Edblad, spoke directly to the jury, and Howard tried to concentrate on his words. Edblad had short gray hair, black glasses, and a rounded face. If he hadn't been a lawyer and a judge, Howard figured he could have been a teacher. He was calm, and he spoke slowly and deliberately, like a father offering words of wisdom to a teenager about to take the car out for the first time. *I'll be fair, I'll be gentle, but I'll be firm.*

Members of the jury, you will hear testimony from witnesses in this trial. It will be up to you to evaluate their credibility and decide how much weight to give what they say. I'm asking you to be patient and listen carefully to each witness and not to come to any conclusions until you have heard all of the evidence.

Howard felt restless. It was hard to come down from the adrenaline high of being here. His gaze flicked around the courtroom, which was smaller than he expected. He and his fellow jurors were seated in blue cushioned chairs inside the jury box. The two counsel tables were placed side by side, barely six feet away from them. He thought it strange to see the prosecutor and defense attorney seated next to each other, like colleagues rather than adversaries. Judge Edblad's platform, inside a wooden enclosure at the front of the courtroom, was only slightly elevated. There were tables and computers for the clerk and court reporter. Everyone was close together.

The room was narrow but high, with twenty-five-foot walls broken up by dark wood panels and white stone blocks. The chambered ceiling featured sculpted trim painted in gold and green. One set of double-wide doors led in and out to the marble hallway of the courthouse. Behind the counsel tables, a few rows of spectator benches were completely filled by the media.

You should rely on your own judgment and common sense to evaluate the testimony of each witness. You will need to decide for yourself whether they are sincere, whether you believe them, whether what they say is reasonable or unreasonable.

His fellow jurors looked as ordinary as he did. Eight women. Six men. Twelve of them white, plus one black man and one black woman. The youngest juror couldn't have been more than twenty-five years old. The oldest, a woman in a blue dress with her hands in her lap, was at least seventy. Howard was seated at the end of the front row, closest to the counsel tables. The lone black woman, who was in her mid-thirties and wore a burgundy pants suit, sat next to him. She had a pleasant smile.

While this trial is going on, there are things you shouldn't do. Remember, you aren't investigators or detectives, so you shouldn't go looking for information about this case. Your family and friends are likely to be curious about what you're doing, but you should not discuss the case with anyone. You shouldn't read articles about it in the newspaper or online or watch news reports.

Janine Snow was directly in front of him.

She was seated at the end of the counsel table beside her attorney, Archibald Gale. If she'd reached out her hand, if Howard had reached out his hand, they could have touched. She wore a light blue suit with a rose blouse underneath. Styled blond hair, each strand in place.

An expressionless, enigmatic face. He could see her blue eyes as she watched the judge. She kept her hands folded primly in front of her. He was close enough to her that he could see the small birthmark near her mouth and the pale pink shade of her lipstick. As beautiful as she was, she wasn't completely ageless. He could see tiny creases in her skin, hiding discreetly under her makeup.

He knew he was staring and that he should drag his eyes away. She must have felt him studying her, because her head swiveled slightly, and their eyes met. It felt to him just as it had in the mall that day. There was something intimate and extremely erotic about it. Her eyes didn't smile or beg him for mercy; she simply answered his own stare, human to human, woman to man. He looked down at his lap, embarrassed.

He hadn't lied in the juror interviews. Not really. He'd acknowledged that he was aware of the case, but that was true of anyone in Duluth. No, he hadn't formed a conclusion about Dr. Snow's guilt or innocence, and that was true. For everything he'd read about the murder, and for all the time he'd tried to divine the truth in pictures of her face, he really had no idea if she'd killed her husband. He was an ordinary man with no connection to anyone involved in the crime. The perfect juror.

"Mr. Erickson," Judge Edblad said, "do you wish to make your opening statement?"

"Thank you, your honor," Dan Erickson said, standing up.

The county attorney remained behind the counsel table, but he spoke directly to the jury. Howard listened as the prosecutor laid out the elements of the case and what the jurors would need to decide. The legal questions. The evidence questions. It all began here.

"This trial is about a relationship that went badly wrong," Erickson told them. "It's about a marriage in which the wife wanted out and her husband refused to let her go. This wife—the defendant, Janine Snow—saw only one way to be free of her husband. Only one way to escape. Murder. That's the story of this case. And the witnesses and physical evidence we will show you in the next few days will make the details of that story very clear. When we're done, you will conclude beyond any reasonable doubt that, on January 28 of this year,

Janine Snow shot her husband, Jay Ferris, in the head and intentionally caused his death."

Erickson was serious and confident. He didn't smile; he wasn't their buddy. He wore an expensive suit, not an everyman suit, as if he wanted Howard and the other jurors to believe that he was just a little smarter than they were, knew just a little more, had been down this road enough times that you could trust whatever he said.

"Most of what happened on January 28 isn't in dispute," Erickson continued. "We have an eyewitness who saw the defendant and Mr. Ferris together, and we have the defendant's own statement to the police that night. She was alone in the house with her husband on the night of the murder. They argued. Minutes later, Jay Ferris lay dead of a gunshot wound to his head in the living room of their house. Not in dispute.

"So what led these two people to that terrible moment? Multiple witnesses will testify that the defendant wanted to end her marriage but that her husband was determined not to grant her a divorce. That the relationship between them was volatile and that each tried to inflict psychological damage on the other. That the defendant's husband, Jay Ferris, knew about his wife's addiction to prescription pain medications and was threatening to expose this information and destroy her medical career. He held her whole future in his hands, ladies and gentlemen. That's the situation Janine Snow faced on January 28. That's why she used a gun to murder her husband.

"Did the defendant know how to fire a gun? Yes, she did. We'll show you a photograph of her firing a gun similar in kind to the gun used to murder Jay Ferris.

"Did the defendant have access to a gun? Yes, she did. You'll hear a witness testify that the defendant knew that her husband owned a gun and that she concealed that knowledge from the police. Her husband's gun has since disappeared.

"Did the defendant take steps to conceal whether she fired a gun on January 28? Yes, she did. By her own statement to the police, she took a shower and washed her clothes that night before the police arrived. So she made it impossible to run chemical tests on her body and her clothes that would have confirmed that she had fired a gun.

"This story isn't hard to understand, ladies and gentlemen. You won't need anything more than your common sense to know what happened that night. Janine Snow caused the death of Jay Ferris."

Howard felt the blank slate of his judgment fill with suspicion as Erickson spoke. Judge Edblad had already warned them that nothing an attorney said was evidence, and yet if the evidence revealed what Erickson promised, it was hard not to believe that the case was exactly as he stated.

Then Archibald Gale stood up.

He was warm where Dan Erickson was cool. He was like Santa Claus in a two-piece suit, with his curly hair, peppery beard, and twinkling eyes. He reminded them that Janine, sitting in that chair beside him, was innocent, and that the entire burden of proof rested with the state. With each sentence, delivered with a sad shake of his head, he cast doubt on that proof.

"Ladies and gentlemen, pay attention to what you do *not* hear from the state in this case. You will not hear any evidence that Dr. Snow owned a gun, because there is no such evidence.

"You will not hear any evidence that Dr. Snow fired a gun that night, because there is no such evidence.

"You will not hear any evidence about the gun used to murder Jay Ferris, because that gun was never found. Think about that. Whoever killed Mr. Ferris took the gun away from the crime scene. On that basis alone, it's reasonable for you to doubt that Dr. Snow could have committed this crime. But there's more."

Gale took a sip of water.

"You will learn that Jay Ferris wrote things in his job as a columnist at the *Duluth News Tribune* that offended people. Outraged them. Cost them their jobs. It's reasonable to wonder whether one of those people killed him.

"You will learn that an unknown vehicle was parked in the neighborhood not far from Jay Ferris's house on the night of the murder and that the police never located this vehicle or who was driving it. It's reasonable to wonder whether that person killed him.

"You will learn that Jay Ferris took pictures of an armed man while hiking in a park near Duluth and that the police never identified this man or interviewed him about his whereabouts on the night of the murder. It's reasonable to wonder whether that dangerous man killed him."

And so it went on.

By the time Archibald Gale sat down, Howard was back to where he'd started. A blank slate. He had no idea about Janine's guilt or innocence. All he could do was stare at her face and wonder. This time, her face wasn't a photograph on the computer screen in the basement of his house. She was real. She was so close that he could smell her perfume.

She was waiting for him to decide.

"Mr. Erickson," Judge Edblad said, "call your first witness, please."

21

Cindy felt physically ill on the witness stand.

At the counsel table, Janine offered her the tiniest of smiles. They were still friends. There were no hard feelings, even though Cindy was the first witness, pounding in the first nail.

Dan Erickson stood up to address her. Cindy knew exactly the kind of man he was. Inside the courtroom, he played his role, leading the jury down the path he wanted them to follow. Outside the courtroom, he was vain, self-absorbed, and manipulative. He was good-looking, and he knew it. He was married, but his eyes and hands wandered over every pretty woman he met.

He took her through introductions. Established who she was. And who her husband was.

"Mrs. Stride, where were you on the evening of January 28 of this year?"

"I was at a birthday party for Deputy Police Chief Kyle Kinnick at the Radisson Hotel."

"Was the defendant there?"

"Yes."

"Was the defendant's husband, Jay Ferris, there?"

"No."

"During the party, did you speak to the defendant?"

"Yes, I did."

"Did you see her consume any alcohol?"

Cindy hesitated. "Yes."

"How much?"

"I don't know, exactly. She was drinking white wine. She had several glasses."

"Did the defendant subsequently ask if you would drive her home?"

"Yes, she did."

"And do you remember exactly what time it was when you drove her home?"

"I remember that the clock in my car read 9:32 p.m. It's not far. We would have reached Janine's house just a few minutes later."

"When you arrived at the defendant's house, did you accompany her to her front door?"

"Yes, I did."

"At that time, did you see Jay Ferris, the defendant's husband?"

"Yes, he came to the door and opened it."

"He was alive?"

Cindy smiled faintly. "Yes, obviously."

"Did you see or hear anyone else in the house?"

"No."

"Were there any other cars in the driveway or parked near the house?"

"No."

"What happened next?"

"Janine went inside with Jay. He closed the door. I left."

"Before you left, could you hear any part of the conversation between the defendant and her husband?"

"I heard loud voices. It sounded like an argument."

"Would you characterize this as a heated argument?"

"I guess so, yes."

"Was there physical contact between them?"

"Yes, Jay grabbed her wrist, and Janine pushed him away."

"Did you see or hear anything else?"

"No. I left after that."

"As you left the house that night, Mrs. Stride, did you see any-one else?"

"No. There was no one else there. I was alone."

"What about other cars?"

"Mine was the only car."

"Did you see anything that raised your suspicions?"

"No."

"Thank you, Mrs. Stride. Now, is it fair to say you consider the defendant a friend?"

"Yes, it is."

"Do you see her regularly on social occasions?"

"Yes, I do."

"Has the defendant ever shared any information with you about her perspective on the state of her marriage?"

"She told me that she considered her marriage to be a mistake," Cindy acknowledged.

"Did she express an intent to seek a divorce?"

"Yes, she did."

"On more than one occasion?"

"Yes."

"Mrs. Stride, in December of last year, did you ask the defendant about the status of a possible divorce from Mr. Ferris?"

Cindy didn't want to say it. She'd known the next question was coming. They'd gone over all of it in her statement to the police. Even so, she hated having to say it out loud, in a courtroom, with the jury listening. With Janine listening.

"Yes. We had lunch, and I asked if she was going ahead with a divorce."

"What did she say?"

Cindy opened her mouth, but her throat was too dry to speak. She reached for the water and drank.

"Mrs. Stride? How did the defendant answer that question when you asked her if she was proceeding with a divorce?"

"She said no."

"Do you remember her exact words?"

"She said, 'I wish I could, but Jay has me trapped.'"

Archibald Gale stood up to conduct the cross-examination.

"Mrs. Stride, while you were driving Dr. Snow home from the party on January 28, did you stop the car at any point?"

"Yes. Janine wasn't feeling well. I stopped, and she got out and threw up."

"So she was a mess?" Gale asked.

"Yes."

"Mrs. Stride, if you threw up on the side of the road, what would you do when you got home?"

Cindy smiled. "I'd take a shower."

"And what would you do with your clothes?"

"I'd put them in the washing machine."

"Thank you. Now, when you arrived at Dr. Snow's residence and you saw Jay Ferris, did he have a gun?"

"No."

"He wasn't waving one in the air?"

Another smile. She saw the jurors smiling, too. "No."

"What about Dr. Snow? Did she have a gun at the party?"

"No, not that I saw. I mean, she had a purse, but it was tiny. It would have been noticeable if something as big as a gun was inside."

"Okay. And you say you left Dr. Snow's house at approximately 9:45 p.m.— is that about right?"

"Yes, that would be about right. A couple minutes on either side of that."

"You have no idea what happened at the house after you left, do you?"

"No."

"If a car drove up to the house thirty seconds after you turned onto Skyline Parkway, you would have no way of knowing that—is that right?"

"That's true."

"Thank you. Mrs. Stride. Did Dr. Snow ever threaten her husband in your presence?"

"No."

"Did she ever tell you that she wished she could kill him? Or that she wished he was dead?"

"No, nothing like that."

"Did she ever seem desperate to you about her marital situation?"

"Janine? Desperate? No."

"Thank you, Mrs. Stride," Gale said. He began to sit down, but then he stopped. "Oh, I'm very sorry, could you tell the jury—did you have a frightening experience at Miller Hill Mall this spring?"

Dan stood up immediately. "Objection, your honor. This line of questioning is outside the scope of direct examination, and it's not relevant to the case."

Judge Edblad waited. "Mr. Gale?"

"Your honor, the incident I'm asking about arose because of the witness's relationship with Lieutenant Stride of the Duluth Police Department—a relationship that Mr. Erickson inquired about under direct examination. In addition, the incident arose because of Lieutenant Stride's investigation into this specific case, which certainly makes it relevant."

"I'm overruling the objection," the judge replied.

Gale continued to Cindy, "You may answer the question."

"I—yes, I did," Cindy said.

"Please tell us what happened."

"I followed a man at the mall, and he confronted and threatened me. He had a gun."

"What was the nature of his threat?"

"He said I shouldn't stick my nose into his business. He said bad things happened to people who did that. And then he showed me a gun."

"I'm so sorry," Gale said. "What a terrifying experience for you. Please tell the jury, Mrs. Stride, why did you follow this man in the first place?"

Cindy felt herself flushing. "I believed that he was a man that my husband, Lieutenant Stride, was looking for."

"Why did you believe that?"

"I saw a set of photographs in a stack of evidence that Jonny—that Lieutenant Stride left on our kitchen table. The photos showed a man in the woods carrying an assault rifle, and there was a note about trying to find him. This looked like the same man."

"This stack of evidence that the Lieutenant brought home to study—do you know what case it was part of?"

"Yes, it was evidence connected to the murder of Jay Ferris," Cindy said.

Gale nodded as he sat down. "Thank you, Mrs. Stride."

"Mrs. Stride, how long did you look at these photographs?" Dan Erickson asked on his redirect examination.

"A few seconds, I guess."

"Ten seconds? Twenty? Thirty?"

"Closer to ten," Cindy admitted.

"Were these crisp, clear, high-resolution photos?"

"No, they were blurry."

"And how long after you saw these photographs did you follow this stranger at the mall?"

"Several days."

"You saw a couple of blurry pictures for maybe ten seconds, and days later, you saw someone that you *thought* might be the same man—do I have that right?"

"Yes," Cindy said.

"Can you say for sure that this was the same man, Mrs. Stride?"

"Not for sure, no."

"Thank you, Mrs. Stride. That's all."

22

Stride had sat in the same witness chair in the same courtroom many times before. Testifying in court was one of the few tasks for which he wore a suit. He owned only two suits, and today he wore the navy-blue one, freshly dry-cleaned. He'd tried to tame his restless hair, and he'd shaved. Appearances mattered. Trials were about evidence, but they were also about perceptions. Finding facts meant deciding whom to believe. Whom to trust.

Dan guided him through a review of his experience, including nearly twenty years with the Duluth Police Department and nearly ten in charge of the Detective Bureau. Stride talked about his background in felony investigations, including dozens of homicide cases. It was all prologue.

"Lieutenant, were you called to the home of the defendant on the evening of January 28 of this year?" Dan asked finally.

"Yes, I was."

"Is this house located in the city of Duluth in St. Louis County?"

"Yes, it is." Stride gave the specific address and described the location of the house. Dan introduced a map of the area enlarged on foam core, and Stride pointed out the residence and described the access in and out—specifically, that Janine's home was located on a dead-end street at the summit of a sharp hill.

"What did you find inside the house?" Dan asked.

"We found the body of Jay Ferris," Stride said. "He had a single gunshot wound to the forehead."

"Can you tell us exactly where the body was located?"

"There's a large marble-floored foyer inside the front door that leads to the living room. The body of Mr. Ferris was located in the living room, approximately ten feet from the edge of the foyer."

Dan introduced photographs of the crime scene and an enlarged floor plan of the house. Stride identified the photos and matched them with positions on the floor plan for the jury. He also pointed out the wineglass found near Jay's body and the other, lipstick-smeared wineglass on the coffee table. He noted a pair of stiletto heels belonging to Janine that had been left on the floor of the foyer.

"Did you find a gun near the body or in the house?"

"No. We conducted a search of the home and the surrounding property but did not locate the murder weapon."

"During your investigation, did you determine whether the victim, Jay Ferris, held a Minnesota permit to carry a handgun?"

"Yes, he did."

"Did the defendant make a statement to you about whether her husband, in fact, owned a handgun?"

"She claimed that Mr. Ferris used to own a handgun but that she made him get rid of it when they got married," Stride said.

"Did you, nonetheless, uncover physical evidence during your investigation that Mr. Ferris continued to own a handgun long after his marriage to the defendant?"

"Yes, Mr. Ferris's brother provided us with a photograph that showed a gun in his possession." Dan introduced the photo of Jay and Clyde Ferris, and an enlargement showed a close-up of the portion of the gun visible in the holster.

"Were you able to confirm when this photograph was taken?"

"Yes, it was taken last October 27, three months prior to the murder."

"Were you able to locate this gun during your investigation?" Dan asked.

"No, we weren't."

"Thank you, Lieutenant. Now, when you arrived at the house that night, was the defendant present?"

"Yes, Dr. Snow was there, along with her counsel, Mr. Gale."

"And did Dr. Snow make a statement to you with her counsel present?"

"She did. Dr. Snow told us that she was dropped off at her house that evening by my wife. This was about 9:45 p.m. She told us that she had some wine with her husband, and they argued. She said she then left her husband to take a shower. Her bathroom is adjacent to her bedroom, two floors down from the living room. She was in the shower for a long time, she said, but she couldn't tell us exactly how long. When she got out of the shower, she said she noticed that two drawers in a jewelry box in her bedroom were open, and several expensive items were missing. She told us that she went back upstairs and found her husband's body."

"At that point, did the defendant tell you that she called 911?" Dan asked.

"No, she said that some time passed before she called the police."

"What did the defendant claim to be doing during this time?"

"She said that she simply stared at her husband's body," Stride said.

"How much time passed between Dr. Snow's arrival at her house that evening and the call to police?"

"Approximately one hour. The actual 911 call was received at 10:47 p.m. A patrol car was at the scene within ten minutes."

"And do we have any way of knowing *exactly* when, during that hour, the shooting occurred?"

"No."

"Lieutenant, based on the evidence gathered in this investigation, and based on your extensive experience in these kinds of crimes, did you form an opinion about the truthfulness of the defendant's statement?"

"Yes. I concluded that her statement was not supported by the evidence."

"Please explain how you reached that conclusion," Dan said.

Stride took a pointer and referred to the floor plans of Janine Snow's house. "Dr. Snow alleged that her husband was killed as part of a home invasion and robbery. However, there was no sign of forced entry, and the door between the garage and the house was locked. So Mr. Ferris would have had to let an intruder inside voluntarily. Then the shooter would have needed to murder Mr. Ferris, proceed down two flights of stairs and along a hallway to the defendant's bedroom, remove jewelry from her jewelry box, and return upstairs and escape."

"And this all would have had to happen in the time the defendant was in the shower?"

"According to her statement, yes."

"Did you find other evidence to discredit the theory that an intruder came into the house?" Dan asked.

"Yes. There was no evidence of a fight or of defensive actions by Mr. Ferris. In addition, there was no physical evidence of an intruder in the house. The walkway to the front door was wet and dusted with dirt and gravel. Traces of snowmelt, dirt, and gravel were found in the marble foyer, but we didn't find any 'tracked' dirt on the living room carpet, on the stairs, or in the defendant's bedroom."

"In your experience, Lieutenant, are persons who commit homicide and armed robbery typically gracious enough to remove their shoes before invading a house?"

Stride suppressed a smile. "No."

"Lieutenant, let's look at other possible explanations for the events that night. Did you run any chemical tests to determine whether the defendant fired a gun on the night of the murder?"

Stride shook his head. "No. That would be standard procedure, but in this case, the defendant told us that she had taken a shower, which would have erased reliable evidence of chemical residue on her hands, body, and hair. She also washed the clothes she was wearing, which would have accomplished the same thing. In light of that, running gunshot-residue tests wouldn't have given us any useful information."

"You didn't find the murder weapon, Lieutenant," Dan went on, "so it must have been removed from the house?"

"That's correct."

"Did the defendant have time to hide a gun and jewelry outside the house before she contacted the police?"

"Yes, she did," Stride said. "We conducted exercises in which a policewoman put clothes in the washing machine, showered, and then drove from the defendant's house to separate locations to secrete evidence and then drove back to the house. We ran that exercise several times, and in no instance did it take longer than thirty minutes. Sometimes, it took less than twenty minutes. So, yes, she had time."

"Now, did you tell us that the defendant admitted to arguing with Mr. Ferris on the night of the murder?"

"Yes."

"Did she say what the argument was about?"

"No, but she said they argued about everything."

"Did she give other indications of trouble in their marriage?"

"Yes, in a later statement, she admitted to an affair with a former police officer named Nathan Skinner."

"Did you subsequently interview Mr. Skinner?" Dan asked.

"I did."

"And did he provide you with any physical evidence related to the defendant's knowledge of handguns?"

"Yes, he provided me with a photograph of Dr. Snow at a gun range, where she is in the process of firing a revolver."

Dan introduced the photograph of Janine at the range, which was presented to the jury. More than anything else, Stride knew that the real impact of the photograph was Janine's expression. Confident. Assured. Almost aroused. She knew how to fire a gun, and she liked it.

"Based on your interview with Nathan Skinner, did you also learn that the defendant owned property in addition to the home where she resided with Mr. Ferris?"

"Yes, we discovered that she owns an apartment on Michigan Street in downtown Duluth."

"Did you conduct a search of this apartment?"

"We did. We discovered a cache of prescription pain medications. There were nearly five hundred pills in fifteen bottles, made up of medicines such as Percocet, OxyContin, and Vicodin."

"Did the defendant subsequently admit to you that these pills belonged to her?"

"Yes."

"Were the prescriptions in her name?"

"No, the prescriptions were all in the name of Holly Jorgenson. She acknowledged that this was a fictitious patient she had created to obtain pills for herself illegally."

"Lieutenant, did you find that fictitious patient's name significant?"

"Yes, the defendant's husband, Jay Ferris, published a column in the *Duluth News Tribune* last July about a prescription-drug addict named Holly. The column threatened public exposure of this information."

"If Mr. Ferris had exposed his wife's addiction and criminal behavior, would there have been consequences for the defendant?" Dan asked.

At that question, Archie Gale intervened. "Objection. This calls for a conclusion outside the witness's expertise."

"Sustained," Judge Edblad ruled.

Dan wasn't deterred. "Has the evidence you uncovered regarding the defendant's abuse of prescription pain medications now become public?" he asked.

"Yes."

"And to your knowledge, have there been consequences to the defendant in relation to her behavior?" Dan asked.

Stride nodded. "Yes, according to a statement by the Minnesota Board of Medical Practice last month, she has voluntarily surrendered her medical license."

He stared at Janine Snow as he said this, and so did the jury. For the first time he could remember, he saw genuine emotion in her face. It was as if her world had already crumbled around her, and nothing else in the courtroom mattered. A tear slipped from one blue eye, and a moment later, she was crying silently.

Gale began to question Stride.

"Lieutenant, you did *not* recover the murder weapon in this case—is that right? It is still missing?"

"Yes, that's right."

"Did any of Dr. Snow's neighbors report seeing her leave the house between 9:45 p.m. and the arrival of the police an hour later?"

"No."

"Did you find evidence suggesting that Mr. Ferris's Hummer had been driven between 9:45 p.m. and the arrival of the police an hour later?"

"I'm not sure what evidence would be available to confirm that," Stride said.

"Well, did you check the hood of the Hummer?"

"Yes, I did."

"Was the engine warm?"

"No," Stride admitted. He added quickly, "However, this was almost an hour after I arrived on the scene. The temperatures were below zero."

"Lieutenant, did your department receive a report about an unidentified Toyota RAV4 parked near Dr. Snow's house on the evening of the murder?"

"We received a report from a teenage driver who thought he remembered passing a RAV4 parked on West 8th Street that evening. The teenager later acknowledged using marijuana that night, so we considered his recollections to be suspect."

"Did the driver say he saw the RAV parked there after ten o'clock?"

"He thought so, but he didn't check the clock."

"Is the corner of West 8th and Skyline within a couple hundred yards of Dr. Snow's house?"

"Yes."

"Did you talk to residents on 8th Street?"

"Yes, we did."

"Did any of those residents own a RAV4 or have visitors who owned a RAV4?"

"No."

"Were you able to identify who owned this RAV4?"

"No."

"Thank you, Lieutenant. You testified that you were unable to locate a revolver allegedly owned by Jay Ferris—is that right?"

"Yes."

"You allege that Mr. Ferris owned a revolver because of a photograph supplied by the victim's brother, Clyde Ferris—is that right?"

"Yes."

"Did Clyde Ferris make a statement to you that his brother routinely carried his gun with him?"

"Yes, he did."

"Did Clyde Ferris also make a statement to you that he went ice fishing with his brother in early January, less than a month before Jay Ferris was murdered?"

Stride hesitated. "Yes, he did."

"Were you able to independently confirm that this outing took place?"

"Yes."

"How did you confirm this?"

"I got a copy of a report filed by Jay Ferris with the Minnesota Department of Natural Resources."

"Did the report indicate that, due to thin ice, Jay Ferris lost his truck and his fishing shanty into the water of Superior Bay at that time?"

"Yes," Stride said, and he knew where Gale was going now.

"Lieutenant, isn't it possible that the gun allegedly owned by Mr. Ferris—which his brother said he routinely had with him—could have been lost in his truck or in his fishing shanty when they went through the ice?"

"It's possible," Stride acknowledged, "although the truck and shanty were both salvaged once the ice came off the bay in the spring. The gun wasn't found."

"Would it have been possible for the gun to be lost in the bay when the vehicle and shack flooded and sank?"

"I suppose."

"Thank you, Lieutenant. You also testified about an affair between Dr. Snow and a former colleague of yours named Nathan Skinner—is that right?"

"Yes."

"You discovered this affair because the defendant brought it to your attention, correct?"

"Yes."

"Did Jay Ferris have a history of animosity with Nathan Skinner?"

"Yes, he did."

"In fact, Nathan Skinner was fired from the Duluth Police Department because of columns written by Jay Ferris. Is that right? Columns in which he cited Nathan Skinner's use of vile racial slurs?"

"In part, yes."

"Did Nathan Skinner assault Jay Ferris after he lost his job?"

"Yes, there was one such incident."

"During the course of your investigation, did you find evidence that Jay Ferris had discovered the affair between his wife and Nathan Skinner?"

"Yes."

"Is it reasonable to conclude that this information would have upset Mr. Ferris?"

"I have no idea."

"Mr. Ferris's wife was sleeping with a man whom Mr. Ferris described in his columns as a racist, and you don't think he would have been upset?"

"I can't speculate about Mr. Ferris's reaction," Stride said.

"Did you interview Nathan Skinner when you learned about his relationship with Dr. Snow?"

"Yes, I did."

"Did Nathan Skinner admit to being angry at Jay Ferris?"

"Yes, he did."

"Did Nathan Skinner have a verifiable alibi after 9:45 p.m. on the night of the murder?"

"We confirmed he was at his apartment for part of the evening, but we couldn't specifically confirm that he was there after 9:45 p.m."

"Thank you, Lieutenant." Gale put down one set of papers on the counsel table, and he picked up another folder. "Can you tell the court, please, did Jay Ferris file a police report last October 5 regarding an individual with a gun?"

"Yes, he reported seeing an individual using an assault rifle in the woods near Ely's Peak."

"Mr. Ferris took photographs of this man, did he not?"

"Yes, he did."

"Were you able to identify this individual?"

"No. The photographs weren't clear enough."

"However, your wife believes that she saw this individual in Miller Hall Mall and that he was carrying a handgun, doesn't she?"

"My wife followed a man who was similar in appearance to the man in the photographs. We don't know if it was the same man."

"Did he threaten her?"

"Yes, he did."

"But you still haven't identified this man, have you?" Gale asked.

"No," Stride admitted, "we haven't."

23

Heather Hubble was a photographer.

Cindy had worked with the young woman the previous year following a fall Heather had taken while shooting the ice caves of the Apostle Islands. Cindy had done PT with her twice a week for three months, and during that time, she'd poked into Heather's life story with her usual curiosity. She learned about Heather's five-year-old daughter, Lissa, and about the short-lived affair that had produced her. She found out that Heather's parents didn't approve of her vegan, out-in-the-woods lifestyle. She pegged Heather as one of the fringe loners dotting the northland, not bothering anyone and not wanting to be bothered.

Heather lived on a dirt road half a mile off the North Shore highway. Dense trees made her small home almost invisible, and the driveway was rutted with mud. It was the kind of house that would have been built decades earlier as a three-season getaway, but Heather lived in it year-round. The cabin had been handed down by her grandfather, and it needed work. Fresh paint. Repairs to the roof and the deck. New windows. Cindy knew that Heather didn't have much money for maintenance.

"Hi, Cindy," Heather said with surprise when she answered the door. "What are you doing in the middle of nowhere?"

Cindy smiled. "I need your help."

"Sure, come on in."

The small living room smelled of berries from two lit candles. With the windows open, a warm summer breeze made music on wind chimes hung from the ceiling. The house was messy, cluttered with old furniture and children's toys. Nature photographs in cheap frames adorned the walls, leaving almost no open space. The photographs were good; Heather had a gift.

Heather cleared space on a plaid recliner for Cindy to sit. There were holes worn in the arms, with white fluff poking out from the fabric like drift from a cottonwood. Heather herself flopped down in a rocking chair and bounced back and forth. She wore shorts and a loose green tank top. Her sandy blond hair was shoulder-length, and her pale, freckled skin had no makeup. She was almost thirty, which sounded young to Cindy now. Once upon a time, it had felt old.

"Where's Lissa?" Cindy asked.

Heather rolled her eyes and grinned. "My parents took her on vacation with them. Disney World. She's going to come back with princess dresses and Mickey Mouse earrings. I'm not sure how I managed to raise a girly girl. That must be her father's DNA coming through. He was always pretty concerned with how he looked."

"How's the photo business?" Cindy asked.

"Not bad. Summer is wedding season. Brides are hell, but their daddies pay good money."

"And your back? It's okay?"

"Yeah, thanks. All the PT really helped. I've been pretty good about keeping up with the exercises, and yoga keeps me limber, too."

"Good."

"What's going on with you?" Heather asked. "You need some portraits done? Sexy glamour shots for the hubby?"

Cindy laughed. "I think that would make Jonny blush. Actually, I have an odd favor to ask. I talked to Kon at *Lake Superior Magazine*, and she said you took a ton of photos at Grandma's Marathon this year."

"Oh, yeah. Lots."

"Do you have many crowd shots?"

"Sure. Crowd shots and runners both. I staked out several spots along the route, and I got onto the roof above the Canal Park shops so that I could get pics as people hit the finish line."

"I'd like to see them," Cindy said. "Are they all digital?"

"Yeah, but you're talking about hundreds of photos. What are you looking for?"

She started to give Heather a brief explanation about the man in Jay Ferris's photographs, but the explanation got longer when she realized that Heather knew nothing about the murder or the trial. Heather didn't get the newspaper, and her awareness of current events didn't extend beyond an occasional report on the MPR classical-music station. Cindy gave her the background of the case and then explained about the man she'd followed in the mall who'd eluded police efforts to find him.

"One of Jonny's sergeants thinks he saw this guy in the marathon crowds," Cindy went on.

"And you thought maybe I snapped him?" Heather asked.

"Exactly."

"That's one needle in a pretty big haystack. Thousands of people cram the marathon route."

"I know."

Heather shrugged. She went to a rolltop desk in a corner of the living room and dug inside several cubbyhole drawers. Finally, she withdrew a USB flash drive, which she deposited in Cindy's hand.

"Here you go," she said. "That's a backup drive of all my marathon pics. Knock yourself out."

24

"You lied to get on to that jury, didn't you?" Carol Marlowe asked.

Howard's head snapped up at the dinner table. He put down a square of Sammy's pizza and stared at his wife. Their six-year-old, Annie, chewed a strand of spaghetti that dangled from her mouth and watched with wide eyes.

"What do you mean?" he said.

"Did you tell them you're obsessed with that doctor?" Carol asked.

"No, I didn't, because that's not true."

"Oh, really? You think so? I've got a good mind to call the judge. How many articles about Dr. Perfect would they find if they searched your computer?"

"That doesn't mean anything," he protested. "So I read some things about the case. Everybody in town did the same thing. I can still be objective."

"Sure, you can." His wife cut a square of pizza in half and stabbed it with a fork. "Annie, stop playing with your spaghetti."

Howard went back to his dinner in silence. Carol was jealous. She resented that he was in the midst of something big, that he had a starring role in a drama that was consuming the city. He didn't believe she'd follow through with her threat about calling the judge, but the thought of it made him nervous. If they looked, yes, they'd find articles about the case on his computer. And pictures of Janine Snow he'd gathered around the Web. He'd be kicked off the jury, which was the thing he feared most. This was the event of his life.

"So, what's your plan, Howard?" Carol continued, not letting the subject drop. "Do you have some fantasy of rescuing her? Will you be the one to convince the jury to let her off, and she'll be grateful to you forever?"

"That's crazy," Howard said. "I'm doing what the judge said. I'm keeping an open mind until I hear all the evidence. Now, would you drop it, please? I'm not allowed to talk about the case, so stop asking me about it."

"Open mind," his wife muttered. "You think she's innocent. You've said so from the beginning. Did you tell the judge that?"

"I never said anything like that!" he protested. "I've always said I don't know what happened. You're the one who convicted her from day one. You and your friends at the grocery store. What is it about her that drives you crazy, Carol? Is it that she's everything you're not?"

The words were out of his mouth before he could take them back, and the implication hung in the air, as toxic as poison. Janine Snow was rich, successful, and beautiful. Carol Marlowe was none of those things. His wife went from angry to hurt in the blink of an eye. She pushed back her chair, which toppled behind her, and stood up with the rigidity of a statue. He wanted to apologize, but he didn't. She stalked to their bedroom in silence and slammed the door, making the house shudder.

"Oh, hell," he muttered.

Annie leaned over and whispered, "That's a bad word, Daddy."

"Yes, I know."

"Is Mommy mad?"

"I guess so." He added, "Are you done with your dinner? You can go watch television."

Annie hopped out of the chair. He cleaned up the dishes, and then he sat in the living room by himself. The smart thing to do was go to their bedroom and apologize, but he knew it would just prompt more anger and more yelling. He didn't have the strength for another fight with Carol.

Howard left the house to clear his head. It was dusk in the neighborhood, but it was summer, and he heard the noise of kids squealing in the nearby yards. He sat in his Chrysler in the driveway with the windows rolled down. Humidity made his neck sticky. Bugs flew inside. He smelled the overgrown lilac bushes on the side of their house.

He thought: *Carol's wrong.* She didn't understand what was at stake. She didn't realize how hard he was trying to do the right thing. Block out everything he knew about the case. Ignore the attraction he felt to Janine Snow and the fascination he felt for who she was. Listen to nothing but the evidence.

They had heard more witnesses at the trial.

They'd heard from a ballistics expert who talked about the bullet recovered from Jay Ferris's brain and about the gun Jay wore in the photograph provided by his brother. Yes, the two were consistent. No, they couldn't be matched without the gun itself. Yes, it was one of the most common guns sold in the country.

They'd heard from the private detective. Melvin Wiley. Yes, Jay knew about the affair and had witnessed Janine's prescription-drug use on the videos. Yes, he'd sworn to get even with his wife.

They'd heard from an attorney named Tamara Fellowes. Yes, she worked for a law firm that was suing Janine Snow over the death of a patient. Yes, she knew Jay Ferris, and, yes, Jay had called her in December. No, she would not discuss the contents of the conversation, but she did testify about what she'd heard in the background of the call—a woman's voice screaming at Jay.

"Don't do this to me, you bastard! Don't you dare do this!"

Did she recognize the voice?

Yes, it was Dr. Janine Snow.

Howard backed onto the street and drove. He headed east out of his Piedmont Heights neighborhood and soon found himself on Skyline Parkway, with the green fairways of the golf course on his left and the steep pitch of the hillside on his right. The Enger Tower

loomed above him. He turned at Hank Jensen Drive and made his way
up to the parking lot at the base of the monument. Other cars were
parked there, people enjoying the summer evening. In a Ford Taurus,
two teenagers groped each other, kissing, their clothes askew. When
the girl saw Howard watching them, she extended her middle finger.
He looked away.

Everything made him think of the trial.

A teenage boy had driven here with his girlfriend on January 28,
just like the boy and girl in the Taurus. They passed a RAV4 on the
way to the tower but couldn't say exactly when or where.

Howard left the parking lot and kept driving. It was as if he were
on autopilot, not setting a course. He was back on Skyline Parkway,
and moments later, his LeBaron drifted to a stop at a spur road that
climbed sharply up the cliffside to his left. At the summit of the road
was the mansion belonging to Janine Snow. He knew he shouldn't be
there, but he turned the wheel and drove slowly to the top of the hill.

There was Janine's house. He recognized it from the television
reports and from the photographs at the trial. What an amazing place,
like a palace built on the roof of the world. Lights were on. She was
home, the defendant out on bail. There were no cars around. He wondered if she was alone. Just her, sitting amid the ruins of her perfect
life. And Howard only a few feet away.

Judge Edblad had told them: "*You are not investigators.*"

Even so, he couldn't restrain his imagination. He sat in the car with
the engine running, and he realized that this was the very place where
everything had happened. On January 28, inside that door, behind its
glass panes, Jay Ferris had been murdered. If Howard had been here
then, he would have heard the shot.

What would he have seen? A stranger running away?

Or Janine Snow pulling out of the garage in her husband's Hummer to hide a gun?

Howard realized that what he wanted more than anything was to
hear the story from Janine's own mouth. He wished he could talk
to her, look into her eyes, and listen to her answer every question. The
frustrating thing was that he knew he never would. She wouldn't take

the stand. Defendants hardly ever testified. She was the one person who really knew the truth, and he would never hear her say what it was.

Somehow, his car engine turned off, and his door opened.

He didn't think it was him getting out and walking toward the house. It was someone else. He felt his feet on the walkway, heading toward the front door. That was what a stranger would have done, coming to murder Jay Ferris. If there was a stranger.

Howard stood at the door. Janine's door. He felt dizzy. His finger quivered; he wanted to stab the doorbell. If he did, she would come. He'd see her appear behind the glass. She would open the door—

—and that would be the end of everything.

He would have crossed a line from which there was no going back. Wheels would be set in motion. Attorneys would talk, and he would be called in front of the judge, and he would be admonished and dismissed, and one of the two alternates sitting in the jury box would take his place.

Howard Marlowe would be just Howard Marlowe again. A footnote in the newspaper, soon forgotten.

Carol would laugh at him.

He felt as if he was awakening from a bad dream. He turned and ran back to his Chrysler, needing to escape before he was seen. Before the police spotted him. Or the media. No one could know he'd ever been here. He got into his LeBaron and shot down the steep street.

Janine watched him go.

She sat in her office, where the security camera at her front door fed video to her computer. She'd installed the camera months ago when she had a parade of unwanted visitors coming to her house after the headlines brought notoriety.

She recognized him, of course. Juror #5. He was the one who sat closest to her in court. She hadn't missed the fact that he liked to watch her. He tried to be discreet about it, but she caught his wandering glances in her direction. At first, she'd written it off as curiosity, but now she realized it was something more. She'd understood men all her life, much better than she ever understood women. This man was in love with her.

She knew she was attractive. Men had fallen for her since she was a high school girl in Texas growing up fast. This was different. Since the murder, men had sent her e-mails, proposals of marriage, and naked pictures. All types of men, married and unmarried, black and white, old and young, from across the country. For the stalkers, she'd become an object of fascination. And now, it seemed, one of those stalkers had made his way onto her jury.

He appeared to be an ordinary man. Physically, he was neither attractive nor repellent. If she'd met him on the street, she would have stared through him as if he didn't exist. Under ordinary circumstances, the only way a man like that would have come into her circle was as a patient, but circumstances were anything but ordinary right now.

She was tempted. All she would have had to do was go to the door. Call to him through the speaker. Invite him into her home. She could have taken his hand and fulfilled his fantasy with a night unlike any he'd ever experienced. Sex meant nothing to her, but she knew it would have meant everything to him. For the price of giving up her body, she would have asked only one thing.

Hang the jury.

He would have done it, too.

Instead, she'd let him go.

Janine knew she should call Archie to have Juror #5 swiftly and quietly removed from the case, but she didn't do that. He might yet be her salvation. She wondered if a man who was in love with her could really believe that she would shoot her husband in cold blood.

25

"Mr. Skinner," Dan asked at trial when Nathan was sworn, "did you engage in a sexual relationship with the defendant, Janine Snow?"

"Yes, I did."

"How did this affair begin?"

"Last spring I was doing part-time night security at the hospital where Janine practices. We got to know each other. One thing led to another."

Nathan Skinner cocked his head with a little smile, as if it were simply nature's way that two attractive people would fall into bed together. His magnetism would be felt by the women on the jury. Stride realized that Nathan was on his best behavior. Dan had probably counseled him to keep his ego and arrogance in check.

"How long were the two of you involved?"

"The relationship began in May. It ended in early December."

"Who ended it?" Dan asked.

"Janine. I think Jay found out and forced her to break it off."

Archie Gale stood up. "Objection—speculative."

"Sustained," Judge Edblad ruled.

"Mr. Skinner, were you acquainted with Jay Ferris?"

"We knew each other, but neither of us would say we were friends."

"Can you explain?"

Nathan sighed, as if the dispute were nothing but a rueful part of his past. "I used to be employed by the Duluth Police Department. Unfortunately, while I was on a vacation in the Wisconsin Dells, I got pulled over by the local cops while I was very, very drunk. It was stupid. Stupid to be driving while drunk—and stupid to say the things I did to the police. I used offensive racial language that I really regret. As I say, I was drunk."

"What happened next?"

"Mr. Ferris got a tip about my arrest, which was filmed by a dashboard cam on the police vehicle. He wrote a column about it—several columns, actually—calling for my dismissal from the Duluth Police. Ultimately, I lost my job."

"When was this?"

"This was back in February of last year."

"Do you blame Mr. Ferris for your being fired?" Dan asked.

"Back then? Sure. I was mad at him and mad at the world. I even took a swing at him in a club a couple weeks later. I felt like he was trying to make an example of me, but you know what? He was right. I deserved it. Like I said, I was stupid."

If Nathan was acting, Stride was impressed with his performance.

"Was your affair with the defendant an act of revenge against Jay Ferris?" Dan asked.

"I guess it started that way. After a while, though, we enjoyed each other's company. I think Janine needed someone to talk to."

"Objection—speculative," Gale interrupted.

"Sustained."

"During the course of your relationship, did the defendant offer her impression of her marriage to Jay Ferris?"

"Yes, she told me she wanted a divorce."

"Did she express any opinion to you about the likelihood of obtaining a divorce?"

"She said it would never happen."

"How, exactly, did she phrase it?"

"She said Jay wanted to own her like a slave. She said she didn't believe she would ever be able to get away from him while he was still alive."

Murmurs rippled through the courtroom, and Judge Edblad quieted the crowd. Dan waited.

"Mr. Skinner, did you ever have a conversation with the defendant about guns?" Dan asked.

"Yes, I told her that I knew Jay owned a gun."

"How did you know that?"

"When I had the altercation with Jay, he showed it to me."

"Did the defendant express surprise at the news that Jay owned a gun?"

"No."

"Did you say anything else to her about it?"

"Yes, I said she should be careful in case Jay found out about us."

Stride waited for the bomb to drop and for a new wave of whispers to wash through the courtroom. Gale, who knew exactly what was coming, waited for it, too. Stride thought he saw a ghost of a smile on Dan's lips.

"What did the defendant say?" Dan asked.

"She said maybe she should get a gun, too," Nathan said. "She asked me if I knew how she could get one off the books."

Archie Gale stood up, well aware that he had a disaster on his hands.

"Mr. Skinner, how much money do you make in your current job?" Gale asked.

"Objection—relevance," Dan interjected.

"Your honor, Mr. Skinner has testified that he lost his job with the Duluth Police Department because of the actions of Mr. Ferris. It's relevant to know the specific impact this had on his financial situation."

"The objection is overruled," Judge Edblad announced.

"I make minimum wage," Nathan said, and some of his casual confidence seeped into bitterness. He didn't like to be humiliated.

"Did you lose your house to foreclosure because of your loss of income?" Gale went on.

"Yes." It was more like a hiss.

"Do you have substantial credit card debt?"

"I don't know about substantial—"

"More than fifteen thousand dollars?"

"Yes."

"Is your current financial situation directly attributable to your dismissal from the Duluth Police Department?"

"Yeah, I guess."

"So, is it fair to say you *hated* Jay Ferris for what he did to you?"

"I suppose so, but that was a long time ago."

"The economic consequences are still very real to you today, though, aren't they?"

"Yes."

"You testified that you got to know Dr. Snow because you were doing part-time security work at her hospital—is that right?"

"Yes."

"Did you ask to be assigned to work at St. Anne's?"

"I—I don't remember."

"Shall I call your boss and subpoena your employment records so we can confirm it?" Gale asked.

"Okay. Yes, I heard about an opening there, and I asked to get it."

"Why?"

Nathan was silent.

"Mr. Skinner," Gale went on, "did you go after that position with the specific goal of seducing Dr. Snow into an affair?"

"It may have crossed my mind," Nathan admitted.

The body language from Janine Snow at the counsel table was eloquent. She oozed scorn. It was easy to see similar reactions on the faces of the women on the jury. For all his attractiveness, there was a dark side to Nathan Skinner.

"Mr. Skinner, were you interviewed by the police shortly after the murder of Jay Ferris?"

"Yes." His voice was clipped. Impatient. He wanted to be done and off the stand.

"Did you say anything to the police at that time about your affair with Dr. Snow?"

"No."

"Did you believe the police would consider you to be a suspect in the murder of Jay Ferris if they found out that you'd been having an affair with the victim's wife?"

"I figured I was a suspect anyway," Nathan said, and then he winced.

"Okay, and as a suspect, would it be in your interest to deflect police attention to someone else?"

"I didn't do that."

"When you were first interviewed, did you say anything to the police about Dr. Snow asking you how she could get a gun?"

"No."

"You only told this story after Dr. Snow informed the police of your relationship—is that right?"

"Yes, but it's true."

"Did anyone else overhear this conversation?" Gale asked.

"No, but Janine knows what she said."

"Mr. Skinner, is there anyone who can verify your whereabouts after 9:45 p.m. on the night of January 28?"

"No."

"Were you drinking that night?"

"I—yeah, I guess."

"How much did you drink?"

"I don't remember."

"Do you own a revolver, Mr. Skinner?"

"I gave my gun to the police. They tested it. It was clean."

"Is that the only handgun you own?"

"They tested all of them. Clean as a whistle."

"How many handguns do you own, Mr. Ferris?"

"Eight."

"Eight guns," Gale murmured. "Mr. Skinner, did you make a statement to Lieutenant Stride that if you had committed this murder, you would have simply dropped the murder weapon through the ice? That the police would never find it?"

"Yeah, I did, but it was a joke—"

"That's all, Mr. Skinner. Thank you."

26

"I found him," Cindy told Stride.

It was late, and he was surprised that she was still up. He'd spent most of the day at the trial and then caught up on the job in the basement of City Hall until nearly midnight. His wife sat at their small kitchen table with a laptop open in front of her. Only the light over the sink was on. She wore a nightgown, and her feet were bare. The house with its open windows was warm and humid, and he smelled old coffee. A stiff wind made the lake roar like a lion not far from their back door.

Stride sat down across from her. Like him, she was nearly forty, and yet in his eyes, she could have been seventeen. She was the same teenager he'd met in school. He could barely remember what his life was like before she came into it. School, college, career—all that time, it was him and her together.

"I found him," Cindy repeated, pushing a photograph toward him across the table.

"Who?"

"The guy at the mall."

Stride studied the photograph and saw a crowd shot taken downtown during Grandma's Marathon. His wife had circled a man with a black marker, and he held the page close and squinted at the face. She'd enlarged the photograph, but the image was crisp and clear. The man was overdressed for the warm June day in a camouflage jacket.

"Where did you get this?" he asked.

"I know a photographer who covered the marathon. I've spent the last six hours analyzing every one of her pictures."

She passed him the original photograph, before she'd zoomed in on the crowd. The picture had been taken from a second-floor window near the corner of Lake Avenue and Superior Street, facing northeast. Swarms of runners filled the street in the center of the frame; they were the jubilant, exhausted ones, within two miles of the finish line in Canal Park. Crowds twenty deep on the sidewalk cheered them on. Cindy had drawn an arrow to show the man in the original photo. He was little more than a stick figure standing by a lamppost in a brick-lined park well behind the flood of people.

The crowd watched the runners.

He watched the crowd.

Stride's eyes snapped back and forth between the two pictures. "You're certain this is him?"

His wife nodded. "I don't know if this is the guy in Jay's photos, but it's definitely the man I followed at the mall. No question about it. I haven't forgotten him, Jonny."

"I know."

He studied the man and understood the aura of repressed violence that Cindy had talked about. Maybe it was bravado; maybe it wasn't. He focused on the people around the man and spotted a heavyset redheaded woman seated on a bench no more than ten feet from the lamppost. She wore a lanyard and fluorescent vest that marked her as race security, but her face was turned away from the camera.

"Did you find him in other photos?" he asked.

"Two more," Cindy said. "I haven't printed them, but I can pull them up on the screen."

She used the laptop touch screen and pushed the computer across the table to Stride. He zoomed in on the photograph, and he could see the man in camouflage in his original spot. The redheaded woman had stood up and was brushing shoulders with him. They were talking, and they didn't look like strangers. Her face was clearly visible. He didn't recognize her, but the marathon team brought in plenty of private security on race day.

"What do you think?" Cindy asked. "Will these pictures help you find him?"

"I don't know about him, but we should definitely be able to find *her*." He stabbed a finger at the security guard in the photograph. "I'll put Maggie on it in the morning."

"Good," Cindy replied, sounding relieved.

He watched a small smile of triumph bloom on his wife's face. She got up from the table and stretched her arms over her head. Her white nightgown climbed up her thighs. He knew she'd had a long day, but he didn't remember when he'd seen her so tired. He reached for her hand and squeezed it.

"Are you okay?" he asked.

"Sure. Never better."

"This was smart of you," he said. "Nice work."

She didn't say anything, but he knew she appreciated the compliment.

"You coming to bed?" she asked him.

"Soon."

"I'll probably be asleep."

"That's okay." He added, "You know I took you seriously about this guy, right?"

"No, I wasn't sure of that, but it's nice to hear."

He kept holding her hand.

"The trial's winding down," he said. "Dan rested the prosecution's case today. Unless Janine testifies, they'll probably wrap up the case tomorrow."

"Do you think she'll testify?"

Stride shook his head. "No. Dan doesn't think Gale will give him a shot at cross-examining her."

"And then?"

"And then we wait for the jury."

Cindy frowned. Her eyes were on the man at the marathon. "I wish you could find this guy first."

27

Maggie ate a Sausage McMuffin in her Chevy Avalanche near the harbor on the Point. It was barely past dawn, but the July day promised to be hot and bright. As usual, she'd only slept for about four hours, and then she'd gone to the drive-through for breakfast. If there was one part of American culture to which Maggie was addicted, it was McDonald's. She couldn't get enough French fries and Quarter Pounders, and somehow, none of it ever padded her small frame.

Through her binoculars, Maggie spied Troy Grange in a Zodiac heading back to the harbor.

Everyone in Duluth law enforcement knew Troy. He was solid. Good values. Hard worker. People liked him. He could have been a cop, but he liked working on and near the water, so he'd signed on as a health and safety inspector with the company that handled security for the Duluth Seaway Port Authority. Sooner or later, Maggie figured, he'd be running the whole department.

Thanks to his reputation, Troy also had an annual part-time job coordinating safety issues during Grandma's Marathon. As a result, he knew everyone who worked security along the twenty-six-mile course.

She crumpled her paper wrappers into a ball and climbed down from her truck. Troy, docking the inflatable Zodiac, saw her and waved, and she waved back. He was a couple of years older than she was and only a few inches taller. He was a weight lifter in his spare time, with a beefy, muscular frame. His skull was shaved smooth, and he had a face that wouldn't win him a cover spread in *GQ*: an oversize, lumpy nose; a couple of broad chins; and florid cheekbones that pushed out from his face like a pair of red jawbreakers.

Troy wasn't anyone's idea of cute, but Maggie had a little bit of a thing for him. She liked nice guys. Stride. Troy. Apparently, she also liked married guys, because Troy and his wife, Trisha, had been married for five years and had recently had their first child, Emma. He was off-limits. Maggie didn't spend a lot of time on self-reflection, but sometimes she wondered if she was doomed to have crushes on men she couldn't have.

"Sergeant," Troy announced as he bounded onto dry land. "I don't usually get a welcoming committee."

"Hey, Troy."

Troy, like Maggie, was an early riser, and he toured the dock areas from the water several mornings a week. His philosophy of security was that the best way to stop trouble was to make sure it never happened. He also liked seeing things with his own eyes, which was why he didn't delegate basic tasks such as reviewing the port facilities.

"So, what's the McPoison this morning?" he asked with a grin. "Hotcakes? One of those new McGriddle things?"

Maggie shook her head. People in Duluth knew way too much about her daily routines. "Sausage McMuffin with Egg, thank you very much."

"I don't suppose you brought me one," Troy said.

"And ruin your organic body? I wouldn't dream of it."

Troy chuckled. "Well, it doesn't seem to hurt yours, Sergeant."

She'd told him for two years to call her Maggie, but Troy stayed formal around cops. For him, it was a respect thing, even though they were friends. Part of her also wondered whether it was his way of keeping extra distance between them. She liked to think that her sex appeal didn't go completely unnoticed.

"How are Trisha and Emma?" she asked.

"Neither one getting much sleep."

"Well, sleep is overrated."

"I told Trisha that," Troy said, "and then I had to duck when she threw a shoe at me."

Maggie laughed. She slid a copy of the photograph that Stride had given her from a back pocket, then passed it to Troy. "Listen, I'm hoping you can help us. This is a crowd pic from Grandma's. See the redhead in the security uniform? I was hoping you know who she is."

Troy glanced at it and handed the page back. "Sure. Jessie Klayman."

"What about the guy she's standing next to? The hard case in the camo jacket?"

He took another look at the photograph. "No, sorry. Him, I don't know."

"What's the story with Jessie?" Maggie asked.

"She's a temp. Moved to Duluth from Fargo about a year ago. She did mall security there. I've brought her in a few times on low-priority overflow work. Nothing sensitive. Between you and me, I don't see her as full-time material. She's not particularly reliable, and if I had to guess, there's an alcohol issue."

"She looks about forty," Maggie said.

"Yeah, that sounds right. I haven't spent a lot of time with her. She's nice enough, but I get tired of hearing about guns."

"Guns?"

"Oh, yeah, she's a bad-to-the-bone gun collector. Always going to shows around the country. She must have an armory at home by now."

Maggie frowned. "Including assault rifles?"

"Definitely. She brags about the hardware. No anti-government or militia crap. I wouldn't hire her if I got a whiff of that. I think she's just your run-of-the-mill gun nut."

"Where does she live?" Maggie asked.

"She's got a little place in Gary. I'm sure I have her address." Troy dug a notebook from his pocket and riffled through the pages. "Here you go," he said, rattling off the number and street.

Maggie wrote it down. "Thanks. And you're sure you don't know the guy with her?"

Troy looked at the photograph again, taking more time. "He's not familiar to me, but I know that Jessie's got a kid. If you ask me, there's some resemblance in the faces. The eyes and nose look similar. Maybe that's her son."

28

By noon, the case was theirs.

Closing statements were done, and for Howard, they were no more than a regurgitation of what he'd already heard. The judge read them instructions on the law and gave them verdict forms. One count of murder in the second degree—guilty or not guilty. There were no more witnesses, no more attorneys, no more exhibits, just the twelve of them together in the jury room. Twelve strangers.

Howard sat nervously at the conference table. The room was no more than a drab meeting space immediately behind the courtroom. Twelve chairs barely fit around the table. There was a leather sofa and a cabinet with a mini refrigerator, microwave, and coffeemaker. An old-fashioned clock ticked off the minutes above the microwave.

He realized they didn't want the jury getting too comfortable. Do your work, make a decision, and go home.

The black woman who'd sat next to him throughout the trial chose a seat next to him again. Every day, she wore a different pants suit; today it was cream-colored, with lace stitching on the collar. She spoke first. "Let's go around the table and introduce ourselves, okay?"

So they did. Some gave just their names. Some talked about what they did for a living. The woman in the pants suit said that her name was Eleanor and that she worked as a secretary in a small accountant's office and had three children. She had a calmness about her, friendly but direct. Her dark skin was mottled. Her hair was short and neat.

"We need to pick a foreman," a man at the other end of the table announced when they'd finished introductions. Howard tried to remember the man's name and thought that it was Bruce. He was the only juror in a tie, and he'd made a point of bragging that he managed a downtown hotel. He was in his sixties, with a gray mustache and a comb-over.

Eleanor said, "Well, who among us would be willing to be the foreman? Maybe we should start there."

Bruce raised his hand immediately. Eleanor stared at the man thoughtfully, and then she raised her hand, too. It was just the two of them. No one else volunteered. Eleanor suggested they each talk about how the foreman could help the group, and when they did, Bruce talked about his management experience, and Eleanor simply said she wanted to respect the process and deliver a fair result.

They passed notepaper around the conference table, and when they'd voted, Eleanor was named foreman by a vote of 10 to 2. Bruce didn't look happy with the outcome.

"We have four questions to answer," Eleanor reminded them as they began their deliberations. "I think we can decide three of them easily enough. Can we take a vote as to whether the state proved that Jay Ferris was dead?"

They did. All agreed.

"And let's also vote as to whether the death took place in St. Louis County in the state of Minnesota."

The same result.

"Finally—and if any of you disagree, we can postpone this question—can we vote that *whoever* shot Jay Ferris did so with the intent to murder him? My own opinion is that if you point a gun at someone's head and pull the trigger, your intent is pretty clear. But that's just me."

They voted, and they agreed that intent had been established.

"That's progress," Eleanor announced with a smile. "That leaves us with one question, and it's the big one. We have to decide whether the state proved beyond a reasonable doubt that Janine Snow caused the death of Jay Ferris. I think it's important that we review all the evidence carefully, regardless of what any of us is thinking at this particular moment. Right? But I also think it would be useful for each of us to share our preliminary opinion, recognizing that our opinion might change as we look at the facts. Okay?"

Howard felt his body tense. Sweat gathered on his neck. This was the moment he'd anticipated, but he had no idea what to say.

Reasonable doubt. The judge had told them: *Reasonable doubt is just what it sounds like. It's doubt based on reason and common sense. The state does not have to prove its case beyond all doubt. Some doubt always exists about most things in life.*

"Let's go around the room," Eleanor said.

Answer yes or no, she told them. Answer yes if you think the state proved its case. Yes if you're ready to declare Janine Snow guilty of murder.

The juror on the other side of Eleanor answered first. "Yes."

And another. "Yes."

One juror declined to answer. So did the next. And then:

"Yes."

"Yes."

Howard stared at their faces. They made it look so easy. They'd sat in the same courtroom as he had, and the case was already clear in their minds. They'd looked into Janine's face and seen a killer there.

"Yes."

"Yes."

Don't be influenced by emotion or passion, the judge had said. *The only thing you should look at are the facts of the case.*

"Yes."

"Yes."

The vote around the table reached Howard. There hadn't been a single person to vote no. Not a single person with doubt. Only two jurors had declined to vote openly, and the rest had made up their minds.

Guilty.

"I—I'm not sure," Howard said. "I guess I have to say no."

There was silence in the room. Howard felt their eyes on him, and his skin burned with embarrassment. Did they know? Did they know how he felt about Janine? *Don't be influenced by emotion or passion.*

"Fine," Eleanor said. "My own vote is yes. Howard, could you tell us about the doubts you have? That may help us think through the evidence."

Howard tried to organize his thoughts. Yes, he had doubt. Was it reasonable doubt? He didn't know. Part of him wanted to believe there was no way that Janine could have pulled the trigger. Part of him wanted to rescue her. Another part of him, the cold part, heard Carol's voice from months earlier. *She did it.*

"They didn't prove that Janine fired a gun," Howard pointed out. "Or that she even had a gun."

The hotel manager Bruce said acidly: "Janine?"

Howard flushed. "The defendant."

"I think we should call her Dr. Snow," Eleanor suggested. "She's the defendant, but she's also a human being, and we're deciding how she's going to spend the rest of her life. Let's not forget that."

"They couldn't prove *Dr. Snow* fired a gun, because she took a shower," Bruce retorted. "How convenient is that? She just happened to do the one thing that would erase evidence of her firing a gun."

Several jurors grumbled their agreement.

Another woman spoke up. "Plus, we saw a photograph of her firing a gun. For me, that's a big thing. You're either a gun person, or you're not. I wouldn't have a clue how to fire a gun. Dr. Snow knew."

"Nathan Skinner also testified that Dr. Snow asked him how to get a gun," Bruce pointed out. "On the QT."

"That's true, but do we believe Nathan Skinner?" Eleanor asked. "He's an important witness, but I'm not sure I find him credible."

"Maybe Skinner killed Ferris," Howard suggested. "Maybe he's trying to frame Dr. Snow."

Bruce shook his head. "That's crazy."

"Why?" Howard asked. "Skinner has no alibi for the time of the murder."

"We saw phone records," Bruce replied. "From early December to January 28, Skinner didn't call Snow. He didn't call Ferris. They didn't call him. There was no contact at all. So all of a sudden, seven weeks after she breaks off the affair, Skinner goes over there with a gun? I don't think so. Plus, we heard testimony from the pizza girl who said Ferris was in his apartment the night of the murder, sick as a dog, watching a hockey game. The game started at 9:00 p.m. What do you think? Before the third period, he suddenly got it in his head to drive to Ferris's place and shoot him? Sorry, I don't buy it."

Howard said nothing. The other jurors nodded their heads.

"All right, but what about Skinner's testimony that Dr. Snow asked him about getting a gun?" Eleanor said. "I just don't think I believe him about that. They were lovers. Frankly, if she wanted a gun, he would have gotten her one. And he didn't do that."

Bruce pursed his lips and shrugged. "Yeah. Yeah, I guess I'm with you on that."

"Let's focus on what we *do* know," Eleanor went on. "In her statement to the police, Dr. Snow admitted that she was home when the murder occurred. She admitted arguing with her husband, which was confirmed by testimony from Cindy Stride. Mrs. Stride also testified that Dr. Snow wanted to get a divorce, but she couldn't because she felt trapped."

"Feeling trapped doesn't mean she killed her husband," Howard insisted.

"She's a pill junkie!" Bruce barked. "Ferris was holding that over her head. You bet she was trapped. And she only had one way out. Bang!"

There was silence again. The twelve of them looked at one another, and Howard felt all of them looking at him. The man with doubt. The only man who wasn't ready to throw Janine into the fire.

29

Stride pulled up to the gravel driveway of Jessie Klayman's house in the town of Gary. It was on Dickson Street, near where the road dead-ended. The house was single-level, with a detached garage and wooden steps leading to the front door. The large yard was mostly scrub grass and weeds, and in back, the lot butted up to a line of trees. He saw two cars in the driveway, a green Dodge Neon and a rusted Pontiac Firebird.

He got out on one side of his Bronco, and Maggie got out on the other.

"Know where we are?" she asked, pointing down the street to 108th. "Turn left there and left again on Becks—"

"Ely's Peak," Stride said.

"Yeah."

He studied the small house. He'd walked up ordinary driveways to ordinary houses too many times to take it lightly. The outside never told him what was happening inside. "Stay alert," he said.

They headed for the front door, where he pressed the doorbell and heard the chime. Thirty seconds passed before a woman answered. She pushed the storm door open and smiled, but her eyes were wary. If this woman worked security, she knew how to recognize cops.

"Can I help you?" she asked. Her voice had the overexcited trill of a bird at dawn.

"Are you Jessie Klayman?" Stride asked. When the woman nodded, he said, "My name's Jonathan Stride, and this is Maggie Bei. We're with the Duluth Police." He showed her his badge, but she hardly looked at it.

"Yeah, I figured," the woman replied, smoothing her dyed-red hair with dyed-red fingernails. She was pudgy and short, and she wore a formfitting Twins T-shirt with jean shorts. "What's up?"

"We just have a couple of questions for you. May we come inside?"

"Yeah, I guess."

She waved them into her living room. A game show blared from the television. The room smelled of beer. So did Jessie's breath. Stride saw the kitchen adjacent to the living room, where dirty dishes mingled with empty Budweiser cans. There was no air-conditioning, and the shadowy interior was warm with stale air that hung in the room.

"You were on the security team during the marathon last month, weren't you?" Maggie asked her.

"Yeah."

"We're trying to identify the man who's standing next to you in this picture."

Jessie took the photograph from Maggie with two thick fingers. The glib smile on her face wavered. "Why are you looking for him?"

"Do you know him?" Stride asked.

"Has he done something?"

"Ms. Klayman, is this your son?" Maggie asked. "Troy Grange thought it was."

She sat down on the old sofa. An empty bag of Doritos was on the coffee table in front of her. "Okay, yeah, that's Ross. So what?"

"Is he here?" Stride asked.

"No."

Stride eyed the hallway that led to the bedrooms. "Does your son live with you?"

"Yes. What is this about?"

"We'd just like to talk to him. Do you know when he'll be back?"

"No, he went for a walk. Do you think Ross has done something wrong? Because he hasn't. He's a great kid."

Maggie withdrew another photograph from her pocket. This one was a blurry picture taken by Jay Ferris near Ely's Peak, showing a man in camouflage aiming an assault rifle. "What about this photograph?" she asked. "Is this Ross?"

Jessie studied it. "I don't know. I can't make out the face."

"Do you or Ross own a rifle like this?"

She shrugged. "We have guns. They're all legal."

"Including a Bushmaster rifle?" Maggie persisted.

"Yeah, so what? I told you, they're all legal."

"What about handguns?"

"Yeah, we have some. Sure. I don't have to remind you guys about the Second Amendment, do I? A person would have to be nuts not to carry a gun in this day and age. No offense to cops, but I don't have time to wait for a patrol car to mosey over here if someone breaks into my house."

"Would you mind if we take a look at Ross's room?" Maggie asked.

Jessie folded her arms across her ample chest. The chirrup in her voice rose higher. "Actually, I do mind. You come in here asking all these questions about my son, and you won't tell me what's going on."

Stride exchanged a glance with Maggie. "Well, thank you very much for your time, Ms. Klayman. We'd appreciate it if you or Ross could give us a call when he's back. We need to meet with him in person."

She shrugged. "Okay, but it's a waste of time. He hasn't done anything."

Stride and Maggie let themselves out of the small house and returned to his Bronco. He turned on the engine, and a song by Sara Evans began playing on the stereo. "Born to Fly." He put the truck in drive but kept his foot on the brake.

"You think it's the same guy?" Maggie asked him. "That Jay Ferris spotted Ross Klayman at Ely's Peak?"

"Probably, but I don't think we'll be able to prove it. We don't have enough for a warrant to test their guns."

"The jury's already out. Do we need to tell Dan about this?"

"Yeah, I'll tell him, for what it's worth," Stride said. "It's up to him whether he wants to disclose it to Gale. I don't think this changes anything at all with regard to the case."

Maggie glanced at the house, where Jessie Klayman stood at her front door, watching them. When the woman turned away, Maggie slid sunglasses over her face. "You don't have any doubts about the case, boss?"

"What, that Janine killed Jay?" Stride asked. "No, I don't."

"None at all?"

"No reasonable doubt," he said. "That's the only thing that matters."

An hour later, Jessie jumped as she felt a hand tickling the back of her neck. She spun around and saw Ross standing behind the sofa. His lips folded into a grin. He could always sneak up on her.

"You scared the crap out of me!" she exclaimed.

"Sorry."

He wore an army hat, with the brim pulled low, and wraparound shades. A black tank top left his shoulders and skinny arms bare, exposing his tattoo of a skeleton dressed for combat. His skin glowed with sweat from the heat of the day, and he smelled of pine. He wore camouflage pants and heavy trail boots.

Jessie went back to her game show. "The police were here for you," she told him.

Ross didn't say anything. She turned and saw her son staring down at her from behind his shades. The grin was gone. His mouth had no expression. She saw a twitch ripple through his bones.

"Did you hear me?" she said. "The police were asking about you."

"I heard you. What did they want?"

"I don't know. They didn't say."

"What did you tell them?" he asked.

She heard accusation in his voice, which annoyed her.

"What do you think I told them? Nothing. I said they should leave us alone."

Ross went to the living room window and pushed aside the curtain to watch the empty street outside. He did that a lot, as if he were waiting for someone who never showed up. She heard the muffled engine of a lawn mower in the neighborhood. Typical summer day.

"I'm sure it's no big deal," she went on. "Somebody probably saw you practicing with the Bushmaster and got freaked."

"They said that?" he asked, his back to her.

"They had a picture. You with a rifle. It was blurry, so I said it could have been anybody. It was you, though."

She got up from the sofa. The credits rolled on the game show. She wasn't sure why she watched; it was people earning money by knowing stupid things. She'd tried to get on a show herself once, but they never wrote back to her. It didn't matter. They had enough money to live.

Jessie came up behind her son, wrapped her arms around his waist, and laid her head against his back. "You're so tense," she said.

He said nothing.

"I'm going to take a shower," she told him. "A cool one. It's so hot."

Still he didn't answer, and she didn't let go.

"Love me?" she asked.

A long time passed, but finally he said, "Yes."

That was all she needed to hear.

30

The vote was 11 to 1.

They'd all declared themselves now, even the two jurors who had originally been undecided. Howard remained the holdout. They'd spent three hours in deliberation. He'd begun to see impatience in their faces, especially Bruce, who acted as if Howard was standing between him and a steak dinner and a bottle of wine. Eleanor, the foreman, remained calm as the others grumbled.

"Howard, you understand that reasonable doubt is a different thing from having no doubt, don't you?"

"Yes, I get that," Howard said.

"No one's asking you to change your opinion simply because we feel differently," she went on, "but I want to make sure we're all looking at the evidence the same way."

Howard pushed his water glass around in circles on the wooden table. He stared down, rather than looking up. "I just don't see it the way the rest of you do."

He got up and went to the lone window in the jury room that looked out on the city. He didn't want to sit with the rest of them. He felt isolated, and being on his own made him more stubborn. They couldn't tell him how to vote. They couldn't convince him that the beautiful woman whose face was always in his head had taken a gun and put a bullet through her husband's brain.

"Howard?" Eleanor said. "Let me ask you a couple of questions, okay?"

"Fine."

"Do you believe that Dr. Snow felt trapped in her marriage and didn't see a way out?"

"Lots of people are unhappy in their marriage!" Howard snapped. "They don't take a gun and shoot their spouse. It doesn't work like that."

Bruce opened his mouth, but Eleanor held up her hand sharply to silence him. "Howard, yes, of course, that's true, but Jay Ferris *is* dead. Someone did shoot him. And my question to you was—do you believe that Dr. Snow felt trapped? Did the state establish that to your satisfaction?"

He shrugged. "Well, sure. I'm not arguing about that."

"Okay. Do you also believe that Jay Ferris was dangling a threat over Dr. Snow's head regarding her addiction to pain pills?"

Howard remembered the newspaper column. Holly. The prescription drugs in the condo. He imagined the pressure Janine had been under. As a surgeon. As a wife. Nowhere to turn, no way to escape, except for the drugs. He'd been on morphine once, when he'd had his appendix removed as a teenager. He knew its allure, the way it could make your whole body float on a cloud.

"Yes. I think he was."

"So let's think about this," Eleanor said quietly. "Dr. Snow wanted out of her marriage, but her husband knew a secret that would have destroyed her life and career. Regardless of whether you're convinced she did kill him, do you believe that she would have seen Jay's death as a way out of her problem?"

How lonely it must have been, Howard thought. To have everything and nothing at the same time. With Jay alive, she was in a cage. With Jay gone, she would be free.

"Yes, she probably did," Howard said.

"Fine. Good. If we're all on the same page about that, then let's think about the night that Jay Ferris was killed. We know that Dr. Snow was in the house. We know that she and her husband argued. A few minutes later, he was dead. The state wants us to go one step further and believe that Dr. Snow killed him."

"I'm just not convinced that she did—"

Eleanor stopped him with a smile. "Hang on, Howard. Let's think about what we have to believe to conclude that there isn't sufficient proof that Dr. Snow killed him. Okay? We have to believe that someone else chose that same foggy, slippery night to go to her house. If it was someone bent on robbery, as Dr. Snow contends, then we have to believe that they saw the lights on and a car in the garage and still decided to proceed with their plan. We have to believe that they either knocked or rang the doorbell—because there was no forced entry— and that Jay Ferris let them inside. This person then shot Ferris in the head, went downstairs without tracking any outside dirt or debris into the house, found jewelry in the bedroom, removed it, went back upstairs, and left. We have to believe that this all happened during the exact period of time when Dr. Snow was in the shower. We also have to believe that whoever did this either chose not to dispose of the jewelry despite committing murder to get it or somehow sold these distinctive, expensive pieces of jewelry without any of the sales coming to light. Okay? Howard, have I said anything that you disagree with?"

He shrugged. It sounded ridiculous when she put it like that, but she was right. "No, that's true."

"Well, my question is this: Do you believe that is a *reasonable* theory of what happened? Anything is possible, but is that a credible alternative in the absence of evidence? Because we see this case differently. We see a successful woman with a terrible secret. She's home alone with her husband. They argue, and she shoots him. Then she showers and washes her clothes to destroy evidence, and she takes the gun and some jewelry and hides them to make it look like a robbery. That's what we think the evidence shows, Howard. Eleven of us believe there is no reasonable doubt that that is what actually happened."

Howard returned to the jury table and sat down. He took the glass of water and drained it empty.

"What about the RAV4?" he asked.

"The witness who saw the car is unreliable about the time and location," Eleanor said. "It makes it hard to take the story at face value. And, really, a car parked on a nearby street? Is that enough to create doubt?"

"There was a man with a gun," Howard added. "Ferris took pictures of him in the park."

Eleanor nodded. "He did, but it's clear that Ferris never even knew who this man was. Why would this person suddenly get it in his head to kill Jay Ferris? And, really, Howard, isn't it stretching coincidence to think that it happened during the exact time Dr. Snow was in the shower?"

Howard wanted to give her an answer. He wanted to keep defending Janine. Carol was right: He dreamed of rescuing her. He'd stared at her face on his computer for months, until he could remember every feature of her eyes, her hair, and her skin. She excited him, interested him, and aroused him in a way no other woman ever had. And now she needed him. She needed him to remain strong in the face of eleven people who were ready to condemn her. She needed him to have faith that the evidence was not what it appeared to be.

Doubt.

But was it really doubt?

He looked at the facts the others saw and knew the truth. Yes, Janine did it. He was grasping for reasons to believe otherwise, but she did it. Even so, could he really be the one to convict her? She deserved better than Jay Ferris. She was a hero. A lifesaver. A beautiful woman. If she saw no other way to escape that despicable man, could he really call it a crime?

They would poll the jury. They always did. They would ask each of them to verify their verdict to the court. He would have to say it out loud. He would have to say it in front of her, so that she'd know he'd betrayed her.

Could he do that?

Eleanor was watching him. So were the others. It was as if she could see tectonic plates shifting inside his mind.

"Let's take another vote," Eleanor said quietly. "Guilty or not guilty."

And so it began. He listened to each voice, man and woman, old and young. Guilty. Guilty. Guilty. They went around the room, and each one announced their decision, free of doubt, free of hesitation. They weren't burdened by what they were doing to her. They weren't shamed by the thought of a good woman brought to this moment by a bad man.

Guilty.

Guilty.

On and on.

As it had each time, it came down to him. He sat in silence while they waited for him. He tried to open his mouth, but despite the water, he was dry. His voice caught in his throat. He thought the world was spinning out of control; he wanted to throw up.

"Howard?" Eleanor asked him.

He needed to speak. Guilty or not guilty.

He saw Janine's face. Her blue eyes. The curve of her lips. There was one person between her and her fate. Himself. Him and his strength. If he surrendered, there was no one.

Eleanor met his eyes.

"Howard?"

31

Miller Hill Mall was a blur.

It was a summer afternoon. Sun burned through the skylights, making orange reflections on the cool squares of tile. Cindy heard Rick Springfield singing through the overhead speakers, but the din of people drowned out most of the music. The food court was thick with teenagers. Girls giggled and screamed. Boys with newly changed voices shouted. They ran and pushed around her table.

So many people. Duluth was a small city, but it had always felt busy to her. Normally she thrived on dense crowds, but recently she'd found herself enjoying remote, empty spaces. Alaska was like that. She and Jonny had flown over glaciers and forests where there was nothing human at all, only thousands of miles without civilization, untouched and unspoiled. It was a place, like the Canadian wilderness to the north of them, owned by the animals and the earth, not the people. The loneliness and sheer size of it made her feel small, but sometimes small was a good thing. She didn't mind being small.

She smelled caramel corn mixing with the garlic of tomato sauce and the sweetness of baking bread. The air-conditioning couldn't keep up with the heat of the day, and she felt warm in her long-sleeve red blouse and jeans. Her black hair felt like a coat on her shoulders, so she pushed it back.

Her plate of Chinese food wouldn't go down. She picked at it, but she had no appetite. Instead, she drank Aquafina from a plastic bottle.

She kept thinking about Janine. She didn't begrudge her friend her weaknesses as a human being. Some people dealt with pressure by taking pills. Some people drank. Some people didn't deal with it at all. In the end, it was the same. The shame of it was knowing that Janine had a gift, and her gift was wasted now. She remembered meeting a young mother and her son in Janine's office, a little boy with a zipper scar on his chest and his whole life in front of him because of what Janine had done for him. His was one story among hundreds of patients who owed their lives to her.

And yet what did it do to someone to know that people lived or died because of you? Cindy knew what it had done to Janine. It had made her an addict. Maybe it had made her a killer, too. She'd been so jealous of Janine's coolness that she didn't realize how many cracks riddled the ice queen.

She found herself watching the young people in the mall. They always made her smile. Every generation had to make the same mistakes, had to get it wrong before getting it right. They blundered on, innocent, happy, foolish. She saw a boy and girl at a table near her. Both of them looked to be about sixteen. Definitely dating. They shared a Blizzard from Dairy Queen with two spoons, and they leaned across and kissed.

That had been her and Jonny ages ago. Two teenagers in love. Cindy tried not to be too obvious about watching them, but something about their cute preoccupation with each other made it hard to look away. Mooning eyes. Whispers. Touches.

The boy checked his watch, then made a noise like, "Oh, no!" He had to go. He slung his backpack onto his arm, kissed the girl again, kissed her several times more, and then jogged to the exit with a wave. He disappeared into the parking lot. The girl was on her own, missing him already. Maybe it would last, and maybe it wouldn't. It would be a summer romance, or, like her and Jonny, it would be a lifetime thing.

Cindy wondered what the girl's name was, and almost on cue, another teenager shouted and waved. "Hey, Laura!"

Laura. Her own sister's name. There were always little twists of fate like that.

Laura, the girl in the mall, had golden brown hair with bangs. The shape of her eyes made Cindy think that the girl was part-Asian. She wore a white T-shirt, which slid off one scrawny shoulder. Her lipstick was pale and pink. She twisted a cheap ring around one finger, and Cindy figured that the boy had given it to her. Laura pulled a book from her purse and began reading. One of the Harry Potter series. That was the craze. Laura popped gum in her mouth as she read, chewed, blew a bubble, popped it. When she saw Cindy watching her, she gave her a big bright smile, and Cindy smiled back.

You saw people, and then you never saw them again. Have a nice life, Laura.

Watching the young girl, Cindy finally decided she'd been putting something off for too long. She grabbed her phone and dialed and held a hand over her free ear. Steve Garske was her doctor, and she expected to get his nurse, but she got the man himself. Steve and Jonny were old friends. Tall, gangly, sweet, heck of a guitar player. His clinic was small, and if no one was around, he answered his own phone.

"Appointment time, Steve," Cindy said.

"You want me to figure out my own calendar system?" Steve asked in dismay. "Okay, hang on. How about next week? Thursday?"

"Perfect." She wrote down the date and time and felt better.

Then Steve asked, "Everything okay?"

If everything was okay, you answered right away, and when she didn't, his voice slid down an octave. "Cin?"

"I—I don't know."

"Tell me about it."

"Well, there's pain sometimes." She lowered her voice and cupped a hand in front of her mouth. "Sharp pain between my legs. I've been nauseated, too. Throwing up."

"When did this start?"

"Winter."

She expected the lecture. You're only calling me now? You let this go on and did nothing? He didn't need to chastise her, because she'd said all those things to herself. "Well, I'll see you in a few days," he told her. "We'll check it out."

"Thanks. Nothing to Jonny about this, right?"

"Of course."

She hung up. Tears welled in her eyes. She stared at the young girl in the mall, Laura. The girl with her sister's name. She tried to make herself smile again, watching this sweet teenager who was in love and learning about sex and reading about boy wizards. What a great life.

"Verdict," someone said.

Cindy looked up. There was a buzz around her. People were talking. They were crowding toward an electronics store with televisions in the window.

She heard it again.

"There's a verdict."

Stride and Maggie walked shoulder to shoulder through the narrow underground tunnel that led from City Hall to the County Courthouse building. The concrete-block walls were painted bright white, and so was the ceiling, which was lit with fluorescent tubes. Utility cables ran in a twisted knot beside them.

Maggie's short legs worked double-time to keep up with Stride. "That was quick," she said. "I didn't expect a decision so soon."

"It was an easy case," he replied. "Archie blew smoke, but that wasn't enough. The jury saw through it."

"So you think it's guilty?"

"I do."

They emerged through the door into the courthouse basement. They took the steps to the lobby, where reporters crowded into the corridor. It looked like election night. Stride hung back, not wanting to give interviews. He saw Dan Erickson deflecting questions, too, as he squeezed through the sea of people. Politicians knew not to brag until it was a done deal.

Archie Gale kept reporters away from Janine. His face was sober. He knew he'd lost. Janine didn't look at the floor the way so many defendants did, about to learn their fate. She looked straight ahead into the cameras that flashed in her face, and when she spotted Stride near the head of the steps, her head tilted in an almost imperceptible salute. She was under no illusions.

"She's a cool one," Maggie murmured.

"Yes, she is."

He'd been in this situation many times before. Most of the time, justice won out. Even so, he took no pleasure in it. Every murder had many victims. He had sympathy for Janine Snow and the pressure cooker of her life and the systematic way that her husband had made it worse. She'd snapped. Even smart, beautiful people snapped.

"Come on," he said. "Let's get up to the courtroom."

"Hang on," Maggie replied.

Her phone was ringing.

She answered and tried to listen above the din. He watched her face and grew concerned. She grabbed his arm, tugging him back to the stairs. When they were out of view of the reporters in the lobby, she waved him urgently downward, and they both jogged to the basement. At the tunnel door, she shoved her phone into her pocket.

"Gunfire," she said. "We need to get out there."

"Where?"

"Dickson Street, boss. In Gary. Neighbors report multiple shots."

"Is it—?"

She nodded as she ripped open the door, and they both sprinted into the tunnel. "It's Jessie Klayman's house."

32

The Pontiac Firebird that had been parked in the driveway was gone. Otherwise, the house looked as it had two hours earlier when they'd interviewed Jessie Klayman. Two police cars had Dickson Street closed at 108th, and two more were parked at the dead end. An ambulance waited behind the barricade. The handful of neighbors on the street had been warned to stay inside and away from windows.

Stride called the phone inside the house. No one answered.

"We think Ross is gone," Maggie said. "Guppo talked to two teenagers who live across the street. They said he usually drives the Firebird."

"Did they see him go?"

"No, but he may have headed out the back. There's a dirt road behind the house that leads through the trees to Gary Street."

"Get his photo out around the city. The car and license, too."

"In process," Maggie said.

They wore their vests. Through binoculars, Stride examined the small house and saw no movement at the windows. All the curtains were closed. So was the door to the detached garage. Overhead, the sun was bright in their eyes.

"We've got two officers staking out the back of the lot," Maggie said. "There's no activity."

"Okay, let's check it out."

They used a neighbor's lawn to approach the house from the east. There were no windows on the east wall other than at the basement level, where there was a door and a lookout window. The detached garage was on their left. As they cleared the neighbor's house, Stride saw one of his officers in position at the rear of the Klayman lot near the tree line. The cop gave a thumbs-up; the rear of the house was secure.

Stride had his gun in his hand. So did Maggie. Guppo and three other cops followed twenty yards behind them.

They reached the Klayman driveway. The house was built against a slope, and a two-level retaining wall and garden led to the front yard. Jessie Klayman kept stone nymphs among the weeds. Stride climbed the first level of the retaining wall at the corner of the brick basement. The windows of the living room were above their heads, and another window at ground level looked into the basement.

No activity.

He pulled himself up to the front lawn. Crossing under the living room windows, he took the wooden steps to the door and pounded sharply with his fist. "Jessie! Ross! Police!"

There was no answer. Looking through the storm door, he saw that the front door was wide open. The room where they'd sat with Jessie was empty, but the television was still on. He shouted again and heard nothing but the laughter of a TV sitcom. The living room showed no sign of disturbance.

Stride opened the screen door and went inside. Maggie followed.

"Jessie!" he called again. "It's Lieutenant Stride."

They cleared the kitchen and the living room, which were both deserted. He used the remote control to switch off the television, restoring silence to the house, except for the rattle of the rotating floor fan. It was dim inside with the curtains closed. He pointed at the hallway, where he could see entrances to two bedrooms.

The first door was painted black, but it was open, and an overhead light was on. He nudged around the threshold into the bedroom, and the interior took his breath away. Maggie entered behind him.

"Oh, shit," she said.

There was no bed, just a mattress on the floor. The walls, like the door, were painted black. The windows had been covered over with black plastic garbage bags duct-taped to the frames. A television sat on an old microwave stand in front of the mattress, and dozens of video games were strewn across the carpet. Gold ammunition littered the floor like popcorn. At least thirty bullet-ridden paper targets were thumbtacked to the wall, along with bizarre posters: a skeleton wearing a Nazi uniform; a naked girl with the head of a jackal and gun barrels for nipples; a skinless zombie in a diaper with blood spurting out of his face; and a Las Vegas casino street littered with torsos and severed limbs.

Across the entire wall, Ross had spray-painted in five-foot red letters: I AM GOD.

"Jesus, who is this kid?" Stride murmured.

But they knew who he was. They'd seen him before, in other cities, in schools, in workplaces.

Stride had made mistakes in his life. He'd arrested people who turned out to be innocent. He'd left cases unsolved. He'd failed to protect people he'd sworn to protect. This was different. This time, he'd missed a threat that Maggie had seen too clearly. That his wife had seen. He knew there was no bright line between social misfit and mass murderer, but he hadn't seen this one coming.

Ross Klayman was out there somewhere. He was going to kill.

"Where are the guns?" Maggie asked. "Troy said Jessie had guns."

They investigated the next bedroom, which was Jessie's room. The gun locker was there, open and empty. No rifles. No handguns. No ammunition. Ross had taken everything when he left the house. If Troy was right, then Ross had an arsenal with him.

Stride saw Guppo in the doorway behind him.

"Alert everybody, Max. Canal Park. Downtown. The mall. The DECC. He's going to show up somewhere."

Guppo turned away, already pulling out his walkie-talkie.

"Boss," Maggie called. Her voice told him the story.

She was in Jessie's bathroom. Stride joined her there, knowing what he was going to find. The bathroom was still humid and damp from the shower. The plastic curtain had been shunted aside. Jessie Klayman was sprawled on her back in the tub. She was naked, and her eyes were open, staring at the ceiling. Wet strands of red hair lay like veins across her face. The blood all over her body, on the walls, on the floor, on the ceiling, on the porcelain tub, matched her hair.

Ross had shot his mother at least thirty times.

Guilty.

Cindy stood in a crowd around the window of an electronics store, watching the live news report on local television. The crawl at the bottom of the screen announced the jury verdict. Janine Snow had been found guilty of second-degree intentional murder in the death of her husband, Jay Ferris.

She'd expected it, but she wasn't prepared for the finality of the result. It was hard to draw a line in her mind from that bitter January night to this hot summer afternoon. She'd driven Janine home. Her friend. She'd watched her go inside with her husband. Minutes later, Jay was dead, and now, months later, her friend had been convicted of his murder. Cindy had been there when it all began.

The reporters speculated about the sentence. The statute called for punishment in cases of intentional second-degree murder of not more than forty years. The sentencing guidelines suggested twenty-five years for a defendant with no criminal history. Archie Gale was on television, vowing an appeal and proposing a sharp downward adjustment in the jail time. Regardless, everyone expected the judge to sentence Dr. Janine Snow to at least twenty years at the women's correctional facility in Shakopee, Minnesota.

Twenty years.

From the beginning, Jonny had said she was guilty. So had Maggie. So had everyone in the city, who'd convicted her in the court of public opinion from day one. And now a jury of twelve Minnesotans had agreed.

Cindy listened to the mutterings of the people around here. The sentiments all sounded the same—that it had ended the way it had to end. She wondered if it was schadenfreude, that joy in watching the downfall of someone who had climbed high. The television showed a picture of Janine in a white surgical coat, blond hair perfect, body perfect. A miracle worker. A millionaire. A murderer.

Dan Erickson appeared on the screen, lecturing about justice applying to everyone, taking no pleasure in the tragedy.

Jay's brother, Clyde, came next, expressing satisfaction with the verdict but reminding everyone that a conviction wouldn't bring his brother back to life. Which was true. Still, if Janine had done this thing, no matter her motive, no matter the circumstances, then she had to pay the price.

The reporters talked about the jury and their willingness to convict without the discovery of the murder weapon. They interviewed the foreman, a woman named Eleanor, who praised the eleven people who'd served with her and the careful job they'd done. She expressed sorrow for victim and killer alike, but she said the verdict was the only reasonable conclusion that anyone could draw from the facts as they were presented to them.

Cindy tried to imagine herself on that jury. Would she have voted to convict? And to her surprise, she realized: Yes.

She heard her phone ringing and slid it out of her purse. Jonny was calling. She assumed he'd been in the courtroom when the verdict was read, and now he wanted to mend fences with her. They'd argued about it for months. It wasn't in her nature to accept that she was wrong and Jonny was right. He was a stubborn man, but he had a stubborn wife, too.

"Okay, I'm sorry," she said as she answered the phone. "You win."

Jonny simply said: "Where are you?"

"What?"

"Cindy, where are you?"

"I'm at Miller Hill Mall. I'm watching the news about—"

"Get out of there," he interrupted.

"Why?"

"Cindy, get out of there right now. I don't want you in any public place."

"What is going on—" she began, but then she stopped.

Her words hung in the air. So did the noise of the mall. The music overhead. The laughter. The television in the store window. She found herself staring at a pretty woman in her thirties who'd been shopping at Aéropostale. She clutched a big bag in her hand. She smiled, joking to a friend, mouth open as if she were singing a karaoke song. That was who she was at that moment, but a moment later, the bag fell from her hand. The light vanished from her eyes. She threw her arms in the air and staggered forward, and dots of red spattered over her body the way thrown rocks make splashes in a lake.

The noise caught up to Cindy's ears. Staccato explosions of gunfire rocked back and forth between the walls. Dust blew, tile shattered, and smoke clouded the air. Her fingers loosened; her phone fell.

The pretty woman near her slumped to the ground. So did another woman. Then an older man.

As they dropped, as the people scattered around her, she saw him coming.

Everyone screamed. Everyone ran.

33

Howard sat with Carol in his car across the street from the courthouse. A crowd lingered on the steps. Some of the jurors had stayed behind to answer media questions, but he didn't want to be interviewed. If he started talking, he'd say the wrong thing. An hour had passed, and already he regretted what he'd done.

He'd said it the first time in the jury room: "Guilty."

And then again in the courtroom: "Guilty."

Janine had watched him as the judge polled the jurors. Her eyes burned him. It was as if she *knew*. He expected her to reach out a hand, to touch him with her cool fingers, to whisper, "Don't betray me."

But he had. He'd squeezed his eyes shut, said the word, and cast her away like all the others. He was weak. When he looked again, she hadn't looked away. He thought he saw the tiniest of sad smiles on her face. Forgiveness.

"You did the right thing, Howard."

It was Carol talking.

He stared at his wife in the driver's seat of his LeBaron. She'd picked him up in white sweatpants and a Dells T-shirt. She looked at him like a hero, and he realized she was proud of him. He'd just sent a woman to prison, and she thought it was the greatest thing he'd ever done.

"I know it was hard," Carol went on. "If you want the truth, I wasn't sure you could do it. You're a softy at heart, Howard. I mean, that's a good thing most of the time, but it takes guts to convict somebody of murder, even when you know darn well she's guilty."

"Let's just go home," he murmured.

She nodded at the reporters near the courthouse flagpole. "Don't you want to go answer some questions? I know this was a big thing for you. You've earned a little fame for being part of it. I can wait here."

"No, I don't want to talk to anybody."

Carol started the engine. Then she turned it off and took his hand. "Hey, listen, I'm sorry. I know I've been a bitch lately. You were in a tough spot, and I wasn't being supportive."

He shrugged. "I don't care about that."

"Well, let me make it up to you. We've got the Dells coming up in a couple of weeks. That'll be fun. We can get Annie a pizza and rent her a movie one night, and you and me can fool around, huh? It's been way too long."

He summoned a smile. "Sure."

"Anyway, I'm glad this is over," Carol said. "No more Dr. Perfect. We can go back to living our lives. Just you, me, and Annie. It's about time, right? I'm ready for things to be exactly the way they were."

Howard didn't answer, because that was his worst fear. He didn't want to go back to his old life. He didn't want to be normal again. He hated the idea of things being exactly the way they were.

"Wow," Carol said.

"What?"

She lowered the window. "Don't you hear it? Listen to all those sirens. Something big's going on."

From her hiding place inside a leather-goods store, Cindy could see bodies in the corridor of the mall, dead where they'd fallen. The tiled floor and columns bore wild streaks of blood. Smears. Handprints. She smelled the discharge that comes with death, mixing like spoiled roses with the sugary aroma of the food court and the leather jackets dangling in front of her. Just as incongruously, the overhead music continued to play happy pop songs. Britney Spears. "Oops! . . . I

Did It Again." The crowd noise that typically drowned out the music had been muted into a muffled chorus of people crying and praying.

Shopping bags spilled their contents onto the floor where they'd been dropped. Swimsuits. Strappy heels. Bottles of lotion. Stuffed animals. She saw cell phones, too, abandoned in the melee. One by one, they began to ring, forlornly, before going to voice mail. Word had spread instantaneously around the city.

Those who could reach exterior exits had escaped, but there were dozens more, like her, trapped in stores. At least ten people huddled near her, hiding behind clothes racks, their arms wrapped tightly around their knees, their faces buried in the crook of their legs. It was as if, by not looking up, they could make themselves invisible. As if the shark eyes of the gunman would pass over them. Or maybe they just couldn't bear to see the end when it came.

She didn't think five minutes had passed, but their imprisonment felt like hours.

He hunted them methodically from store to store. She couldn't see him, but he wasn't far away. He fired and moved, fired and moved, fired and moved, like a soldier occupying a beachhead. Seconds of silence stretched out between assaults, giving her faint hope, but then a new hailstorm rained down not fifty feet away—gunfire, store windows shattering, victims screaming, individual bullets that could only be kill shots directed at those who had nowhere to run. And then his boots making new footfalls. Tap, knock, tap, knock.

He worked his way toward them. They didn't have much time. Each assault was a little closer, a little louder.

Cindy saw a fifty-something woman pressed against the wall of the leather store, like a prisoner lined up for a firing squad. The woman's sanity had flecked away, scattering into confetti. Her jaw was slack. Cindy tried to catch the woman's eye and give her a smile of encouragement, but there was nothing but faraway panic in the woman's face. She was a rabbit facing the open jaws of a fox.

And then she began to talk to herself. The noise was jarring.

"Nicky, come in from the rain," the woman murmured. "Are you cold, Nicky? Come in from the rain."

What she said made no sense. Her words came out as a whisper, but then she spoke more, and each time, her volume got louder. "Hide in the barn, Nicky . . . don't be afraid of the spiders . . . hide in the barn."

She sounded like a child.

"I smell apples. Isn't that funny? Apples!"

Cindy gestured urgently with her hands to make the woman stop. Others in the store hissed for silence. The woman didn't hear them; she simply stood at the wall, shaking uncontrollably, retreating into some long-ago memory.

"Climb up here with me, Nicky. Be careful! Don't fall!"

Another voice murmured from a hiding place, "Oh, my God, oh, my God."

And then another whisper, in rage and fear: "Shut up, you stupid bitch, shut up, shut up, shut up, shut up."

But the woman was nearly shouting now. Turning them into targets.

"Crows. I hear crows, Nicky. LISTEN TO ALL THE CROWS."

Cindy felt around in her pockets, but she knew she'd dropped her phone. Even so, she had to do something; she couldn't wait. She spotted a lost phone just outside the doorway of the store, maybe three feet into the mall corridor. She leaned beyond the rack of coats where she was hiding, far enough to see through the store window. The gunman, wherever he was, wasn't in view. She broke cover, crawling for the doorway, and stopped in its shelter.

"NICKY, COME IN FROM THE RAIN."

The phone was just out of Cindy's reach. She listened for the warning alarm of the killer's boots but heard nothing to give away his location. Maybe he'd fled. Maybe he'd gone down another corridor of the mall, hunting for new victims.

Or maybe he was waiting for her just outside the store.

Cindy took a breath and dove. She scooped up the phone and rolled back into the protection of the doorway. It took no more than two seconds. Her body tensed, waiting for gunfire, waiting for the window to shatter into popcorn above her. Nothing happened, but the silence almost felt more ominous than the noise of bullets. Her chest hammered as if she'd just done her morning run.

She punched the numbers for Jonny's cell phone. It rang, but he didn't answer, and she realized he wouldn't recognize the caller ID on the phone. When the call went to voice mail, she left a hushed, one-sentence message—"It's me, answer the next call"—and then she tried again, hoping he'd pick up.

Finally, on the fourth try, he did. His words tumbled out in a rush.

"This is Jonathan Stride, who is this?"

"It's me," Cindy whispered, keeping the phone close to her mouth and her eyes on the store window. The mall filled her senses. She could hear water gurgling somewhere—a fountain. Britney was done singing; now it was Bono and U2. "With or Without You." She felt cold tile under her knees, and her arms were sticky with someone else's blood she'd dragged into the store. She smelled leather and death.

"*Cindy!* Where are you? What's going on?"

"I'm hiding at Wilson's. You need to get in here right now. He's killing everybody he comes across."

"Can you see him? Do you know where he is?"

"No, but he's close. He was firing inside one of the stores near us just a couple of minutes ago. People are dying, Jonny."

"HIDE IN THE BARN, NICKY."

"What the hell is that?" he asked.

"There's a woman freaking out in here. You need to hurry."

"Get into the back of the store and hide. We're moving on all the entrances right now. We'll be there in less than sixty seconds."

"NICKY, LISTEN TO THE CROWS."

Cindy waited desperately for the clatter of doors and guns as the police stormed the mall, but, instead, like the rattle of bones in a cemetery, she heard the solitary march of boots again. His boots, clapping the floor. Tap, knock, tap, knock. He was heading for the leather-goods store.

He was almost here.

"We don't have sixty seconds, Jonny," she said calmly.

"Hide! We're coming!"

She shut off the phone. There was no panic now for her and no terror. If he loomed over her, if he fired, she would be dead in seconds; she knew that. It didn't matter. Calmness ruled. Calmness became her.

Sixty seconds became fifty. She glanced at the store, draped in jackets and purses, and saw the frozen shapes of the others sheltered there. At the back, behind the sales counter, she could buy time for herself. A few seconds, but that was all she needed.

Jonny was coming.

Fifty seconds became forty.

She willed herself to move and save herself, but then everything changed for her. On the opposite side of the mall, she saw the doorway of a Victoria's Secret store. Models of crazy perfection wore almost nothing in the window posters, but the spatter on the glass made them look as if they were covered in blood. In the doorway of the store, standing up, terrified, was a teenage girl.

It was the girl who had innocently sat in the food court, making out with her boyfriend. The sweet half-Asian girl reading about Harry Potter. The girl with her sister's name. The girl with an entire amazing life ahead of her.

Laura.

That girl—Laura—stood paralyzed no more than twenty feet away. She stared at Cindy, and Cindy stared back at her. Laura wore a skirt that left her long legs bare, and her knees practically knocked against each other. She wore heels that weren't meant for running, but she was going to run. Her pretty oval eyes darted back and forth, looking for escape. She was a deer by the highway with a truck coming, startled, ready to bolt.

The exit door wasn't far away. Laura thought she could make it, but Cindy knew she couldn't.

Tap, knock, tap, knock.

Cindy spread her fingers wide on both hands and pushed the air, as if she could shove Laura back into the store, as if she could make the girl turn around and hide. She shook her head frantically, needing her to understand. She mouthed the word over and over: *No! No! No! No!*

Forty seconds became thirty-five. Time slowed down until she could almost see the world drift to a stop.

Don't run! Don't run!

Laura ran.

The teenager took six steps in her gangly heels before the bullet took her down. She wailed, her head flung back. Red bloomed on perfect peach skin, and one leg caved under her. She toppled, her shoulder struck the floor, and she squirmed on her back, clutching her thigh.

Tap, knock, tap, knock.

There he was. He marched into view, a soldier all in camouflage, a warrior armed with an assault rifle and ammunition slung over his chest. He had a handgun outstretched at the end of his right arm. He came for Laura, the wounded animal, to deliver the killing shot. Laura wriggled away and cried and begged. He was ten feet from her.

Thirty seconds.

Every other thought in Cindy's brain went away. Every thought of herself and Jonny vanished. Cindy knew only one thing: Teenagers weren't supposed to die. Her sister wasn't supposed to die.

The girl on the floor of the mall was *not* going to die.

Cindy charged. She took off like a sprinter and crossed the space between her and the gunman in one breath. He heard her coming, he felt her coming, and as he turned, bringing the gun with him, she launched herself into the air. She was small, but so was he, and they collided heavily, both crumpling to the tile. She was on top of him, but he hit her hard with the side of the gun, and the impact made her limp.

Twenty seconds.

Somewhere in her mind were the shouting and the thunder of the police. Somewhere close by was Jonny. But not close enough.

The gunman pushed her off him as if she were nothing but a toy. He rolled onto her chest, crushing her, holding her down. She smelled the sourness of his breath and saw his tattoos glowing with sweat. She grabbed his forearm, but he was stronger, and so she bucked her head forward and sank her teeth into his wrist, tearing away skin. He howled. The gun fell. In rage, in pain, he clapped her forehead with the heel of his hand, and her skull shot back against the stone floor.

Circles of burning light burst like ripples in her head, and each ripple dizzied her. There was no more time, no more countdown of seconds, just a merry-go-round that wouldn't stop. She was vaguely aware of him above her, aware of a Velcro pocket ripped open, of another gun in his hand. His knees were on either side of her chest. She struck him, but her hand was like a mosquito, easily brushed away.

Footsteps pounded. Chaos. Noise. Voices.

The gun was in her face.

Bullets rang from the police, but no bullets touched him, as if he were shielded. She saw his lips bend into something like a smile. The end was near, but so much could happen at the finish. The barrel touched her cheek, like a kiss. His finger caressed the trigger. More bullets came, more guttural shouts, but the tumult was meaningless. There were only two people in the mall. Him and her.

He leaned down and whispered.

"I am God," he told her.

Then in a single, smooth motion, he shoved the barrel of the gun into his own mouth and blew off the back of his head.

34

Janine had never given much thought to walls. As a rule, she didn't like them. She preferred to stare through windows. Her office had large windows, and so did her house, and there was something about the openness of the view that made her feel free. Which she wasn't. Not anymore. She realized as she looked around the drab holding cell that walls were about to become a big part of her life, and she would need to make peace with them.

Clothes, too. The uniform of prisoners at the women's correctional facility in Shakopee consisted of jeans, a denim shirt, and sneakers. She had no need of fashion anymore. She'd already decided to donate her wardrobe to charity for sale at an auction. The executive from the American Heart Association told her they'd make a lot of money that way. He'd looked sheepish about admitting that people would bid astronomical sums to own the clothes of a surgeon-turned-murderer. Janine wondered who those strange people were and whether they would actually wear her clothes in public.

Archie waited for her to regain her focus. She had found herself mostly unable to think since the verdict. Even knowing the likely outcome, she really hadn't taken time to consider what it meant for her. And now, with all these changes in front of her, she found she could barely concentrate. She was being carried along by a river, and it would take her wherever it wanted.

"The appeals process will continue," Archie said. He looked calm, but there was no jovial smile and no jokes today. He wore his pressed, tailored suit, which reminded her that he was part of a club—the outside world—of which she was no longer a member. She didn't hold it against him.

"On what grounds?" she asked.

"There are always grounds. We'll analyze the transcript. Technicalities may seem like small things, but they can loom large on appeal."

She allowed herself a smile. "And, really, Archie, how often does this bear fruit?"

He rubbed his salt-and-pepper goatee. He didn't bury the truth for her under false hope. "Not often."

"No. I didn't think so."

"This Ross Klayman incident may change things, however," Archie said.

Janine thought about the mall, where she'd often walked and shopped. She thought about Cindy wrestling a gunman and saving a teenager's life. A hero. From time to time, Cindy had talked about being jealous of Janine and about how physical therapists helped people but they didn't really save people. Which was all wrong, in Janine's view. She wondered if Cindy felt differently about herself today.

"What a terrible thing," Janine said. "What makes a man do something like that?"

"I don't think there are any answers to that question. Even so, the fact that Jay saw this man with a gun—and that Klayman did this—"

"Ross Klayman didn't kill Jay. Let's not kid ourselves."

Archie studied her with his sharp blue eyes. "You don't know that for sure, Janine. Do you?"

She got the message. It's not about reality. It's about the law. "I just don't want to exploit this tragedy."

"It's not exploitation. It's a reasonable question given the facts and given Klayman's behavior."

"I hear you, Archie," she said. "Now can we get back to the real world?"

The lawyer nodded. "Judge Edblad will probably announce a sentence at the hearing next month. The guidelines call for a sentence between twenty-two and thirty years, and, given your history and the lack of aggravating factors, I think we can expect a sentence on the lower end. I'll argue for a downward departure from the guidelines, but, candidly, I don't expect it." Archie hesitated. "Here's something for you to consider, Janine. A confession and statement of remorse might get sympathy from the court."

She smiled sweetly. "Even if I didn't shoot him, Archie?"

They stared at each other for a long time before her lawyer shook his head. It was one of the only times she'd been able to see inside his mind. He thought she was guilty. "No," Archie replied. "I can't advise you to say something that isn't true."

"Well, then. What does all of that mean in terms of time in prison?"

"You can typically expect to serve at least two-thirds of your sentence before being considered for supervised release. So if the sentence is twenty-five years, that would be almost seventeen years of doing time in Shakopee."

Some of her coolness faltered. She hadn't dwelled on the reality, but seventeen years was a lot of reality. The prime of life gone. She would no longer be young or beautiful at the end. She would be a felon in her mid-fifties with little money left and no profession. It was almost harder to imagine stepping back onto the street than spending her remaining life behind the prison walls.

"Seventeen years," she murmured.

Archie was silent. No doubt he'd seen this drama play out many times before.

"What will it be like?" she asked.

"Prison life is mostly about routine and rules," he replied.

"How exciting."

"You can have visitors."

"There's no one to visit me," she said.

He had no answer for that one. She had no parents. No siblings. No friends who would travel to see her. And no husband, obviously.

"Do I have to worry about my physical safety?" she went on.

"In general, no, but there are always risks. Most of the inmates are nonviolent offenders, but Shakopee is the only women's prison in the state. Women who commit violent crimes go there, too."

"Like me," Janine pointed out.

Archie heard the sarcasm in her voice. He leaned across the table and took her hands. He played the grandfather now. "Listen, Janine, I won't pretend that this is anything but what it is. Hard. Long. Painful. That said, it is not the end of your life. As impossible at it may seem right now, you'll have to find a way to embrace it."

"Embrace it," Janine said. She smoothed her blond hair. "What would that look like, do you suppose?"

"I have no idea."

"Well, you're honest, Archie. The fact is, I'm a doctor. That's all I am. It's my whole life. I never wanted to be anything else. And now I can't be that anymore. So what do you suggest I do?"

"I'm sorry. I don't know. However, you're not the only doctor in prison. Some find other ways to use their professional knowledge. Others decide to explore a completely different side of themselves."

"You're assuming I have one," Janine said.

Archie waited. Then he asked, "Are you a danger to yourself?"

"You mean suicide?"

"Yes, that's what I mean."

"No, Archie. That's the good thing about being an incorrigible narcissist. We can't imagine depriving the world of our presence."

"I'm serious," he said.

"So am I."

Archie tried to see if there was any real threat behind the jokes, but smarter men than he had tried and failed to decipher the riddle of Janine Snow. She took pride in that.

"You're wrong," she told him.

"About what?"

"This *is* the end. It's like death, really. People go away, and we go on with our lives. That's what's going to happen to me. I'll go away, and people will forget about me. I hate that."

"That's not true. How many lives have you saved? Those people and their families aren't going to forget you. I imagine many of them still thank you in their prayers every night."

She shook her head. "I wish they wouldn't do that. It's a waste of time. Patients are always sending me gifts, knitting me sweaters, lighting candles for me. I wish they'd stop and accept it for what it is. Some debts aren't meant to be repaid. It's better not to try."

He didn't have an answer for her. Instead, he gathered his papers and stood up. "I'll be in touch as I know more," he said.

"Of course."

Janine's gaze traveled from wall to wall. She wasn't any closer to accepting them. Each time she looked, it seemed as if the walls had pushed inward, making the space around her smaller.

"So, what would it take?" she asked. "To throw out the conviction."

"The appeals process—"

"Not the appeal," she said. "I'm not talking about legal loopholes. I mean, what would it take to really prove that I didn't shoot Jay? Enough for a judge to release me."

Archie looked down at her, trying to gauge if she was serious. After all, he still believed that she was the one who'd pulled the trigger. "Honestly?" he asked. "The gun. And the jewelry. In someone else's hands."

Howard sat in Judge Edblad's office. He'd dressed in a tie again, the way he had during the trial. His collar was moist where his neck sweated. The office in the courthouse was formal, with an oak desk and a flag, but he also saw pictures of the judge with his family and posters on the walls from Disney World. It was strange to think of the judge as a human being.

"Mr. Marlowe," Judge Edblad said, entering the office from the corridor and taking a seat across from him at the conference table. He wore a suit, not the robe he'd worn in the courtroom. "My clerk said you wanted to talk to me."

"Yes."

Howard tried to go on. He'd rehearsed the words, but now they left him. He didn't know what to say.

"Well, what can I do for you?"

"It's about the trial of Dr. Snow. I'm having second thoughts."

"Second thoughts? In what way?"

"I voted with the others to convict her. I said she was guilty, but now I'm not sure."

The judge tented his fingers on the table. He didn't roll his eyes or tell Howard that he was a fool. There was a patience about the man that Howard liked. "Why is that?" he asked.

"I just—I just wonder if she really did it. And now, with the news of that killer in the mall—"

"That was a horrifying incident," the judge agreed. "If the police uncover any evidence to suggest that Mr. Klayman could have murdered Mr. Ferris, then Dr. Snow's attorney will certainly file a motion to throw out her conviction. However, that's not anything you need to concern yourself with."

"I know. I'm just having doubts."

"I understand. I'd like you to answer a few questions for me. Did any of the other jurors pressure you to vote to convict? Were you subject to any threats or intimidation?"

"Oh, no. I mean, I was the only holdout at first, but they didn't pressure me. Eleanor was good. She talked me through the evidence. In the end, I thought I was doing the right thing, but now I don't know."

"So when I asked you in the courtroom to confirm that you shared in the unanimous verdict, did you answer fully and truthfully that you were voting guilty?"

"Yes . . ."

Judge Edblad nodded. "You made a difficult decision, Mr. Marlowe. Now you're having second thoughts about it. It's not uncommon. We call it buyer's remorse. Unfortunately, in the absence of any actual misconduct in the jury room, it doesn't constitute sufficient grounds to void the verdict."

Howard tensed. "Except—except I want to change my vote."

"It's too late. The trial is over."

"What if I talk to Mr. Gale?" Howard asked.

"You can certainly do that. I'll inform him of our conversation, too, as well as Mr. Erickson. However, a juror changing his mind after the fact isn't enough for a new trial. I'm sorry."

Howard stood up. He felt crushed. "I see. I'm sorry to bother you, Your Honor."

"It isn't a problem, Mr. Marlowe. Being a juror is a weighty responsibility. Everyone in this courthouse understands and respects that. You did your civic duty, and now you can go on with your life."

The judge stood up, too, and walked Howard to his office door. He clapped him on the shoulder, showed him out, and shut the door behind him. Howard could see the jury room in front of him, where the deliberations had taken place. It was empty. He wanted to go inside, sit down again, and change the past.

Go on with your life.

That was what Carol had said, too. *We can go back to living our lives.*

They all wanted him to forget about Janine, but Howard couldn't do that.

35

Cindy sat on the green bench at the end of the Point in the midst of a small patch of sand by the bay. She checked her watch, but Jonny was late. He usually was. She'd gotten used to it over the years.

This was Jonny's place, where he went to stare at the calm waters. As teenagers, they'd first talked about marriage here, in that awkward way that young lovers grope toward their future. When Jonny's mother died, they'd come here to talk about the good and bad of her life. Now it seemed like the right place for them to talk about other things.

It was dusk. The August days were getting shorter, stealing the sunlight. Long shadows filled the park behind her. At her feet, crowns of golden alexanders swayed as the breeze blew, and the bay ripples gurgled at the beach. As warm as it was, she shivered. There were moments late in every summer when you got the first kiss of fall, a little finger trailing up your spine that reminded you of what lay ahead.

She'd visited the teenager from the mall that afternoon. Laura. The girl was home now, out of the hospital, and recovering nicely from the bullet wound in her leg. Reporters had wanted to talk to both of them and take pictures, and Cindy had given them a firm no. She didn't want publicity. She'd spent half an hour with Laura and her parents, and they'd fallen all over themselves to thank her, which made her uncomfortable. She didn't want thanks or tears. The only thing she wanted was for Laura to go on and live her life. The ups and downs. The happiness. The sadness. She'd hugged the girl at the end and whispered, "Don't let this define who you are."

Which was easier said than done, she knew. That moment in the mall would likely be the seminal moment of the girl's life. She'd have nightmares. She'd be in therapy for years. She'd wonder why she was spared when others died. That was okay. You couldn't ask those questions and wrestle with the answers if you weren't alive.

She and Jonny hadn't talked about it. They'd agreed to put it aside in a box. She knew he wanted to ask her how she could have taken such a crazy risk with their future, but he couldn't. Not when he would have done exactly the same thing at the same moment. But that was his job. For her, it was a choice, but in the moment, she'd felt as if she had no choice at all.

Cindy heard the engine of his Bronco and saw him pull into the dirt of the parking lot beside her Outback. He got out and smiled at her and crushed a cigarette in the sand. He mussed his wild black hair. God, he was handsome. That was what she'd thought years ago, when she'd met him in school, this intense, brooding teenager who was obsessed with doing the right thing. Whatever that might be. Now he was in the prime of his life, and she didn't think he'd ever looked better than he did at that moment. Cocky and confident, wounded and deep. He was such a strange, wonderful mix, this man of hers.

He sat down beside her on the bench and stretched out his long legs. His boots were dusty. He had a can of Coke in his hand, and he took a drink and then offered it to her.

"You think I want your spit, Jonny?" she asked.

He laughed, but she took the can anyway and finished it.

Together they watched the dying light on the bay. They didn't talk for a while. He held her hand, and their skin was damp and warm. The evening was alive with summer sounds—insects in the bushes, the whine of a floatplane overhead, the pop of illegal firecrackers on the lakeside over the dunes.

Finally, she asked, "Do you know anything more?"

Jonny nodded.

"Did he . . ." she asked.

That had been the question in her mind since it happened. Did Ross Klayman kill Jay Ferris? Her mind had spun out theories in which Ross was guilty. Jay spotted him somewhere. Found him. Followed him. Ross had eliminated the one man who could stand in the way of his planned rampage.

Which meant that her friend, Janine, was innocent.

"No," Jonny told her.

He didn't give her any room for doubt. She felt a wave of disappointment but not any sense of surprise. "Are you sure? You sound sure."

"The Bureau of Criminal Apprehension tested every handgun we found in Klayman's car that could have been used in the murder. None of them matched."

"That doesn't necessarily mean anything, does it? He could have gotten rid of the weapon."

Jonny shook his head. "There's more. We went over Jessie's credit card bills. There was a charge from a gun show in Arkansas on January 28. The Arkansas police talked to several of the vendors, and they all knew Jessie and Ross. They confirmed that Ross was with his mother at that show. He was a thousand miles away from Duluth when Jay was killed, Cin. He didn't do it."

"Oh."

And that was that. Ross Klayman didn't do it. Janine did.

"I'm sorry," he said.

"No, you were right all along. I was wrong."

"You weren't wrong about Ross Klayman," Jonny said flatly. "Nine people died. Thirty more were wounded. Maybe if we'd found him earlier, we could have stopped him. I feel responsible."

She squeezed his hand hard. "Don't you ever do that to yourself, Jonathan Stride. Do you hear me? It's not your fault."

"No?"

"No. It's not."

"I'm having a hard time accepting that."

"Mentally ill people don't wear signs," she said.

He shrugged. He knew it was true, but she knew it wouldn't stop him from beating himself up.

They were silent again.

Then he looked at her. "You never told me what he said to you. Just before he killed himself."

"Who, Klayman? Nothing."

"Nothing?"

"I don't remember."

He didn't push her, and she was glad. She was lying, and he knew it, but maybe he realized that some moments couldn't be shared with anyone. If she closed her eyes, she could picture his face and hear his voice. I am God. The strange thing was, as he'd said it, she almost believed him. Not that she thought God was cruel or uncaring. And yet cruel things happened.

Cindy realized she couldn't put it off any longer. She'd told Jonny to meet her here for a reason. Not anywhere else. Here.

"Listen," she said, dragging the words out of her chest. "There's something I need to talk to you about."

She'd gone over and over in her head about how to tell him, but she still didn't know what to say. How do you break that news to your husband? She'd had an appointment with Steve Garske. And it wasn't good.

"Something's not . . ." she began. Something's not right. With me. Something's very wrong. Something bad.

"Hang on," Jonny said. His phone was ringing. When he answered, she recognized Maggie's voice on the line, which had a strange kind of intimacy. It was odd how Maggie was always coming between them. She'd never really thought about it that way, and it wasn't fair, because Maggie represented the job. The job came first. It always did.

He hung up.

"A teenage girl has gone missing in Lakeside," he said. "She went jogging, and she never came home."

"What's her name?" Cindy asked. She always wanted to know the name. Victims were never faceless or nameless to her.

"Kerry McGrath."

"Well, go," she said.

"I'm sorry."

She shook her head. There wasn't any call for apology. She knew the life.

"What did you want to tell me?" he asked.

"It can wait."

He got up from the bench and headed across the sand for his Bronco. She watched him go. Hands in his pockets. Boots leaving footprints. That body she knew so well, with its muscles, furrows, and scars. His head cocked, watching the lazy turns of a hawk in the dark of the Duluth sky.

Suddenly, she ran after him with a sense of urgency. He heard her coming and turned around in surprise, and she swept her arms behind his waist and lifted herself up on her toes to kiss him. She gave him a long, hard, wet, Cindy kiss that went on and on. You could feel kisses like that all the way down to your toes, and you could close your eyes and remember them like candy on your lips.

They were the kind of kisses you never forgot, no matter what happened next.

NOW

36

THE PRESENT

"We finally got an ID on the victim outside the bar," Maggie told Stride and Serena.

She stood in the doorway of Stride's cottage on the 3300 block of the Point. It was a July evening after dark, and the windows were all open, letting in lake air through the screens. Stride sat in his red leather armchair near the fireplace, under the mantel that was decorated with a sign that read: Believe. Serena sat on the walnut steps that led up to their unfinished attic.

He reached over to the small table next to him for a cigarette before he realized that he didn't smoke anymore. Strange. After fits and starts, it had been three years since he'd had a cigarette, but sometimes he simply forgot that he was a different man now. You are always one moment away from being who you were, so the price of maturity is constant vigilance.

"Who was she?" Serena asked. She wore a purple tank top and shorts, leaving her strong arms and legs bare. The skin of her long legs was mottled by scars from burns she'd suffered in a fire two years earlier. Her flowing black hair was mussed.

It had been three weeks since Serena saw a young blond woman shot and killed outside the Grizzly Bear Bar in West Duluth. She'd chased down the shooter, but he'd escaped, leaving his gun behind but with the woman's wallet and phone lodged in his pocket. They were no closer to finding him, and the woman herself had been a Jane Doe since the murder. Nothing in her baby-blue suitcase had helped them give her a name. Until now.

"Kelly Hauswirth," Maggie said. "Twenty-two years old. From Denver."

"She was a long way from home."

"Yeah." Maggie danced uncomfortably from one foot to the other.

"You can come inside," Serena told her. "I don't bite."

"I think that's what the wolf said to Little Red Riding Hood," Maggie replied, but she wandered into the cottage, handed off copies of a Colorado driver's license to the two of them, and sat down on Stride's sofa with her feet propped on the coffee table. It was like the old days, but it wasn't.

A palpable frost chilled the air between her and Serena. The two of them had nursed an uneasy friendship since Stride and Serena began a relationship four years earlier, but the fractures between them had split open the previous fall. In the wake of a near-fatal accident that left him struggling with flashbacks and nightmares, Stride had made the one mistake in his life that he'd always sworn to avoid. He'd slept with Maggie. Within days, Serena had moved out, and he and Maggie had launched a short-lived affair.

But things changed, and then they changed again. That was the way of the world. He and Serena were back together. They shared the cottage with a pregnant teenage girl named Cat Mateo, whom they'd rescued from the Duluth streets. And Maggie, who was in many ways still his best friend, was an outsider now.

"Where's the kid?" Maggie asked, glancing into Cat's empty bedroom at the front of the house.

Serena rolled her eyes. "Out. Again."

"We think she has a boyfriend," Stride added, "but she won't tell us who it is."

"Welcome to parenthood," Maggie said.

Stride knew that Maggie didn't trust Cat. She was also still pretending that everything was fine between her and Stride, when it clearly wasn't.

"Kelly Hauswirth worked at a telemarketing company in Centennial," Maggie went on. "She told her coworkers she was going on vacation. Didn't say where or with whom. Word is, she kept to herself, didn't socialize much. It was almost two weeks before anyone reported her missing, and it took the Denver police a while to connect the disappearance to our report."

"What about family?" Serena asked.

"Her parents are in Montana. They don't talk with her more than once a month. The Denver cops sent a pic of the body to the police in Missoula, who ran it by Mom and Dad. They confirmed it was their daughter."

"Do they know what Kelly was doing here in Duluth?"

Maggie shook her head. "Nope."

Stride studied the driver's license photo of Kelly Hauswirth. Serena had described her as the suburban girl next door, and she was right. The woman's blond hair was straight, her eyes wide and blue, her face round. Pretty but not a stunner. She didn't flirt with the camera. However, she'd left behind lace thongs and ribbed condoms in her baby-blue suitcase. The shy cheerleader type was in town for a man.

A man driving a stolen Grand Am.

A man who'd shot her in the back of the head.

"Have the Denver police been able to trace her movements?" he asked.

"She charged a bus ticket from Denver to Minneapolis on her credit card. That's nineteen hours of hell. The police talked to the drivers on the route, but no one remembered Kelly specifically."

"How about on the Minneapolis end?"

"Nothing. There are no other charges on her credit card. If she took another bus to Duluth, she paid cash."

"She was obviously coming here to meet someone," Serena said.

Maggie nodded. "Yeah, one of her coworkers thought Kelly had hooked up with a guy online. The Denver police dug into her phone records and say she was texting hot and heavy with someone, but all the details he gave her were completely fictitious. Name, location, occupation—all made up. They're going to e-mail me a transcript. The number connected to a throwaway phone, and it hasn't been used since the murder."

"He lured her," Stride said.

"Looks that way. She got catfished."

"How'd she hook up with him?"

"They don't know. Probably a chat room, but they haven't found it yet. This girl was easy prey. Very naive. The guy texted her photos of himself, but it's really some male model you can find all over the Internet."

Maggie held up a photograph of a twenty-something man with mop-top brown hair and a trimmed, wispy beard. He wore a simple white T-shirt and had dreamy blue eyes that belonged in a boy band. He was good-looking but not threatening.

"And that's who she thought she was going to meet?" Serena asked.

"Yeah. Must have been a shock. You think you're about to hook up with your Prince Charming. Instead, some stranger robs you and kills you."

"This was more than a robbery," Stride said. "Nobody goes to that much trouble to grab a wallet."

Maggie nodded. "Yeah, we may have something else here. Something bad. Troy Grange called me today. He heard about our case. He thinks there may be a connection to a query he got from Interpol about security for outbound ships at the port."

Stride's face darkened. "What kind of query?"

"Homicide. Troy says there's another victim."

"Why haven't we heard about it?"

"Because the murder didn't take place here," Maggie explained. "They found this other woman in Amsterdam. Her throat was slit, and she was dumped in one of the canals. But guess what she was wearing? A Grandma's Marathon T-shirt from Duluth."

By midnight, Cat hadn't come home. They knew she'd turned off her phone, because their text messages weren't being delivered, and the tracking app didn't show them where she was. The girl was deliberately pushing boundaries and buttons.

"I don't get it," Stride murmured. "I don't understand her behavior."

"That's because you were never a teenage girl," Serena replied with a smile.

They sat on Adirondack chairs on the front porch of the cottage. The street was quiet, and the waves of Lake Superior thundered out of sight behind them. He flicked away a hungry mosquito.

"One minute she's sweet and innocent," he said, "and the next she's the Girl with the Dragon Tattoo."

"Teenager," Serena said again.

"I know, but she's so intent on keeping the baby. And she's not ready for it."

"No. Not at all."

"I can't help but think—" he began, but he cut off his words. He didn't believe in anyone else making decisions for a woman. Even a woman who was really just a girl. He continued to believe that Cat should give up the child for adoption, but she kept insisting that she wanted to be a mother.

"You can go through bad times as a teenager and come out okay," Serena pointed out. "I did."

"Yeah, but a lot of girls don't."

"That's true."

He felt like a father to Cat, which made him feel old. Plenty of other things made him aware of his age, too. In the eight years since he'd lost Cindy, gray had begun to win the battle over black in his hair. The leg he'd broken last summer had healed, but in the dead of winter, he sometimes found himself limping. In a few months, he'd turn fifty. There was something about the change in decade that made it harder to pretend you were young.

Life had reminded him over and over that he wasn't bulletproof. It wasn't such a bad thing. He'd begun to accept his mistakes and imperfections. He didn't bang his head against every wall. He and Serena, both wounded, both alone, had found a measure of peace with each other. If they could keep it.

And Cat.

He hadn't realized how much he'd needed someone like Cat in his life until he found her shivering in his bedroom closet three months earlier, on the run from a killer. Now he couldn't imagine being without her. Which was what made her behavior so frustrating. He couldn't protect her from everything. Not even herself.

Serena took his hand. "I should have trusted my instincts at the bar."

"How so?"

"I knew Kelly Hauswirth didn't belong there. I should have talked to her."

"You couldn't possibly have known she was in danger, and talking to her wouldn't necessarily have changed a thing."

Serena shrugged. She didn't always take her own advice about living without regrets. "What about the murder weapon?" she asked.

"The BCA is running prints and ballistics. We don't have a report yet."

"And the Grand Am?"

"Stolen from a parking lot at the convention center. No one saw anything. No prints inside. It's a dead end."

"I wish I'd seen his face."

"Well, we may not have anything on him, but we know who she is now. That's something."

"Kelly Hauswirth," Serena said again. "She looked like a Kelly. Sweet little Kelly falls in love with a guy online, and he gets her to come to Minnesota to meet him. And then—what? She realizes that the guy in the car isn't the man she's supposed to meet, and she tries to run?"

"It looks that way," Stride said.

Serena shook her head. "I don't know. Nothing about this feels right to me. I think this guy is an iceberg, Jonny."

He knew what she meant. Most of an iceberg floated underneath the water, and it was the part you couldn't see that you had to fear.

37

Howard Marlowe typed into a Microsoft Word document on his computer:

> The prosecution couldn't put a gun in Dr. Snow's hands, but they did put one in Jay's hands. Was that gun the murder weapon? Most of the jurors thought so.
>
> Not me. I think that Archibald Gale's speculation at the trial was right. Jay lost his gun when his truck and fishing shanty went through the ice. People made a big deal of the fact that the gun wasn't recovered during salvage, but that doesn't mean anything. If your house floods, do you think everything stays put? No. The gun floated away. It's buried under the silt of Superior Bay.

He studied what he'd written, and he liked it. Next came the evidence he'd uncovered in his research.

Four years ago, he'd taken a lawn mower to Jay's brother, Clyde, for repair. By then, Clyde didn't remember Howard from the jury. Howard got to know him, went out with him, and peppered him with questions over drinks. Clyde admitted after half a bottle of Captain Morgan that he was pretty sure Jay had the gun with him that afternoon in the shanty. And he admitted that he never saw his brother with the gun again after that day.

Howard passed along the information to Archibald Gale, who said what he always said. It wasn't enough for a new trial. So the appeals came and went, and nothing happened.

Janine Snow remained in prison.

"What are you working on?" Carol asked Howard from the door-way of his office. She'd gone to bed early, but she had trouble sleeping most nights. "As if I didn't know."

"The book," he said.

His wife folded her arms across her pajama top. Dark half-moons rimmed her eyes. "The book. Will it ever be done? How long is it now? Fifteen hundred pages? No one's going to read it."

He didn't take his eyes away from the monitor. "It's not about whether I publish it or not. It's a hobby."

"A hobby? It's one in the morning, Howard. You spend every min-ute you're awake researching and writing that book."

"So what? I need something to fill my summers while school's out."

"Really? How about doing something with your family? How about doing something with *me*?"

"We were just in Door County," he told her.

"One weekend. Three days. It rained. And the only reason we went is that you tracked another white RAV to somebody in Sister Bay."

"I told you. It's my hobby."

Carol shook her head in frustration. When he looked at her, he saw how much she'd aged in the last nine years. The extra ten pounds she'd always carried had become twenty. Her face, without makeup, was pallid, like beach sand. She was right that he was ignoring her. They didn't have much in common anymore. Their intermittent sex life had dwindled to nothing; he couldn't remember when they had last slept together. Their daughter, Annie, was a sullen teenager, too preoccupied with her own life to worry about them. Carol didn't have anything else. She still worked as a cashier at the Super One. She quilted. She went to church. And she nagged him about the book like a squawking parrot on his shoulder.

She didn't understand that the case was the most important work he'd ever done in his life. It was his life. It made him feel young again. His office had become a library of evidence, all of it neatly organized and categorized by subject. The witnesses. The exhibits. The gun. The RAV4. Two years ago, he'd started turning his investigative work into a book.

But a book needed an ending, which he didn't have yet. It would end when Janine was free.

"What did you do today?" she asked, making the question sound like an accusation.

"I went to a pawnshop in Grand Rapids."

"Every week you're in a different pawnshop," she snapped. "You're never going to find anything after all this time. What do you hope to accomplish?"

"The missing jewelry is still out there," Howard retorted. "Those are expensive pieces. Sooner or later, whoever has them is going to figure it's safe to sell them."

Carol opened her mouth to shout at him, the way she usually did, but this time she held her tongue. He'd heard it all before. The jewelry wasn't missing; it was at the bottom of a lake, where Janine had tossed it, along with the gun. He would never find it. He was wasting his time.

His wife closed her eyes. She took a long, slow breath. He realized she was crying.

"Tell me why," she said.

"I've told you before."

"Tell me again," she said.

He got up from the chair with a sigh. There wasn't much room to walk in the office anymore. Too many boxes. Still, he knew what was in each one. He went to his wife in the doorway, but they didn't touch. They were strangers who shared a house and a child. It had stopped bothering him long ago. Couples grew older. They grew apart. If they were lucky, they stayed friends.

"I put her in prison," he explained. "Me."

"No, you didn't."

"It's my fault. I wasn't strong enough to stand my ground. If I can prove that she's innocent—"

"She's not innocent, Howard. She's guilty. She's immoral. She's the devil."

"Stop that," he snapped.

"She took you away from me!"

"Don't be ridiculous."

Carol laughed without a glint of humor. She spread her arms, pointing at the stacks of boxes, and her voice was wild with desperation. "Is all of this really more important than your marriage? Is this fantasy about her more real to you than I am?"

"Oh, for heaven's sake," he said.

She put her arms around his waist and held him tightly, and he let her do it. Her head sank against his chest. It felt the way it had years earlier. When a minute had passed, he gently peeled away her hands, and then he went back to his desk.

"Why don't you come to bed?" Carol murmured. An invitation.

"I will. In just a little bit."

She was silent, but she didn't leave. Then his wife said, "I know you see her, Howard."

He looked up nervously. "What?"

"I know you visit her in prison."

Howard wanted to deny it, but he didn't think she was fishing for the truth. She hadn't pulled this idea out of the air. She knew. Besides, his face was a confession, and he didn't want to hide it from her any longer. She stared at him, and they both didn't say a word, and then she turned and left him alone in the basement.

Cat lay on her back, watching the stars. Her boyfriend lay beside her. She had no idea what time it was, but she knew it was late. She'd turned off her phone, because she didn't want Stride and Serena spying on her. They didn't need to know that she was only fifty yards from their cottage, sprawled with Al on the beach, with the lake waves almost reaching their bare feet.

He placed a hand on the bare skin of her swollen belly. The baby thumped from inside, and he grinned and said, "Cool."

Al wasn't the father of her child. She didn't know the father's name; he was just one of the men who'd paid her for sex in the bad days. Funny, that the man would never know he had a child. A son. She didn't know what she'd tell her boy about his father when the time came. Or about herself.

Cat felt Al's fingers caressing the side of her breast, but that was as far as it went. He hadn't pressured her for sex. Just kissing and petting. If he'd wanted sex, she would have said yes. Some boys got freaked out about being with pregnant girls, but Al said it wasn't that. It was respect, he said. She'd told him that sex didn't mean anything to her, not after years of doing it for money, so he said he wanted to wait until it did.

She wondered if that meant he was getting what he needed from someone else. She didn't want to ask.

He sat up on the beach and helped her do the same. Superior was loud. The cloudless sky shimmered with stars. She felt a strange rush of contentment, but it was shadowed by the guilt of hiding things about herself from Stride and Serena. And from Al, too. Keeping secrets was a hard habit to break. In the past, her secrets had kept her alive.

"My buddy gave me a couple joints," he said. "You want a puff?"

"No, thanks. I shouldn't. But you go ahead."

He lit one and held the smoke in. When he exhaled, sweetness surrounded her. He had a warm beer can in the sand, too, and she'd allowed herself a swallow but nothing more.

"Anna's not speaking to me," Cat said.

Anna was the waitress at the Grizzly Bear Bar.

Al said nothing. The joint did its thing. He looked as if he were far away, on one of the stars, where all their little problems didn't matter.

"She's not even reading my texts," Cat went on. "She's pissed because I didn't tell her I was living with two cops."

Her boyfriend sighed as he returned to Earth, as if this was a conversation he didn't want to have. "Well, why didn't you tell her?"

"I didn't want to scare her away." Cat scrunched up her pretty face in annoyance. "It's not fair. Serena doesn't want me hanging out with any of my old friends. She told Fred at the bar that she'd have the place busted if he let me inside again."

"Sorry." Al added, "Do Stride and Serena know about me?"

"No."

"Do you think they'd say you shouldn't see me?"

"I don't know. Probably."

"Well, you're not going to be able to hide it forever," he said.

"Have you told your mother?"

He grinned, because she'd just given him a taste of his own medicine. "Okay. No."

"So there."

He put an arm around her shoulders and pulled her closer. She liked him a lot, even though they'd only known each other a couple of months. He was two years older than she was, tall and scrawny, with long legs made for basketball. He wore his black hair trimmed to a point on his forehead, and his goatee made a wiry square against his dark skin. His voice was soft and mellow, and it made her think of distant thunder. He wore cheap, baggy clothes from Goodwill, except for his Converse high tops, which were the one treat he allowed himself at Christmas.

She'd met him because of Anna. Anna volunteered at local churches, and every couple of months, she twisted Cat's arm to go along with her on community projects. It wasn't Cat's favorite thing, but she did it to stay friends with her. In May, she'd spent a weekend painting Al's mother's house from top to bottom. Cat and Anna supplied the labor, and the church donated the paint. Al got them burgers at the Anchor Bar for free when they were done.

Despite working two jobs, Al never had much money. The mortgage ate up most of his paycheck, and a backlog of credit card bills took the rest. His father had died of a stroke five years earlier, which was when the debt began piling up. His mother had emphysema and couldn't work. His younger siblings were still in school, which was where he wanted them to stay. Between his days working maintenance at Duluth's Lake Superior Zoo, and evenings and weekends washing dishes at the Anchor, he didn't have much time to spend with Cat. Stolen moments like this were precious to her.

The beach was mostly deserted. A mild lake breeze rustled her chestnut hair. In the dark, fifty yards north of them, she could see another couple making out under the starlight. She knew Al had to go soon, because he worked in the morning, but she wished they could stay here all night.

"I liked your mother when Anna and I met her," Cat said. "Don't you think she'd like me?"

"She'd love you, but she says I don't have time for a girlfriend."

"Especially not a pregnant one, huh?"

"Oh, that's not it. Not really. She just doesn't want me stuck on the bottom rung like her and Dad. Mom always says God has big plans for me, and if I don't work hard, I'll never find out what they are."

"Do you believe that?"

"It's the way I was raised, so, yeah, I have to believe it. She'd whack me if I didn't. Except God must be pretty disappointed in me."

"Why do you say that?" Cat asked.

He shrugged. "Sometimes I do stupid shit that I really regret. I'm not worthy of big plans."

"Join the club," Cat told him.

"You? Come on."

"It's true. God doesn't have any plans for me. I'm just a screwup."

"Don't talk like that," he chided her. "You're special. Way more special than me. Why would you say that?"

"It's just hormones. I go up. I go down. I'm pregnant, so it comes with the territory."

"Oh."

"Hey, can I ask you something?" she said.

"Sure."

"Do you love me? Because I kinda think I love you."

His eyes widened. "Cat, I—"

"Never mind. Don't answer that. I'm sorry. Wow, that was a really dumb thing to say. I'm pressing the Delete button."

Except you couldn't delete things like that after you said them.

Al looked unhappy with her, and Cat didn't blame him. She thought to herself: *There I go again, screwing everything up.* She stood up awkwardly and brushed sand from her skin. Al stood up, too. He looked as if she'd punched him in the gut.

"We should go," she said.

"Cat, listen, it's not that I—"

"No, don't say anything. Please. Forget it. I was being stupid. I just want to get out of here. You have to work, and I'm sure Stride is waiting to read me the riot act."

"I'll come with you. I'll explain it to him."

"That would just make it worse."

"Well, let's go back to my car," he said. "I'll drive you home."

"No, you go ahead. I'll walk."

"Alone? Not a chance."

"It's two houses, Al. I could shout, and Stride would hear me."

He looked reluctant, but he allowed her to persuade him. He kissed her goodbye, which was normally magic, but she'd spoiled the moment for them. Stupid, stupid, stupid. He left her, his shoulders slumped, and disappeared southward along the beach. She watched him until he turned and headed for the street. She wondered if he'd call her tomorrow or if she'd driven him away for good.

It wasn't just talking about love before he was ready to hear it. That was a big mistake, but she was keeping other secrets, too.

She needed to tell him what she'd done.

38

Stride shook Troy Grange's hand.

He didn't see Troy often, but there was a bond connecting them. They'd both known personal losses that had upended their lives. Stride had lost Cindy to cancer almost eight years ago. Last summer, Troy's wife, Trisha, had been murdered, leaving him to raise two young girls alone.

Troy greeted Maggie, too, and Stride didn't miss the warmth in Troy's face. He was pleased to see it. Troy was finally opening up again, which took a lot of time after the death of a spouse. He wondered if there was something more between the two of them. Troy and Maggie had worked together as colleagues for years, but it looked as if their friendship had drifted into attraction. At least for him. There was no way Maggie hadn't picked up on Troy's feelings, and Stride wondered whether the interest was reciprocated.

"Sit down, guys," Troy told them in his foghorn voice. He was the senior health and safety manager for the Duluth Seaway Port Authority, but his office was small, and he was rarely inside the building. Instead, he was out among the port's docks, where thousands of tons of goods moved in and out of the city by boat and rail every day. Lumber. Coal. Iron ore. Cement. Grain. Limestone. The long boats brought in loads and took them out into the waters of Lake Superior and from there to destinations around the world.

Along with that traffic came smuggling problems. Drugs. Weapons. People.

"Maggie was telling me about this girl Kelly Hauswirth from Denver," Troy said. "Do you have any more leads on the guy who killed her?"

"Not so far," Stride said. "We're waiting for ballistics on the murder weapon."

"We're assuming he's the same guy who lured Kelly from Colorado to Duluth," Maggie added. "Someone established a fake online ID and built a relationship with her. When she figured out that this guy wasn't who she thought he was, she tried to get away, and he shot her."

"I assume you interviewed everyone in the bar that night," Troy said.

"As many as we could," Maggie replied. "A lot of them melted away before we got there."

"The Grizzly Bear is a watering hole for foreign crew off the boats," Troy said.

"Yeah, and they're a tight-lipped bunch. Nobody claimed to know the woman or who she was meeting."

"Figures."

"Why do you think there may be an Amsterdam connection?" Stride interjected. "Maggie says Interpol reached out to you about another murder overseas."

Troy grabbed a photograph from his office printer and passed it across the desk. The corpse in the picture was barely recognizable, with features bloated and bleached by time in the canals. A knife gash had split open her throat. Her strawberry hair was pasted to her skin. Her swollen torso had split open seams on her T-shirt, but Stride could still see the Grandma's Marathon logo. The woman—or whoever had given her the shirt—had been in Duluth before she was killed.

"When did they find this woman?" Stride asked.

"Last week."

"Have they identified her?"

"No, the Dutch were hoping we could help them with that. The condition of the body doesn't make it easy. They're assuming she's American because of the T-shirt and the quality of her dental work, but they don't really know for sure. They also don't know how long she was in the Netherlands. The marathon T-shirt was one of last year's printings."

Maggie leaned across the desk. "Can we get the JPEG?"

"Of course, Sergeant."

Stride smiled. Troy was invariably formal around them about official business. Stride was Lieutenant. Maggie was Sergeant. He was the kind of gruff ex-seaman who wore nothing but plaid shirts, jeans, and boots, but he had a serious way about him that Stride respected. He wasn't tall, but he had the bulky build of a weight lifter. Nobody messed with Troy.

The security manager clicked a few keys on his computer. Stride's and Maggie's phones both chirped with an incoming e-mail as he sent them the photograph.

"Do the Dutch police or Interpol know anything more about the circumstances of this woman's murder?" Stride asked.

"Maybe. They found a tattoo on her wrist associated with an Estonian crime syndicate. Very brutal and very sophisticated. This group began with synthetic-drug exports and high-end robberies, but Interpol thinks they've branched out into an international smuggling network. Illegal metals. Drugs. Weapons."

"And women," Maggie guessed.

"Yeah. Exactly. Their guess is that this woman was kidnapped and dumped into a forced-prostitution ring overseas."

"They think she was smuggled out through the Duluth port?" Stride asked.

"Well, that was their question to me. I couldn't rule it out." Troy folded his meaty hands together. "Look, port security guys talk all around the world. We've got tech guys who trawl the Deep Web—you know, the places that Google doesn't reach. It's practically a Craigslist for slavery. Women, girls, boys, babies, even pets. If you've got the money, you can write up specs for whoever you want like you were placing an order for custom drapes. And syndicates like this Estonian group will go out and grab someone who fits the profile and smuggle them out. It could be a girl in Sydney. Or Cape Town. Or Cancun."

"Or Denver, Colorado," Stride said.

"Yeah. Exactly. They just disappear. Order fulfilled. Huge payday for the smugglers. And once they've outlived their usefulness, the girls wind up like this woman in Amsterdam."

Stride got up and went to the window in Troy's office. He could see train cars covered with graffiti. Silos. Pyramids of taconite. The sheer volume of everything that passed through the port made a single human being seem like a needle in a haystack. Easy to hide.

"I'm not saying that's what happened to Kelly Hauswirth," Troy went on, "but I think we have to consider the possibility. She was lured here, and somebody did that for a reason. Plus, I don't like the fact that the meeting place was a bar where a lot of the overseas sailors hang out."

Stride nodded. "We'll need a list of the ocean-going boats that were in port when the murder took place. And when each of them is expected back in Duluth."

"You got it."

"I want to talk to your contacts at Interpol, too."

"Sure." Troy stood up, and he shoved his hands into his pockets. "Listen, I hope I'm wrong about this, but if someone is smuggling girls through here, they didn't start with Kelly, and they're not going to stop there. It's peak shipping season. For all we know, they've already got other girls hidden in the city, and they're just waiting to get them out on a boat."

Her name was Erin. She was from Grand Forks.

She knew who she was, but otherwise, she was disoriented. Her mind swam, making her dizzy. She couldn't tell the difference anymore between consciousness and dreams. She opened her eyes, but the world was black. A blindfold. When she tried to speak, to shout, to scream, she couldn't make a sound. Something filled her mouth, muffling her cries. Her wrists pressed against each other behind her back, and she couldn't move them. Her ankles were tied, too.

Panic rippled over her. She squirmed and struggled in a fit of despair. Blind. Mute. Bound.

This was a nightmare.

No.

Erin knew she was awake. She lay on a wooden floor on her side. Her blond hair spilled across her face. Dirt and splinters pressed into her skull like sharp fingernails. Her neck spasmed with pain. This was real. She could hear things. Somewhere close by, she recognized the trill of a cardinal in the trees, penetrating the walls around her. It sang to her, but she couldn't sing back. The world was still out there.

She rolled onto her back, and her knuckles dug into the small of her spine. The weight of the gag stuffed into her mouth made her choke. She was afraid she would vomit. With a thrust of her body, she rolled again, all the way onto her face, where dust blew into her nose. It became difficult to breathe, and the stricture in her throat made her suck in each breath faster. She hyperventilated. Her heart raced.

Erin heaved herself onto her side. She had no sense of the space around her. How big. How small. She was inside, somewhere, and the room was hot. Damp sweat covered her skin. When she tried to bring her knees toward her chest, her ankles resisted. They were tethered on a short leash to something heavy and solid, immovable. She kicked at it and realized her feet were bare. Her shoes had been taken. She wriggled around and sat up.

She knew who she was but not where she was or how she'd gotten here or how long she'd been in this place. Time had no meaning. My name is Erin. I am a dental hygienist in Grand Forks. I am on vacation to see . . .

That was it. Matt. Mattie_1987. Matt the paralegal. Funny, sweet, athletic, such a shy, sexy face. Most men didn't understand her, but Matt did. He seemed to know what it was like to be her, all the insecurities, all the nervousness when she looked in the mirror, all the doubts about where she was going in life. She'd never believed she could fall in love with someone online, but that was before she found Matt in the chat room. It was easier to talk to him than to anyone in her real life. There was something about the anonymity of the darkness and the screen that made her tell him secrets. She shared things with him that she'd never shared with her family or friends. Not that she had many friends. Or family, other than a distant sibling and parents who didn't really understand her.

That's me, too, he'd said. *I know how you feel.*

He was like her soul mate.

But her soul mate had never showed up to meet her. She felt as if she'd lost hours in her brain. Lost days that were gray in her memory. She had a cloudy memory of a bar. Drinking. Waiting. Growing sad and anxious as time passed and the evening waned. More drinking. Where was he? She'd driven to Duluth to meet him. He'd said he would be there for her.

Texting over and over again. No response. *I'm here, Mattie. Where are you?*

Then the blackness had descended. And now the terror. Not knowing where she was or how she'd gotten to this place or why she'd been imprisoned. It was an empty road between there and here.

Outside, she heard the scratch of footsteps on dirt. The cardinal, alarmed, stopped singing. Her first thought was of rescue, but she knew that no one was coming to release her. She listened, hearing the footsteps pause. There was a stretch of silence and then the metallic rattle of a lock being undone.

The hinges of a door squealed. Light stabbed the blindfold but only for a moment as the door was closed again. She felt herself shivering. He was inside with her, coming closer. She thought she heard breathing, but her own breathing reverberated inside her head, like the panting of a trapped animal. She couldn't run. She couldn't cry for help.

He was near her. Inches away.

Fingers touched her hair, almost seductively, and she jumped. The gag loosened, but it still filled her mouth. Something cold and sharp pricked her neck, deep enough to make her gasp at the sting. The breathing came back, right beside her, warm and measured in her ear.

A disembodied voice filled her head.

"If you scream, I'll cut your throat."

39

"She's never been in my bar," Fred Sissel told Serena.

The bar owner folded up the faxed photograph of the dead woman in Amsterdam and slid it back to her with one finger, as if the paper carried a communicable disease. He took a towel from his sleeve and ran it over the varnished counter. It was midafternoon on Wednesday. The place was mostly empty.

"You sound pretty sure," Serena said. "It's not a great photograph. I don't think I could answer one way or another."

"Then why show it to me?" Sissel asked.

"Sometimes we get lucky. We got this photo two days ago, and we're canvassing the area to see if anyone remembers her."

"Well, I don't."

Sissel tweaked his mustache and smoothed his slicked-back, graying hair. He didn't hide the fact that he wanted Serena to leave. The murder of Kelly Hauswirth had brought a lot of cops and news cameras to his bar. His customers didn't like it, and they'd voted with their feet.

"What about others?" Serena asked him.

"What do you mean?"

"Other young women who didn't fit in with the crowd here. Women like Kelly Hauswirth."

"It's a bar," Sissel said. "People come and go. I look at the credit cards, not the faces."

"You took a pretty good look at my face," Serena pointed out.

Sissel's mouth flickered into a smile. "Well, you've got a face worth looking at."

"Come on, Fred. Kelly Hauswirth had a suitcase with her. She stuck out in your crowd like a church lady at a biker rally. All I'm asking is whether you've spotted any other girls who match the same profile."

Sissel tugged on his sleeves. "Sorry."

Serena cast her eyes around at the handful of men at the tables. She leaned across the bar and lowered her voice. "Look, this woman in Amsterdam with her throat cut? The police there think she was a sex slave. Do I need to tell you what that's like? Kelly Hauswirth may have been headed for the same life. You've got foreign sailors in and out of this bar every day. Somebody knows something. I want to know what you've heard. Rumors. Gossip. Whatever."

"I don't hear anything. It's not good for my business. Or my health."

Serena sighed with frustration. She reached into a pocket and pulled out a card. "If your ears start working again, give me a call."

Sissel bent the card between two fingers and flicked it to the floor. Laughter rippled around them. "Whatever," he said.

Serena stalked out of the bar. Throaty catcalls followed her to the street. She emerged into the afternoon sunlight and shut the door sharply behind her. It was hot under a blue sky. She slid sunglasses over her face and walked diagonally across the street to the road that led down to Irving Park. Power lines streaked over her head.

She saw the park's wall of trees. Tucked inside them, invisible, were the muddy steps to the creek. She remembered the chase, but she wished she remembered more. His face. His smell. Anything about him. She only knew that he was ruthless. He'd killed without hesitation, and he could kill again.

Serena understood the plight of lost girls. Like Kelly. Like Cat. She'd been lost herself as a teenager, and she knew all about predators. The drug dealer who'd used her as his whore was long gone, but he lingered in her life in ways she couldn't escape. She was still closed off from people. She didn't trust easily. She'd tried for years to get past things she couldn't get past, before realizing they were now simply part of who she was.

Jonny lived the same way, for different reasons. He was wary of the future, wary of believing that anything would last. His affair with Maggie had shaken her, but there was a certain inevitability about it. Maggie was in love with him. Sooner or later, that attraction was bound to blossom into something when Jonny was vulnerable. Serena blamed herself a little for not preventing it. She'd tunneled inside herself when he needed her. She couldn't pry him out of his own shell, because she'd been locked in hers.

But not anymore. She'd come a long way in six months alone. She'd made peace with a lot of things about who she was and who Jonny was. There was really just one ghost left between them.

Her name was Cindy.

"You're the cop, aren't you?" said a voice behind her.

When Serena turned around, she saw the waitress from the bar who was a friend of Cat. "I am," she replied. "It's Anna, isn't it?"

The girl nodded. "Anna Glick."

Anna was older than Cat. Maybe twenty or twenty-one. She was anorectically skinny, all bones. Her makeup was goth, and the look was supplemented by studs in her nose, eyebrows, and lips. Spiky orange hair jutted out from under a wool cap. Serena could see in the girl's eyes the smart, cynical expression of someone who knew how to read people and calculate the odds of getting what she wanted from them.

"So, how's Cat doing?" Anna asked.

"Fine."

"She lives with you, huh?"

"Yes, she does." Serena added, "Cat says you helped her out when she was on her own. Found her places to stay."

"I did what I could. Not just for her."

"I'm grateful. I'm glad someone had her back in those days. But Cat doesn't need that kind of help anymore."

Anna's lips bent into a smirk. "In other words, stay away from her?"

"It's not about you. I just think it's better if Cat cuts the cord with her past entirely. I hope you understand."

"Yeah, I hear you. Whatever you say. Just so you know, Cat came to see me, not the other way around. And just so you know something else, I have a house and, like, four jobs. Waitressing. Data entry. Medical coding. I'm not going back to who I was."

"Sorry, I didn't mean anything personal."

Anna shrugged. She had a chip firmly lodged on her shoulder. "You over here talking to Fred?"

"That's right. How long have you worked at the bar?"

"About a year."

Serena removed the photograph from her pocket of the dead woman in Amsterdam. She showed it to Anna, who didn't flinch. The girl had a tough shell.

"Do you remember seeing this woman around here?" Serena asked.

"What did Fred say?"

"Does Fred's memory affect yours?"

"He doesn't like us talking about what happens in the bar. Especially to cops."

"Well, Fred's inside, and you're out here with me," Serena said.

Anna examined the picture again. "I don't think so, but I'm only here three days a week. Welcome to the part-time economy. If she was here, it was when I wasn't working."

"What about the girl who was killed outside the bar? Kelly Hauswirth. You served her that day, right?"

"Yeah, vodka and lemonade. She didn't touch a drop. I already talked to you people. I carded her when she got to the bar, but I didn't remember her name or where she was from. All I look at is the birth date."

"How long was she there?"

"Couple hours."

"Did you talk to her?"

"Sure. We were BFFs. 'What can I bring you?' 'Vodka and lemonade.' 'You still okay on that drink?' 'Fine, thanks.'"

Anna had a supple voice. Harsh and gravelly when she was being herself, as if she could scare off the world. Sweet and convincing when she channeled Kelly Hauswirth. When you lived on the street, you learned to be whoever your next meal ticket needed you to be.

"Did Kelly say who she was meeting?"

"No."

"Anybody hit on her?" Serena asked.

"You saw what she looked like. Lots of guys hit on her. She shot them all down."

"Are there guys in the bar who don't take no for an answer?"

"Sure, we've got plenty of those. I ran interference with anyone who was getting too fresh. The boys don't mess with me. If I tell them to back off, that's what they do."

"So you had to help Kelly with some of them?"

Anna tugged her wool cap lower on her forehead. "I told some of the drunker ones to leave her alone. It was no big deal."

"Have you seen others like her in the bar? Girls waiting for somebody? Maybe a girl from out of town, with a suitcase?"

"No, but like I said, I'm a part-timer."

Serena nodded. She didn't think Anna was sharing everything she knew, but talking to cops was an occupational hazard for the girl. "Tell me something, Anna. Does Cat have a boyfriend?"

"You should ask her about that," Anna replied. "Not me."

"She says no."

The girl shrugged. "Then I guess she doesn't."

"If Cat shows up here again, I'd appreciate it if you give me a call."

"So you can come drag her out?"

"Exactly."

"You're a real mother superior," Anna said.

"No, but I've been in Cat's shoes," Serena told her. "And yours."

40

Janine Snow waited for her visitor.

To her surprise, she found that she looked forward to visits from Howard Marlowe. He came twice a month during the summers, less frequently during the school year. He told her about his research, his book, his determination to find evidence to set her free. When he ran out of things to say about Jay's murder, which wasn't often, he talked about his life, his dreams, his students, his daughter, and his wife.

In the early years, she'd thought of Howard's visits as a slim thread connecting her to the real world. Then she realized that the real world was here inside the walls of the prison at Shakopee. Howard was a resident of a fantasy world. A world that didn't exist anymore. A world in which she was free.

She was the same woman she'd been in Duluth, and yet she was completely different. Age showed on her face more, because she couldn't hide it now. Gray had painted over much of her blond hair. Her skin was natural, which meant the wrinkles near her eyes and mouth were there for everyone to see. She was still fit and trim, because she exercised regularly, but she fought with the weight of carb-heavy prison meals. Her nails were nothing more than the slimmest of crescent moons. She read voraciously. One of the benefits of Shakopee was an excellent library. She read history. Mysteries. Philosophy. Science. She'd never had much time to read in the past, and now she had nothing but time. Her old life had revolved around medicine and sex, and suddenly she had to make peace with a world where neither of those things played any role in her life. She kept up on medical journals for a year and then decided she never wanted to see them again. Even her sex drive waned.

Relationships with other inmates didn't come easily to her. She was a woman who'd only been comfortable around men—people she could control, people she could manipulate—and now she lived in a community of women. She'd kept herself aloof at first. She couldn't hide that she considered herself superior to the others, and they knew it. She didn't like them. They didn't like her. Even so, time passed, and time could smooth mountains. She joined the prison book club, and she found that the perspectives of other inmates were often deeper and more complex than her own. They defied her caricatures of who they were. When she finally opened her own mouth, she tried to show them that she was more than the bitch they thought she was.

A few became something close to friends. Some came and went after serving time for lesser offenses. Others stayed. Like her.

No one wrote. No one visited. Except Howard.

She found it strange that he was the only person, after all this time, who still doubted her guilt. Who still believed in her. He was the juror who'd put her in here. And yet he kept coming, more determined than ever, more in love with her than ever. She could have sent him away, but the loneliness would have driven her crazy. She looked forward to seeing him. She even had a degree of fondness for him. The humane thing would have been to insist that he not waste his life on a foolish quest, but eight years hadn't changed everything about her. She was still selfish.

"Janine," Howard said.

She'd been far away, and he was standing above her. She smiled at him, got up, and shook his hand. His skin was clammy, as it usually was. She had the feeling that shaking her hand was the most erotic experience in this man's life.

"How are you?" he asked as they sat down.

"Much the same."

"It's hot out. But nice."

"Good."

"You look great," he said.

"Oh, well. Thanks."

It was the usual small talk, followed by the usual silence. She didn't mind. Years ago, she'd thought that Howard Marlowe was the most boring person on the planet. She still thought so, but boring didn't seem entirely bad anymore. After a while, you looked forward to the predictable things. It was summer, so Howard wore his summer clothes, a collared, short-sleeve shirt, black jeans, white tennis shoes. He'd had his curly brown hair cut before coming to see her, as he usually did. Five years ago, after consulting with her, he'd had LASIK surgery done, and he didn't need glasses now. He had a suburban paunch that he tried to suck in when he was with her.

She knew he fantasized about her. He'd admitted it. She found it a little pathetic, but every now and then, she would make some coquettish gesture that she knew he'd remember. A meaningful look in her eyes or a tiny puckering of her lips. Or she would tug at her denim shirt in a way that emphasized the swell of her breasts. Harmless, but she felt she owed him something.

"The book's going well," he said.

"Good."

"You don't mind my doing it, do you?"

"Of course not."

"I run chapters by Mr. Gale. Should I run them by you, too?"

"No, you don't have to do that."

"I understand."

"It's not that I don't appreciate it, Howard. It's just that I don't want to relive it."

"Oh, I get it."

"That doesn't mean I'm telling you to stop."

"No, I'll keep going," he assured her. "When I publish it, it will bring lots of new attention to your case."

Janine smiled at him. She held out no hope that Howard would ever finish his book, or if he did, that he would ever publish it.

"I wanted to tell you," Howard said. "Carol knows about us."

"What?"

"She knows I come down here to visit you."

"Oh."

"I don't know how she found out."

"Oh," Janine said again. She didn't know what else to say.

"She wants me to stop, but I'll keep coming, I promise. Don't worry about that."

Janine found herself indescribably sad. Sad about everything. Sad that she was ruining this man's life and marriage. Sad at even the possibility that he might stop visiting and leave her completely alone. Sad that she was here.

"Look, Howard," she said, watching him hang on her words. "I want you to think about this. Maybe you shouldn't come here anymore."

"What? No. No way."

"You're hurting your wife."

"I don't . . ." he began, and she realized that he was about to say: *I don't care.* He stopped without going on, but she knew it was true. She'd become his Mona Lisa. She was everything to him, beginning and end.

This was wrong. She had to put a stop to it.

"Really, Howard," she said in a sterner voice. "Go home to Carol. Forget about me."

He shook his head fiercely. "I won't do that."

"This isn't fair to you or to your wife. It means a lot to me that you visit, but I've let this go on way too long."

"Janine—"

"No, I mean it. You have to stop."

"I can't," he insisted. "I'm not going to give up. I won't quit until I find something. I won't stop until you're free." He paused and added breathlessly, "Until we're together."

Janine tried to keep the horror from her face. That was the fantasy behind all of this. He would get her out of prison. He would rescue her. And they would live happily ever after, just the two of them. She had to kill that dream right now.

"I'm never getting out of here," she said finally.

"Don't talk like that! Don't give up. I promise, I'll find proof that you're innocent."

"Howard," she said sharply, in a voice that was barely a breath. "Don't you understand? I'm not innocent. I'm guilty."

Stride didn't look up as Maggie came into his office on Friday night. It was late and already dark. The woodland outside the building was invisible. The Duluth Police Department had moved in the spring to a new location in the open land north of the city. He missed City Hall but not the building's rats. It had been several months, but moving boxes still littered his office floor. He never found time to unpack, which was an excuse for the fact that he didn't like to deal with change.

Maggie didn't say anything to him as she sat down.

"Troy got back to me with crew lists for the boats that were in port when Kelly Hauswirth was killed," Stride said. "I'm working with the FBI and with Interpol to cross-reference for criminal records. It's a long list, but it's a place to start."

Maggie was still quiet, but he didn't notice her silence.

"Speaking of Troy," he went on. "I haven't teased you about him, have I? I think he's got a thing for you. He was giving you the eye when we saw him."

He waited for the usual sarcastic reply, and when he didn't get it, he wondered if he had crossed a line with her. Their own breakup, and his reunion with Serena, were still too fresh.

He looked up and said, "Mags?"

Her golden face was a ball of confusion. Her bangs were in her eyes, but she didn't blow them away.

"What's up?" he asked.

"I got the ballistics report from the BCA on the murder weapon. The one that Serena found. The one that killed Kelly Hauswirth."

"Okay."

"They got two hits."

"Really? Excellent."

Maggie was quiet again. Then she said, "The gun matches a bullet fired during a smash-and-grab robbery at a Chicago jewelry store more than eight years ago where a security guard was wounded. This was right before Christmas."

"Interesting. What was the other hit?"

His partner shook her head. "It doesn't make any sense. I don't understand it."

"Understand what?" Stride asked.

"I asked the BCA if they could run the test again. They said it was a lock. No question about it."

"Mags," he repeated. "What the hell are you saying?"

"The gun that Serena recovered in the Kelly Hauswirth case," Maggie said. "That's the gun that killed Jay Ferris."

41

Serena knew that Jonny was awake. Their bedroom was dark, and they both lay atop the blankets. It was a warm night. The windows were open. She heard the trill of crickets in the bushes outside.

He'd told her about the case. Janine Snow. Jay Ferris. The investigation and trial. They'd talked about old cases before, but not that one. Typically, he only told her about cases that were unsolved, but the murder of Jay Ferris had been open-and-shut from the beginning. He'd never doubted what happened. There was only one loose end from the entire investigation—the missing gun—but even that detail hadn't stopped a jury from convicting Janine Snow.

Except now the gun had been found. Serena had found it.

She slid her hand across the bed and laced his fingers with hers. "Question," she murmured.

"Okay."

"You said there were two hits on the gun. How come the ballistics database didn't pick this up years ago during the original investigation?"

Jonny pushed himself up in bed. He reached over and switched on his nightstand lamp. A moth tapped against the glass. There were shadows on Jonny's face and in his eyes.

"It's the usual backlog bureaucracy. The bullet from the Chicago shooting didn't get logged for years, and when it did, they didn't do a cross-region search. Just Illinois. Somebody didn't want to bother sifting through false hits."

"Chicago," Serena said. "What's the connection?"

"There is no obvious connection that I can see. A jewelry store near Calumet Park on the south side of Chicago was robbed at gunpoint on December 20 almost nine years ago. That was just over a month before Jay Ferris was killed. A security guard tried to intervene and took a bullet in the thigh. The guard ID'd the perp from mug shots, and Chicago police found him a week later living with his aunt not far from Wrigley Field. He was wearing a Rolex watch he'd grabbed at the store. Real smart."

"But no gun."

"No gun. They didn't need it to make a case. They had the guard's ID and jewelry from the store. The shooter took a plea. In his statement, he said he'd sold the gun for cash the day after he hit the store. He didn't know the buyer and couldn't describe him. It was just one more gun on the Chicago streets. No one tried to track it down."

"And yet a month later that same gun was here in Duluth being used to shoot Jay Ferris," Serena said.

"Exactly."

"Can you find the Chicago perp to get more details on the sale?"

"He's off the grid," Jonny replied. "He did three years, got out, and never even bothered with a single parole meeting. There's an outstanding warrant, but the police don't think he's anywhere near Chicago."

Their bedroom door was closed, but they heard movement in the living room. Cat was up. She was a restless sleeper, and they often found her awake in the middle of the night. She'd suffered from nightmares for most of her life. When she couldn't sleep, she turned on the television or ate cold pizza from the refrigerator or sat in silence on the back porch. Hearing her footsteps, Jonny looked at the door, wanting to check on her.

Serena got out of bed. She opened the bedroom door a crack, saw Cat sprawled on the living room floor in front of the television, and closed the door again. She draped herself across the end of the bed at Jonny's feet.

"So, what happens next?" she asked.

His face showed his frustration. "The gun has torpedoed the entire case against Janine. Archie's filing an emergency motion for her release. The county attorney thinks he may get it. If the gun didn't have a history, it probably wouldn't be enough to convince a judge, but the fact that it was used in a violent crime prior to Jay's death—and now in another murder years later—changes everything."

"I hate to admit it, but I agree with Archie," Serena said. "It looks like Janine never had that gun at all."

Jonny shook his head. He was stubborn. "Not necessarily. The buyer in Chicago was a man, but street guns change hands all the time. Janine probably bought the gun later. Or Jay bought it for himself, and then Janine used it."

"And then what? You don't murder your husband and sell the gun on the street. You get rid of it."

"She may have tried to get rid of it, but somebody else found it."

"Or somebody else shot Jay," Serena told him. "You may not like it, but that's a real possibility."

He was quiet. Then he said, "I'm going down to Shakopee. I want to talk to Janine."

"She won't tell you anything. The gun is her ticket out. She's not going to jeopardize that."

"I know, but even if she won't talk, I want to see her face when I ask her about it. Believe me, I know Cindy. I'll know if she's hiding something."

Serena gave him a sad smile. "Cindy?"

He closed his eyes, realizing what he'd said. "Sorry. Janine. Freudian slip."

She knew that the discovery of the gun had awakened ghosts for him. The murder of Jay Ferris, and the conviction of Janine Snow, didn't exist in a vacuum. She could do the math. Jay Ferris had been killed in January. One January later, Jonny lost his wife. In between were some of the hardest days of their lives.

"This must bring back some tough memories," she said.

"Sure," he admitted.

"Want to tell me about it?"

She waited to see if he would keep talking. Or if he would shut down the way he usually did.

"You know the timing," he said. "It was a bad year."

"I know."

He hesitated, and then he plunged ahead.

"There was a shadow about Cindy in those days. She was so up and down. I thought she was angry because she thought Janine was innocent and I was trying to put her in prison. But it wasn't just that. She was holding out on me. I was focused on the case, and all the while . . ."

Serena said nothing, but she knew. All the while, Cindy was dying. She looked in his eyes for tears but didn't see any.

"I told you about Ross Klayman, didn't I?" he went on, staring at the ceiling of their bedroom. "The shootings at Miller Hill Mall?"

"Yes," she murmured, wondering where he was going with this story. "Awful thing."

"Cindy was there. The wrong place at the right time. She saved a girl's life and probably others, tackling Klayman the way she did. And you know what? I was angry with her. I was glad that girl was alive, but I was furious. I felt like she had put our lives in jeopardy by risking her own. It was stupid of me. Selfish."

"Hardly," Serena said softly, holding back tears herself.

"I've thought about that day a lot ever since."

"Of course."

"I think Cindy knew what was happening to her. That's why she did it. That's why she took the risk in the mall. Steve Garske told me later that there would have been symptoms. Warning signs. And she did nothing. She let months go by, until it was too late."

"Don't lay that burden on her, Jonny," Serena said. "It wasn't her fault. It wasn't yours. It wasn't anyone's fault."

He didn't reply.

She realized that she'd missed something important all these years. This wasn't just about grief and loss for him. It was about anger, too. He was mad at Cindy for dying. For leaving him alone.

It was strange. For the first time, she saw Cindy not through Jonny's eyes but through her own. She'd put Cindy on a pedestal for years, but that wasn't fair to either of them. Cindy was a woman, like her. Strong and afraid. Full of goodness and mistakes. If Cindy were alive now, Serena wouldn't be in this bed. But Cindy was gone.

Life followed its own twisting path.

"Nine years is a long time for a gun to stay out of circulation," she said.

"Janine knows where it's been," Jonny insisted.

"Does she? Or do you not want to accept the possibility that you were wrong about her?"

"I'm not wrong."

Serena spoke softly. "If this is really about you and Cindy—"

"It's not," he snapped. "I know you think losing Cindy is clouding my judgment, but it's not. I didn't make a mistake back then. I've been wrong about plenty of things in my life, but not about Janine Snow."

42

A poster of Guy Fieri stared down at Maggie from the wall of the Duluth Grill. The punk-haired host from the Food Network had pro-filed the restaurant on *Diners, Drive-ins and Dives*, and since then, tourists had swarmed the place, grabbing most of the tables. Even so, the Grill was still a hangout for the Duluth police, and the servers all knew Maggie. They always found her a booth near the window.

She dug her fork into a cinnamon roll that was twice the size of her fist. To wash down the sweetness, she took a slug of coffee from an artsy Duluth Grill mug. With her mouth full, she checked her watch.

Nathan Skinner was late.

She wolfed down the pastry while she read the *News Tribune*. When her plate was empty, Nathan still hadn't arrived, and she began to get impatient. She moved on to her third coffee refill. Her bacon and eggs replaced the cinnamon roll, and she nibbled at the bacon while she devoured the paper's editorial page.

Finally, she heard a familiar laugh near the front door.

After all these years, Nathan was still a star to Duluthians who were old enough to remember his championship season. He couldn't walk through a restaurant without being grilled about decades-old college hockey games. She wondered if it annoyed him or if he relished reliv-ing his glory days on the ice.

Nathan slid into the booth, across from her, wearing his old, familiar, masculine grin. "Maggie," he said.

"Hello, Nathan."

"Long time."

He hadn't changed much physically. He was shaving his head, and Maggie guessed it was because he was losing his blond hair. His punched-down face looked baby-smooth, enough to make her wonder if he'd had a nip and tuck. His blue eyes still twinkled magnetically, and he had kept himself in shape. His career prospects had obviously improved, because he was dressed better than in the old days, in form-fitting khakis and a yellow silk shirt. He looked like a Republican heading for the golf course, not a washed-up security guard.

"What have you been up to?" Maggie asked.

"I run a business now."

"Yeah? What kind of business?"

"It's sort of like a corporate dating service. I help entrepreneurs in the northland find venture capitalists who have money."

"Interesting career change," Maggie said. "How'd you get into that?"

"A college buddy helped me out. Said he didn't want to see God-given talent like mine go to waste. I'd like to say it's all about spread-sheets and ROI, but really, my end is mostly about cigars, luxury boxes, and hookups. I know how to schmooze people. I talk the talk."

Nathan grinned again, and Maggie didn't doubt that he'd found his niche. He was still in a fraternity, selling to other frat boys.

"Nice to see you doing well," she said without enthusiasm.

"Probably not as well as you are. Your husband left you a pile of money after he got shot, didn't he? Condo over the Sheraton next to all those hospital docs? Pretty nice for a cop."

"You're well informed," Maggie said, but she wasn't surprised. Two winters ago, her husband, Eric, had been murdered. It was the biggest news story in the city. She'd been the prime suspect. And when she was cleared, she'd sold Eric's sporting-goods business and banked several million dollars.

"Well, that's part of my job. I keep track of where the money goes in town. Eric was on my radar, so now you are, too. If you're looking for investments, you should call me. I can get you in on the ground level of some exciting projects."

Nathan was smooth. He'd left the rivalry between them far behind. At least on the outside.

"I'll keep that in mind," Maggie said.

"I'm sorry about you and Stride, by the way. You guys flamed out, huh?" She couldn't hide her annoyance, and he said, "Cops talk, Maggie. You know that."

She did know that, but she hated being the subject of office gossip. She felt her face grow hot.

"Hey, I wasn't trying to poke the bear," he went on. "Seriously. I'm sure it was tough on you."

"What, do you watch *Dr. Phil* now, Nathan?"

He laughed. "I wouldn't go that far, but I've spent enough time on the downside of life to know it sucks."

"Fine, it sucks," Maggie said. "Move on. You're not my therapist."

"Are you still holding a grudge against me? Come on, we're both too old for that now. People really do like me, Maggie. I know that may be hard for you to believe. Actually, you might like me, too, if you gave me a chance. I've changed."

"What's the old saying about leopards?" she asked.

He grinned and shook his head. "No, really. I'll be the first to admit, I was a pig in my misspent youth. Racist. Sexist. You name it. I was angry at the world and blamed everybody but myself. But time mellows people. Even me."

"Well, let's light up some weed and sing Arlo Guthrie songs, Nathan. Since we're being so mellow."

"Come on. You think I could do business with the attitudes I had back then? It doesn't work that way. The economy is diverse. The world is diverse. So am I. My wife's Hispanic. I met her on a trip to Guatemala. I even speak respectable Spanish these days. So if you want the old Nathan Skinner? *No más.*"

Maggie wondered whether to believe him. In her own experience, people didn't change. They just became more of who they really were, for better or worse. She knew that was true of herself, too.

"Actually, I do need the old Nathan Skinner for a few minutes," Maggie told him. "The guy who spouted racial obscenities at Wisconsin cops and cheated with Janine Snow. That guy."

Nathan leaned across the table with a serious expression on his face. She had to admit that she still felt the old, unwanted attraction to him. He knew how to turn on the physical charm. There was also more calm and restraint about him than he'd shown in the old days. She couldn't push his buttons so easily now.

"I heard about you guys finding the gun in the Jay Ferris case," he told her. "I know what you want to ask me, but the gun's not mine. It never was."

"So where do you think it came from? And where has it been all these years?"

Nathan eased back into the booth. He swiped a piece of bacon from Maggie's plate, which annoyed her, because she loved the bacon at the Grill. "Honestly? I have no idea."

"This was a street gun," Maggie said. "Not a suburban Gander Mountain special."

"Do you think Jay had gang connections you never heard about?"

"Not according to his brother, Clyde. And we never got a whiff of that during the original investigation."

"Well, street guns don't usually show up in a domestic murder case," Nathan said. "More in gangs and armed robberies. Or maybe murder-for-hire. Wasn't there some old lady who thought Janine killed her husband on the operating table? Did she pay some money to have Jay whacked?"

Maggie nodded. "Esther Rose. She passed away last year. It wasn't her. We checked her finances nine years ago, and there was no evidence that she paid anyone to get rid of Jay."

"Then I don't know what to tell you," Nathan said. "The gun disappears for years and then shows up at another murder scene? I don't get it."

"There's something I need to ask you about. Just between us. Did Janine Snow really want to know how she could get a handgun off the books?"

"That was my testimony in court," he replied cautiously.

"I know. Was it true?"

"Even if it weren't, do you think I'd admit perjuring myself? Sorry."

"I'm not trying to bust you. I just want to know if Janine could have figured out a way to buy that gun."

"You're talking about a Texas girl, Maggie. They're half animal under those pretty faces. If Janine wanted a gun, she wouldn't be shy about asking around. That woman knew how to get what she wanted. So, yeah, the gun could have been hers, but I don't think it was."

"Why not?"

"Because there's one thing about Jay's murder that always bothered me. And it has nothing to do with the gun."

"What's that?" Maggie asked.

Nathan shook his head. "I didn't have any trouble believing that Janine was the one who shot Jay. Frankly, I didn't blame her for it. The man treated her like shit. But Janine's a smart woman. Scary-smart. There's no way—no way—she would have let you guys pin it on her. Losing control? Shooting Jay in the head and coming up with a lame story that nobody believes? Sorry. That's not Janine Snow. She would have had a plan for the whole thing, and she wouldn't be sitting in prison right now. As much as I hate to admit it, she may have been telling the truth all along. The gun wasn't hers."

"Hello, Cat," Anna Glick said. "You shouldn't be here, you know."

Anna sat on a plastic chair on the weedy front lawn of her house in Morgan Park. It was a two-story house barely wider than an old Chevy, with a sharply peaked roof and brown stucco walls. Ivy vines draped over the wall facing the street.

"You haven't called me back," Cat complained. "You haven't answered any of my texts."

Anna had a Chromebook on her lap, and she wore shorts and a skimpy tank top that showed off her pale, bony limbs. "Uh, maybe because the cops you live with told me I should stay away from you?"

"My friends are my own business," Cat insisted stubbornly.

"Maybe, but I don't need trouble."

"Hey, I won't tell them. They don't need to know who I see. Come on, I'm bored. I just want to hang for a while."

"Okay, fine, stick around if you like," Anna agreed with a sigh. "How'd you get here, anyway?"

"Bus."

"Is that smart?" she asked, eyeing Cat's baby bump.

"We're only three blocks from the stop. It's not like I'm handicapped or something."

Anna shrugged. She nodded at a second patio chair leaning against the house, and Cat went and grabbed it. The day was hot. Both of them wiped sweat from their foreheads. Anna had a can of Bud on the lawn beside her, and Cat ducked into the small house to pour orange juice from the carton in the fridge. Outside, she sat next to Anna and sipped the drink in silence. Anna tapped away on her keyboard, playing a fantasy game. Cat didn't interrupt her.

"So, where's Al?" Anna asked without looking up from her computer game.

"I don't know. Working, probably."

"Are you guys still an item?"

"I guess," Cat said.

Anna's eyes flicked away from the Chromebook. "You guess?"

"I haven't talked to him. He's busy." Then she added, "I did something stupid. I asked if he was in love with me. It freaked him out. We haven't talked since."

"Guys don't want serious. They want right now."

"Al is different. We're not even having sex. We're waiting until it feels right."

Anna's fingers hovered over the keyboard, and then she kept typing. A smirk flew across her lips. "You think he's going to get hornier as that basketball of yours gets bigger? I don't think so. Most guys are afraid the baby will reach out and grab their dick while they're pumping."

Cat frowned as Anna giggled at her own joke. Then she asked, "So how's Fred over at the bar?"

"Fred is Fred. He's pissed about the cops and reporters hanging around. Are they any closer to finding the guy who did it?"

"Stride and Serena don't tell me anything about that," Cat replied.
"They're cops. No surprise."

"I miss the bar."

"Well, Fred won't let you back in. Sorry."

Cat knew that Anna was right, and she wasn't happy. She chafed under the restrictions on everything she did. It was summer. No school. She was free, but she felt as if she'd been locked in prison.

"I'm low on cash," Cat admitted.

"Seriously? Again?"

"Yeah."

"Don't the cops give you an allowance?"

"It's not much," Cat said. "I don't think they trust me with money. They figure I'll buy cigarettes. Or drugs."

"Uh-huh." Anna took off her wool cap and primped her spiky hair. "Well, there's a church project this weekend if you want. Cleaning out a house in West Duluth. You might pick up a couple bucks that way."

Cat hesitated. "I don't like doing that stuff."

"Hey, the last job worked out okay, huh? Painting that place in Superior? Plus, that's where you met Al. You complaining about that?"

"No."

"Well, it's your call," Anna said. "Do whatever you want."

"I'll think about it."

Anna flipped down the cover of her Chromebook. "I don't have to be at work for a couple hours. You want to go get a burger and a Coke somewhere? I'm buying."

Cat grinned. "Great!"

"Where do you want to go?"

"How about the Anchor?"

Anna shook her head. "You just want to run into Al."

"I miss him."

"Cat, he's a guy. Guys like him come and go like beer cans. Especially when you start throwing the l-word around with someone who hasn't even poled you yet."

"I told you, we're waiting—" she began, but Anna waved a hand in front of her face to stop her.

"Listen, I didn't want to tell you this, okay? I knew you'd get upset."

"Tell me what?"

Anna fixed a drooping strap on her tank top. "Couple weeks ago, Al was over at the Grizzly Bear talking to Fred. I think he was looking to pick up some part-time work. Anyway, my car had a flat, so Al drove me home. It was late, and he came inside with me, and we had a few drinks and put on some flicks. Next thing I know, his tongue was down my throat, and his hands were inside my T-shirt."

Cat shot to her feet. "Al made a pass at you? Al?"

"Sorry, kiddo," Anna told her, "but, yeah, he did. Like I said, we were both pretty drunk. He's probably been nursing a major hard-on, wanting to get into your pants. The thing is, I won't lie to you, Cat. As passes go, this wasn't exactly a dropped ball in the end zone."

"What are you saying?" Cat asked, but she already knew.

"I'm saying it was a completed pass. Al spent the night with me."

43

When Janine entered the visiting room, Stride noticed the physical changes of eight years, the same way he did when he looked at himself in the mirror. They were both older. She wore no makeup. No jewelry. Like every other inmate, she was dressed down. In the past, watching Janine walk was like following a celebrity who could part a crowd with her presence. She had an otherness that set her apart from ordinary people. Now she was one of many.

"Hello, Jonathan," she said as she sat down across from him.

"Hello, Janine."

He could see her taking his measure, the way he'd done to her. She was probably thinking similar things. He was older. Bruised and not as cocky. They sat in silence for a while, and others in the waiting room stole glances at them. Everybody knew who they were. There were no secrets here.

"I can't tell you how sorry I was to hear about Cindy," Janine said finally.

"Thank you."

"She was probably my only real friend. Not that I'm comparing my loss to yours. I know what a love match the two of you were. My heart ached for you when I heard. Really. I wrote to you, but

I didn't expect a reply. I just wanted you to know that my grief was sincere."

"I got your letter," Stride told her.

"Good."

More awkward silence followed. Once upon a time, they'd been something like friends. Now he didn't know what they were.

"Are you involved with someone?" she asked him.

He didn't answer, and she sighed and looked away.

"So I'm still the enemy, am I?" she went on. "I thought after all this time things might be different. Well, it may not matter coming from me, but I know Cindy would want you to be in love. I envied the two of you. How you could be different and yet the same. Obviously, I never mastered the art of relationships."

He was silent again, and then he said, "I'm involved."

"I'm glad. Is it serious?"

"Yes."

"Even better," she said. Her glance traveled around the room. "I suppose it doesn't happen very often, coming to see people you put in prison."

"No, not very often."

"Of course not. Why would you? I don't get many visitors."

"What about Howard Marlowe?" Stride asked.

Janine's eyebrows rose in surprise. "You know about him? Well, of course you do. I forgot I have no privacy here."

"Howard has built quite a hobby out of you," Stride told her. "He got copies of most of our investigative records through Archie. He calls us all the time. He wants us to investigate new leads. I gather he's writing a book."

"Yes, he is."

"He visits you here, too."

"He does. Is it strange, a man like that who can't let go?"

"It happens," Stride said. "People get obsessed."

"On one level, I'm grateful. For the company. For someone who believes in me. On the other hand, I feel as if I'm cheating him out of his life."

"You don't have to see him."

"I know. And yet when I think about taking him off the list, I just can't do it. A part of me can't let go. I'm hoping he'll decide on his own that I'm not worth it."

Stride wondered if she was sincere. The old Janine would always have put herself first.

"I assume Archie has been in touch with you," he told her.

"Yes, of course."

"So you know we've identified the gun that was used to kill Jay," he went on.

"After all these years. It's quite a mystery."

He expected to see a glint of triumph in her face. She knew that this discovery, whatever it meant, opened up new legal doors for her. For the first time, she had a realistic chance at a new trial or even a complete dismissal. The idea of early release from prison was no longer a fantasy. Except he was surprised by what he saw. Anxiety. Even fear. The life inside was the life she now knew. She really had become an indoor cat. Outside was uncertain. Outside was scary. She couldn't simply walk back to her old life, and she knew it.

"I was hoping you might be able to shed some light on that mystery," Stride said.

Janine shook her head. "I'm sorry. You know I can't do that."

Which was the answer he'd expected.

"I suppose Archie reminded you not to tell me anything that might jeopardize your release," he said.

"Yes, he did."

"There's a solution to this puzzle. I'm going to find out what it is."

"I wonder if you will," she replied. "I'm not doubting you, but nine years is a long time."

Stride stared at her eyes, looking for answers. "Can I be honest with you, Janine?"

"I'm sure you will be."

"I think you're guilty. I always have."

"I know that."

"And if you're guilty, that means you must know what happened to the gun that killed Jay and where it's been all these years."

"In other words, where did I hide it?" she asked. "Or whom did I give it to?"

"Exactly."

"Even if I knew, you realize it would be foolish of me to tell you. Legally speaking."

"I know that."

"So why ask me? Why did you come down here?"

He couldn't keep the frustration out of his voice. "Because this is about more than finding an old gun in the woods and running a ballistics test. This gun was used to kill a woman just a few weeks ago. The man who did it is on the loose. The lives of other young women may well be at stake. I have just one clue. His gun. Eight years ago, that gun was in your living room. It's the gun that murdered your husband. If I knew where it went after that, then I stand a chance of figuring out who used it last month."

He hoped he would get through to her. She was already in prison, and he wanted to believe there was enough regret in her heart over what she'd done that she would choose to save someone else's life. He saw her hesitate. He knew—*he knew*—that she had the answers he needed.

Janine leaned across the table and, violating the prison rules, took both of his hands in hers.

"I'm sorry, Jonathan," she told him. "I know what you think of me, but I'm telling you the truth. I was telling you the truth all those years ago. That gun was never in my hands. I'm not the one who shot my husband."

44

Howard had long ago memorized the jewelry that Janine Snow lost when her husband was murdered, but he still reviewed the photographs every time he entered a pawnshop. Six items. All expensive. A black-pearl ring in a white-gold setting. Matching black-pearl earrings and necklace. A bracelet of twisted gold chains interspersed with diamonds and sapphires. A hummingbird pin with a breast of real rubies. An emerald brooch in the shape of the letter J. Each piece was a custom design.

He parked in the ramp garage of the Fond-du-Luth Casino and emerged onto Superior Street. The casino was next to him, belching cigarette smoke when the doors opened. He'd never been inside. He didn't gamble. It was a sweltering afternoon, and he thought about stopping at a bar, but beer fogged his head. He needed to be sharp as he perused the jewelry locked under the glass of the pawnshop counters.

For eight years, he'd visited the same shops again and again. Duluth. Cloquet. Grand Rapids. Hinckley. Even down to the Twin Cities. Dozens of them, from the upscale mall shops buying gold and silver to the alley joints that served up fast cash and payday loans. The owners all knew him, although he'd never told them what he was looking for. Howard was paranoid that if any of the owners knew they were fencing property stolen in a murder case, they'd make those items quietly disappear before he could identify them.

He climbed 2nd Avenue in the heat. He wore a red Kohl's polo shirt, tan khakis, and sneakers with reinforced arches for his flat feet. The shoes were new, and the soles squeaked. Zenith Pawn was at the next corner, garish with neon.

Black-pearl ring in a gold setting.

Hummingbird pin.

Emerald J brooch.

All these years, all these fruitless hours spent hunched over display cases, and he'd never lost faith.

Howard thought about his last visit with Janine and the odd confession she'd made. It shocked him, until he'd realized that she was simply trying to drive him away. He'd been too honest with her about his frustrations with Carol. Janine blamed herself for his dissolving marriage, and maybe she was right. Even so, he refused to let her send him away.

"Say whatever you want," he had told her. "I'm not going anywhere."

Howard opened the glass door of the pawnshop. Inside, the air-conditioning made his damp skin cold. It felt good. Another customer was at the counter, a silver-haired lady dickering with the owner over the price of an old penny. The shop overflowed with inventory. Jewelry. Guns. Video games. Stamps and coins. Leather. Cutlery and knives. Electronics. Some items were new, but most were used, the litter of the Great Recession. Three balls were the universal symbol of boom times gone bust.

"This is a 1933 wheat penny," the old woman insisted. "I looked it up. It's worth twenty dollars. I cleaned it up for you, too. Nice and shiny."

The owner was bald and big and reminded Howard of a pro wrestler like Jesse Ventura. He wore jeans and a black leather jacket. Somewhere inside the jacket, Howard assumed the man carried a badass gun.

"Beverly, sweetie," he replied in an Aussie accent, "it's twenty dollars in uncirculated condition. This penny looks like it's been through a stretchy machine at Fun Land. And cleaning it makes it worth less, not more. I've told you that."

"Twenty dollars," she repeated.

"Sweetie, I can give you two dollars and a cup of decaf, and that's because I'm in a good mood."

The old woman continued to argue. Howard ignored her. He saw the owner shoot him a wink and a grin.

Howard slipped reading glasses onto his face. He bent over the long counter crammed with one-off jewelry items, and the glasses slipped down to the end of his sweaty nose. He tried to stay focused. After a while, the jewelry all looked alike. The same stuff week after week, most of it cheap paste.

He checked the tag on each item. Ring—four hundred dollars. Necklace—seventy-five dollars. Elvis tie tack—"priceless." The owner had a sense of humor. Each piece was nestled in a velvet sleeve, and when Howard had surveyed the entire counter, he moved on to the next one.

Watches. Earrings. Murano-glass charms.

But again—nothing.

It had been nothing all day in the other shops. It had been nothing every month since he began his search years ago.

He'd hoped today would be different because of the gun. The police had finally found the gun that killed Jay Ferris, years after the crime. The same gun had been used in a murder in West Duluth the previous month and in a Chicago robbery shortly before Jay's death. No one could explain it.

Howard didn't know how or why this particular gun had made its way from one crime to the next, but he felt vindicated. He'd been right all along that Jay's own gun had played no part in the shooting. This was something different. This was what you'd expect from a home invasion, just as Janine had insisted. A stranger came to the door. Killed Jay. Stole the jewelry. Disappeared, along with the gun.

Now the gun was back.

Where had it been for eight years? Howard didn't know, but he was willing to bet that wherever the gun had been hidden, the missing jewelry had been hidden there, too. If someone had used the gun recently, then it made sense that the jewelry might show up at the same time. The truth was coming to light.

"Howie!" the owner bellowed at him. The man was known as Caffy, which was short for his last name, Cafferty. "Mate!"

Caffy loomed on the other side of the counter like a brown bear. Wheat Penny Lady was gone, clutching two dollars in one fist and a foam cup of Green Mountain Nantucket Blend Keurig coffee in the other.

"Want an old penny?" the owner asked, flipping it in the air with his thumb and catching it in his giant palm. "Only twenty bucks."

Howard stopped his search and looked up, his mouth falling open.

A grin bent across the owner's face. "Kidding, mate. This penny ain't worth a dime. If you've got a chair that wobbles, stick it under one of the legs."

"So why'd you give her two bucks?" Howard asked.

"Oh, Beverly's all right. Likes a yank on the crank in the casino now and then. Who knows? Maybe she'll take my twofer and win a Cadillac or something."

Howard smiled. He actually liked Caffy. Most of the pawnshop owners he met were too slick by half, but Caffy dealt straight with people. If he didn't have a soft spot, he had a thinner plate of steel than most around his heart. They'd talked over the years. Sports. Chinese history. Irish poets. Caffy was surprisingly well-read and well-traveled, which Howard found fascinating. The man had led the kind of unattached wanderer's life that Howard envied.

Even so, he'd never shown the photographs of Janine's jewelry to Caffy. You could like someone face-to-face and not trust them when your back was turned.

"That watch over there," Caffy boomed. "That would look good on your wrist."

"Who wears watches anymore?" Howard asked.

"Ah, they're coming back. You'll see. Smartwatches, though—that's the new thing."

"No, thanks."

Caffy never took rejection personally. "Sure, whatever. You're in earlier than usual, ain't you? Thought it would be another couple of weeks before you showed up again."

"Yes, I'm early," Howard admitted.

He was at the end of the last counter. He'd looked through hundreds of pieces of jewelry, ranging in price from five to a thousand dollars. He'd found nothing even as interesting as the wheat penny.

"Might help if you gave me a clue what you want," Caffy told him. "After all these years, the I'll-know-it-when-I-see-it game gets old, doesn't it?"

"One needle, lots of haystacks," Howard said.

"Come on, mate, give me a hint. Cheap, expensive?"

"Expensive. Very expensive."

"Oh, well, why didn't you say so?" Caffy told him. "I do have a little private stock this week. Best customers only. Which don't exactly include you, Howie, but you want to see it anyway?"

"I do—thanks, Caffy."

The owner retreated into the back. As he did, he pressed a button that locked the shop door, which told Howard exactly how far trust went between them. He could see the big Aussie disappearing inside an oversize steel vault, and he emerged a moment later with a typewriter-size box. He set it on the glass counter in front of Howard and opened the top, revealing several dazzling felt rows of jewelry that were probably worth more than everything in the storefront counters combined.

"Nice stuff, huh?" Caffy said.

"Very nice."

"Look but don't touch, mate."

"I won't."

Howard bent over, securing his reading glasses on his face. This collection wasn't thirteen-to-a-dozen rings and bracelets. This was beautiful work. Multicarat diamonds. Rubies and emeralds that glowed as if the inside of the stone were on fire. Gold that belonged on the bare neck of a perfect young starlet.

"People really pawn this kind of stuff?" Howard asked. "Why?"

"You're in the museum of lost dreams, Howie."

Lost dreams or hot property, Howard thought. He took his time examining the pieces, because each was beautiful and distinctive, with a story behind it that he wished he knew. Divorce? Inheritance?

Mistress? He wanted to pick the stones up in his hands, but he restrained himself.

Even so, there was nothing and nothing and—

Howard stopped. He stared at the fourth velvet row, where engagement rings nuzzled with bejeweled pinky rings. He stared, stopped, and stared again. His mouth went dry. His heart took off, beat, beat, beat, beat.

There it was. After all these years, there it was.

Black-pearl ring. The setting—two thick white-gold bands intertwined to form a wreath. The stone as dark and ominous as the sea, swallowing all light. One of six pieces of jewelry missing since a winter's night, January 28, almost nine years ago.

Janine's ring.

45

The bartender directed Serena to a dirt lot behind the Grizzly Bear, where she found Fred Sissel. The bar owner sat on a picnic bench with his long legs stretched out and his dress shoes coated with dust. A cigarette perched between his lips, and his tie was slung over his shoulder to avoid ash. He sat uncomfortably close to Anna Glick, who texted on her smartphone. Sissel had his hand on the young woman's thigh, and his face sported the kind of grin that men use when they're being cocky and cool. Anna didn't remove Fred's hand, but the way she held her body didn't offer encouragement.

Serena had done her research on Sissel. He was fifty-three years old. He'd lived his whole life in Duluth. He'd worked in sales and marketing for a small advertising agency until he lost his job in the recession. At that point, he'd scraped together enough savings and debt to buy the bar on Raleigh Street. He had more debt than savings, and the revenues had gotten worse, not better, in the six years he'd owned the bar. He was unmarried. The smile, the slick hair and mustache, the stained ties, were all lines on the business card of the perennial bachelor. His colleagues said he thought of himself as a ladies' man, but that was mostly in his head. He had a paper-thin ego that could be blown away by the mildest breeze.

BRIAN FREEMAN

"You said you had information for me?" Serena called to Sissel. She'd received a text message from the bar owner an hour earlier.

Sissel whispered to Anna, who clambered off the bench. Serena saw the man's hand graze Anna's ass as she wandered away, still engrossed in her phone.

"You can do better," Serena murmured as the girl passed her.

Anna shrugged, as if nothing could be more obvious. "I do."

Serena crossed the lot and sat on the opposite bench. Sissel, still sucking on a cigarette, smoothed his hair and rubbed two greasy fingers together. The smoke on his breath mingled with the scent of beer.

"Some guy came into the bar this afternoon," he told her. "He was asking a lot of questions about that woman who was killed. Kelly Hauswirth."

"Who was he? A sailor?"

"No, he wasn't from the boats."

"What did he look like?"

"He was hard to miss. Blue glasses, turquoise pants, a white button-down shirt. Short, maybe five-six, skinny."

"So what did this guy do?" Serena asked.

"He came in midafternoon when the place was pretty empty. He ordered a beer, and then he asked me if I knew which table this woman Kelly was sitting at before she got shot. It was weird, but, hey, people have their kinks. I told him which table it was, and he took his beer over there and sat down. When I went to take his order, he grilled me with more questions. Did I talk to the woman? How long was she there? Did I see what happened to her? That struck me as more than the average freaky curiosity, so I went out back and sent you a text. By the time I got inside again, the guy was gone. He finished his beer and told Anna to make his burger to go. Paid cash."

Serena frowned. They often found hangers-on at murder scenes, but this one sounded odd. "Did he say where he was going?"

"No, but I talked to one of the guys who came in right after Blue Pants left. He saw him get into a red compact. Headed toward Grassy Point."

Serena stood up. "Thanks for the information, Fred."

"You're welcome. Maybe you'd like to have dinner sometime."

"Maybe I wouldn't," Serena replied.

She left Sissel on the bench and went around the side of the bar to the street. In the distance, the Bong Bridge slashed across the bay to Superior. She put out an alert with the description of the man and the car, and then she drove her Mustang into the industrial area near Grassy Point. This was where the business of Duluth got done. Boats belched iron ore down gravity feed ramps. Trains and trucks came and went. Lumber got stacked like matchsticks, and taconite was piled into black pyramids. The air always smelled of cut wood, and engines thundered like storms that never moved off. White columns of steam rose from the industrial plants and merged into the white clouds.

Where the road turned toward the bay at 50th Street, she got lucky. A hundred yards away, she spotted a red Corolla. There was a splash of blue on the hood, where a man in turquoise pants sat watching the rolling train cars. She parked her Mustang not far away and got out. She let a truck pass, then crossed the road to approach him.

"Afternoon," she called to the man.

He was probably about thirty years old but looked younger. He had a baby face and nervous eyes behind the blue-framed glasses that matched his pants. He looked as if he wanted to jackrabbit across the train tracks toward the water.

"Uh, hi," he said.

Serena let him see her police shield. "Do you mind coming down here for a minute?"

"Uh, okay." He slid off the hood, scattering French fries from a white foam box. "Is there a problem? Am I not supposed to be here?"

"May I see some identification?" Serena asked.

"Sure. I guess."

He dragged a wallet out of his pants and gave her his driver's license. His name was Mort Sanders, and he was from the Twin Cities suburb of Eden Prairie. Mort looked like a geek who'd never outgrown his high school science classes. His short hair was curly and mocha-colored.

"What do you do for a living, Mr. Sanders?" she asked.

"I'm a field service tech for a big gaming company. I test and repair their video slot machines."

"Is that what you're doing in Duluth?"

"Uh, no. I'm just up here doing tourist stuff."

"I understand you were in the Grizzly Bear Bar asking questions about the murder of Kelly Hauswirth," Serena said.

"You know about that?" His voice screeched like a badly played violin. "Holy crap, I knew this was a mistake. I swear, I didn't kill her!"

"I didn't say you did, but I'd like to know why you're so curious about this crime. Did you know Kelly?"

"Sort of. I mean, I never met her, but I knew her. Online. I'm on the road for work a lot, so I'm stuck in hotel rooms. I like to follow the chat rooms. It's a big party in there, you know? Everybody's drunk and hitting on everybody else."

"So you met Kelly in one of these chat rooms?"

"Yeah. She was Dream_on223, and I was . . ."

He stopped.

Serena asked, "What was your handle?"

"Beccababe911."

"You pretended to be a woman?"

."Yeah, but it's no big deal. Most people use fake IDs. They're not dumb enough to put their real identity out there, okay? Kelly wasn't Kelly online. If you talked to her, she said her name was Corinne, and she was from Maryland. And it's not like gender-bending is so odd. The fact is, women will talk to other women. They're on their guard whenever men approach them. So Beccababe can get to know women, which Mort Sanders can't. I've made a lot of great women friends that way."

"By lying to them," Serena said.

"I lie about my outer self but not about my inner self."

Serena rolled her eyes and waited for the noise of a passing train to diminish. "Let's get back to Kelly. Why are you here asking questions about her murder?"

"I was reading a copy of the *Star Tribune*, and I saw an article about this murder victim in Duluth being identified. Kelly Hauswirth from Colorado. I saw the pic, and it was her. It was a shock. I felt really bad. So I just wanted to find out more about what happened to her."

"You said Kelly had a different identity online," Serena reminded him. "How did you know who she was? Did she tell you her real name?"

Mort wet his lips with his tongue. "No."

"So how?"

"It's kind of a hobby of mine."

"What is?" Serena asked.

"I collect people."

"Collect them? What does that mean?"

"You're going to think it's weird," he said.

"Oh, we're way past weird."

"Look, I swear, it is totally innocent. I never do anything to them. I told you, it's just a hobby."

Mort slid a smartphone out of his pocket and punched a button to pull up his photo stream. He held it so Serena could see the screen, and he used his thumb to flick through a series of photographs. They were all unposed shots of ordinary people in ordinary places. A middle-aged woman in a grocery store. A teenager coming out of school. An older man in a suit getting on a bus. And then—Kelly Hauswirth. Serena recognized her. She saw Kelly jogging on a treadmill at a suburban gym.

"Where did you get this photo?" Serena asked.

"I took it."

"How?"

"I told you: I'm a collector. It's what I do. The thing is, when you meet people online, most of them use fake personas, right? Different names. Different hometowns. Sometimes different ages and genders. But most people who create fake IDs also use some elements of the truth. It's easier than making everything up. Maybe they tell you their real job but not the real place they work. Or real stories about friends or family. Or the real car they drive. Get it? For me, the fun is to see whether I can meet a person online with a fake ID and figure out who they really are from the clues they give me. And if I do, when I happen to be in that city on a casino job—well, I track them down. Take a picture for my collection. See?"

"You stalk them," Serena said.

"That's an ugly way to describe it."

"It's the accurate way to describe it."

"No! I told you, it's innocent. I don't have any contact with them. I don't want to be part of their real lives. I just want to know who they are. It's harmless."

Serena felt an urge to go home and take a shower. And never to boot up a computer again. "So you *collected* Kelly Hauswirth."

"Right."

"You figured out that she wasn't Corinne from Maryland. How?"

"She wasn't too tough. Parents are always a good way in. People lie about themselves but not about their parents. We talked about her being estranged from them, and she mentioned that they lived in Montana. Another time, she mentioned their first names. And then another time, she told me what her dad did for a living before he retired. I keep notes on all this stuff. It's like a jigsaw puzzle. She gave me enough to find her parents, and they helped me find her when I called them. Old people like to talk about their kids."

"So when you figured out that Corinne was really Kelly Hauswirth, you went to Colorado and followed her and took her picture."

"Uh, yes. I told you, it's just a game."

"Then you read that she'd been murdered, and you figured you'd come up here and ask around about what happened. Because you felt bad for her?"

"Yes, exactly."

Serena shook her head. "Sorry, Mort. No way. What are you not telling me?"

The man danced back and forth on his feet. "Okay, I was a little scared, too."

"Why?"

"I wanted to make sure that someone wasn't going to come after *me*," he told her.

"Who would do that?" Serena asked.

Mort took off his blue glasses and cleaned them. He repositioned them on his face with both hands. "Kelly told me about this guy she met online. She was really into him. Used the l-word. She told me who he was, the things he said, romantic stuff. I knew it was all bogus."

"How?"

"Because the same guy hit on me, too. His handle was Lakelover. I tried to collect him, but he was way too cautious. Nothing he said about himself checked out. I knew why Kelly fell for him, though. He was cool, a good listener. As much a girlfriend as a boyfriend. He never pushed me for sex, which is pretty rare, but he asked me lots of questions about myself. Something about it felt . . . off. I had a bad feeling about him."

"Did you warn Kelly?"

"I tried, but I sort of let on that I knew who she was. She got totally creeped out, and she blocked me. When I read that she'd been murdered, I thought about this Lakelover guy. I began to think—what if he was able to track me down the way I do with other people? I've been looking over my shoulder ever since."

Lakelover.

That was a good handle for someone in Duluth.

Serena studied the young man next to her and realized he was genuinely scared. He was probably on the razor's edge of violating privacy laws—and he was definitely on the far side of the moral line—but she didn't sense any violent intent from him.

"Here's some free advice," she told Mort. "Take your collection and punch the Delete button. And next time you feel like going into a chat room somewhere, go buy a book. Sooner or later, with what you're doing, something bad is going to happen to you. Let Kelly's experience be a lesson, okay?"

Mort swallowed hard. "Yeah, okay."

But she knew he wouldn't stop.

"Now get out of here before I feel the need to arrest you for something," she said.

"Listen, there's one other thing you should know," Mort went on. "I was in another chat room last month, chatting up another girl. Cute, innocent, a lot like Kelly. She told me about her online boyfriend and how cool he was. His handle was Mattie_1987. The thing is, I know it was the same guy. Different room, different alias, but the personal details were identical."

"Mattie_1987 was Lakelover?" Serena said.

"I'm sure of it. No way two different guys would use the same background, same story, do the same seduction routine. It was him."

Another alias. Another girl.

"Who was she?" Serena asked.

Mort drummed his fingers nervously on his blue pants.

"Come on, don't play innocent with me now," Serena said. "This other girl. Did you collect her?"

He nodded. "Okay, yeah. I did. I never got her picture, but I found out a few details about her. Her name was Erin. She was from Grand Forks."

46

The *Ingersstrom* floated in the black water of Burns Harbor in Indiana.

As a saltie—an oceangoing cargo boat, not the freshwater ships that stayed in the Great Lakes—it was long at six hundred feet. The green-and-red steel of its hull was marred by discolored waterlines and orange swaths of rust. Three thirty-foot cranes towered above the deck like praying mantises. The German-flagged ship had started its Atlantic crossing in Rotterdam and made its way through the Seaway, unloading shipments of steel coils in Canada and New York. In two more days, it would cross Lake Michigan and Lake Superior and pass under the lift bridge into the port of Duluth.

One of the ship's crew leaned against a portable toilet two hundred yards from the *Ingersstrom*. The toilet smelled. So did he. His tight-fitting white T-shirt was thick with grease, and he hadn't showered in three days. It was after dark, and he was largely invisible where he stood, but the port was alive with spotlights and metallic noise and the silhouettes of men who looked like busy ants. His blue-gray eyes moved slowly, studying the movement around him. Every hour in port made him nervous, but there were no surprises tonight.

Nearby, heavy boots scraped on gravel. A man waddled toward him from across the railroad tracks near Boundary Road. The crewman shoved his hands into his jeans pockets and curled the fingers of his left hand around an ice pick. The man approaching him was squat and heavyset, with a beard and greasy black hair. He recognized him as one of the engine crew from the *Ingersstrom*, but he didn't drop his guard. He made sure the man was alone before he released the wooden handle of the pick.

"Hello, Bernd," the man said to him.

Bernd grunted a greeting back.

"Any troubles here?" the heavyset man asked. "All good?"

"All good," Bernd said.

"You eaten?"

"Yeah."

"I had a sausage sandwich in town," the man told him. "With cheese fries. Better than the shit on board."

"Anything is," Bernd said.

"Calm seas, eh? No worries?"

"No," Bernd said, but he didn't like small talk. The man had gone into the city of Gary for a reason, and Bernd was impatient to get what he'd paid for. "You have something for me?"

"Yeah, I got it. No problems."

The beefy man reached into the pocket of his jacket and extracted a package wrapped in a blue plastic bag.

Bernd took it from him immediately. "It works?" Bernd asked.

"What, you think I tested it? Like I should shoot somebody?"

Bernd shrugged. "Cartridges?"

"In the bag."

He examined the automatic inside. It would do. He preferred revolvers, but the bigger clips of the black gun would be more useful. And his last revolver had been bad luck. After he'd blown off the face of the blond woman who was trying to run, he'd lost the gun on the wet steps when that other bitch tackled him.

Bernd shoved the gun into his belt and pulled his T-shirt over it. He squeezed the box of cartridges into his back pocket. He felt more secure having a weapon again. He had gone a long time without a gun, but those purchases were easier in the USA than in Amsterdam.

The two men stood silently beside each other. The business of the docks went on around them.

"So," the other man said. "Duluth again, eh?"

"Yeah."

"Another delivery?"

"Yeah."

The fat man thought about this. "Captain says he's hearing things online. More surveillance. More questions."

"A body turned up in Amsterdam," Bernd said. "One of ours."

"So they'll be searching. People will be on guard."

"Let them search."

"You say that, but it's all our asses if things go bad. Maybe we should wait."

"It doesn't work like that," Bernd snapped.

The fat man didn't look happy. He wasn't alone; others among the crew had begun muttering about the authorities. Bernd didn't like extra heat, but skipping the delivery wasn't an option. Their buyers were already impatient. The Saudis paid a freaking fortune for the American girls on their shopping lists, so they got what they wanted. Bigger risks meant bigger payoffs.

"Well, keep your eyes open, eh?" the fat man said, waving goodbye, heading across the busy port for the *Ingersstrom*.

Bernd grunted a salute.

His full name was Bernd Frisch. He was twenty-six years old. His narrow, pale face was heavily dotted with freckles, and his chin was rounded. He had blond hair shaved to his scalp on the sides and sitting in short, tight curls on top. His lips were thin, his nose a small shallow bump on his face. Unlike most of his crewmates, he didn't have a tattoo anywhere on his skin, and he was mostly hairless. He was tall, with a lean, hard body.

He'd spent most of his childhood in Germany, and he spoke German and English fluently, thanks in part to a succession of American tourist girlfriends. He'd left school at fifteen, when he concluded that he was smarter about the real world than most of his teachers. For five years afterward, he drifted. Berlin. Prague. Riga. Tallinn. Needing money, he'd joined an Estonian gang as muscle to take care of their street-level problems. When the gang expanded into smuggling operations, he'd helped them bribe, blackmail, and threaten their way onto the *Ingersstrom*. The ship was now the backbone of their North American ventures. That included fresh-faced girls who could fetch as much as fifty thousand dollars with certain Arab buyers. They'd trafficked girls six times in two years.

His only failure had been the one who'd tried to run. The loss of a prime package didn't sit well in Tallinn, and other gang members had paid for smaller mistakes with a plastic bag taped over their heads. Bernd was lucky. He was too valuable to lose, but the ice under his feet was thin.

He felt his American cell phone vibrate in his pocket. He checked his surroundings and then slid the phone into his hand. He'd been waiting for his Duluth contact to check in by text:

Are you on time?

Bernd keyed in a response: *Two days. Be ready.*

Always.

What about the package?

Already in storage.

Bernd typed: *I expect no problems this time.*

There was a long pause before the reply.

The last package arrived late. Not my fault.

Bernd didn't want excuses. The situation with the woman from Colorado had been a disaster, and he couldn't afford a repeat. None of them could. As it was, he was afraid the situation in Duluth had become too hot. He wondered about the police investigation and how far it had gone.

Have you had visitors?

Yes.

How much do they know?

Enough to cause problems. Plus, we have a new situation.

What?

There was a problem with the gun I gave you. It had a history. I didn't know.

Bernd felt his anger rise. More problems. More mistakes. Whenever he relied on other people, they disappointed him. He'd invested time and money in the Duluth operation, and it was too late to walk away now. The only thing to do was to see it through.

Stick to the plan. Collect the girl. And then tie up loose ends.

He wrote:

Make sure the package is ready. I'm coming.

47

Cat listened to the whistle of trains across the street from Al's house. She rested her feet on the broken footrest of an old recliner and sweated in the stifling living room. Dirty bowls and plates were stacked on a tray table in front of the sofa. The beige carpet was littered with video games and toys.

The walls were white, not yet scuffed with dirt and fingerprints. She saw family photos in frames that hadn't been rehung yet. If she inhaled, she still caught the tiniest whiff of fresh paint. A couple of months earlier, she'd been here, with the furniture pushed into the center of the room under a plastic tarp, and a roller brush in her hands. She'd painted the downstairs, and Anna had painted the upstairs bedrooms.

That was when she'd met Al. He came home late, exhausted from his second job at the Anchor. She remembered the smile on his face when he saw the walls all white and clean. It was something new in a house that didn't see many new things. She remembered the look in his eyes when he saw her, too. Men usually looked at her the way a lion looks at food. Al's eyes were different. He didn't assume that she was for sale. He didn't even notice the little pooch that said she was pregnant. He'd looked at her with a sense of wonder, as if she were the most beautiful thing he'd ever seen in his life. Cat—tired, dusty, with flecks of white paint in her hair and on her golden skin—saw that look and fell in love with him right then and there.

She was such a fool.

Al's mother wandered into the living room from the kitchen and handed Cat a can of warm Mountain Dew. The woman fell into a corner of the sofa that was nearest the recliner. "Silence. Isn't that grand? Everybody's finally asleep."

Cat sipped the pop and smiled nervously. "It's not like that a lot, huh?"

"No, hardly ever. Except late at night like this. Mostly, it's jabber, jabber, jabber." She put a hand gently on the wall behind her. "Gotta tell you again how sweet that was of you to paint this place. Real nice."

"It was nothing," Cat said. She wasn't looking for praise for painting the house. Right now, she wanted to forget all about it.

Al's mother was friendly, but her eyes weren't naive. She sized up Cat like a butcher who didn't need a scale to know how much ground beef was in her hand. "Is Al the daddy?" she asked, pointing at her bump.

"Oh, no, he's not."

"I'm glad to hear it."

The woman took short, shallow breaths, but despite her emphysema, Cat caught an aroma of cigarette smoke on her clothes. It was hard to stay away from the things you shouldn't touch.

"How old are you, Cat?" she asked.

"Seventeen."

"I had Al around the same age. Believe me, I know the drill. Is the daddy still in the picture?"

"No, he and I aren't together," Cat said. She wasn't going to tell the truth about her baby's father and the life she'd led before. It didn't matter. Somehow she had a feeling that Al's mother was shrewd enough to figure her out.

"I don't envy you what you've got ahead. It'll be tough. No point in pretending otherwise. Me, I was lucky. My man stuck with me."

"I want the baby," Cat insisted.

"Good for you, but if you're thinking about my boy as your meal ticket—"

"I'm not."

"Hey, I don't blame you if that's what's in your head."

"It isn't."

Cat didn't know if Al's mother believed her, or if she even believed it herself. She thought that she was in love with him, but she was scared, and scared people can convince themselves of lots of things. Al was cute. Nice. Hardworking. Respectful.

And he'd slept with Anna.

Damn it, damn it, damn it.

"I just need to talk to him," Cat said.

His mother eyed her. "What'd Al do?"

Cat looked at her hands in her lap. "Nothing."

"Girl shows up at my house late at night and wants to talk to my boy? Come on, you might as well tell me. Otherwise, I'll get it out of him myself."

"I should go," Cat said. "It was a mistake to come here."

"Do what you want, sweetheart."

Cat tried to get up on her own and couldn't. She pushed, but her body sank back into the recliner. The effort made her cry. Emotion gushed out of her like water through a broken hose. "He slept with my best friend!" she wailed, feeling like a child.

Al's mother sighed. She didn't look surprised, but she waited for Cat to get control of herself and wipe her face before she said anything. "I'm sorry to hear that. I thought I raised my son better than that. You want me to talk to him?"

"No."

"Well, I'll talk to him anyway. I expect more from that boy."

Cat sniffled. "I'm sorry. I should go. I don't even know why I came here."

"No, you sit there and wait. Al always gets home about now. You give him hell, girl. He deserves it. And when you're done with him, he'll have to answer to me, too. But don't misunderstand me, okay? I don't approve of you and him. I'm not in favor. He can't support you and your baby. He's got other things to do with his life."

Cat said nothing. She was miserable, and all she wanted to do was leave, but she heard the noise of a truck door outside. Al was home.

Suddenly, Cat didn't want to see him. It would hurt too much, because she hated him, and she loved him. Then the door opened, and there he was, looking startled to see her sitting there with his mother. He stood in the doorway, not moving, and his mother shoved herself off the sofa. She clucked her tongue at her son and then slapped him in the face.

Al rubbed his stinging cheek as his mother turned on her heels and left them alone. "What was that about?" he said. "Why'd she do that?"

"You know why."

Al sat down on the sofa, looking like a deer frozen by headlights. "What's going on? I'm sorry I haven't called you. I've been busy."

"You've sure been busy," Cat said. "Anna told me what happened."

Al swallowed hard and closed his eyes. He looked as if he'd begun to sweat through every pore simultaneously. "Oh, shit."

"All that talk. 'It's okay to wait, Cat. I want it to feel right for you. We don't need to have sex.' Nothing but talk."

"Cat, I'm really sorry," he insisted. "It was one time, and it was a mistake. I never meant for anything to happen. I was over at the Grizzly Bear talking to Fred, and Anna's car crapped out. So I took her home."

"You took her home and fucked her," Cat snapped.

Al took hold of his head with both hands. "Look, what do you want me to say? It just happened! She said, how about a drink? I figured, what the hell, one drink. Next thing I knew, we'd finished off a six-pack, and we started making out. It was stupid. You have to believe me, I don't care about Anna. I care about you. I love you. You wanted me to say it? There, I said it."

"Yeah, because it means so much to me now," Cat snapped.

"How can I make this right?" Al asked.

"You can't. You can drive me home, and you can keep your mouth shut the whole way, and then you can go away and leave me alone. I don't ever want to see you again. I wish I'd never met you."

"Cat, please—"

She pushed against the arms of the recliner, but she still couldn't get up. Al jumped to his feet, took her hands gently, and helped her. As soon as she was standing, she pushed him away, not wanting him to touch her. His arms dropped uncomfortably to his sides, as if he had no place to put them.

"I made a mistake," he repeated. "People make mistakes."

"Take me home," she muttered.

He yanked his keys from his pocket. She made her way to the front door, and he followed her silently. His head was hung low in shame. He felt bad, and she was glad. All she wanted to do now was hurt him. Punish him. Having Al betray her was worse than anything else, because she'd begun to count on him being there for her. He'd let her think that a boy could be with her for who she was and forget about who she'd been.

Instead, he'd proven what she'd always believed.

Nothing good ever lasted.

48

Stride studied the photograph of the opaque black pearl enrobed in twines of white gold. The ring was unmistakable. Once upon a time, Janine Snow had worn it on the third finger of her right hand. He'd seen a photograph of her from a hospital ball a decade earlier, adorned in matching black-pearl jewelry and a revealing sequined burgundy cocktail dress. The night of Jay's murder, according to Janine, this very ring had been part of the jewelry stolen from her bedroom by the man who killed her husband.

Then it had vanished, never to be found again. And now, like the gun, it was back.

The timing was no coincidence. The gun. The ring. Something had happened to bring them into the light.

"I talked to Pat Burns," Stride told Serena and Maggie in his office.

Pat Burns had taken over as St. Louis County Attorney from Dan Erickson two years earlier.

"What did she say?" Maggie asked. "What did the judge decide?"

She sat with her legs dangling in the chair immediately in front of Stride's desk. Serena sat on Stride's sideboard with her back against the office wall. The two women in his life avoided looking at each other.

"He signed off on Archie's motion and ordered Janine's release," Stride told them. "She'll probably be out tomorrow. The judge ruled that a third party clearly had control over the murder weapon all these years and that the violent history of the gun before and after Jay's death makes it impossible to sustain the original trial verdict. He agreed with Archie that if the evidence of the gun had been available to the jury back then, Janine would have been acquitted."

"So she gets out," Maggie said.

"She gets out. Pat will have to decide whether she can mount a new trial. And whether she even wants to, given the evidence."

Serena spoke from the credenza. "I know you guys don't want to hear this, but isn't the most logical explanation that Janine really was telling the truth? Somebody had the gun back then, but not her. Whoever it was killed Jay Ferris and stole the jewelry."

Maggie looked as if she wanted to argue for the sake of arguing, but then she said, "Yeah, Nathan said the same thing. He thinks we were wrong about Janine. I don't know, boss. I hate to say we blew it, but I think we blew it."

Stride knew what Cindy would say. *Told you so, Jonny.*

"Let's forget about Janine for the time being," Serena said, interrupting his thoughts. "We've got other problems."

"Meaning?"

"Meaning my weird little nerd, Mort Sanders, was on to something," Serena told them. "Mort was chatting online with a woman named Erin from Grand Forks. He says she was being chased by the same stalker who was involved with Kelly Hauswirth. Kelly hooked up with a guy who called himself Lakelover, and Erin's boyfriend was Mattie_1987, but Mort swears they're the same guy."

She held up an enlargement of a driver's license from North Dakota, which showed an attractive blonde, just over twenty-three years old, oval face, blue eyes, with a smile that was innocent and sexy at the same time. Stride couldn't help but notice the similarity between this woman and the Colorado photograph of Kelly Hauswirth. They could have been sisters.

"This is Erin Tierney," Serena said. "She's a dental hygienist from Grand Forks. She's been missing for at least two weeks. Her Nissan Versa hasn't turned up anywhere. I don't think that's a coincidence."

"You think Erin's the replacement for Kelly?" Maggie asked.

"Could be."

"Did she talk to anyone at home about having a new boyfriend? Or about taking a trip to Duluth?"

Serena shook her head. "No, Erin sounds like a loner, like Kelly. That may be part of the personality type this guy looks for. These girls live out fantasy lives online. In real life, they're shy. Not many friends."

"Two weeks is a long time," Stride said. "If she was in the city, they may already have smuggled her out."

"Or they've got her stashed somewhere," Serena said.

"What about these online user accounts?" Stride asked. "Can we trace them?"

"They're fakes," Serena replied. "Their online bios don't check out at all, but the details match up. I think Mort is right that we're looking at the same guy. And there's definitely a Duluth connection. I was able to get the ISP data for both accounts, and all of the log-ins come from the Twin Ports area. Both sides of the bridge. Whoever this guy is, he's smart. He hunts for free Wi-Fi and never hooks into the same network twice, and there's nothing in the pattern to suggest where he's really located. He could be anywhere in Duluth or Superior."

"Have we shut down the two accounts?" Maggie asked.

"No, but we're monitoring their activity. So far, Lakelover and Mattie are both lying low. They haven't been online in days. In fact, not since Erin Tierney disappeared. Again, I don't think that's a coincidence."

"Troy still thinks there's an international connection because of the murder in Amsterdam," Stride said. "We've got data from the night Kelly was killed. The boats in port included four salties outbound to Europe. The *Relko*, the *Venstaat*, the *Ingersstrom*, and the *Pietra Ragazza*. It's possible they could use lakers instead of salties and transfer the girls elsewhere in the Seaway, but the more times they move them, the bigger the risk."

"Is there anything suspicious about the individual boats?" Maggie asked.

"Not on paper. Chances are, the corporate owners don't know a thing about what's going on belowdecks."

"What about recent activity?" Serena asked.

"None of these boats has been back in Duluth since the murder. Two of them are due in this week, the *Venstaat* and the *Ingersstrom*. The *Relko* is in Asia and isn't expected back this season. The *Pietra Ragazza* will return in September."

"That makes it likely that Erin Tierney is still in Duluth," Serena pointed out.

"I hope so," Stride said, "but we also could be wrong about the transport network. Or they could have their hooks into multiple boats. Regardless, you're right: Let's plaster Erin's photo all over the city. Same with her car. If she came to meet this Mattie_1987, someone may have seen her."

Maggie waited until Stride was done, then said, "We've got another angle working for us, too. The black-pearl ring."

"Were you able to trace it?" he asked.

"Yeah, I talked to Caffy at Zenith Pawn. Once he found out the jewelry was connected to a murder investigation, he started talking. He got the black-pearl ring back in May from a Minneapolis accountant named Neal Fisher, who was in town for some Democratic political hoo-ha at the convention center. I talked to Fisher. He was dating a girl, and he bought the ring in Canal Park for her, but before the convention ended, she sent him a Dear Neal e-mail. So he pawned it before he left town. He figured he was making out pretty well, because he didn't think the guy who'd sold it to him knew what it was worth."

"Where'd he buy it?" Stride asked. "One of the antique shops?"

Maggie shook her head. "No. Neal knows a buddy of ours."

Stride leaned forward. "A buddy?"

"Remember Curt Dickes?"

Stride did. So did Serena. Curt was a janitor at one of the Canal Park hotels, but he also ran an endless series of low-level scams to feed his need for cash. He'd been a pimp hooking up tourists with UMD girls. A petty thief stealing stingray pups from the Great Lakes Aquarium. A scalper of counterfeit Yanni concert tickets. He wasn't violent, but he was the kind of streetwise kid who would never go straight. Stride had known him since he was fifteen.

"Curt sold this guy the ring?" Stride asked. "Where the hell did he get it?"

"That's what I'm trying to find out," Maggie said. "Curt's been under the radar for a few days, but I just got a call. He's got a new thing going. Duluth ghost tours. I'm going to track him down now."

"Good."

Maggie stood up and headed for the door, but then she stopped. She shoved her hands into the pockets of her jeans and blew the bangs out of her eyes.

"You want to come with me?" she asked Serena. "We could be like Rizzoli and Isles or something."

Stride saw the surprise in Serena's face. He was surprised, too. Maybe there was a chance of a thaw between them. He didn't know what Serena's reaction would be, but she wasted no time sliding off the credenza. The two women stood next to each other, short and tall.

"Okay, let's go," she deadpanned to Maggie, "but I get to be Angie Harmon."

49

It had taken Janine two whole years to stop dreaming about her old life when she fell asleep at night. Her unconscious brain would whisk her back to her mansion on the hill or stand her in scrubs over the open chests of patients in the operating room at St. Anne's. Even awake, she would find herself making false mental leaps whenever she read a book or a magazine.

I should look for those shoes the next time I'm at Macy's.

Abruzzo in Italy—that should be my spring vacation.

I need to try the lobster ravioli at Bellisio's.

Then she would wake up, or she would remember: Those things are never going to happen again. Don't dream, don't fantasize, because dwelling on what you can't have will drive you insane.

Except now life had turned on its head again. It was happening so quickly that she was disoriented. Nothing seemed real. She hardly dared to believe it. Right now, she was at Shakopee, and at the same time tomorrow, she would be on the other side of the security doors. She wondered how long it would take her brain to give up images of prison when she dreamed.

"Will they attempt to try me again?" she asked Archie on the phone.

"If Dan Erickson was still the county attorney, I'd say yes," Archie replied. "With Ms. Burns in charge, I think it's less likely. The evidence works in your favor now. Assuming they can't ultimately show that you somehow acquired that gun after it left Chicago."

"I didn't."

"Or that you hid it after the murder. Or sold it. Or gave it away."

"I didn't."

"Then I think you're safe, my dear."

Janine wasn't so sure.

She could hear the doubts in Archie's voice. Not about her legal situation, but about her innocence. Her own attorney had never really believed in her. He'd given her a robust defense, but he thought she was guilty as sin. She'd told him over and over that she hadn't pulled the trigger on that gun. She'd never so much as held it in her hand. Even so, Archie still suspected that she had simply outsmarted everyone else. Like a magician, she'd killed Jay and made the gun and the jewelry disappear. Until now.

Everyone else would think the same thing. She had no illusions about the public opinion of Dr. Perfect. People would still stare and wonder how she got away with it.

"Welcome to the next chapter of your life," Archie told her. "What are you going to do with it?"

That was a good question. She didn't know the answer.

She was accustomed to thinking day to day and ignoring the future. The thought of walking out into the world with no plan terrified her, because throughout her life, she'd always had a plan for everything.

The media would be waiting for her. She'd be mobbed. The release of Janine Snow would be big news. The surgeon murderer set free. She wasn't ready for the questions they'd shout at her—What do you think really happened to your husband? Will you sue for wrongful imprisonment?—and she had no answers to give them.

She'd asked Archie if he could buy her some time. Get her past the media horde and hide her somewhere. She needed a few days to get her head around the idea of living outside the walls again, and then she could talk to the reporters. She couldn't avoid the world forever, but she needed time. She needed to get used to different walls.

She would go back to Duluth. That was still home. For now.

Archie would put her up in a hotel. She'd paid enough to earn that treatment from him, at least for a while. She could stare at the waters of Lake Superior and order room service and drink wine. One day, then the next, then the next, until she figured out whether there was anything left to live for.

However, she had one immediate problem that wouldn't go away. Howard Marlowe.

Howard, bland and boring. Howard, obsessed and driven by desire. This was his fantasy come true. Janine, free; the two of them, together. She'd never actually told him they had no future together, because all that time in prison, she'd had no future to give him. He was her little indulgence, someone to feed her ego.

Howard, Howard, Howard. Nice, unremarkable Howard, writing a book he would never finish, to rescue a woman who would never be in love with him. He would give up everything in his life for her. His wife. His child. When you're an addict, nothing else matters except your addiction.

She couldn't hide from Howard. He'd find her. That very first night, he'd be at the door of her hotel room. Probably with flowers, the poor fool. And champagne. As if she'd anticipated that moment the same way he had.

Janine knew she would sleep with him. She couldn't send him away without it. She'd toyed with the man for eight years, and if she let him live out his fantasy with her for one night, that wasn't such a great sacrifice. It was nothing but sex. Years earlier, when he'd showed up on her doorstep during the trial, she'd thought about taking him into her bed. If she'd done it, would she be in prison right now?

Okay, Howard. This is what you've dreamed about. This is what it's like to be with me. She could live with that. And in the morning, when she broke his heart, she wondered if he would still think it was worth the price.

Howard sat in his basement office, waiting for Archibald Gale to pick up the phone. A classical symphony played while he was on hold. He'd already listened to ten minutes of Beethoven, but Gale's assistant assured him that the lawyer was eager to speak with him. That was a big change from the days when he would make five or six calls to Gale's office without getting a callback.

Finding the ring had changed his status. He would always remember the look of grudging admiration on Gale's face when he showed him the ring.

Howard wasn't stupid. He knew that Janine's lawyer patronized him, full of hollow encouragement for his research. Yes, you keep digging, Howard. Yes, I have faith in you. And then he laughed behind his back. The truth was that Gale had never believed that Howard would discover anything remotely useful to Janine's appeal.

So it was a triumphant moment to put the ring from the pawnshop in Gale's hand and say: "I did it. I found it."

That moment had changed everything between them. Suddenly, Howard wasn't a crackpot, operating on the fringes of the case. Suddenly, Gale had called in an associate and taken Howard's statement. Gale had clapped him on the back. Joked with him about lawyers and judges. Poured him a shot glass of expensive Scotch and sat and chatted with him as if they were fellow members of Duluth's exclusive private club, the Kitchi Gammi.

Howard asked, "Do you think she'll finally be released?"

Gale, brimming with effervescence, replied, "Yes. Yes, this time I really do. Between the gun and the ring, I do."

"I always knew she was innocent."

And then Archie Gale, with the strangest of grins, a little tipsy from his third shot of Laphroaig, said, "Yes, yes, innocent. Or exceedingly smart."

Which Howard thought was an odd thing to say.

But it didn't matter. It was really happening. Janine would be free tomorrow. He was dizzy with desire. Every nerve ending felt as if it were on fire with anticipation. He swiveled in his office chair and put his feet up on the basement wall and hummed along to Beethoven.

"Howard," Gale said when he finally came on the line. "The man of the hour. You heard the news?"

"Of course!"

"Well, you definitely played a role in making this happen. Janine and I are very grateful."

"Do you know what time she'll be released?" Howard asked.

"I do, but I'm not giving out that information to anyone. I'm trying to keep the media at bay. You understand."

"Well, I'm not just anyone," Howard told him. "I want to be there. To pick her up."

There was a long silence on the line, and when Gale spoke again, his ebullience had tempered into something cooler. "That's very gracious of you, Howard, but it's not necessary. I'm handling all the details."

"I want to see her," he insisted.

"And you shall see her, of course. Very soon. I'll talk to Janine, and I'm sure we can arrange a time for her to thank you in person."

Howard's fingers clenched around the phone. "To thank me in person?"

"Exactly."

"I need to see her tomorrow. Do you know how long I've been waiting for this?"

The politeness vanished from Gale's voice, and he became a lawyer again. "I'll pass along your wishes to Janine, but when and if you see her is entirely up to her. I know she's grateful, as am I, for all the hard work you've put in on her behalf. But you shouldn't presume a personal relationship that doesn't exist."

"It does exist," Howard snapped.

"Well, I'll talk to Janine, and I'll be back in touch. I promise." Then he added, somewhat more kindly, "Listen, Howard. Take my advice. People are different in prison than they are in the real world. The two often have very little in common. You need to be aware of that."

"Just call me back!"

"Of course. I will."

Howard spun around in his chair and slammed down the phone. He was disgusted. After all Howard had done on her case, Janine's lawyer had humiliated him again. As if he were nothing but a groupie. Well, Gale would find out the truth soon. He'd talk to Janine, and Janine would set him straight.

"You bastard. You worthless bastard."

Howard looked up and jumped. Carol was there.

"I didn't see you . . ." he began, but his words drifted away. Sweat made a film on his skin. "I'm sorry."

"You're leaving me," she said. "For *her*."

She didn't phrase it as a question. She didn't beg him to change his mind.

He could barely look at his wife's face, but when he did, he saw that her familiar eyes had turned dead. There were no tears. They'd been through tears many times, her crying at night, him pretending to comfort her. There wasn't even any anger left. She didn't yell at him. Or curse. They'd been through that, too. She simply stared at him with fish-blank eyes. Her arms hung at her sides. Every emotion, every feeling, had burned down to gray ash.

"I can't believe you did this to me," Carol murmured.

"This was never about you. It was about *me*."

"Remember that when you see her tomorrow," his wife said.

50

"So," Maggie said.

"So," Serena replied.

The two of them sat at an upstairs table at Dunn Bros on London Road. The coffee shop was styled like a modern log cabin. Serena sipped a cup of black decaf from a ceramic mug. Maggie drank a caramel frappe and wiped the foam on her upper lip with her tongue. She had a blueberry scone, too.

Serena didn't know how Maggie could eat the way she did and stay stick-skinny. If Serena made a daily stop for breakfast at McDonald's or the Duluth Grill, she'd be ordering her jeans in plus sizes.

They'd already scouted several Duluth landmarks, hunting for Curt Dickes, the low-level con artist who'd fenced Janine's black-pearl ring. So far, they hadn't located his Duluth ghost walk for gullible tourists. After they checked the empty parking lot at the Glensheen estate—no sign of Curt—they stopped for coffee on the way back to downtown.

Maggie nibbled her scone and played with her Android phone. Serena flipped through apps on her iPhone. They had the upstairs level of the coffee shop to themselves. The relationship with Maggie made Serena feel like a teenager again, which was silly. She put down her phone and studied Jonny's partner, who was her own age and whose love life had been a train wreck for as long as she'd known her. She didn't think that Maggie had ever really been in love with Jonny. He was simply a crutch so she didn't have to confront how bad she was at falling in love with anyone else.

"Are you seeing anyone?" Serena asked her, breaking the awkward silence.

"Why do you care?" Maggie replied, not putting down her phone.

"I'm just curious."

"Well, you know me, Serena. A day without sex is like a day without sunshine."

"Funny."

"I've slept with most of the men in Duluth. I'm thinking of branching out to Cloquet."

"Fine. I'm sorry I asked."

Maggie sighed and shoved her phone into her pocket. "You're right. I think my bitch switch is on automatic these days. No, I'm not seeing anyone. And it's not because of you-know-who. I'm taking a break from dating."

"Jonny thinks Troy Grange is interested in you," Serena said.

"Yeah, Troy's been dropping hints. He must be a masochist."

"He's a nice guy."

"I know he is. I like his kids, too. He talked about the four of us driving down to the state fair this year."

"So?" Serena asked.

"So I told you. I'm taking a break. If I do anything, I'm going slow. Peck-on-the-cheek, knees-closed slow. For the time being, call me Sister Maggie."

Serena had a hard time imagining Maggie as anyone's idea of a nun.

"What about you guys?" Maggie asked, sipping her frappe. It was sensitive ground, her asking about the two of them. When Serena didn't answer immediately, she added, "I mean, how is it with Cat living there? Instant family and all."

"It's a struggle," Serena admitted. "I don't think Jonny realized how difficult it was going to be. He had this idea that if we helped her, she'd turn herself around. It's not that simple."

"No, it's not," Maggie said.

"I know you thought it was a mistake for us to take her in," Serena said.

"Yeah, and I still do. Sorry."

"There are days when I agree with you," Serena acknowledged. "Even so, we love her, and she loves us. Unfortunately, that's not always enough."

Maggie said nothing more. They finished their drinks through another stretch of silence. Then Serena went on. "This case has brought back a lot of memories for Jonny. Memories of Cindy."

"I'll bet."

"I don't like competing with a ghost. Then again, I didn't like competing with you, either."

Maggie laughed, but it wasn't a happy laugh. "You were never competing with me, Serena. I was never in the game. Even when Stride and I were together, there wasn't a day that he wasn't still in love with you."

Serena didn't hear bitterness in Maggie's voice. Just honesty. Maggie grabbed the empty cups from the table and stood up.

"Oh, and for what it's worth," she went on, "you're not competing with Cindy, either."

"I think I am."

"Only in your head. Not his. Did Stride love Cindy? Yeah, of course he did. Was it a nightmare to lose her? Yeah. But that doesn't change how he feels about you. I saw it all winter when you weren't here. Trust me, it was extremely annoying."

Serena allowed herself a faint smile. "Sorry."

"It's not your fault. Anyway, it's not Cindy coming between you two. It's the fact that Cindy died. That's his problem."

Serena stared at Maggie, and for just a moment, it felt like they were friends again. Which they weren't. But at least they'd moved beyond being enemies.

"I don't understand."

"Stride thought he had everything, and then it was taken away from him," Maggie said. "He's not sure he believes in the future anymore. He's worried it'll be stolen from him again."

"That's always a risk."

"I know, and Stride doesn't like risks."

"He asked Cat to live with us," Serena said. "That was a big risk. He was thinking about the future when he did that."

Maggie cocked her head, as if Serena were the densest woman on the planet. Maybe she was. "You're right. Doesn't that tell you something?"

Serena let those words sink in. When they did, they made their way up the length of her body and gave her a little chill. Sort of like the breath of a ghost, invisibly touching the nerve endings of her skin. Maggie had said things she didn't need to say, and Serena could only imagine how hard it had been for her. In her shoes, she wasn't sure she would have been equally gracious.

"You know, you really ought to call Troy," Serena told her. "Go to the state fair with him and the girls."

"You think so?"

"I do."

Maggie shrugged. "What the hell, maybe I will. But only for the cheese curds. Damn, those things are good."

They found Curt Dickes after dark near the lift bridge separating Canal Park from the Point.

It was a windy night. Waves in the narrow ship canal struck the concrete walls and sent clouds of cold spray into puddles on the sidewalk. Overhead, a bone-white light illuminated the crisscross metal span of the bridge superstructure. Threads of fog moved in and out of the steel Xs, making them invisible.

A cluster of twenty tourists huddled near the canal. Some had umbrellas. Curt Dickes stood in the middle of them, or Serena assumed it was Curt. He was dressed in a skeleton costume that included a skull mask covering his face and a top hat at a jaunty angle on his head. In his left hand, he clutched a plastic sickle that was taller than he was.

"Do you hear that?" Curt shouted.

Clearly, he had a microphone under his mask; his voice was amplified, and he used an echo effect that repeated his last words. "Do you hear that . . . *that . . . that . . . that?*"

"That's not the wind. Oh, no. That's the scream of Lars Olson. His ghost never leaves the bridge, and on nights like this one, you can hear him pleading for mercy. Who's Lars Olson, you may ask? He was the ex-chancellor of UMD. He died a horrific death at this very spot. Someone tied a rope around his neck and hooked him to the span, so that when the bridge went up . . ."

Curt put a bony fist near his neck and tugged sharply, letting his head dangle sideways.

"He was hanged . . . *hanged . . . hanged . . . hanged . . . hanged.*"

One of the children in the group of tourists gasped. "Did that really happen?"

"All of my stories are true!" Curt announced. "You can run, but you can't escape the dead . . . *dead . . . dead . . . dead . . . dead.*"

Maggie waded into the crowd. "Oh, give me a break, Curt."

Curt spotted Maggie and Serena, and the skeleton froze in place. With a flourish, he removed his top hat and gave them a deep bow. "Ladies and gentlemen, may I present the lovely Maggie Bei and Serena Dial, two of Duluth's finest, dedicated to keeping tourists like yourselves safe from the criminal underworld. Ms. Bei, Ms. Dial, have you decided to join our happy group to hear more absolutely true tales of ghosts in the Zenith City? Tickets are just twenty-five dollars each, payable in cash only, no refunds."

"Lars Olson was a character in an Ellen Hart novel," Maggie announced. "She killed him off by hanging him from the lift bridge at the beginning of *This Little Piggy Went to Murder.*"

Curt scratched the top of his head with his sickle and offered a nervous giggle. "Well, sometimes fiction is stranger than truth, you know. I mean, stories do come to me secondhand from time to time."

A restless murmur rippled through the crowd.

"What about the ghost of the marathon runner?" a woman asked. "Was that one true?"

"Totally true!" Curt assured them. "I've seen him myself."

"Marathon runner?" Serena asked.

"Barnabas 'Batty' Burns," Curt replied confidently. "Eighty-seven years old. Tried to run all 26.2 miles of Grandma's Marathon. Made it to within ten yards—ten yards!—of the finish line and dropped dead of a heart attack. Tragic. To this day, he runs the last block of the marathon over and over, trying to make it to the finish line, and he disappears into wisps of smoke just before he gets there. I've seen him dozens of times."

"You are so full of crap, Curt," Maggie told him. She grabbed the skeleton by his bony arm, and Serena took the sickle and poked him in the back.

"Folks, hang out here for a while; we need to borrow your tour guide."

With Maggie on his left side and Serena on his right, Curt was quick-walked along the wall of the canal. Waves slapped loudly on the pier and doused all three as they marched away from the bridge. When they were out of earshot of the tourists, Maggie grabbed the top hat and yanked the skull mask from Curt's head. Curt, a twenty-five-year-old beanpole, tried to tame his greasy black hair. Musk cologne oozed from his skin.

"Jeez, guys," he complained. "I'm trying to do a show here."

"Duluth has a cool history," Maggie told him. "Next time, try to stick to it, okay? No more Batty Burns the Long-Distance Runner."

"Hey, I'm a storyteller. There's nothing wrong with that. Stride told me I should make an honest living."

"Well, you're getting closer," Serena agreed. "Don't worry, we're not here to bust your ghost walk. It's your other job we want to talk about."

"I'm not pimping anymore. I swear."

"Not that one," Serena said.

"I found those boxes of camping gear behind the Duluth Pack store. I swear, I thought they were throwing them away."

"Not that one, either," Maggie said. She held up an enlarged photograph of Janine's ring on a piece of paper that quickly became sodden in the spray thrown from the canal. "Your other job, Curt. Fencing stolen merchandise."

Curt put two skeleton hands on his chest in mock dismay. "Whoa, what? You got the wrong guy." He added an echo with his microphone: "*Wrong guy . . . wrong guy . . . wrong guy.*"

"Save it," Maggie snapped. "You sold this ring to an accountant named Neal Fisher. He identified your photo, Curt, so quit playing innocent. Oh, and by the way, he ripped you off. He gave you two hundred bucks, and this thing is worth at least a few thousand."

"That asshole!" Curt bellowed. "I know you can't trust lawyers, but I figured accountants were okay."

"Where did you get the ring?" Serena asked.

"Um, let me see. I think I found it on the street."

"You found it?" Maggie asked. "It was just lying there?"

"That's right. Over near the Depot. I figured it slipped off somebody's finger. Their loss was my gain."

"This ring came from a stash of jewelry stolen nine years ago," Maggie told him. "The husband of the woman it belonged to got his head blown off during the robbery. People have been looking for the jewelry ever since, Curt. And now it shows up in your hands? That's not a good thing. It makes me think you needed money back then, so you drove up there with a gun—"

"No way!" Curt retorted. "You know that's not my scene, Sergeant. No violence. Not a chance."

"So where did you get the ring?" Serena repeated.

"Okay, somebody sold it to me. I gave them fifty bucks. And then I sold it to the accountant for two hundred. That's commerce. Nothing wrong with that. Although now I wish I'd asked for a lot more."

"Who sold it to you?" Maggie asked.

"Just somebody I know."

"Who?"

Curt winced. His wet hair was shiny. "Look, are you sure you guys want me to tell you? Because I don't think Stride's going to be too happy about this. You neither, Serena. If I tell you, don't blame me, okay?"

"What are you talking about?" Serena asked.

"The girl who sold it to me," Curt said, "it was *your* girl. Cat. She's the one who had the ring."

He repeated her name, and it echoed.

Cat . . . Cat . . . Cat . . . Cat . . . Cat.

51

"I'll talk to her," Stride said.

He studied the closed door to Cat's bedroom at the front of the cottage. He was seated in his red leather chair near the fireplace, and Serena stood against one of the dark wood columns that framed the nook where the fireplace was located. They could hear music through Cat's door.

"Do you want me to do it?" Serena asked.

Stride stood up. "No, I want to deal with this myself."

At Cat's door, he knocked and heard her young voice answer from inside. He opened the door. Cat's bedroom was small, with chambered windows facing the street, and two twin beds on the left and right. Cat was stretched out on her back on one of the beds, working on a book of *Super-Advanced Brain-Tingling Sudoku Puzzles*. She always did them in pen.

It was a reminder to him. This girl was smart. She had a gift, if she ever wanted to use it.

"Hey, Stride!" she said happily.

Cat rolled off the bed and gave him a hug. She did that most nights when she saw him. He felt bad that he wondered sometimes about her sincerity. He didn't doubt that Cat loved him and Serena, but love was a complex thing for a girl like Cat, who'd been caught up in years of guilt, shame, and fear. He didn't know if she could love anyone without trying to manipulate them.

Cat sat down on the end of her bed. She switched off the music. "What's up?" she asked.

Because she knew something was up. She could read his face. And he saw in her nervous brown eyes the uncertainty of a teenager who was keeping lots of secrets and wondering which one he'd uncovered.

Stride sat on the other bed. "I was thinking about your mother today," he told her. "I cared about Michaela a lot."

"I know you did."

"There's not a day where I don't feel regret about what happened to her."

Cat hooded her eyes. "Me, too."

"Michaela told you to find me if you were ever in trouble," Stride said, "and you did. I'm glad you did, Cat. I didn't always believe that things happen for a reason, but more and more, as the years go by, I do. Even when the worst things happen. I find myself realizing that the turns of life take us where we're supposed to go."

Cat was silent. She didn't understand what he was saying, and when she didn't understand, she got scared.

"Do you like it here with us?" he asked her. "Do you feel safe here?"

She nodded urgently. "Of course. You know I do."

"Then what's going on with you, Cat?" Stride asked quietly. "I need to be able to trust you, and I can't. Neither can Serena. All summer, you've kept crazy hours, not telling us where you are. You're hanging out with people you shouldn't. You're making bad choices. Why? We gave you a second chance, Cat. *I* gave you a second chance."

"I know you did, but I don't deserve it. I'm not worth anything."

He watched her eyes welling with tears, and he put up a hand. "Stop that. Listen to me. I don't want to hear you talk like that. I don't hold your past against you, and I never will. Who you were the day before you came here doesn't matter to me, but what you do right now does matter."

"I told you, I'm not worth it!"

"Well, I'm here to tell you that you are worth it," Stride said, "but that doesn't mean there aren't consequences, or that you get a free ride. You're going to have to figure out a way to put the past behind you. You're going to have to decide that your life—and your son's life—mean something. And you're going to have to look into my eyes and realize that I'm not going anywhere. Other people have turned their backs on you. Not me. And not Serena."

He watched her. Her head was bowed, and she wouldn't look at him. Maybe one day she'd be able to stare into his eyes and be her own person, but she wasn't there yet. He exhaled in disappointment.

"Serena talked to Curt Dickes tonight," he went on. "You know what he told her, don't you?"

Cat chewed her lower lip. "Curt bought some things from me when I needed money. It was just a couple times."

If Cat said it was a couple of times, Stride knew it was many times. And that meant she'd been stealing.

"What do you need money for?" he asked.

"Just day-to-day stuff. Buses. Music. Jewelry sometimes. I like jewelry."

"If you need money, you can come to us," he said.

"I know, but I don't like to do that."

"Are you buying drugs?"

"*No*. How can you ask me that?"

"Because you've been lying to me, and I don't trust you."

"I'm not using drugs. I'm not."

Stride tried to stay patient. He couldn't deal with all of this now. There was only one thing that mattered. "Okay, listen to me. You sold a black-pearl ring to Curt a couple of months ago. Where did you get it?"

"I don't remember."

Which was a lie. Her face was flushed, and she couldn't look at him.

"Was it just the ring, Cat? Or was there other jewelry? I can describe all of it to you. Matching black-pearl necklace and earrings. A diamond-and-sapphire bracelet. A hummingbird pin. An emerald brooch. Does that sound familiar?"

"I only had the ring," she insisted. "How did you find out about it?"

"Because that ring is connected to a gun, Cat. The gun and all the jewelry I just talked about disappeared during a murder nine years ago. Now we've found the gun again. It was used in another murder last month."

Cat's eyes widened. "You mean at the bar—when Serena—"

"That's right."

"No! That can't be. That's impossible." She wrung her hands together and looked close to panic.

"That gun showed up outside the Grizzly Bear Bar, Cat. Now some of the jewelry that went missing along with the gun can be traced to you. *You.* Do you realize the situation that puts you in?" He got up from the other bed and sat down next to her. "Do you know anything about this gun? Or about the man who used it?"

She shook her head again and again. "No! I don't know anything about a gun! Nothing!"

"Then where did you get the ring?"

Cat looked dazed. And then she looked angry. "Talk to Al."

"Al?"

"He's my boyfriend. At least he was. He cheated on me. The ring came from his house."

"Did he give it to you?" Stride asked.

"No, I—I took it."

"You stole it? Why?"

"I told you, I wanted money. And I like jewelry. You remember I always used to carry my father's ring with me, right? I did that for years, but then I had to give it back. So I wanted—I wanted another ring to have. And I took it. Except I realized I couldn't wear it, not with Al around. So I sold it to Curt so I could buy something else."

"Oh, Cat," Stride murmured. He was disappointed, and she knew it.

"I'm sorry!"

He put his hands gently on the girl's shoulders. "Are you telling me the truth? Because you know what happens next, don't you? I get a search warrant tomorrow, and we tear Al's house apart from top to bottom."

"The ring was in his house," she insisted. "That's where I got it."

"What about the other jewelry I talked about? The earrings, necklace, brooch. Did you see any of those other pieces in the house?"

She shook her head. "I only had the ring."

"And the gun?"

"I never saw a gun! I didn't!"

Stride believed her. There were still secrets in Cat's eyes, but he didn't think she was lying about the gun. "This is important, Cat. Did Al ever say anything about this woman who was killed? Kelly Hauswirth?"

"No!"

"Did you ever have reason to think that he could be involved in criminal activity?"

"No, no, that's not him! He's not a bad person."

"Cat, listen," Stride told her. "We think someone was trying to kidnap Kelly Hauswirth when she was killed. Possibly to sell her as a slave. That's as terrifying and cruel as it sounds. Someone in Duluth was making that happen, and whoever it is had access to that gun."

"Al would never do anything like that."

"There's another girl missing right now, Cat," he went on. "Her name is Erin. We need to find her. So please, think. Is there anything Al said—anything he did—that would help us find this girl? Do you know where she might be?"

Cat wrapped her arms around his waist and hugged him. "No. I swear, Stride, there's nothing. I don't know anything about a missing girl."

52

It was morning, but Erin had no way of knowing what morning it was. Her world was black.

Every movement of her body brought pain now. Her skin was blistered where she'd struggled fruitlessly against her bonds. Cuts had scabbed over and broken open again on her face. Her muscles, once so supple and strong from her visits to the gym, had balled into knots, like shoelaces tied so tightly, they couldn't be undone. She knew she had a urinary tract infection. Peeing brought a knifing sting.

Twice a day, the voice came back. The door would be unlocked and locked again, but the darkness was unrelenting. She was given food and a chance to relieve herself, with a knife at her throat and her limbs tied. Most days, she couldn't hold it until then, so she found herself doused with a bucket of cold water to fight the smell. Even in the heat, she shivered so hard that she thought her bones would break.

She'd screamed once when the gag was removed. As she did, she found herself choked, every atom of air cut off until her limbs twitched, while the voice hissed obscenities into her ear. She didn't scream again. She became docile, learning the routine, living by it.

Eventually, the animals at the zoo understand there is no way out.

One time, she'd murmured, "Why?"

She got no answer.

Another time—maybe it was yesterday, whatever yesterday was—she'd said, "When?"

Because she knew this was the beginning, not the end.

This time the voice told her: "Soon."

Above her head, a summer rain began. It was still summer; the heat and drenching humidity told her that. She could smell the freshness of the rain from outside, and she could hear its drumbeat assaulting the roof. A squall, loud and sustained. She couldn't see lightning through her blindfold, but a growl of thunder made her prison tremble. It sounded like a devil's throaty laughter.

Hammering raindrops squeezed through the roof. Drips leaked on her face, and she grabbed for them with her dry, swollen tongue. She heard a toneless plink-plink, too, water making music on metal. The change in pitch among the falling water told her there was something large inside the room with her, and she knew instinctively what it was. Her car was hidden with her. Her Barney-purple Nissan Versa. No one would find it. No one would find *her*.

In the beginning, she'd prayed for Matt to find her. Mattie_1987. Her confidant, her friend, her lover. When he arrived at the bar and found she wasn't there, he'd spread the alarm throughout Duluth and call the police. He'd pass her photo from hand to hand. Strange, how long it had taken the truth to sink into her brain. Even when it was obvious, she'd refused to believe it. There was no Matt. He was a figment of her imagination. An online fantasy. She'd been lured and trapped here by the voice.

What bothered her more than anything was how easy it had been to be tricked. She felt like the perfect fool. Growing up, she'd thought girls were naive to fall for men's scams. She couldn't understand how women could believe the same tired lines from guys in bars. And now she'd allowed herself to fall in love with a lie. To be drawn into something far worse than a one-night stand.

More thunder. The devil chuckled at the joke. *No one's coming for you, Erin.*

She had tried to escape, but the steel of handcuffs and chains was unbreakable. She'd screamed and struggled, achieving nothing. She'd cried. Wept. Prayed. God didn't answer and left her in hell. When the gag came off twice a day, she'd beg for mercy and bargain with the voice. Let me go. Please. I'll do anything. What do you want?

That was all buried somewhere in the past. Her tears had dried long ago. She'd realized that the darkness allowed a grieving process: struggling, protesting, challenging—and finally accepting the reality. Her life was over. What was left to her wasn't life at all. She'd felt herself going dead inside as the darkness continued, until she felt nothing at all.

Erin had a choice. Early on, she'd known that the choice was available to her. The last choice. When she explored the tiny universe allowed by her chains, she discovered that she was affixed to a heavy steel table. It was immovable. Bags of sand or concrete had been laid on top of it. The table was weighted, as heavy as her car, imprisoning her where she was.

However, the metal corner of the table above her head came to a sharp point. It was jagged, hooked, like the end of a dentist's pick. The jab of metal was useless against the steel holding her in place, but that wasn't what she needed it for. God had given her a way out of this hell, if she had the courage to use it.

The rain kept on, as hard as ever, but the thunder quieted. It was as if the devil knew what she was going to do.

Erin twisted her body, pushing herself onto her knees in the dirt, until she could nudge her chin over the smooth, cold tabletop. She smelled concrete dust, but she took a breath anyway, savoring it. Funny, how you took life for granted. Breathe in, breathe out. She slid her face leftward, hunting for the prickly corner, like the needle of a cactus. It bit into her neck. Her salvation. Metal might not penetrate metal in this case, but it could penetrate flesh.

Home squirmed into her brain. Her apartment in Grand Forks. Good days. Swimming in the river. Red wine on Saturday nights. She couldn't let those thoughts control her. Home didn't exist. That life—her life—didn't exist anymore. She pressed against the point of the table, which bit harder. Her body wanted to jerk away, but she didn't let it.

The little claw took hold of her neck. Erin slung her head in a single, sharp pivot. The pick held, then ripped, then tore. Pain awakened her, but pain was a friend. Rain leaked onto her body, warming her skin, but she knew with a wild sense of freedom that the rain had stopped.

This was blood.

This was escape.

Bernd Frisch didn't smile at the Coast Guard officer. Smiling was what guilty people did. He wasn't concerned by the search of the boat or the extra security. His fake Dutch passport would come through the computer databases as clean as spring rain. The entire crew had cleared customs inspections over and over again, and today would be no different.

He answered questions. Politely. Offering nothing but facts. Where the ship had been. Where they had docked. What they loaded and unloaded. The voyage of the *Ingersstrom* was routine.

The one surprise was the photographs they showed him. The officer presented him with pictures of women. Had he seen them? Had he witnessed any of the crew interacting with these women? Had he seen them here in Duluth or elsewhere in Europe?

No. No. No.

Did he have any knowledge of human trafficking activities on this or other foreign ships operating in the St. Lawrence Seaway?

No.

Bernd recognized the photograph of the woman he'd delivered from Duluth last year—the woman who'd been found murdered in Amsterdam. He recognized Kelly Hauswirth, whom he'd shot in the back of the head. He recognized the woman who would be smuggled on board after dark tonight, before the boat set sail into the waters of Lake Superior at 2:00 a.m.

"These women are unfamiliar to me," he said.

And that was that.

Bernd was cleared. He took his backpack and left the boat. They didn't search him, so they didn't find the gun at the bottom of the pack, fully loaded now. If they had spotted the gun, he would have told them that America wasn't a safe place. Didn't they watch television?

He swaggered down the gangplank to the busy port. Steam rose from the ground in humid clouds. The sky over the lake was black where a storm blew eastward away from the city. It had rained, but the rain was gone.

Welcome to Duluth.

Bernd slipped out his phone and texted. *I'm here.*

53

As soon as they climbed out of Stride's Expedition at the house in Superior, Maggie knew she'd made a terrible mistake nine years earlier.

This was where Cat's boyfriend lived, but she recognized exactly where she was. She remembered the sea-foam-green two-story house on the corner. The coming and going of the trains across the street. The overpass of Highway 2. The arborvitae, even taller now, towering over the roof.

"I've been to this house before," she said.

Stride and Serena both stared at her. "What? When?"

"After Jay Ferris was killed."

Maggie's memory painted the picture for her. Back then, it had been winter. Mountains of snow were piled on the street corners. The engineer who waved at her from a passing train wore an orange down coat and gloves. The sky was slate-gray over her head, like it was today. And across the street, parked beside the two-story house, was a white Toyota RAV4.

The RAV wasn't there anymore. There were no cars on the street or in the driveway. Even so, she remembered being here, questioning a man on the front porch. She and Guppo had interviewed dozens of RAV4 owners in Duluth and Superior, trying to pinpoint one of them who might have been parked on the street near Janine Snow's home on January 28.

"The owner's name was Seymour Pugh," Maggie recalled. "He was on our checklist back then. He owned a white RAV, and he had a criminal record for burglary. I talked to him about Jay's murder."

"Cat's boyfriend is Al Pugh," Serena said.

Maggie nodded her head in frustration. "Al must be his son. That's the connection."

She'd misread Seymour Pugh all those years ago. He'd fooled her.

She was angry with herself, but there was no way she could have put the pieces together back then. Pugh was just one of many interviews, one playing card dealt from a full deck. She remembered liking him. He was a family man. A man who'd stayed with his wife and kids instead of running out. A man who got a solid job after his run-ins with police and prison.

A job. Maggie remembered Seymour Pugh's job, and it meant something important to her now.

"Pugh told me that he drove a truck," she said. "He was all over the Midwest delivering machine parts. Including Illinois."

"You think he was the one who bought the gun on the street in Chicago," Serena concluded. "That's how the gun got to Duluth."

Maggie banged her fist into her palm. She was stupid. Pugh had given her a song and dance about his values, about supporting his family, about finding God. She'd believed him. And now she was convinced that he'd lied to her. The clues fit, and they all pointed in one direction. The white RAV4. The connection to Chicago, where the murder weapon had been sold. The stolen jewelry that came from Pugh's house.

She'd been talking to the man who murdered Jay Ferris.

"Come on," Stride said. "Let's go inside."

The two streets leading to the house were barricaded a block away. They had a dozen officers with them, all in militia gear, with vests on. They weren't taking any chances with what might be waiting behind those doors. The team fanned out around them, staking out positions on all sides of the house. A wooden fence surrounded the yard, and half a dozen officers made their way through the gate.

Gray clouds layered the sky. The street steamed with puddles. Stride, Serena, Maggie, and Guppo approached the front door, which was secured with burglar bars. So were the windows. Maggie drew her Glock and aimed it at the door, and Guppo did the same. Stride pounded on the wall and shouted for anyone inside.

Those were the tensest moments. The silence. The waiting. Either this would go well, or it wouldn't.

Ten seconds later, they heard the knock of the dead bolt being undone. The door inched open. A young black man stared out at them, eyes wide. Just a sliver of his body was visible. He saw the guns and their stony faces.

"Al Pugh?" Stride demanded.

"Yeah—yeah, what the hell—"

"Put your hands up, open the door slowly, and come outside."

The young man did as he was told, but he looked scared. Maggie thought he couldn't be more than nineteen years old. He was tall but underfed, all skinny arms and legs. He was good-looking with his trimmed goatee and black hair against smooth cocoa skin. It was easy to see why a girl like Cat had fallen for him. He wore a T-shirt and loose-fitting cargo pants, and, dressed like that, he looked a lot like the man Maggie had interviewed years earlier. But this young man would have been a child when Jay Ferris died.

Al nudged onto the porch, and Stride grabbed him by the scruff of the neck and dragged him down the steps. Stride spun the boy around, kicked his legs apart, and frisked him from head to toe. No weapons. He put a strong hand on Al's shoulder and pushed him down on the front step at their feet.

"Who else is inside?" Stride asked.

"My mom and my sisters. What's going on?"

"We have a warrant to search the property."

"Search? For what?"

Stride ignored him and barked at Guppo. "Gather the people inside in one room, and make sure someone stays with them. Search everything inside and out. Attic, basement, garage. Keep an eye out for false walls and false floors."

"False walls?" Al asked. "What are you talking about? What are you looking for? We don't have anything like that."

Guppo led the team inside. Maggie heard shrill protests from a woman. Al's mother.

Stride crouched in front of Al Pugh. "Are you Cat's boyfriend?"

"Cat? Is that what this is about? What did she say? Hey, I'm sorry I cheated on her, man. I don't know what she told you, but I didn't do anything. I didn't touch her, either!"

"How did you meet her?"

"Here, at my mom's house. It was a church painting project. I thought she was cute, and we started going out. Tell me what she said, man! I didn't do anything!"

Maggie held up a photograph of Kelly Hauswirth. "Do you know this woman?"

"What? No! No, I—aw, wait, isn't that the chick who got shot? That was all over the news, right? I recognize the face, but I don't know her."

Serena held up a photograph of Erin Tierney. "What about her?"

Al shook his head. "No way. Never seen her."

"She's missing."

"I'm telling you, I don't know who she is! That's the truth."

"We're taking your laptop, Al," Stride said. "We'll find out all about the chat rooms. You might as well tell us about it. And who you're working with."

"Man, I can't tell you what I don't know! I don't even *own* a laptop."

"Cat says she took a ring from your house," Stride said. "A black-pearl ring. Where did you get it?"

Al stared at them. "Ring? I don't have any ring. Shit, man, laptops and pearl rings. Does it look like we got the money for stuff like that? I'm lucky if we got mac and cheese for dinner."

"This ring was stolen during a murder in Duluth almost nine years ago," Stride told him. "The gun that was used back then is the same gun that murdered a woman outside the Grizzly Bear Bar last month. The ring and the gun are *connected*, Al. And Cat says that ring came from this house."

Al tried to stand up, but Stride shoved him down. "Aw, man, are you kidding? I don't know anything about a ring, and I sure as hell don't know anything about a gun! You guys are crazy!"

Maggie looked up as they heard a commotion inside the house. The front door was wrenched open, and a woman in her late thirties stormed onto the porch, long hair flying. Guppo, in hot pursuit behind her, grabbed her flailing wrists, but when that didn't stop her, he bear-hugged the woman and lifted her off the ground. Her legs kicked, and one high heel flew off like a missile. Her voice got louder and screeched for the heavens.

"You people let me go, and get out of my house!"

Al stood up again, trying to calm her. "Mom, Mom, knock it off. It's okay."

"Put me down!" she screamed at Guppo.

Guppo did, but he didn't let her go. Al bounded up the steps before Stride could stop him, and he put his arms around his mother. She kept screaming. Police officers ran from different parts of the neighborhood. Finally, Stride shouted, raising his voice above the chaos, and everyone stopped in place.

It was silent. Al's mother panted. Her face was furious. Her raspy voice dissolved into a coughing fit.

"Listen," Al said, sounding calmer and older now, a boy who wanted to protect his mother. "I don't know what Cat told you guys, but you are on the wrong track. I swear. I don't know anything about this ring she has, and I sure as *hell* don't know anything about a gun."

Maggie stared at Al's mother. She was young, but she looked old. The woman wiped spittle from her lips and stared back at Maggie.

"You know about the gun," Maggie said to her quietly. "Don't you, Mrs. Pugh?"

Al started to interrupt, but then he saw his mother's face, and he let her speak. She stood up straight and smoothed the housedress she was wearing. She was tall, like Al. The boy couldn't hide his confusion. This was all new to him, but it wasn't new to his mother.

She knew exactly what was going on.

"Yes," she told Maggie. "Okay, yes, I do. I know all about that gun."

*   *   *

They sat inside. One of Mrs. Pugh's daughters made tea. The search of the house was over, but it had revealed nothing of importance in either murder investigation. There was no hideaway in the house or grounds in which the kidnapped women had been kept. Erin Tierney wasn't here. She never had been. There was no jewelry from nine years earlier.

Everyone stared at Al's mother, waiting for her story. There was an oversize photograph of Seymour Pugh with his family in a frame that leaned against a freshly painted wall. Maggie recognized the man from her visit years before. He still had the same smile, but life had corroded him at a fast pace. She wasn't surprised to learn that he'd died of a stroke three years after she met him.

Mrs. Pugh stared at the photograph, too, and Maggie saw pride in the fierce little smile she gave Seymour. This was a woman who loved her husband, no matter what he'd done.

"What you're thinking is what it is," Mrs. Pugh finally told them. "It was Seymour who did it. He shot that man. Took the jewelry. Guess it doesn't matter now, although I didn't want Al and the girls finding out about their daddy. Seymour's long gone, God rest him. I know Jesus forgives him. Jesus understands what he did."

Mrs. Pugh fell silent. She wiped her eyes.

"The gun?" Stride asked. "Where did he get it?"

"He bought it on one of his road trips. Never told me about it. I would have made him get rid of it."

She sat primly with her knees pressed together. Her fleshy body would have been toned once, and her worn-out face with its tumbling black hair would have been pretty. Maggie could imagine her and Seymour, hooking up, having kids, bumping into the struggles of life. It wasn't easy then, and it wasn't easy now. Mrs. Pugh's chest wheezed. She sucked in the air around her but never seemed to get enough.

"Did you know what he was planning to do?" Maggie asked.

"No, no, 'course I didn't. He wouldn't dare tell me. He knew I'd kick his ass if I heard about it."

"Then why did he do it?"

Mrs. Pugh gave them a rattling sigh and stared at her lap. "For his family—what else? For me, for Al, for the girls."

"You needed money?"

"Sure, we did. A man does what a man's gotta do when it's his family. Jesus understands."

"When did you find out?" Stride asked.

Her shoulders gave a little shrug. "Don't remember. Few weeks later, I guess. Some cop came by the house, asking questions. Seymour said it was nothing to worry about, but I knew he was lying. That night, after the kids were in bed, I got it out of him. He told me what he'd done. Showed me the gun. The jewelry. He was too scared to unload any of it. I told him to bury it all somewhere. Get it out of the house. Throw it in the lake. Whatever. I didn't want it here. I thought he got rid of everything, but I was wrong. He kept it. After Seymour died, I was going through his stuff in the attic, and I found a shoebox hidden in the rafters. There was the gun. The jewels he'd stolen. I tell you, I swore a blue streak at that man!"

Serena leaned forward. "What did you do with the box?"

"I shoved it up on a shelf in my bedroom closet. I didn't feel safe getting rid of it myself, and it's not like I was going to tell you people what I found. Figured you'd lock me up if I did."

"What happened to the gun and the jewelry?" Stride asked.

"Far as I know, it's still in the box."

"It's not. We found the box. It's empty." Stride's head swiveled to her son. "Al, if you know anything about that box—about what was in it—"

The young man shook his head. "I don't know a thing. I never saw it. I never even knew it was there."

Maggie saw Stride and Serena exchange a sober glance, and she knew what that look meant. Cat. If it wasn't Al, it was Cat. Cat found the box. Cat found the ring. And along with the ring was the gun that had murdered Jay Ferris and Kelly Hauswirth.

"When was Cat here painting the house?" Stride asked, wearing a frown that looked as if his world were ending.

"Sometime in May," Al said.

"Did Cat paint your bedroom while she was here, Mrs. Pugh?" Serena asked the woman in a soft voice. "Could she have gone into your closet and found the box on the shelf?"

Al's mother scratched her chin and thought about it. Then she said, "No, the pretty young one was painting downstairs. Sweet girl. I liked her laugh. It was the other girl who did the bedrooms upstairs. The pasty one with the Halloween hair. She was a little creepy, I have to say."

"The other one?" Serena asked.

"Anna," Al interjected quickly. "The waitress at the bar. Anna Glick."

54

Cat pounded on Anna's door and waited impatiently for her friend to answer. The quiet neighborhood in Morgan Park where Anna lived was deserted. No cars. No kids playing. Black clouds blew across the afternoon sky, and high winds made the mature trees sway and talk. Drizzle spat on the ground.

"Come on, come on," Cat murmured.

She was afraid that Anna wasn't home, but, finally, she heard the click of the latch and saw her friend peering out at her from inside. Anna didn't open the door immediately, and when she did, she only opened it a few inches.

"Cat," Anna said. "What's going on? Why are you here?"

Cat shoved the door open and pushed past Anna into the small house, which smelled of cigarette smoke and the must of old furniture. Anna wore a cotton robe that barely covered her hips. It was tied loosely, and her bare skin made a narrow V from her small breasts to the knob of her belly button. Her spiky orange hair was mussed, as if she'd just gotten out of bed.

"They know!" Cat told her. She paced back and forth on the worn shag carpet and chewed her fingernails. "I knew this would happen. I knew they'd find out. I'm so stupid!"

"What are you talking about?" Anna asked.

"Stride and Serena know about the jewelry you found at Al's house. I sold the ring you gave me, and they traced it back to me through Curt. I'm such an idiot. I told you, I hate these scams!"

"You didn't mind them when you were raking in extra cash," Anna pointed out. She grabbed a half-empty pack of cigarettes from a coffee table and lit one. "I told you, church projects are the perfect cover. You paint people's houses and see what shit they keep hidden away. Most of the time, they don't notice that anything is gone until months later. If they even notice at all."

Cat shook her head. She was sick with guilt. She liked the money she'd made with Anna—almost five hundred dollars in just a few months. Even so, she'd known from the beginning that the stealing would crash down on her head sooner or later. She wished she'd never agreed to be a part of it.

"We need to come clean with the cops," Cat said.

Anna laughed at her and blew out smoke. "Yeah, right. That's not going to happen. What, exactly, did you tell them?"

"I told them I took the ring from Al's house. I sold it."

"Did you mention me?"

"No!" Cat said. "I didn't. I would never rat you out, but you know they're going to figure out you were there, too. And they asked me about a gun! Did you find a gun at the house? They said it was the same gun that was used when that woman got murdered at the Grizzly Bear."

Anna stared at her. She didn't even look like Anna anymore. "I really wish you'd kept your mouth shut, Cat."

"I'm sorry, but what else could I do?"

"What are the cops doing right now?" Anna asked. "Where are they?"

"Searching Al's place. They got a warrant this morning."

Anna's face turned sour, and she talked softly, as if to herself. "It won't take them long to make the connection to me. They'll be coming here." Then she announced loudly, "Bernd, come on out. We have to go. We've got trouble."

Cat heard the floorboards in the old house shift. In the doorway that led to the bedrooms, she saw a man. A stranger. He wore only briefs and made no effort to cover himself. His skin bore fresh nail marks on his chest. Anna's. He was handsome, with a taut, muscular body, but he conveyed menace like no one Cat had ever seen. His ivory-pale, freckled face was devoid of expression, and his blue-gray eyes watched her with the coiled-up ferocity of a tiger.

"Who is . . ." Cat began, her voice cracking.

"This is my boyfriend. Bernd, we've got a problem."

"Another problem?" the man said, spitting the words at her. "What did you do this time?"

Cat watched Anna fold like a flower. She'd never seen her friend intimidated by a man. "It's not my fault, but the cops are coming. We'd better get out of here right now. Both of us. Permanently."

Bernd marched closer to them. Cat felt nauseated by fright. She spotted men's clothes in a pile on the floor, and Bernd squatted and dug in the pockets. Cat began to back toward the door, but Anna darted behind her and threw an arm around her head, burying her neck in the crook of her elbow. Cat couldn't move and couldn't breathe. Bernd stood up, and he had a gun in his hand, which he pointed at Cat's head.

Cat whimpered and tried to speak, but she couldn't.

"On your knees," Anna told her roughly.

Cat sank to the floor. Her arms wrapped protectively around her stomach. Her chestnut hair spilled across her face, and sweat beaded on her forehead. She kept staring at the gun.

"Tie her hands," Bernd said, snapping his fingers at Anna. "Quickly. Leave her ankles free for now. She's going to have to go with us. Where's the other girl?"

"In my storage unit across the street."

Bernd waited in stony silence while Anna ran to the kitchen and returned with a roll of duct tape. Anna bound Cat's wrists tightly with tape, which was sticky and rough on her skin.

"I warned you," Bernd snapped at Anna. "You put the whole operation at risk with your stupidity. I told you not to freelance."

Anna flinched. "Look, I'm sorry, okay? Your people pay good money, but it's not enough to live on. I found you the other girls—"

Bernd made a slashing motion across his throat. Anna stopped talking. The man stepped into his jeans from the floor. As he zipped himself, he squatted in front of Cat and held her chin between his fingers, pinching so tightly that she grimaced in pain. He shoved her face left and right, and then he put his hand on her stomach, and she tried to squirm away.

"We'll use this one as a bonus," Bernd said. "She's pretty. Pregnant is a plus. Some buyers like that. And the baby will be worth something, too."

"*You leave my baby alone, you bastard!*" Cat screamed into his face.

Bernd slapped her hard, leaving a welt and choking off the words in her throat. "She's spirited, too. That's good. They like the ones who fight. Maybe she'll make up for the one you lost us."

"You shot the other girl!" Anna barked. "If you'd kept control of Kelly, there never would have been a problem. I texted you about the cop in the bar. You needed to get her out of there, and, instead, we wound up with a mess on our hands."

"The mess started with the gun you gave me," Bernd replied. He reached out and grabbed Anna's neck with his hand, pinching his fingers shut like a vise until she began to twitch, unable to breathe. When he finally let go, she jerked away, coughing and crying.

"Fucker!" she moaned.

For the first time, Bernd laughed.

"Anna, why are you doing this to me?" Cat asked her. "What is this about?"

Anna rubbed her neck and looked furious at her humiliation. "Jesus, why are girls like you so naive? You're going to take a trip, Cat. All the way to a desert kingdom. Don't worry, you won't be alone. Erin will keep you company."

Erin.

Cat knew that name. Serena had mentioned that name. Stride had shown her Erin's photograph.

"That's the girl who's missing. Serena said that she had an online boyfriend who kidnapped her—"

"Boyfriend?" Anna retorted. "*I'm* her boyfriend."

"You?"

"Yeah, me. All these girls are so perfectly clueless. Do you know how many pathetic single women have told me they loved me? How they've been searching their whole lives for a man like me? They'll swallow anything I tell them."

"Enough!" Bernd snapped. "We don't have time for this. Gag her. I'll make sure the street is empty. We'll put her in the truck and get the other girl, and we'll head for the boat."

The man shoved the gun into his belt and marched out of the house. Cat and Anna were alone. Anna unrolled another stretch of duct tape and cut it with her teeth. The tape dangled from her fingers. She grabbed a dirty sock from the floor and wadded it up in a ball in her fist.

"Open up," she said to Cat.

"How can you do this to me?"

"*Open your mouth.*"

"I'm your friend."

Anna pinched Cat's jaw until her mouth opened, and she shoved the sock deep inside, making her choke. Then she slapped the tape across Cat's lips and dragged the girl roughly to her feet. She pushed Cat toward the back door.

"Time to go."

55

Two and a half hours between Shakopee and Duluth marked the difference between Janine's old world and her new world.

Archie was at the prison to give a statement to the media and handle the paperwork for her release. He arranged for her departure in an unmarked van from the loading dock. They drove past the unsuspecting reporters and made their way to the parking lot of a nearby Best Western hotel, where he had new clothes waiting for her and a room in which she could change. She showered and put on a blouse with three-quarter sleeves and a vibrant red-and-gray print. She left it untucked over tapered black dress slacks and heels. She wadded up the clothes she'd worn out of Shakopee and put them in a plastic garbage basket; they could be burned, for all she cared.

Archie waited outside with a town car and driver. He had champagne opened and a tray of hors d'oeuvres. She emerged from the hotel, wearing sunglasses, and got into the backseat of the car with him. They headed north to Duluth, but they didn't speak for miles. She wanted to savor the silence, which he seemed to understand.

Somewhere near Forest Lake, on the northern edge of the Twin Cities, Archie got a text on his phone. He eased back in the leather seat, champagne in hand, and studied her over the rims of his half glasses. His curly gray hair nearly grazed the roof of the car.

"My police sources tell me they're executing a search warrant on a house in Superior," he said. "It has something to do with the gun and jewelry that were found."

"Oh, yes?" Janine watched the wilderness flowing past her. The lakes. The pines and birch trees. "Does that matter to us?"

"Not really. I told you that you're likely safe in any event. However, if they find the person who really pulled the trigger, it removes any final legal issues hanging over your head. A complete exoneration may be useful in whatever you choose to do next."

"Ah," she said mildly.

"Do you know what you plan to do next?" he asked her.

"Well, being free doesn't make me a surgeon again. Not to be crass, but the medical board never really cared whether or not I murdered my husband. They only cared that I was popping pain pills while operating."

"But you're clean now."

"I am, but I'm almost nine years out of touch with my field."

"You can catch up."

"No offense, Archie, but right now, I just want to find a way to make it through today."

He smiled at her the way a grandfather would. "Yes, of course. My apologies."

They didn't speak for the rest of the journey. One hundred and fifty miles took her back to Duluth. It made her sad to drive into the heart of the city, because she could see her estate on the hillside from the freeway. The house she'd designed. The house that was supposed to be her lifelong sanctuary. It belonged to someone else now. She'd been forced to sell it years ago to settle the malpractice case against her. It would never be hers again. Not that she wanted it now.

The town car took her to the hotel and shopping complex called Fitger's Inn. That would be her home while she assessed her future. Archie had arranged a press conference at his office the following day, but she needed at least one day and night of privacy. Anonymity. He'd already checked her into the August Fitger suite on the hotel's top floor, with a king bed, whirlpool tub, and a view toward the vastness of the lake, and he'd stocked the room with clothes and toiletries. When they arrived, he handed her an old-fashioned key.

"I'll call you in the morning," Archie said, "but contact me before then if you need anything at all."

"I will. Thank you."

"You might need cash, so here you are."

He gave her five hundred dollars. And still there was doubt in his eyes.

Janine didn't go to her room. She'd been locked up for too long to lock herself inside again. With sunglasses hiding her face, she shopped both levels of the complex. She bought an expensive bottle of white wine and a hand-blown Hungarian wineglass. Downstairs, at the bookstore, she selected a long literary novel to pass the evening. The blond-haired manager was friendly, but Janine was pretty sure the woman recognized her. Even so, she was discreet.

After an hour, she went upstairs to her suite, opened the wine, and drank. She dragged an armchair to the floor-to-ceiling windows and stared at the majestic blue water. Five stories below her, people wandered the boardwalk, and children screamed and laughed. It was summer—the perfect season. A ship came in under the lift bridge. A ship went out.

Still she drank. Soon she was buzzed, and some of the weight lifted from her shoulders.

She didn't know how long she'd been drinking alone when she heard a knock at the suite door. There was no doubt in her mind who it was. She'd told Archie it was okay to let him know. She got up, feeling wobbly, and made her way to the door and opened it.

"Hello, Howard," she said.

"Janine." He said it in a hushed voice, like someone standing in front of a Michelangelo sculpture.

He had flowers in his hand, a sunny bouquet of yellow roses, white daisies, and purple irises. He wore a suit that was old but had been recently cleaned and pressed. A faint grease stain marred his blue tie. His penny loafers had been shined. His center-parted hair rose high on his forehead and nestled in brown curls.

He handed her the flowers, and she said, "How sweet. Thank you."

She found that she was almost glad to see him. Everything had changed in her life, but Howard was the constant, and there was something comforting about him. She felt warmth that wasn't really affection but that might have been gratitude. She pulled him by the elbow into the suite and shut the door.

"No one saw you?" she asked.

"No."

"Do you want wine?"

"Sure."

She poured him a glass and poured herself another, emptying the bottle. She returned to the windows, and he followed her and stood next to her. The king-size bed with its brocaded green comforter was near them by the adjacent wall. They sipped wine in silence. He finished his glass and took her hand. His skin was warm. He'd never touched her before, but she knew what it meant.

Janine put her own wine down and faced him. She reached up to stroke his face. Her fingertips caressed his shoulder. She tilted her head slightly, leaned in, and kissed him softly, lips to lips. His eyes were closed. She smelled mint on his breath.

"Are you sure this is what you want?" she whispered.

"It's the only thing I've dreamed about for years."

The power of his fantasy made her flush. She felt no arousal herself, but she enjoyed the long-dormant sensation of controlling a man. She took over, which was what she always did in bed. She led the way. She dominated. Only one man had ever been different, after a lifetime of submissive husbands and lovers. Her equal.

Jay.

He'd given as good as he got. She'd been turned on by his strength in the early years, but after a while, she grew tired of the game. There could only be one alpha in a marriage, and she had no interest in relinquishing the crown. That was when things careened downhill.

It was strange, sharing herself with Howard. She was older now, simply going through the motions. And yet it was heady to watch the adoration in his eyes. She loosened his stained tie, slid it from under his collar, and tugged it like a rope in her hands. Teasing him, she wrapped it around his wrists and yanked it tight. She kissed him again, harder this time. With tongue. She held up his hands and sucked on the fingers one at a time. He quivered.

She let the tie fall and stepped backward, putting distance between them when he wanted to embrace her.

"Take off your clothes for me," she instructed sharply.

Howard rushed to comply.

She found her thoughts going far away. She paid no attention as he undressed, fumbling with his shoes and belt. Different futures wandered through her brain. A doctor. A surgeon. A teacher. A consultant. Archie was right. She had things to offer the world. She still had power, knowledge, determination, and drive. Prison hadn't changed who she was. Time hadn't diminished her.

She was Janine Snow. Dr. Perfect.

Howard stood in front of her, naked.

"Lie on the bed," she told him, and he did.

Yes. She knew now. She could do anything. Jay was a memory. Jay, who'd sapped her confidence, who'd degraded her. Jay was dead, and she was free. She could be whatever she wanted, and what she wanted was to be a doctor again, to hold life in her hands, to be God. No one could deny her that. The board would restore her license. The patients would come to her, because they wanted to live, and she could answer their prayers.

"This is what I live for."

She said it out loud. Howard thought she was talking to him. Talking about sex. Maybe she was.

She stood over this naked man on the bed, who was fully under her spell. She gave him a wicked smile. She touched him with warm hands, her fingers spread, playing him like a piano. His chest. His stomach. His legs. His thighs. His eyes were wide open, drinking in what she was doing to him. Fully clothed, she bent over and enclosed him in her mouth. Just a kiss, just for a moment.

I will show them all. I will get my life back. Jay had cost her eight years, but eight years was punishment enough. She had nothing else to answer for. No other sins.

Janine undressed, taking her time. Howard followed each undone button like a revelation. The loosening strap of her bra, then the cups as they fell away. The zipper on her slacks. The lace of her panties, which she peeled down inch by inch, until she was nude in front of him. She climbed onto the bed, straddled him with her thighs, and hovered with her breasts dangling and the V between her legs teasing an inch above him. Making him wait.

This wouldn't take long.

They would couple, and she would let him hold her briefly. Then she would tell him the truth. It was a fantasy, but the fantasy was over. She'd crush his world, but better to do it fast, leaving him with the glow of fulfillment. She would thank him, kiss him, and send him back to his gray little life.

Goodbye, Howard Marlowe.

Janine lowered herself and felt him sinking inside her. He gasped, almost as if he were in pain, and called out her name. Like a prayer. This was ample payment for his devotion.

She rode him slowly, then more quickly, and as she did, her mind drifted to other things. She thought to herself that she could order the chicken with fig and brie from the hotel restaurant that evening. Maybe the ahi tuna appetizer, too. And another bottle of chardonnay.

Then she could put on soft music and enjoy the solitude as night fell, and she could plan for tomorrow.

56

The small row of six storage units was immediately across the street from Anna's house. The facility was built from cinder blocks, with double-wide green wooden doors, on a dirt lot that was overgrown with weeds. Dense trees swarmed the units, dropping leaves and branches on the mossy roof. Where the lot ended, the ground fell off into a steep ravine.

Anna backed her SUV to the last unit in the row. She got out, making sure they were alone. Bernd was in the backseat with Cat, and he dragged her out of the truck by the collar of her T-shirt. The gun was in his hand. Outside, the dirt under Cat's feet was wet and spongy. Rain spattered her face, and wind swirled the treetops that grew out of the gully, making a roaring noise.

"Erin's inside," Anna told Bernd as she opened the tailgate of the SUV.

"Let's get her and get the hell out of here."

A packing crate filled the rear of the truck. The unfinished wood was stamped with the name of a foreign manufacturing company and labeled for steel shims. A bungee cord looped the square box, and Anna yanked heavily on the cord to drag the crate from the rear of the truck, where it dropped into the mud. She used a crowbar to pry open the lid. The crate was empty.

Cat saw her future, and she knew it was inside that box. Cat and Erin, the two of them, imprisoned together. The thought of being nailed into the wooden coffin, rolling with the waves of the sea, set off panic in her chest. She wanted to shout, but she couldn't. She wanted to run, but she had nowhere to go. Her legs bowed; she began to fall. Bernd grabbed her elbow and jerked her to her feet.

"Open the door," he told Anna impatiently.

The double doors of the storage unit were secured by a padlock, which Anna undid with a key. She swung open one of the green wooden doors. Cat saw the rear bumper of a purple Nissan Versa with a license plate from North Dakota. Otherwise, the interior was black.

Anna went inside and plugged an orange extension cord into an outlet, which illuminated a floodlight hanging from the ceiling. The breeze blew in, making the floodlight sway. Anna headed for the back of the storage unit, and Bernd pushed Cat inside, pulling the door shut behind them. The space smelled of mold and metal. Strange shadows played across the walls through streams of dust. At her feet, an army of black bugs pushed through the dirt and feasted on scraps of meat and bread.

Anna got to the front of the Versa and stopped cold. A strangled gasp blew from her mouth, and her fists clenched. "Oh, fuck."

"What is it?"

Anna stared at the floor and shook her head.

Bernd pushed Cat by the neck, and she stumbled forward, trying to keep her balance. When she came up next to Anna, she screamed into her gag. A woman lay at their feet, chained to a metal table that was weighted down with bags of cement. She was on her back, spread-eagled, her skin gray. A two-inch gash was open on her neck, and blood pulsed from the wound, pooling under her head and staining her long hair.

"You stupid bitch . . ." Bernd muttered to Anna.

He let go of Cat and swung his arm in a haymaker to the side of Anna's skull. The blow knocked her halfway across the hood of the Versa. Her wool hat flew off. Dizzied, she slid to the dirt. She tried to right herself, then crawled on hands and knees to the woman on the floor. She put her fingers on the woman's neck, coming away with blood on her nails.

"She's still alive," Anna told him. "She's still breathing."

"And we're supposed to move her like that?" Bernd demanded.

"Well, I don't know—we could—"

"Shut up," Bernd said. "Stop talking."

"Bernd—"

"*Shut the fuck up.*"

Anna staggered to her feet. She grabbed the hood of the car for balance. Blood was everywhere now. On Anna's skin, her knees, her arms, her clothes. She'd bitten down on her own tongue when Bernd hit her, and blood dripped from the sides of her mouth.

"I'm sorry," she pleaded with him.

Bernd's face was knotted up into a mask of rage.

"I didn't know. How could I know?" Anna went on. "We still have Cat. You said yourself, she'll be worth a lot. Come on, let's get out of here."

"Not you."

"You can't leave me here!" She took Bernd's shirt in her bloody fists and shouted in his face. "You think I'm going to prison for the rest of my life for you? Fuck that! I'll give you all up. Every one of your sorry asses. I'll tell them everything!"

"I know," Bernd said.

He brought the gun up and fired through Anna's stomach. The noise reverberated in the shut-up space. Anna screamed in agony and laced her hands over her belly as she staggered backward. Streams of blood squeezed through her fingers. She stared down at herself in disbelief.

"You son of a bitch—"

Bernd straightened his arm and fired again, directly into her head. The shot was like a bomb. Cat watched Anna's face explode in a shower of bone and brain. Her friend's knees crumpled, and Anna slumped to the floor in a dead pile. Cat squeezed her eyes shut and looked away. She felt deaf from the bang of the gun, and her skin was pricked with stinging, pinpoint burns.

The killer's hand locked around her wrists. "Let's go."

Bernd dragged Cat by her bound hands, and her shoes scraped on the dirt. He got to the door of the storage unit and kicked it open with his heel. She squinted into the gray light of the afternoon. The rain was heavier now, sheeting sideways in the wind.

The SUV was there, its tailgate open. The packing crate lay on the ground, the wooden lid next to it. Cat knew what came next. Bernd cocked his arm and flipped the pistol in his grip, ready to crash the butt of the gun into her head. Cat swung at him with her arms, but it was like striking an oak tree. His body barely moved. She lost her footing in the mud as she hit him and stumbled to her knees. Protecting her stomach, she tried to skitter away from him, but he grabbed her under her shoulders and hoisted her into the air. Her legs kicked. She landed blows without felling him. He dropped her down again, and with one bloody hand around her neck, he pointed the gun into her face.

She felt the heat of the barrel burning her.

And then she heard it. They both heard it. Sirens. Loud, wailing, roaring closer, not even a block away. She stared past the dirt lot to the street, barely able to hope for rescue, but there they were. The strobe lights of squad cars flashed between the tall trees, one after another, brake lights squealing as the cars swung wide. In the midst of them, she saw a truck she recognized.

Stride's Expedition.

"There!" Al shouted, pointing at an ivy-covered house at the corner of a T intersection with Edward Street. "That's where Anna lives."

Stride jerked to a stop and bumped over the curb on the boulevard. With his window open, he gestured police cars past him, where they swerved into position, blocking both streets. He opened the driver's door. Serena and Maggie climbed out of the backseat behind him.

"Stay here," he told Al. "Don't move."

All of Stride's attention was focused on Anna's house, which was built on a shallow slope of lawn and had steps leading from the sidewalk to the front door. The wall nearest the street was completely draped in dense vines, obscuring the windows. He led the way toward the door, with Serena and Maggie close behind him. Rain slashed his face. He'd nearly reached the door when he heard Al shouting from inside his truck. The kid's high-pitched voice was muffled by the window, but he screeched a name over and over, and Stride recognized what Al was saying.

"*Cat! Cat!*"

Stride swiveled toward the street. So did everyone else. He saw a dilapidated row of storage units, a muddy, weed-covered driveway, a forest of soaring, waving trees, and an SUV parked near the last unit with its tailgate swung open. Beside the truck, a tall man backed away toward the edge of a steep ravine.

The man had a gun in his hand.

And he had Cat.

The passenger door of Stride's truck swung open. Al screamed Cat's name and bolted across the street, his arms and legs flying. Stride shouted after him, but the kid didn't stop. Then they were all running: Stride, Serena, Maggie, the cops. Stride skidded down the lawn of Anna's house and hit the pavement in a sprint. Ahead of him, Al kept shouting.

"Cat! Cat!"

Al pumped through the mud, his sneakers splashing. He was almost at the SUV when the man holding Cat raised the pistol and fired. The first shot missed wide. Al threw himself behind the truck bumper, but a moment later, he charged again, and the man fired again. This time the bullet drilled into the meat of Al's shoulder. Al jerked at the impact, his face twisted in pain, and his knees buckled. His hand clutched his shoulder, and he fell against the truck door.

Stride didn't dare shoot. He kept the SUV between himself and the gunman as he evaluated Cat's situation. She was bound with her hands in front but otherwise looked unharmed. She wriggled frantically in the man's grasp, but he had her neck in a chokehold as he pulled her toward the edge. When the man spotted Stride, he laid the barrel of the automatic against Cat's cheekbone.

The two of them kept backing toward the ravine. Thick trees soared from the pit of the valley and loomed over their heads. Dense, leafy brush leaned in around them. Compost and dead branches, dumped at the fringe of the slope, made the earth like quicksand.

"Stop!" Stride shouted at him. "Stay where you are!"

The man cast a glance behind him, where the ground fell away. He was up to his ankles in mud. He took the gun from Cat's head and squeezed off another shot, which pinged against the metal siding of the SUV. With one more shot, he shattered the truck's windshield, pelting Stride with glass.

Stride ducked behind the truck and waited an excruciating five seconds. The man didn't fire again. When Stride stood up, the slope ahead of him was empty. The deep gully had swallowed them up.

57

Stride went down and down and down.

He half fell, half hiked down the sharp slope. The soft earth gave way under his feet, and he stayed upright only by grabbing on to wet brush. Leaves slipped through his fingers. The deeper he went, the darker it got, blocking out the charcoal sky. When he glanced behind him, he saw Serena and half a dozen cops starting down the hill, but soon they disappeared behind the crowns of trees. He was alone.

Where the ground finally leveled, water gurgled over his feet. He was no more than a hundred yards from the open coastline where the St. Louis River widened into Spirit Lake, but for now, he might as well have been in a rain forest, trapped among trees so dense that he couldn't see ten yards in front of him. He listened, but the noise of rain and wind drowned other sounds.

He saw fresh footprints in the mud of the creek, heading east toward the lake. That was their trail.

Stride yanked out his phone and called Maggie. "They're moving east. There's an abandoned set of railroad tracks by the lake. We should be able to get people in from the north."

"On my way," she told him.

He followed the ravine, shoving branches aside and wiping water out of his eyes. He felt blind and deaf. The rain got harder, drumming like thunder on a million leaves over his head. The creek water deepened, filling his boots. Every few steps, he stopped and squinted to peer through the forest ahead of him. There was no sign of them.

And then—

The flaky trunk of a birch tree burst into bark and wood chips two feet from his head. The crack of a gun rippled over the noise of the storm. He squatted and caught a glimpse of a man's legs, anchored in the creek, facing toward him. Cat was still with the man, struggling to escape. They were fifty feet away. Another second later, the man turned and disappeared, dragging Cat behind him.

Stride gave chase, but the wilderness fought back. Spindly branches scraped his face and drew blood. The water and mud sucked his boots into the ground, clinging to him with each step. His arms hacked through the foliage, forcing a path. It couldn't have been more than five minutes that he'd been inside the woods, but it felt longer. He no longer saw anyone ahead of him, but he kept low as he pushed forward, in case the man fired blind shots to slow his pursuers. He was glad he did, because four more gunshots echoed wildly around him, swallowed by the woods. He didn't know how close any of the bullets had come.

Finally, beyond the trees, he saw water and sky. He spilled out of the forest and found himself on the graveled fringe of old railroad tracks, steps from the dappled surface of Spirit Lake. The wooded land mass of Wisconsin was visible a mile across the water. Streaks of rain surged from the low clouds. Almost immediately, as he reached the clearing, gunshots rang out again. He ducked, taking cover.

The man with the gun pulled Cat northward on the railroad tracks. On his left was the impenetrable forest, and on his right was the expanse of the lake. He had nowhere to go, but he ran anyway.

"Stop!" Stride shouted. "Give it up!"

In answer, the man fired at him again and kept running.

Stride followed. The railroad tracks were overgrown with weeds. The lake beat against the land, and the rain gushed across his body. He jogged, then threw himself flat as the man twisted back and squeezed off another shot.

Behind him, Stride saw Serena emerge from the trees. Six other officers appeared, too, crouched and ready. They spread out between the woods and the lake, and all of them pushed northward. Stride moved again, closing the gap between himself and the man with the gun. Beyond the man, a quarter mile away, he spotted Maggie and a team of officers converging from the other direction.

They had the perp in a squeeze now, police coming from both sides. The man with the gun saw it, too, and he stopped dead on the tracks. He looked ahead. He looked back. There was no escape in any direction.

He put his gun to Cat's head. "Everybody stop!"

Stride held up his hands to freeze those behind him. Up the tracks, Maggie did the same. Nobody moved. The man had a dozen guns trained on him, but he knew they wouldn't fire with Cat in jeopardy. The man's face swiveled back and forth, north, then south. He tugged Cat tighter against his chest and jabbed the gun barrel into her hair above her ear. She squirmed in his grasp.

Her eyes met Stride's. He was only fifty feet away, close enough to fire if he got a clean shot. Which he didn't have. He tried to will himself into her brain. To tell her to be calm. To tell her that nothing was going to happen to her. To tell her that this would all end with her safely in his arms.

He wanted to believe that.

The standoff drew out. The rain poured across them from left to right like a wave, carrying a sweet smell of pine. The forest was a lush wall of green, dark against a dark sky, practically dipping its roots in the lake. The railroad tracks made parallel lines that seemed to meet at the horizon. Stride dug his feet into the gravel of the tracks, steadying himself. He pointed the barrel of his gun squarely at the man's head, but all he saw was Cat's face. Too close.

He took a quick glance behind him. Serena was twenty feet back, down on one knee, her gun also aimed at the man's body.

"Let the girl go!" Stride shouted at him. "Put your gun on the ground, and put your hands up."

The man gave no sign of surrendering. Trapped in the man's arms, Cat used the heel of her shoe to hammer his shin, but her kicks did nothing to dislodge him. The man whispered in her ear, then moved the gun from the side of her head to the soft skin of her face, and she stopped struggling.

"You can come out of this alive," Stride called. "If you put down your gun, no one's going to shoot you."

Stride watched the man's stony face as he weighed his options. He was trapped, pinned down, with nowhere to run.

"You want this girl alive," the man shouted to Stride.

"I want everybody alive."

"Call off the dogs," he demanded. "Give me a way out of this."

"You have one way out. Put the gun down. Let the girl go."

"Are you ready to let this girl die? And her baby?"

Cat flailed again, erupting in fury, but he kept her locked in his grip. As she struggled, Stride noticed one thing that the man with the gun had missed. Cat's hands were almost free. Their run through the woods had shredded the tape binding her wrists, and if she twisted hard, they'd come apart.

She knew it, too. He could see it in the blackness of her eyes. There was something in her face that he'd never seen before—something determined and violent. This man had threatened her child, and she was ready to fight back.

They were running out of time.

"I want all of these cops out of here!" the man shouted.

"You can get a lawyer. You can do a deal with the feds. But not if you hurt the girl."

"As soon as I put down the gun, I'm dead. You think I don't know that?"

He sounded like an animal backed against a wall, and Stride didn't like it.

"If you surrender, you're safe. You have my word. No one's going to shoot you."

But the situation was spiraling out of control, and Stride couldn't stop it.

Cat's hands were free. She'd severed the tape and was flexing her fingers. She'd gone limp in the man's grasp, but the looseness was a ruse. She wanted to go for his gun. And she'd lose.

Serena saw it, too, and she murmured a warning. "*Jonny.*"

"Cat, don't move," Stride called to her. "We'll get you out of this. Stay calm."

A mistake.

He regretted it as soon as the words left his mouth, and the man didn't miss his slip. Cat. Stride had admitted that he knew this girl. She wasn't a stranger. She was more than an anonymous hostage.

"You want to save *Cat*?" the man shouted. "Then get these cops out of here! You've got ten seconds before I pull the trigger. Kill me if you want, but she'll be on the ground, too. Is that what you want?"

"Stop! Don't do this! Cat, don't move, it's okay."

"Ten . . ."

Cat's fingers curled like claws. Fragments of torn tape dangled from her slim wrists. Her breathing accelerated.

"Nine . . ."

"Put the gun down!" Stride shouted at the man.

"Eight . . ."

Cat stared at Stride, and he stared back. *Don't*, he tried to tell her, but she wasn't listening; she was too far gone with fear and fury.

"Seven . . ."

"Jonny, he's going to do it," Serena whispered.

"Six . . ."

And he was. Stride knew that. The man was insane. When he reached zero, he'd pull the trigger, regardless of the consequences. And before that, Cat would wrestle him for the gun, and he'd overwhelm her in seconds. It all ended the same way. With both of them dead.

"Five . . ."

Everything was careening to a finish. One way or another.

"Four . . ."

Stride bent down and put his gun beside him on the railroad tracks. He straightened up and put his hands in the air with his fingers spread wide.

"Look at me!" Stride shouted. "Look! No gun!"

The countdown stopped. The man stared at Stride.

"Now the others, too," he called. "All of them. Tell them to drop their weapons."

"First, we chat," Stride said. He took a step closer to the man.

"Stay where you are!" the man shouted. He kept the gun at Cat's head. "She and I are going to walk out of here. Just her and me. And you're going to let us go."

Stride shook his head and took another step closer. "I can't let you do that. I just wanted to prove that I'm not going to shoot you."

"Stop!"

Stride took another step closer.

"I told you to stop!"

And another step closer.

Then the man finally did what Stride wanted. He took the gun away from Cat's head and pointed it directly at Stride's chest. "I said, *stop!*"

Stride froze. No one had a clear shot yet. Cat stared at him with a question in her eyes. *Now?*

"Let me talk to her," Stride said. "I need to talk to Cat and make sure she's okay. Take off the gag."

He didn't dare look at Serena, but he hoped she was keeping a dead aim on the man for the instant when Cat was free.

"I need to talk to Cat," Stride repeated. "Otherwise, that's a deal-breaker. Take off the gag!"

The man relented. He ripped the tape away from Cat's mouth and yanked out the gag inside. In doing so, he had to let go of the choke-hold holding the girl in place. Stride wanted Cat to fall where she was, but, instead, with her hands free, she grabbed the man's wrist and sank her teeth into his thumb and knuckle, biting down hard until her teeth were stopped by bone.

The man wailed. The gun fired wildly into the air. His hand, spurting blood, let go, and the pistol dropped at his feet.

Stride ran. So did Cat. The girl threw herself into his arms, and Stride spun her around and lowered her to the ground and sheltered her with his body. He couldn't see behind him. He couldn't see the man drop to the tracks as bullets missed high, couldn't see him grab the gun with his uninjured hand and swing around to aim at Stride's back.

An easy shot. A paralyzing shot. A kill shot.

The beach was alive with gunfire. Deafening, overlapping.

The man aimed, but he never fired again. A dozen bullets hit him at once. In his chest. In his head. The gun fell again, and so did he.

Stride waited, protecting Cat, until the echoes died to silence.

58

Cat fidgeted in the hospital bed.

"I'm fine," she said. "I don't want to be here. When can I get out of this place?"

Stride held her hand. "You're not going anywhere until the doctors check you out. You and the baby. We want to make sure you're both okay."

"I want to go home—" she began, but then she stopped nervously. She looked away, not meeting Stride's eyes. She wasn't sure if she had a home anymore. She didn't know whether, after everything she'd done, Stride would let her stay.

"Don't worry, you'll come home soon," he told her. "Maybe tonight, definitely tomorrow." Then he added, "And we have a lot to talk about."

Her pretty face was unusually pale, her long hair dirty and matted. "What's going to happen to me?"

"I don't know," he replied honestly, "but I can tell you a few things. You're going to make a list of every house you were in and everything you and Anna stole. You're going to go to every one of those homes in person and apologize. You're going to return anything you still have, and you're going to make restitution for anything you don't. You're going to do community service every weekend from now until you graduate from high school. And that's just my punishment. A judge will have more to say."

She nodded. "Okay, Stride."

"I'm the easy one," he added. "Serena will be much tougher."

Cat gave him a tiny smile, and it was good to see that smile lighting up her face again. When he'd first met her, he'd thought she had a magical smile. Then her lips bent down in genuine confusion. "Why the heck aren't you kicking me out?"

Stride thought: *Maybe because you keep telling me to.*

"Let's make a new rule," he said. "You never ask me that again. Okay?"

She nodded. "Okay."

Serena joined them in the hospital room. She sat next to Stride, and he slid an arm around her shoulders and pulled her close. He could feel her exhaustion, emotional and physical. He was sure that some of the bullets that killed Bernd Frisch were hers, and she knew it, too. It didn't matter who was on the receiving end or how justified it was or how much the man deserved it; firing a bullet into another human being took a bit of your soul and never gave it back. It wasn't her first time, but it wasn't something that grew easier with experience.

"Erin Tierney?" Stride asked.

"The doctors say she'll make it," Serena said. The relief in her voice was palpable. "She was conscious for a while, but she's sleeping now. She doesn't remember much, which is a good thing. I talked to her parents, who are flying in tomorrow. We'll get a therapist here, too."

"I'm glad she's alive," Cat said from the bed.

She didn't ask about Anna Glick. She knew Anna was dead. Stride realized that Cat had seen way too much death this year—more than anyone should face in a lifetime. And yet fate played out strangely. If Cat hadn't made her mistakes, things would likely be different for Erin now. Other women would still be in danger. By accident, Cat had led them to an evil that was far worse than stealing jewelry or cash under the guise of painting houses. Which didn't excuse what the girl had done.

They'd linked Bernd Frisch through his passport to the *Ingersstrom*. The ship was on lockdown in the harbor. The feds and Interpol would be asking questions, and, with luck, the answers would blow open a European crime syndicate and save more lives overseas.

Strange fate.

Cat stared at Stride and Serena. "Can I ask you two a question?"

"Of course," they said together.

She played with her fingers and then placed both hands over her stomach. "Am I really ready to be a mother?"

Stride looked at Serena, not sure which of them should answer. Finally, he said, "That's your call, Cat, not ours."

"I want your opinion," she said. "And I want you to be honest with me."

Serena leaned forward and put her hand on top of Cat's. "Honestly?" she said. "No, you're not."

"I knew you'd say that. You're right."

"Not because you're a bad person," Serena went on, "and definitely not because I think you would be a bad mother. It's just that you're too young to take on that kind of responsibility. It will cheat you and cheat your son."

Cat suddenly looked older than her years. "I'm thinking now that maybe adoption would be a better way for me to go. Are there ways to adopt where he can know who I am?"

"Yes, open adoption is becoming more common," Serena said.

"What about you two? Would you two consider adopting him?"

Stride and Serena both stared at her, wondering what to say. "Cat, that's a sweet thing to suggest," he began, "but we can't—"

"I mean, you two are going to get married, aren't you?" Cat continued, as if she hadn't already taken away enough of their emotional hiding places.

Serena waited. And watched him. As if she were very interested in the answer he would give. She could have let him off the hook. She could have smiled or made a joke. But, no. They'd left the subject of marriage off the table ever since getting back together, but sooner or later, they would have to decide what this relationship was.

In the end, Cat gave him an out.

"I'm sorry," she said. "I know it's none of my business."

Stride hadn't said a word, and he felt the faintest cool breeze of disappointment blowing toward him from Serena. He got up and went to the hospital window. Behind him, he heard Cat whisper, "Did I say something wrong?"

He heard Serena's reply. "No, he's just not ready."

Stride let their hushed conversation go unanswered, even though he wanted to turn around and gather both of them up in his arms. All he could think about was how much he hated hospitals.

"Can I see Al?" Cat asked suddenly.

"Maybe a little later," Serena told her. "You should get some rest."

"No, no, I'm fine. I want to see him. He saved my life, too, you know. I don't want him thinking that I hate him."

Stride turned back from the window. "Al's lucky. The bullet went through his shoulder muscles but nothing vital. He'll be okay."

"Please, can I see him? Five minutes."

Stride and Serena both nodded. "Five minutes."

Cat didn't waste time. She slid out of bed and pushed her toes into slippers, and the three of them went into the hospital corridor. At the nurses' station, Stride checked on Al Pugh's room. When they reached the boy's doorway, and Cat saw Al in bed, she flew to his side.

"Al!" she exclaimed. She bent down and hugged him, then let go as he flinched in pain. "Oh, sorry! Sorry!"

He laughed, which made him wince again. "That's okay. Don't worry about it. Wow, you look good. I'm so glad you're okay."

"You, too!"

Al was propped up in bed. His hospital gown was tied loosely at his neck, and the bandages on his left side extended from his neck to his elbow. Otherwise, his eyes were bright. Stride saw him for the first time as a handsome young man, with his neatly trimmed hair and beard. Friendly smile. The lanky physique of a basketball player. He understood Cat's attraction to him.

Cat danced on the balls of her feet and stared at the floor. "Listen, Al, I'm sorry about all sorts of things. Lying to you. The things that Anna and I stole. I was such a jerk."

"Hey, I was a jerk, too. I just hope someday you can forgive me."

Cat nodded. "How's your shoulder? Are you okay?"

"It hurts," he admitted.

"You heard about Anna?"

"I did."

A nurse came into the room, and Serena touched Cat's shoulder gently. "Come on, we should go and let Al rest. Trust me, I know what it's like to get shot. It takes a lot out of you."

"Yeah, okay."

She bent down and kissed Al lightly on the lips. Stride could see the kid's face bloom with happiness. Al took Cat's hand and didn't want to let her go. It was a little gesture that made Stride realize that Cat had actually chosen well in finding her first real boyfriend. Al was solid. Hardworking. Not perfect, but no boy could be nineteen years old without doing stupid things. Something about the two of them made Stride smile and think about being nineteen himself. With Cindy. Back when he believed in the future.

He was still watching them when it happened.

The nurse undid the knot at Al's neck to check on the bandage, and the fabric of the hospital gown slipped down, exposing his bare torso. Exposing something that didn't belong on the chest of a healthy teenager. It took Stride a moment of shocked disbelief to understand exactly what he was seeing. Then, with the swiftness of a bullet from a decade-old gun, everything in the present and past made perfect sense.

This innocent young man. He was the key. He was what they'd all missed back then.

"Jonny?" Serena asked, watching his face.

The nurse retied Al's gown, but Stride had already seen the zipper scar.

The scar of someone who'd had heart surgery.

59

They found Al's mother in the hospital cafeteria.

She was with her three daughters, who ranged in age from ten to sixteen. When she saw Stride, Serena, and Maggie converging on their table, her lips puckered into a frown. Under her breath, she spoke to her children, and the girls picked up their trays and moved.

She continued eating calmly as the detectives joined her. She didn't even look up when Stride said, "Janine Snow operated on Al, didn't she? She saved his life."

Toiana Pugh put her knife and fork back on the tray and folded her hands in her lap. She took a long breath, and a tear slipped from her eye.

"Yeah, she did. That woman was an angel sent from heaven. My little Sherman Aloysious was going to die. We were going to lose him. And that beautiful woman gave him back to us."

"Why didn't you tell us this before?" Stride asked.

Anger flashed on Al's mother's face. "So you could give her more trouble? Haven't you done enough? That woman doesn't belong in a jail cell. She should be helping other families. Other kids."

Stride leaned back and ran his hands through his hair. The front legs of the chair came off the floor. He looked around at the cafeteria. Most of the people eating there were nurses in scrubs, but there were families, too. He knew what it was like to spend hours in a place like this. Waiting. Praying. Crying.

"I understand," he told her. "Really, I do. But we need to know exactly what happened."

Toiana jabbed a finger with a long purple fingernail at him. "You know how many docs we talked to back then? I can't count. No insurance? Sorry, we can't help you. My boy could turn blue in front of them for all they cared. But not Dr. Janine. She said she'd take care of Al. We had no money, no insurance, and she said, don't you worry about that. I'm not ashamed to say, I was on my knees crying. Seymour, too. And Dr. Janine was as good as her word. She did the surgery. She saved him. Never asked us for one penny."

"I can hardly imagine how grateful you must have felt," Stride said.

"Grateful? That's not half of it. We owed her everything. Seymour and me, we told her, what can we do? How do we pay you back? She said, you just make sure Al lives a good life. That's all. But we told her, if there is anything—*anything*—you need, you call us. No matter what."

There was a long silence at the table.

Finally, Maggie asked, "And did she call you?"

Toiana grabbed her fork and picked at the lasagna on her plate, but she'd lost her appetite. "There were lots of follow-up appointments after the surgery. Dr. Janine talked about that husband of hers. What a beast he was. How trapped she was. Smart people can be the absolute worst when it comes to relationships. Here's this amazing doc, but in her personal life, she wasn't any different from the wives and girlfriends who end up at the shelters."

Or that's what she wanted you to believe, Stride thought.

"We knew things were bad," Toiana went on, "but what happened next—"

She stopped.

"Mrs. Pugh?" Maggie murmured.

"Not sure I should tell you any more."

"Do you want to talk to a lawyer?"

"I don't trust lawyers. Besides, I didn't know a thing about what went on back then. I don't blame Dr. Janine for what she did. Guess I don't blame Seymour, either. He felt he had a debt to pay. We owed her in ways you can't measure."

They didn't press her, but they waited.

"Dr. Janine came by our house," she told them. "This was a couple weeks before Christmas. It was a surprise. She'd never been there. Said she wanted to see how Al was doing. Me, I felt like it was a visit from the queen, you know? Everybody was so excited. And then she and Seymour—they went out and sat in her car. Talked. Must have been an hour or more. She left after that, and Seymour came back inside, and that man had some kind of big burden on his shoulders. I asked him what they talked about, but he put me off. Said it was nothing. The thing is, he was never really the same man after that. Never, ever. He had secrets."

It wasn't hard to imagine how that conversation had gone. Janine asking for help to get rid of her husband. Seymour Pugh feeling that he had no choice but to do what she wanted. This doctor who had saved his son's life wanted repayment in blood. A killing. A murder. And the next time Seymour Pugh was in Chicago, he bought a gun on the street.

"After Jay was killed, did your husband tell you what happened?" Stride said.

"Eventually, he did. Like I said, it was after that cop came to see us. It all made sense then, how Seymour had been acting. I screamed at him until he told me the truth. Chilled my bones—that's what it did. But would I have said no if he'd told me before he did it? I don't know. Al was alive because of that woman."

"Did he tell you exactly how the plan worked?"

Toiana nodded. "It was supposed to look like a burglary gone bad. Kill the husband, steal some jewels. Dr. Janine didn't want him to stay long, so she said she'd put some jewelry in a bag and leave it in the mailbox for him. She had a party to go to. That was when she wanted him to do it. She knew her husband would let Seymour into the house if he said our boy was one of Dr. Janine's patients. It was all supposed to be done before she got home, but things went wrong. I mean, you can't fool God, can you? She didn't pull the trigger, but she went to prison anyway. Seymour wanted to help when they arrested her. Pawn the jewelry or something, or make sure the gun got found. I said no way. I mean, I felt bad for Dr. Janine, but I wasn't going to let Seymour throw away our lives. He'd get caught. I knew it. And you people would put her in jail anyway. How was that going to help anybody?"

"So what went wrong?" Stride asked. "Janine was already back home when your husband arrived at the house."

"Seymour didn't know that. He was real late getting there, and he thought about scrapping the whole thing, but he figured he'd better try to do it. He didn't think he'd have the stomach to go back some other time. Her car wasn't in the garage, so he thought she was still at the party. He figured it was safe."

"Why was he late?" Maggie asked, and then she pounded the table. "The bridge."

Stride looked at her. "What?"

"The bridge! The bridge was closed that night. A semi overturned. We were up there for a couple of hours, remember? Seymour Pugh must have been sitting there in his white RAV4. Stuck. I bet if we grab the news photos, we'll find his car. He was supposed to be at Janine's house hours earlier, when she was at the party, but he couldn't get there because of the bridge. So when it finally opened up, he drove to her house. He didn't know that Cindy had already taken Janine home."

Stride realized that Maggie was right. He also felt a new wave of resentment against Janine Snow, because he realized that Janine's plan had relied on manipulating Cindy from the beginning. *His own wife* was supposed to be Janine's alibi that night. The wife of the city's chief detective—who could argue with that? Janine would ask Cindy to take her home, and they'd find Jay's body together. Instead, Jay answered the door, alive, and the whole plan went to hell.

Janine must have figured that Seymour got cold feet. Except when she went to take a shower, Seymour showed up after all, took the jewelry out of the mailbox, shot Jay, and disappeared. Exactly as they'd arranged weeks earlier. And he could imagine Janine's horror, discovering the body, and realizing that her plan for the perfect murder had made her the prime suspect instead.

"Where is she?" Stride asked Maggie. "Where's Janine?"

"Archie has her in a suite at Fitger's."

Stride stood up. "I think we should welcome her back to Duluth."

60

"I thought I was going to have to apologize to her," Stride said as he parked on Superior Street outside Fitger's Inn. "For being wrong about Jay's murder. For stealing eight years of her life."

The three of them got out of his truck. Stride climbed the steps toward the hotel lobby with Serena and Maggie beside him. A bellman opened the door for them. The rich burgundy carpet, the grand piano, and the old-fashioned table lamps made him feel as if they were walking into the parlor of one of Duluth's robber-baron estates. The hotel check-in desk, nestled behind iron grillwork, was like the teller window of a bank in the Wild West.

He saw carpeted stairs leading to the next floor. He knew where Janine would be, in one of the top-floor suites overlooking the lake.

Serena touched his elbow. "Are you okay?"

Stride shook his head. "This woman used Cindy. Cindy was her friend, and Janine deliberately tried to make her part of her plan to get away with murder. What's worse is that she probably is going to get away with it. God knows what this does to double jeopardy. We convicted her of shooting Jay, but we were wrong. She never had the gun. And yet she was guilty of his murder anyway. I don't know if we can ever put her back in prison for it."

He started up the stairs.

"She still got eight years," Serena pointed out.

"Eight years of what should have been life without parole," Stride replied. "This was first-degree murder. Premeditated."

He reached the hushed hallway of the hotel's second floor. The Fitger's manager, Tami, met him there, descending from the upper floors of the inn. They'd known each other for years. The petite blonde's normally ebullient face was serious. "Oh, Stride," she said. "That was quick."

"What do you mean?" he asked.

"I only just called your office."

"We're not here for a call," Stride said. "What's going on?"

"We've got a disturbance upstairs. Screaming."

"Is it Janine Snow's room?" he asked immediately.

She nodded.

"Who's up there?"

Tami shook her head. "I don't know. Archie Gale checked her in earlier this afternoon. She was shopping for a while, but for the last couple of hours, I thought she was up in her room alone."

"Stay here. We'll check it out."

The three of them headed upstairs. They were on the fourth floor when they heard the gunshot.

Stride broke into a run and took the steps of the last staircase two at a time. At the landing, he heard a second shot. He reached the fifth floor with Serena and Maggie immediately behind him. Janine's suite was six feet away at the head of the staircase. Its door was ajar. He smelled the smoke of gunfire inside, and he drew his own gun. He listened, but the room was quiet now.

Stride nudged the door with his boot. It was heavy. Through the crack of the opening, he could see someone standing on the far side of the room. He led the way with his gun and called, "Police. We're coming in."

The person inside didn't move or react. Stride opened the door the rest of the way. Inside the suite was a large living area with a sofa and a coffee table decorated with fresh flowers. The dark light of the afternoon poured through a skylight. An open, empty bottle of wine sat on the table, with two glasses on either side of it. He thought of the bottle of wine in Janine's house on the night Jay was killed.

Just beyond the door, a body lay on the carpet. Stride recognized the dead man on the floor. It was Howard Marlowe, the ex-juror in the murder trial who'd never given up his obsession with the case. He'd been shot in the forehead, like Jay.

Beyond the living area where Howard's body lay, the carpet led to a king-size, four-poster bed and a fireplace. Floor-to-ceiling windows looked out on Lake Superior between heavy drapes. He could only see the end of the bed; the rest was blocked by a tall walnut bureau. A woman stood at the foot of the bed. He didn't recognize her. Her shoulders were slumped. She looked to be almost fifty years old, and she wore a baggy, untucked T-shirt over blue jeans. Her gray-brown hair was pushed back behind her ears. She stared at the bed, her arms limp at her sides.

A revolver was on the carpet where she'd dropped it.

"Step away from the gun, ma'am," Stride told her, but she didn't move. She didn't seem to hear him. She was in a daze as he came closer.

"Who are you?" he asked.

"My name is Carol Marlowe," she replied.

Stride got close enough to see the rest of the bed, and he understood what had happened. Janine lay among the tangled sheets. Naked. Dead. The two of them—Janine and Howard—had both been shot in the head. Howard's wife had killed them in the aftermath of their lovemaking.

"That bitch ruined our lives," Carol murmured. "She took everything from me."

There was nothing he could say. Stride kicked the gun on the floor away from her. Maggie came up behind Howard's wife, who offered no resistance to the handcuffs that Maggie locked around her wrists. Carol Marlowe was limp as Maggie led her away, but as they reached Howard's body, she came to life and began to wail and cry. Maggie had to physically restrain her as she fought to get to her dead husband.

"Howard! Oh, God, Howard! I'm sorry!"

The door closed. The screams continued in the hallway.

Stride and Serena were alone with the bodies. The suite smelled of gunpowder and sex. The patio door was partially open, letting in sweet lake air and the humid reminder of rain.

He checked Janine's pulse for final confirmation, but she was gone. Her eyes were closed with a strange look of peace. Her nakedness still had beauty, and her skin was as warm as life. He felt an urge to cover her, but there was no modesty in death. She was guilty. She was innocent. She was a heroine. She was the devil. She was all of those things.

His anger at her bled away into regret. Stride never got emotional at crime scenes, but this time he felt an unexpected sense of loss. As if the universe were saying there were no such things as new beginnings. He didn't want to believe that. Maybe the lesson was simply that you couldn't escape the sins of your past. Sooner or later, they caught up with you.

He couldn't look away from the woman on the bed. The strange thing was that he couldn't see Janine's face without seeing Cindy in his mind, too. January 28. Almost a decade ago, when everything was different. He could see his wife in the shadows of their bedroom that night. The moonlight shining on the bare skin of her shoulder. He could smell the smoke of his own cigarette as he told her about Janine and Jay.

They were both so young then. They didn't know what lay ahead. How everything was about to change.

That was then. This was now.

61

Stride sat on the green bench at the end of the Point. His legs were stretched out, and the rippled waters of Superior Bay lapped at his boots. Yellow wildflowers sprouted along the beach. The late-summer sun had fallen behind the western hills, leaving an orange glow in the clouds. He was alone, but if he stared deeply into the semidarkness, he could almost imagine Cindy beside him, the way she'd been for so many years. Her legs pulled into a lotus position on the bench. Her hands on her knees, her chin tilted toward the sky. Her long black hair cascading to her hips.

Here I am, Jonny, she would say. *Don't you see me?*

It wasn't real, of course. It was simply another Thursday evening. Serena was out at a movie. Cat was in her room at the cottage, doing her puzzles. Life hadn't changed at all.

And yet he could still close his eyes and make Cindy come alive. As if no time had passed. As if the real dream were all the years that had happened in between. Elsewhere in his life, she'd become a ghost who haunted him less and less, but here, by the water, she was always waiting for him. Here there was never a need to say goodbye.

Stride watched the bay, trying to memorize every wave. They'd been here together so many times. Lived so much of their lives in this place. Talked and cried and laughed. Remembered.

How old were we when we first came here?

Seventeen. Cat's age.

You asked me to marry you here.

Yes, I did.

What did I say?

You said not yet.

I'd only known you a week.

That's true.

He knew what love at first sight was. He'd asked Cindy again at the end of the summer, and that time she'd said yes, although they didn't tell anyone they were engaged. Not her father. Not Stride's mother. It was their secret for a while.

Good things have happened at this bench.

And bad things, too.

Yes, and bad things. That's life.

He came here at turning points. Good, bad, up, down. In many ways, this was ground zero for who he was. Put a pin in a map, and this was where you would find the soul of Jonathan Stride. In Duluth. On the Point. By the water. Not staring out at the lake but inward at the calm harbor and the industry of ships and docks. Life in the northland.

He wondered what Cindy would have said about Janine, now that they knew the truth. Her friend was guilty after all; her friend had used and deceived her. And yet he knew the person Cindy was. She would still be sad. She would still cry that Janine was gone. He felt that same sadness himself, but it wasn't really for Janine's death. She'd simply been one last open door to another time in his life. A door that had finally closed.

Tell me you're not still pining after me.

That was what Cindy would say. And the answer was no. Not anymore. For a long time, he'd refused to let go of her, but not anymore.

"I need to tell you something," he said aloud, as if she could hear him.

But there was no need to say it. Wherever she was, she was at peace with herself and with him. She would understand what he wanted to do next. She would say he'd already waited too long. *You've got someone in your life you're scared of losing again. And that's a good thing.*

Yes, it was a good thing.

He wished he could touch Cindy again, or smile with her, or have her with him for a few more seconds—but when he stared at the empty bench, she was gone. She'd been gone for years. There was nothing around him but the bay and the sand. It was the story of their relationship. She was there, and she was there, and she was there, and then she was gone.

He was alone.

Except, he wasn't. Not anymore. Not if he didn't want to be. Not if he believed in the future.

Serena found Maggie in the basement bar of Tycoon's on Superior Street, across from the casino. Stride's partner sat alone with a Starfire Pale Ale at a candlelit table near one of the rough sandstone columns. The pub was located inside Duluth's old City Hall, and the downstairs bar with its low ceilings had once served as the town prison. You could still see century-old names scratched into the stone by people who'd lived here among the dripping water and the rats.

Maggie held up her pint glass in a toast. "Well, well, Serena Dial. 'Of all the gin joints in all the world.' How did you find me?"

Serena sat down across from her. She didn't drink, but the bartender knew her, and he brought her a tall Diet Coke with crushed ice. "You weren't at your condo, so Tycoon's seemed like a safe bet."

"I thought about Black Water, but I was more in the mood for a beer tonight than a martini."

Serena didn't think the Starfire in front of Maggie was her first of the evening. "Can I tell you something? Speaking as an alcoholic with experience in such things."

"Go for it."

"You drink too much."

"And you think I don't know this?" Maggie asked.

"No, I'm sure you do, but if you're like me, you don't start paying attention until your friends mention it."

Maggie finished her beer and twirled her index finger in the air at the bartender to order another. "Well, when one of my friends mentions it, I'll cut back."

Serena nodded. "Slam noted."

"I'd hate to think I was being subtle when I'm this drunk," Maggie told her.

"Too bad, because I could use a friend. I think you could use one, too."

Maggie blew her bangs out of her eyes. "I don't need anybody."

"Good for you, but that doesn't work for me. Things have been weird, but it's not all your fault. Anyway, if you want me to leave, I'll leave."

"No, stay. If all this old stonework finally crumbles, I can hide under your breasts."

Maggie giggled. Serena, who was briefly annoyed, laughed, too. And that set off a fit of laughing that left them both breathless. When they could talk again, Maggie chuckled and leaned dangerously far back in her chair. "Can I just say something? It's been a shitty couple of years for me."

"I know that," Serena said.

"I mean, really. Shit-*tee*. I thought rich people were supposed to be happy. Maybe I should give it all away."

"So you can be poor *and* unhappy? I don't think so."

"You're right."

"The state fair starts next week," Serena reminded her.

"Yeah, so? I can drink beer right here."

Serena tapped Maggie's phone on the table. "Call Troy."

"He deserves better than me."

"He likes you."

"Which makes him a party of one."

"Do you want me to call him for you? I'll call him."

Serena picked up the phone from the table, and Maggie grabbed it out of her hand. "I'm not ready," she insisted.

"I think you're just chicken."

"Cluck," Maggie said. The bartender brought her another Starfire, and she stared at it with a frown on her face. She knew Serena was right. She'd been drowning her sorrows in a lot of alcohol.

"So, why are you here?" Maggie asked.

"I miss our talks," Serena said.

"Does Stride know you were coming to see me?"

"No. I didn't want to get his hopes up, in case we wound up in a girl fight."

"You'd have to call Guppo first. He'd pay good money to see that."

Serena smiled. "Did Jonny tell you about Cat and the baby?"

Maggie shook her head. "We steer clear of the subject of Cat. Is everything okay?"

"Fine, but Cat's thinking of giving him up now. Adoption."

"Sounds like a better plan to me."

"She asked if Jonny and I wanted to adopt him."

"You mean, so she can be around for the good stuff, while you guys do all the work?"

"Wow, you're cynical," Serena said. "But it doesn't matter. We're going to tell her no."

"Do you both feel that way?"

"Yeah, we do. I can't have kids, so I've never really thought about it. Jonny thinks it's a younger man's game. So we're in sync on this."

"And yet here you are, talking to me," Maggie said, with a pointed look in her eyes. "What's wrong?"

Maggie didn't miss much. For all of the troubles between them, they knew each other like sisters. And neither one was shy about telling the other when she was making a fool of herself.

"Honestly, I worry that Jonny saying no to kids is really his way of saying no to me," Serena admitted. "Like he and I aren't going anywhere."

Maggie shook her head. She gave in and drank a healthy dose of Starfire. "For such a hot chick, you're way too insecure."

"Look who's talking."

"Insecure? Me? No, just realistic."

Serena tapped Maggie's phone again. "Troy."

"Fine, okay, you win. I will call him." Maggie dialed a number on the phone using her index finger and got Troy Grange's voice mail on speakerphone. "Troy, it's Maggie. I'm in. You, me, and the girls. Deep-fried stuff on a stick next week."

She hung up.

"Satisfied?" she asked Serena.

"You'll thank me."

"Maybe. Now quit reading anything into Stride saying no to Cat. It has nothing to do with how he feels about you."

"What about you?" Serena asked.

"What about me?"

"You wanted to adopt a baby last year after Eric got shot. You were all in. You were going to do whatever it took to find one."

"Yes, and I got turned down by every agency in the state. Strangely, they didn't like the idea of handing a child to a single woman with a dangerous job and a very public history of bad romantic decisions. I decided they were right. End of story."

"Not if you don't want it to be," Serena said.

Maggie leaned forward. "*Me* adopt Cat's baby? Is that what you're suggesting?"

"That's what I'm suggesting."

Maggie drank more beer. "No."

"Just like that?"

"Just like that." She put the mug down, and her voice softened, and she covered Serena's hands with her own. "Look, tomorrow I will deny ever being sensitive. Okay? The fact is, Cat living with the two of you, and her baby living with me, is not healthy for any of us. Which I think you know perfectly well. But it was very sweet and very noble of you to suggest it."

"I was serious," Serena said, even though she knew that Maggie was right.

"I'm sure you were, but, no. I think it's great that Cat is willing to look at adoption. She should choose a nice, stable young couple somewhere in the city who can give that kid lots of love."

Serena smiled. "You're going soft."

"Bite your tongue."

Serena stood up from the table. "Okay, I should go. I'll let you finish your beer in peace."

"Actually, I'm done," Maggie said. "A friend told me I'm drinking too much."

Maggie threw cash onto the table, and the two of them climbed the stairs to the street level of the pub. They didn't talk. They emerged onto Superior Street, where there was a nighttime buzz of noise and neon. People came and went from the casino and jaywalked between the cars stalled at the red light. A police car turned from the hill, and the two of them waved.

The Sheraton Hotel, where Maggie had her condo, was two blocks away. The Chinese cop shoved her hands into the pockets of her jeans. It was a cool evening, hinting at an early fall. "Night, Serena. And thanks, by the way. I know this wasn't easy for you."

"It was easier than you think," Serena said.

Maggie turned away and clip-clopped in her block heels toward the Sheraton. Serena watched her go and then retrieved her Mustang from the casino parking lot. She heard the Zac Brown Band singing on the car radio. She hummed along as she drove back to the Point, narrowly missing being bridged by an ore boat arriving from out on the lake. At the cottage, she parked and went in through the back door. She was surprised that Jonny's Expedition was gone.

Inside, she checked on Cat, who was still playing Sudoku puzzles from a magazine balanced on her very pregnant stomach.

"Do you know where Jonny is?" Serena asked.

"He went out," Cat told her with the strangest of smiles.

"Out? Did something happen?"

"I don't know," Cat replied, but her voice said something else. It sang to her, as if to say, *I know a secret.*

"Where did he go?"

"He said he left you a note."

"Okay," Serena said, but she was confused. She pointed at the lamp beside Cat's bed and said, "Lights out, kiddo. The puzzle will wait. It's past midnight."

Cat winked. "Yes, Mom."

Serena shut the girl's door. She realized that she felt an odd lightness in her heart. She started to undress by unbuttoning her blouse, but then she went into their bedroom and saw a slip of paper folded on her pillow. She opened it and found Jonny's handwriting inside.

I'm at the green bench. Meet me there?

It took only a moment for the lightness she felt to become the weight of all the things that were uncertain in her life. Maggie was right: She was insecure. The green bench was a place for turning points. Jonny went there in good times and bad times, and she couldn't help but wonder which this was.

Good or bad.

I know a secret, Cat's expression sang again. The secret was waiting for her at the end of the Point.

Serena realized that her first instinct was to run away. Even from good news. Even from things she wanted. She almost got into her Mustang and drove away from Duluth without ever finding out what Stride wanted to say to her.

Instead, in the still of the night, she went to meet him.

FROM THE AUTHOR

Thanks for reading the new Jonathan Stride novel.

You can write to me with your feedback at brian@bfreemanbooks .com. I love to get e-mail from readers around the world, and, yes, I always reply personally. Visit my website at www.bfreemanbooks.com to join my mailing list, get book club discussion questions, read bonus content, and find out more about me and all of my books.

You can "like" my official fan page on Facebook at www.facebook .com/bfreemanfans or follow me on Twitter or Instagram using the handle bfreemanbooks. For a look at the fun side of the author's life, you can also "like" my wife, Marcia's, Facebook page at www.facebook .com/theauthorswife.

Finally, if you enjoy my books, please post your reviews online at sites such as Goodreads, Amazon, BN, and other sites for book lovers—and spread the word to your reader friends. Thanks!

ACKNOWLEDGMENTS

I'm fortunate to work with many talented people in all areas of the publishing industry, including editors, agents, publicists, librarians, and booksellers around the world. My books wouldn't be in your hands without them, and I'm grateful for all of their help and support.

Jeff Edblad, the Isanti County Attorney (and fictional judge!) was kind enough to offer technical insights on the legal and courtroom issues in this book. In Duluth, I'm very grateful to the Honorable David Johnson, Tony Mancuso, and Dana Kazel at the St. Louis County Courthouse; to Machelle Kendrick and Colin Bates at Miller Hill Mall; to former Duluth Police Chief Scott Lyons; to Chuck Frederick and the people of the *Duluth News Tribune*; to Sally Anderson and everyone at the Bookstore at Fitger's; to Ann Hoak and the team at Barnes & Noble, Miller Hill; to Tami and the entire staff at Fitger's (www.fitgers.com); and to Pat and Bill Burns for their hospitality at "Stride's Cottage" (www.cottageonthepoint.com).

My advance readers always give me great insights on the first draft before I turn the book in to my publishers. Big thanks to Mike O'Neill, Alton Koren, Ann Sullivan, and Matt and Paula Davis—and, most of all, to my best and very first advance reader, Marcia.

Finally, Marcia and I are so grateful to the people of Duluth for their support in the ten years since my first Stride novel, *Immoral*, was published. I've brought some dark things to a truly magical city, and yet you keep welcoming us back! Thanks for making us feel at home.